BOOKS BY LAURENCE GONZALES

The Last Deal   1981
Jambeaux   1979
4.4.4.   1977

The Last Deal

THE LAST DEAL

by *Laurence Gonzales*

ATHENEUM
New York
1981

Library of Congress Cataloging in Publication Data

Gonzales, Laurence, 1947–
    The last deal.

    I. Title.
PS3557.0467L3   1981   813'.54   81–66017
ISBN 0–689–11199–1   AACR2

For my Brothers

gregory
michael
philip
albert
stephen
federico

and for my Sister

janet bailey

Early
Flights

1

DANNY'S MOTHER was not quite seventeen years old when he was born. She worked at a resort north of Acapulco, a collection of half a dozen stucco houses backed into the jungle cliffside high above the ocean. Between the narrow beach and the water's edge was a barrier of smooth brown boulders on which crabs and iguanas sunned themselves. The Pacific surf would explode across them, then retreat, hissing back to the sea, but the crabs and lizards never seemed to move.

In the spring of 1947 a law student named E. Forrest Paine arrived there with his ailing wife. As an aviator during the war he had been shot down and was presumed dead; in reality he spent seven months in a German prison camp. A year after his return a group of physicians put at one in five his wife's chances of living beyond another six months. By the time Nancy and Forrest Paine reached Mexico, shattered and exhausted, she had beaten those odds and was fond of telling Forrest that she could put all her trust in physicians into a thimble and still add soda. Even at their Mexican retreat, though, all Nancy Paine could do was to sit on the veranda or lie propped up on the sand.

"Forrest," she would sometimes say when he came down to the beach to sit with her, "I'm going to have the best tan of any dead woman we know."

Most mornings Forrest awoke with the distinct and paralyzing sense that he was trapped inside someone else's most

sinister midnight dream. He'd sit up in bed, thinking he
was still in prison camp or in the cockpit of his B-17 Flying
Fortress, inverted, going round and round on his way back
to earth. When he wasn't on the verge of hysteria or in a
deep depression, he was bored silly. Though he tried to read
his law books, he spent most of his time sitting on the
quarry tile deck of the house, sipping rum and watching the
sixteen-year-old housegirl work with a grace and economy
of movement that were, to him, irresistible. When she would
throw her weight to a task—yank her arms down, popping
a clean sheet straight out into a plane of cotton cloth suspended in midair above the bed—her bottom would stick
out for balance and Forrest could feel himself come alive
with a desire to hold someone hot and healthy in his arms.

That he eventually did so was a measure of how out of
character the situation had put him. It was a fleeting moment
of pleasure. The sweat began to appear on her forehead, her
cheeks, her naked brown chest. He saw that she wasn't a
goddess at all but merely pretty and young. She was also
a virgin. She knew nothing of lovemaking and lay under him
as if under the knife of a surgeon, mystified, stoic, uncertain.
When Forrest reached his orgasm almost immediately upon
entering her tight, hot body, she looked frightened and
asked, "What's wrong? Are you all right?"

For the rest of his stay he was uncomfortable whenever
his eyes met hers. When he and his wife returned to Chicago,
Forrest applied himself to his study of the law, as if pure,
unpunctuated concentration would deflect his thoughts—
all of them. After only a few weeks, however, the owner
of the resort wrote a polite, chatty note, which only at its
end (and there quite offhandedly) mentioned that the girl
had become pregnant.

Leaving his wife with some fabricated story, Paine took
a commercial airliner—a noisy, smoking propeller-driven
collection of groans and rattles—all the way to Mexico just
to make sure the girl did not have an abortion, which in
those days (and especially in Mexico) could easily have
meant the end of the girl as well as the child. Forrest already
had enough death in his life. He set out to convince the

girl to go to the U.S. side of the border so that their child could have American citizenship. The girl did not want the child—did not even want to go through the bother of having it—but she did wish to visit America, where she had a half brother who lived in Harlingen, Texas, which was in America, if just barely.

Alberto de la O (Beto to his friends) worked there with the Mexicans who picked fruit and vegetables in the Rio Grande Valley. The girl agreed to stay in Harlingen, but soon after the boy was born, she became homesick and returned to Mexico, leaving the baby (whom she had named Daniel) in Beto's care. Neither Danny nor Forrest nor Beto ever saw her again.

Nancy Paine died in 1956, the same year that Alberto de la O was killed as a result of a farm labor dispute. More than twenty years later, when Danny turned his mind back to that time in Texas, he saw Beto, a big man holding a shotgun in the first light of morning, walking soundlessly toward a water hole. Beto had an old single-shot 410 that he allowed Danny to carry, though he never put shells in it. One morning when Danny was eight years old, he begged and pestered his uncle until Beto agreed to let him try a shot. He knew Danny would miss, frightening the birds, but he wanted to make sure the boy learned how to use a firearm properly.

Beto gave Danny the blue paper shell. In the center of its shiny brass base was the button of a primer. Danny placed the cartridge in the breech with the care and reverence of an altar boy. As they crept into sight of the pond, they could see birds near the water's edge. Beto put his hand on Danny's shoulder and nodded, indicating they had come far enough.

Danny shouldered the slim scatter-gun and closed one eye in grave concentration. He put the bird just above the blue black barrel and began applying steady pressure to the trigger, just the way Beto had taught him, dry firing. Without warning, the gun went off and jerked into the air. Danny held on, lowered the gun and looked where he'd shot. He felt his pulse in his throat. The bird lay dead. Beto was so surprised he didn't even raise his gun to fire at the other birds, which fled in every direction. The dead bird was stretched out on its back in an odd position, like a fossil impression in limestone.

An hour later Beto had shot two more birds and held fire for one deer that came to drink.

"Why don't you shoot the deer?" Danny asked.

"We couldn't carry deer."

"Other people shoot deer."

"Other people have trucks," Beto said.

"Why do the animals go to the water hole every day if they know they might get shot?"

"It's the way they live," Beto said.

"But they might get killed," Danny argued.

"Well, I guess if it's as good a way to live as any, then it's as good a way to die as any," Beto said. He laughed at what he'd said. Danny did not. He registered it in a way only young minds can, the way unexposed film can register an image and—once exposed—can never register others with such clarity again.

The Rio Grande Valley was planted with produce and sprayed by crop dusters. The planes would appear out of nowhere with a sudden, tremendous roar, streaking low over the ground, and then disappear across the next line of trees, straining toward heaven with a power unimaginable to Danny. He often stood and watched for hours, waiting for another plane to come by. He had no idea where the planes came from or what made them move through the air. It was the most profound mystery in his world and he burned to know its secret.

One day he saw a plane land in a nearby field and ran to get a closer look. There was an unusually strong wind that knocked him about as he ran toward the pilot, who was relieving himself beside the plane. Danny stopped short and stared at the airplane. He had never seen one on the ground before and was surprised to find that where there had been nothing but a rounded nose before, there was now a propeller. He wondered why he hadn't seen the propeller as the planes flew over the fields.

The man zipped his trousers, squinted up at the sun and then smiled down at Danny. He spat and the wind whipped the spit away before it reached the earth.

"You spray the plants?" Danny asked.

"Yeah, I do," the pilot said, "but not with that thing." He jerked his thumb at his small aircraft. "That one's for fun. For the air shows. You ever see the air shows?"

"No."

"Oughta see it, pardner." Again he jerked his thumb at the plane. "This baby goes."

Danny asked, "How does it go?"

The pilot studied the little boy, who had a great, unruly mop of dark hair, a wild tangle of curls and waves, blown about by the incessant wind.

"How does it go?" Danny asked again.

The man squatted down beside Danny and, gesturing with his hands, outlined the mechanics of flying in terms as simple as he could find. When he was done, however, he could see that Danny wasn't satisfied. The pilot picked Danny up and swung him into the cockpit. It was with open-mouthed awe that Danny regarded for the first time the interior of a real airplane, its knobs and switches and dials.

The pilot explained again, moving the stick to demonstrate how a plane is flown. He said it was simple. The propeller turns, pulls the plane through the air; then the air lifts the plane.

Danny stared at him with a blank expression. "But how does it *work?*"

The pilot, not an eloquent man, plucked Danny from the plane and put him back on the hard, dry earth.

"You just watch 'er," he said.

He climbed into his airplane and fired the engine. Danny saw the propeller turn, then catch and spin into a translucent disc. Suddenly he understood why he had not been able to see the propeller as the planes flew over. The plane rolled and was airborne immediately, rising almost vertically but making little forward progress against the wind. The pilot turned the plane around and it shot along, passing over

Danny with a magnificent roar. It turned 180 degrees again and approached Danny, going very slowly and descending. The nose began to point upward. The plane neared Danny no more than twenty feet off the ground as the engine labored. Danny watched the nose go higher and higher as the pilot lay back in his seat, the throttle wide open, until finally the airplane stopped and simply hung there, fifteen feet off the ground, dancing a little this way and that, as the pilot jockeyed the controls. Danny had not known that planes could stop in midair like that.

The engine revved a little more, the nose increased its upward angle and the airplane began to drift backwards. It inched back across the field like a raft being carried out to sea. Then the pilot cut back the throttle, the engine noise slackened and the plane settled, fifteen, now ten feet off the ground, still settling, finally, miraculously grazing the earth itself, whereupon the pilot killed the engine. He stood on the brakes at the same time and the plane squatted on the hard-packed earth, rocking on its struts, parked.

Before Danny recovered from his surprise the pilot started the engine again and was gone, into the sky and over the tree line, with Danny running after him as hard as his little body would carry him, shouting, "Wait! Wait!" until he could no longer run or hear the airplane in the distance.

Many years later, when Danny himself was a pilot and uncertain if he'd seen or imagined that, he checked to make sure. The National Weather Service records showed that the area was on the back side of a hurricane that had just made landfall. This explained why the winds had been that strong. Danny even tried it himself once at an airport northwest of Chicago when a thunderstorm lay across the approach path to the runway. It was a very dangerous stunt, but not by any means the most dangerous Danny would attempt. He managed to get a Cessna 150 Aerobat to a standstill over the numbers but had to go around when the wind suddenly shifted.

The year Nancy Paine died, Forrest was working for Eisenhower's reelection campaign with the fervor of someone who was going to go places. Danny was 1,100 miles away in Harlingen, Texas, being entertained by Beto's half brother, who had come to visit. Danny knew him only as *Tío* Jim, a dashing young man wearing a Mexican Army uniform and a fine, neatly trimmed mustache. *Tío* Jim told Danny stories about the fliers in the military, but no matter how many stories Danny heard, he would beg for more. The night before *Tío* Jim left, Danny lay awake and heard him pleading with Beto to be more careful, not to stir up "union" trouble and not to get himself killed.

Danny had heard talk of trouble before but had not made sense of it. He did not, for example, know what a union was. Nor did he understand the purpose of Beto's drills. There was a crawl space beneath the shack in which they lived. Beto kept things down there—his shotguns, an old sleeping bag, a few tools. It was accessible through a trap door covered with a small rug. Beto had told Danny time and again to go down there and stay down there in the event of "trouble."

Whenever Danny tried to remember Beto, he remembered the shack and the crawl space and a hot night near Harlingen, when the air was merciless and still.

He had barely fallen asleep in his bed when Beto shook him awake and rushed him down to the crawl space. Danny kept asking, "What, *Tío?* What is it, *Tío?*"

"Shh, shh, go back to sleep," Beto told him as he placed him beneath the trap door. But Danny did not sleep. He lay in the dust, holding onto the barrel of Beto's twelve-gauge shotgun for what seemed like hours. He may have dozed off, he was never sure later. Suddenly he heard someone slam through the door of the shack. Without thinking, he pushed the trap door open an inch or two and saw a large Mexican man standing in the doorway, holding a revolver.

Beto lifted his pistol, but the other man fired and Beto went to his knees. Smoke and the smell of powder filled the little room. Danny's ears rang. He saw Beto's pistol skitter across the floor and stop against the stove. The big man

raised his revolver again, and then Danny was knocked back
into the crawl space so violently that at first he thought he'd
been shot. Then he realized that he had pulled the trigger
and fired the twelve-gauge he'd been holding.

Danny forced the trap door open again. The man was
standing in the doorway. His face was as round and gray as
the moon. He clutched his right wrist with his left hand and
watched the blood foam from his arm and onto the bare
wood floor. The hand itself lay on the floor, torn and shredded
but still clutching the revolver that had shot Beto. The man
stood for a moment in shock, without even seeing Danny,
then turned and stumbled out the door and into the night.

Beto lay face down on the floor in the haze of moonlight
coming in through the open door. Cautiously Danny moved
toward him. He was too afraid to cry or panic. He asked
Beto if he was going to be all right.

"*Hijo*," Beto said. And then he died.

Danny shook his uncle, hollering, "Beto! Beto! I'll kill
him! I will!" He continued shaking Beto and shouting, until
the lake of blood leaking from under his uncle's body reached
and soaked his knees. Danny leaped up in horror and bolted
out the door, screaming that he would kill "him," until
people began to emerge from their shacks to see what the
boy was hollering about. A woman who had often taken care
of Danny tried to stop him, but he spun out of her arms,
hysterical, shouting at her, "No! I'll kill him! Let me go!"

It was ten miles to San Benito, where they picked Danny
up. He was exhausted by that time and simply nodded or
shook his head in response to the sheriff's questions. He
listened as the sheriff and his deputy discussed what to do.

"It's 'at fucking Mendoza," the deputy said.

"Harlon, I wish to hell you wouldn't use vulgar language
in front of the goddamned kid," the sheriff complained.

"You sure he's not deaf?"

"Shut up, Harlon."

"Maybe Mendoza'll bleed to death."

The sheriff shook his head. "Between his drugs and front-
ing for the growers, it's a goddamned miracle he hasn't been
shot more often."

"He'd be back over to the Mexican side by now."

"If they'd take care of their own kind, we wouldn't have to be fussin' with 'em."

From the moment the deputy had mentioned the name Mendoza, Danny's attention had gathered like clouds banding together into a storm. He knew he would never forget the face. Now they had provided him with a name.

Danny was put into an orphanage in Corpus Christi, where he stayed until one day when a tall, handsome man arrived. He said he was going to take Danny away from there.

"What for?" Danny asked, thinking the suggestion odd.

"I'm your father," Forrest explained.

"You *are?*"

"Yes." Forrest nodded.

"Well, where have you *been?*" Danny asked with a very concerned look, as if Forrest had been lost all those years; obviously the man had been lost, very, very lost, for now he wept and hugged Danny, who struggled away, saying, "Don't cry, it's all right now." Which only made Forrest sob more intensely. He stood up and turned away, withdrawing a handkerchief from his pocket and wiping his face. He composed himself and once again sat next to Danny. He knew that Danny could not possibly feel about him the way he felt about Danny. He needed something more to break the ice. It was by a happy coincidence that he said exactly the right thing.

"How would you like to take a ride in an airplane?" he asked. "And come home with me?"

Danny had been in an airplane only once and, for reasons he did not understand, had lost his chance to get off the ground in it. He certainly wasn't about to make the same mistake twice. Without hesitation or comment he nodded.

When they reached the airport ramp, Danny saw an enormous airplane, a great silver machine with four propellers and what appeared to be thousands of people boarding. He knew that if that monster ever left the ground, then flight was indeed a miracle.

Forrest gave him the window seat and Danny watched with rapt fascination as the plane rolled along, not in some field of grass but on a stretch of concrete road. The engine noise grew louder and the plane picked up speed as buildings passed them, going the other direction. Perhaps, he thought, the machine would simply drive them along this road to wherever they were going. But then he felt his heart leap into his throat. He could feel his seat lifting. Out the window the earth pitched away beneath them. It had actually happened. They had left the earth.

For twenty minutes Danny sat bolt upright, staring out the window, as familiar objects grew smaller and less distinct below. He closed his eyes, trying to visualize himself from the outside. He fell asleep.

Forrest watched him sleep, feeling for the first time since the spring of 1947 a kind of inner peace. When Danny awoke later, he came out of it with a start, saying "*¡Tío! ¡Tío!*" He looked out the window to see the sun low off his left shoulder and realized where he was. The plane rolled out of a bank above the red-tinged blanket of shocking white cumulus. Danny yawned. He turned to Forrest. "Can the pilot make the plane stop?"

Forrest laughed. "No, that's impossible. Planes can't stop while they're flying."

Danny said, "Yes, they can. I saw one."

"No." Forrest smiled and patted Danny on the arm. "Once they take off, they have to keep going until they land."

Danny looked out the window, ignoring what Forrest had said. He had learned long ago that adults were sometimes difficult to deal with. It seemed, in fact, that the older they got, the less they knew.

Danny had spoken so little Forrest didn't want to let him sink back into what he assumed was a disturbed state of mind. "Come on," he told Danny. "Let's see if the pilot will give us a look at the cockpit."

Not only did the pilot let them look around the cockpit, but the copilot gave Danny his seat. It was almost the beginning of a scene; Danny did not want to move when the copilot needed his seat back for the final approach. Forrest coaxed him back to the cabin by telling him that he had his own plane.

Danny was reluctant to believe that but considered the discussion worth pursuing. When the plane landed and Danny was still not fully convinced of the existence of this airplane, Forrest decided to take Danny to the smaller airport and show him. Danny talked his way into the airplane and then announced that he was spending the night in it. Forrest laughed and explained that there was a bed at home —a whole room for Danny.

Danny was unimpressed. "What if somebody steals the airplane?"

"Then we'll buy another," Forrest told him.

Danny considered that. He looked up at his father. "You got that much money?"

"I have some," Forrest said. He took Danny by the shoulder. "Come on."

It was not until many years later that it occurred to Danny that he thought he was getting an airplane when actually he was getting a father. In those first moments, when this man had asked him if he wanted to take a ride in an airplane, Danny had assumed the entire trip would be no more complicated than that. Further, when Forrest asked if Danny wanted to be taken home in the airplane, Danny failed to understand that to Forrest the emphasis was on the word *home*, while to Danny it was on *airplane*. Danny thought he had somehow miraculously acquired an airplane. Forrest thought he had somehow miraculously acquired a son. Just getting those signals straight would take the two of them another twenty years.

Danny learned to fly in his father's Taylorcraft. At first, of course, he could not even reach the pedals, but Forrest bought him a logbook in which Danny recorded the time he spent in the right seat "flying." Forrest allowed him to hold the yoke during takeoff and landing and had him perform a few of the easier tasks in the cockpit. Danny experienced his first in-flight emergency at the age of nine, when, taking off from a small airstrip in Grayslake, Illinois, Forrest's Taylorcraft "blew a jug," as he put it. When the old plane's engine threatened to shake itself loose from its mounts, Forrest shut it off and made a forced landing in a field of soybeans. It reminded Danny of the flying he'd seen back in Harlingen, where pilots had landed on anything that was flat. Forrest was so terrified of Danny's being hurt that when the aircraft stopped and he saw that they both were safe, he became ill. That day he put the Taylorcraft up for sale and made a down payment on a new Cessna.

In the evenings Forrest would sit with Danny and teach him how to compute true airspeed, wind triangles, density altitude and runway requirements—all simple arithmetic calculations basic to any flight. Together they set up a little workshop in the basement, where they dabbled in gadgets for their new plane. They wanted to install a pair of shrakes on the Cessna to depress the stall speed; Forrest arranged to buy a power tool from a local man to do the job. One Saturday afternoon the man came by to deliver the tool.

Danny was sitting in the kitchen with paper and pencil, laboring over his preflight calculations, frustrated with his less-than-stellar mathematical ability and eager to blast off for his afternoon flight with Forrest. Douglas Wolf rang the back doorbell and entered with his son.

"Hello," he said to Danny. "I'm Doug Wolf. Where's your dad?"

Wolf's son hung back as if there might be something dangerous in the kitchen. He stood a full head taller than Danny, who said nothing at first as the two boys glared at each other, Danny with undisguised antagonism, the other boy with a kind of mute and defiant disdain. Douglas Wolf looked around the kitchen as if Forrest might step out of the refrigerator. He looked down at the two boys and told Danny, "That's my son, Charles. You're Dan, right?"

Danny nodded. "My father is in the living room."

"Thanks," Wolf said, and left the kitchen to find Forrest.

The two boys regarded each other for another moment. Charles walked over to the kitchen table, moving as if he feared his own size. He looked at the paper on which Danny had been calculating density altitude. "It's two thousand feet," he told Danny.

"What?"

"I said it's two thousand feet. You made a mistake."

"Well, how do *you* know?" Danny demanded.

"I just know."

Danny wanted to ask this big, dumb intruder just who he thought he was, coming in here and telling him what the density altitude was after he had spent half the morning struggling with the computations. Danny stomped over to the table and looked at the figures. He picked up his pencil and did the calculation again. He looked at the boy. Charles was right.

"You fly?" Danny asked.

"I *wish*," the boy said.

"I fly."

"I *bet*."

"I do so," Danny insisted.

"Bull."

Danny turned suddenly and left the room. He found his father and Mr. Wolf talking in the living room. When Forrest turned his attention to Danny, he asked, "Can that boy go with us this afternoon? He says I don't fly."

"It's up to his father whether or not he can go, but what do you care what someone else says?"

Danny had no answer. He only knew that anybody who could do those calculations that fast in his head ought to be taught a lesson.

Forrest turned to Doug Wolf. "Do you think Charles could come with us? You could come, too. It's a four-seater."

"He'd love it," Wolf said. "He just loves airplanes."

Danny returned to the kitchen. Charles had redone all his calculations and had found two more mistakes. Danny worried the calculations until he was convinced the boy really was right. He turned to face the intruder. "People really call you Charles?" he asked.

"My dad does. People call me Chip."

"Sure."

Soon after they met, Danny was insisting that Chip go with him wherever he went, including flying lessons. Chip's father began contributing to the cost of fuel and the two boys demonstrated a voracious appetite for any problem Forrest and other pilots could throw at them. Forrest took them to air shows at Rockford and played all sorts of games with them. The Gear Game, for example, in which he would name an aircraft and they would have to say how many engines it had, whether or not it had retractable gear and whether the propeller was fixed or controllable; or the Reciprocal Game, in which Forrest would name a radial and they would have to give him the reciprocal instantly. Since there are 360 degrees on the compass, a reciprocal is 180 degrees in the other direction. Knowing reciprocals is basic to instrument flight and is also one of the pilot's primary lifesaving tools, allowing him to employ without hesitation what Forrest called the Cleveland Defense, which amounted to nothing more than pulling a quick about-face and "getting the hell out of there." In the Reciprocal Game, Chip put Danny to shame.

Danny and Chip had to calculate the weight and balance of the aircraft and figure the distances needed for takeoff and landing, considering weight, as well as temperature, wind, elevation, runway conditions and gradient and atmospheric pressure. Chip could do them all in his head. Danny had to use a slide rule, but by the time they were ready to fly alone they both knew as much as professional pilots.

Just out of eighth grade, Danny and Chip took summer jobs together as line boys at Pal-Waukee Airport and there insinuated themselves into the left seats of all sorts of sophisticated aircraft. They seduced an old line pilot named Stewart Robbins into teaching them advanced techniques. Stew was a tough old buzzard, but Danny and Chip soon learned that he could not resist the temptation to teach. His training regimen was exact and grueling, though, and some days up in the air with him, Danny and Chip would wish they had taken up sailing instead.

Stew kept little rubber discs in his pockets. He was in the habit of whipping these out at critical moments and sticking them over the faces of the flight instruments. It taught Danny and Chip not to lean too heavily upon the slender reed of technology. If the plane had two wings and the motor was running, you should be able to land and walk away from it—even if the motor wasn't running, for that matter. Stew had another habit of cutting the power at odd times, saying cheerfully, "The squirrel just died, sweetheart, if you lived here, you'd be home by now." He'd then wheeze and chuckle as one of the boys frantically searched for a suitable field or a stretch of highway that didn't have power lines strung across it every which way. Before they got the hang of it, both Danny and Chip had died a thousand deaths.

Stew also taught them how to land with no lights at night, without altimeter or airspeed indicator, with no radios, no navigational aids—just the engine purring and the ground coming up fast and black.

By the time Danny and Chip were sixteen years old—legal age for soloing—they could handle singles, complex and high-performance singles, as well as multiengine aircraft. They had accumulated sufficient actual instrument hours with Stew and Forrest to be rated to fly blind. Both had taken full aerobatic courses in a Stearman Stew had commandeered.

It was the summer before their senior year in high school, and while the other boys were practicing indolence with their shirts off around the burger stands, and peering into the lungs of a 427-cubic-inch automobile engine, Danny and Chip were out at Pal-Waukee Airport, calibrating VOR receivers, shooting practice ILS approaches and doing precision spot landings. By the time Chip departed for his annual visit with his relatives in Kansas, Danny had begun his research at the University's Deering Library. He had known for a long time he would have to do it. His name—his real name—was de la O. That, at least, had been Beto's name. He traced the name to a group of sixteen families, who, in 1731, had been transplanted by the king of Spain from the Canary Islands to Texas. From there the families had spread to Mexico and intermarried with Indians.

It was well into the summer of 1964 when he realized his researches had taken him only halfway through 1850. He stepped up his work schedule, staying late at the library and making up stories about girls to feed Forrest. Danny pored over old reference books and maps in the subbasement stacks until he had narrowed the field to a handful of names that could be traced to his own relatives. The web seemed to have its center in a town called Puebla, where a ranch had been established by part of the family in the 1920s. The name was de la Garza and the family was purported to be wealthy. At least one thing was certain. Anyone with the name de la Garza was related to Danny, if only by connections in the remote past.

Danny could not wait any longer. He took the plane, telling Forrest he was flying to Kansas to see Chip. He made it all the way to Benito Juárez Airport in Mexico City. From there he made his way to Puebla. To Danny's surprise, the ranch was nothing more than a tin shed with fifth-generation tractor tires stacked on the corrugated roof and a goat tied in front, nibbling on the pitiful shoots that crawled up between rocks and scorpion nests. Danny had to wonder if the goat would starve to death first trying to survive on that diet or if the family would die first trying to survive on the goat.

The shack belonged to an old couple named de la Garza, who assured Danny that the place had once been a real ranch before the land had been liberated. To Danny's amazement, his research had been correct. The family did have relatives named de la O and had even heard of Alberto, the boy who had run off to the U.S.—a wild boy, they seemed to recall, who wanted to organize laborers. They did not appear to know that Beto had gotten himself shot, so Danny said nothing about it, though they encouraged Danny to look for him in Corpus Christi. Danny pressed the couple to try to remember any names of Beto's relatives, but they could come up with only one, a kid in Cuernavaca—at least he had been a kid the last time they saw him. His name was Santiago Amesquita Garza. He had been in the army somewhere. They knew nothing more.

Danny tracked the name through Cuernavaca, where the name Garza was so common the search seemed hopeless. Apparently a great number of de la Garzas had simplified the name to Garza, which made the process that much more complicated. At first, Danny succeeded only in annoying a lot of Garzas with phone calls and visits. He even checked with the army and they laughed at him. Find a soldier who'd been in the Mexican Army in 1952? Ridiculous.

Having had no luck with the name Garza, Danny fixed on the name Amesquita, mostly because it was an unusual name in Mexico and that, he reasoned, gave him a better chance of success, like looking for something under a streetlamp because the light is better, even though it was lost elsewhere in the dark. Amesquita would be the man's father's name, Danny knew, so he might be using it. The reasoning turned out to be sound.

Amesquita was a friendly man with a family. He wore an expression of perpetual concern, as if someone were repeatedly dry sniping him from a great distance. This had taken shape in the last year like a cachexia of the face, wasting it from within. His wife had mentioned it to him and Amesquita had become self-conscious about it, trying to smile more, but getting it wrong and at the wrong times. His worried look had grown out of the drug-smuggling case on which he'd been working.

Amesquita had been with the drug enforcement detail for almost his entire career, but he had never seen anything like this. Recently brown heroin—called Mexican Mud and refined from opium grown in Mexico—had begun to show up on the streets of Chicago, New York, Los Angeles. The case Amesquita had worked for the past year involved Mexican Mud and went beyond anything he had imagined people would do for money.

When Danny found him, Amesquita was at a restaurant, alone. It was simply a wood-and-thatch roof shading a slab of concrete that elevated a few tables above the blistering clay street of a small village. From a radio with a blown speaker came the sounds of *vihuela, guitarrón, marimba,* harp and out-of-tune voices, pathetic and listless, straining for falsetto notes in long phrases that trailed off as if electrical power in Mexico were as uncertain as political power.

Dogs with brisket as thin and delicate as Chinese kites

roamed the streets, in and out of scant spots of shade. Amesquita ordered and an obese woman brought two iced bottles of Negra Modelo. She giggled at Amesquita, whom she obviously knew. He smiled his crooked, nervous smile at her and she retreated, apparently satisfied with their mysterious communication. Amesquita told Danny that he had known Beto many years earlier.

"*Era mi tío*," Danny said.

"*¿Tú?*" Amesquita asked. "You're Beto's boy?"

Danny nodded. "Daniel de la O."

"*Hijo.*" A blaring crepitation of trumpets took up, accompanied by the voice of a man screaming at the top of his lungs about a headache remedy called Mejorál. "What do you want with me?" Amesquita asked. They watched as the fat woman set plates of chicken *mole* before them.

Danny sipped his beer. He rolled a tortilla into a neat cylinder, dipped it into *mole* sauce, bit off the end and chewed. "I was looking for something." He shrugged. "I don't know." He picked up the beer and sipped again. "My family." Danny knew he was lying, being intentionally vague with the man. Well, why not? he thought. Why not just tell him? You've come all this way for it.

"Looking for what?" Amesquita asked.

"I want to find the man who killed Beto," Danny said, looking up from his plate.

"No, you don't."

Danny was surprised. "You know him?"

"Ah." Amesquita hesitated.

"His name is Mendoza," Danny told him.

Amesquita's eyes widened. "How do you know that?" he asked.

"The sheriff told me the day Beto was killed. They picked me up in San Benito and I heard them talking about Mendoza. I was very young. I didn't understand everything they said, but they said he would be back on the Mexican side."

"Daniel," Amesquita cautioned him, "you are very young still. And that was a long time ago. You still don't understand. You don't know what you're dealing with here. What do you expect to do if you find this man?"

"Kill him," Danny said. He could feel his heart beating in his neck now. He had said it for the first time. All those years he had only half admitted to himself what he was doing, what he was waiting for. Now he was big enough, he knew. He knew he could do it. He had flown all the way to Mexico to do it.

Amesquita sat in stunned silence, uncertain if he should laugh or get angry, unsure if the boy before him knew what he had just said—this child, who sat there in all sincerity, telling a federal investigator that he had come to Mexico intent on committing premeditated murder.

"Do you have a gun?"

Danny shrugged again, the way teenagers shrug when they do not know but wish to appear merely unconcerned.

"Well? How do you propose to kill this man?"

"I'll kill him."

Amesquita put his hand over his eyes and wiped the sweat from them as if he were very tired. *"Hijo,"* he whispered to himself. He was just beginning to realize the magnitude of the problem he had on his hands with this boy. "All right," he continued. "I'm going to level with you." He looked up sharply at Danny. "But you have to promise me you'll stop trying to find this Mendoza. It's ridiculous and impossible, and you don't know what you're dealing with."

"I can't promise you that."

"You've got to listen to me," Amesquita insisted.

"Dígame," Danny told him.

Amesquita sighed. "Beto was my half brother, Daniel."

Danny stared at him as if he hadn't heard correctly. "What?" he asked. "How come I never met you?"

"You did, you just don't remember." Amesquita smiled his odd smile. "I told you about airplanes and you couldn't get enough of it. I wore an army uniform." Amesquita looked off in the distance, as if he wished the world were still as simple and quiet as that.

"Tío Jim," Danny whispered. *"Tío* Jim?"

Amesquita nodded. "Didn't you know that Santiago means James?"

"No." Danny laughed. "I guess I never knew anyone to

use that name." He stared at his uncle. "Christ, yes, I can see the resemblance."

"I hope I haven't gotten that old," Amesquita said.

"You look different," Danny said. "I didn't recognize you. If you were Beto's half brother, does that mean you were my mother's brother?"

"Yes."

"Where is she?"

Amesquita looked off across the street and said nothing at first. An intense heat lay upon the street and set it trembling with light. "Dead," he finally admitted.

Danny sat for a moment, motionless. Then he whispered, almost inaudibly, "Who killed her?"

Amesquita closed his eyes. "No one killed her. She died when she was nineteen years old. A fever. It was a long time ago, Daniel. She didn't have American doctors around. I don't really know what it was. She got sick and she died."

Danny looked down at his chicken *mole*. The glaze of fat had coagulated on the surface of the chocolate sauce. "Montezuma," Danny said softly, "ate this sauce with the meat of children." Danny looked up sharply because Amesquita's chair squealed on the concrete floor. Danny thought he might have begun to choke on something. Amesquita's face contorted in pain. Danny had no idea why he was reacting that way to what he'd said.

The waitress waddled over toward them. She was so obese that the fat sloshed against the limits of her body as if she were a great hogshead of liquid being wheeled carelessly across the room. She grinned at Amesquita, then looked at his plate and asked if there was something the matter with the food. Amesquita tried to smile, but it came out all wrong. He patted her hand, which was rolled and pleated with fat.

"So," Danny said when she had left. "*Tío* Jim a cop."

"Yeah, *Tío* Jim a cop," Amesquita said. He pushed his thumb and forefinger into his eye sockets and shook his head. "I loved Beto," he said. "They shot him down."

"I was there," Danny told him.

"Where?"

"I was in the room when Mendoza shot him. There was

a trap door underneath the house. Beto put me down there. I shot Mendoza's hand off with Beto's bird gun."

"You did that thing?" Amesquita asked in shock.

Danny nodded.

"You were only a baby, Daniel."

"Yeah. I was eight. The gun went off accidentally."

"*Imajínate,*" Amesquita whispered. "I'm sorry." After a moment of quiet he added, pointing a finger at Danny, "But I've been trying to get Mendoza for *years*. He's a very bad man. You have no idea what you're talking about doing. Mendoza would think more about breaking wind than about killing you. Or me. There is no way to get to him. We just have to wait until he makes a mistake."

"Why did Beto leave Mexico in the first place?" Danny asked, as if he hadn't heard his uncle's warning.

"I don't know. I never knew."

Danny picked a piece of chicken out of the coagulating sauce and took a bite. He chewed it thoughtfully. Chocolate, chile, raisins, cinnamon, almonds. Such strange flavors. "Can I stay with you for a day or so?" he asked.

"*Cómo no,* you can stay. But you know, things are very different down here. Do you understand what I mean?"

Danny nodded, but Amesquita knew he could not possibly understand. All young men think they understand. "Tomorrow," he told Danny, "you'll come with me. I have some people to visit. Places to go to. I want you to see for yourself, so you know what you're getting into down here."

"Fine by me," Danny said with that false air of worldliness teen-age boys can mimic so well before they learn that there is no such thing as strength.

✦

REPORTS OF MISSING CHILDREN were not uncommon in Cuernavaca. For nearly a year, however, there had been a standing order that all such reports be routed to the federal police, specifically to Amesquita. Since his work had nothing to do with children, this had served only to generate jokes among the men about his changing sexual preferences. The morning he showed up with Danny, a five-year-old girl named Linda Márquez had been reported missing. The duty officer called down and, in an attempt to tease Amesquita, said, "Hey, Jimmy, we got another missing children for you, guy. You want it to go or do you eat it here?"

Amesquita was not in the mood for that sort of joke, though, and he told the man to mind his goddamned business and pass along the report. He gave Danny a cup of coffee and told him to wait. He then went to see the woman who was waiting in a private interviewing room. She was Señora Márquez, widowed, mother of the missing girl. Amesquita came away from the interview drawn and pale. When Danny saw him, he asked, "What's the matter with *you?*"

Amesquita simply said, "Come on," and led him out to an unmarked government car. Danny said nothing.

It was the eighth time Amesquita had heard the same story. He lived in fear of hearing it. And with each new woman who told it, Amesquita knew a deeper layer of dread.

He had shown nothing of this reaction to the woman, however. She was encouraged to believe that there was a simple explanation for the disappearance of her daughter, in spite of the fact that the police had had her repeat her story to federal government officers ("Just a formality"). Linda, the daughter, had gone off the day before and hadn't returned. She had gone to the zoo with friends, a man and woman Señora Márquez and Linda knew well. It made no sense, she said. She had a terrible premonition. Several times during the interview she became hysterical. Amesquita had had to give her a shot of whiskey at one point. He had managed a crooked smile and patted Señora Márquez on the arm after she gave him the details he needed. It was absurdly simple. Certainly the couple would turn up with an explanation. And with Linda.

Amesquita left abruptly, stopping only to tell the duty officer to get the woman to a doctor and get her sedated immediately. In every detail the story was like the other seven. A well-dressed American couple had befriended Señora Márquez and Linda. They spoke impeccable Spanish and

German. They drove a new Mercedes. They stayed at La
Manzana and had the mother and daughter over for the
beautiful midday meals served at that aristocratic old hotel,
where albino peacocks wander the lawn and monkeys and
macaws entertain the guests under royal palms and the intense, high-altitude skyforms so commonly seen above the
dry parts of Mexico. The man was witty and charming, the
woman beautiful, and soon Señora Márquez felt as if they
were old family friends. They invited her and Linda to visit
them in New York, giving them an address, which, when
Amesquita checked it later, turned out to be the address of
the public library. In return, Señora Márquez invited them
to dinner at her house. The man played Spanish guitar quite
respectably and taught Linda to pluck it a little. He promised
to give her lessons when they returned to Mexico. In that
fashion the four of them passed a few days together before
the couple left for New York.

A month later word arrived that the couple was once
again coming to Cuernavaca. Linda was so excited she could
barely do her schoolwork. Señora Márquez made elaborate
preparations for their return, whipping her staff into a frenzy
of activity, fixing special dishes and even repainting the guest
room, in which she insisted the couple stay. They protested,
saying they were perfectly happy at La Manzana—and it was,
indeed, a beautiful place to stay—but Señora Márquez per-
sisted and they eventually agreed to stay with her and Linda.

A week of grand times followed. The couple took them
to all the places one could want to visit in Mexico City and
the surrounding countryside. They strolled the Alameda and
the couple bought a piece of black Oaxacan pottery for
Señora Márquez. They spent one early morning climbing to
the top of the Pyramid of the Sun and then ate a picnic
lunch in its shade. They scaled the endless stairs at Cha-
pultepec and saw the castle, guarded by *federales* with automatic rifles, who lounged sullenly around the mysterious
fountain of the cricket.

The man had even begun to teach Linda some elementary
guitar chords, which she played with some difficulty but with
great delight, her delicate fingers plucking carefully, not

strumming with undirected vigor as most small children would.

The day of Linda's disappearance Señora Márquez had an appointment to go to in the morning. The couple offered to take Linda to the zoo while the mother was away. They agreed to meet at a restaurant. The couple never showed up. At some point during the interview Amesquita asked for descriptions of the couple, their car—anything that might lead him farther along what had so far been a trail as blank and cold as freshly fallen snow. Her descriptions of the couple were of little use—they looked like people in American magazines, she said. Pretty people. Their car was a dark green Mercedes, but there were many such cars in the affluent neighborhoods. The license plate, however, was American, though she had no idea of the specific differences among the states there. It was orange, she said.

"What is it?" Danny asked, breaking into Amesquita's thoughts.

Amesquita shook his head. They were driving along the highway, but he could not seem to remember how he had gotten there. It worried him. He had been having more and more spells like that, where he would be off in another world for miles at a stretch and would wake to realize he had been driving on automatic pilot. "I can't tell you," he said to Danny. "It's something very bad. Some very bad men."

He had put in a lot of time during the past year tracking down dental records. His guess was that the couple had checked into La Manzana as Germans, under a German name. Hence the Mercedes. The owner of La Manzana was German—a man named Werner. Finding a well-dressed German couple in Cuernavaca was easy; there were thousands of them. That was the worst part. He had all the pieces of the puzzle before him and nowhere to begin putting them. He could see the plastic steering wheel bend in his hands. He forced himself to relax. It was impossible, he knew. Which was why he had to chalk it up to fate when he heard the radio call. Often he didn't even turn on the radio. Most reports did not concern him. At first he did not even hear what was being said—a traffic accident of some sort. Then the echoes of it jolted through him and he grabbed the microphone and asked to have the report repeated.

Danny listened to the clipped, static Spanish of the dispatch describing a dark green Mercedes, a New York license plate number and the details of the crash. He heard Amesquita call back and ask what color the license plate was. The dispatcher said it was orange. Amesquita responded by ordering that the scene be sealed—nothing was to be touched except the injured couple. "And I want guards inside the ambulance," he said into the microphone. The radio responded by telling him that an ambulance had already left with the couple. "Shit," Amesquita said. He told the man on the radio to make sure guards were posted at the hospital—he wanted those people alive.

"What's going on?" Danny asked.

"There's been an accident."

When they reached the scene, Amesquita told Danny to stay in the car.

"Aw, come on," Danny began in protest, but Amesquita cut him off quickly and walked away. Danny sat back and tuned the car radio until he found *mariachi* music, a powerful, morose cadence.

The Mercedes was completely destroyed. A plume of steam emerged from under the sprung hood. It was a miracle it hadn't exploded. Amesquita found it difficult to believe the couple hadn't been killed outright when the truck jackknifed into their lane on the road to the airport.

He was given the purse and wallet the couple carried. There were two first-class tickets to Chicago. In another fifteen minutes they would have been through the gate. Half an hour and they would have been airborne. That afternoon they would have once again disappeared into the crowds at O'Hare International. It was only something like this, Amesquita knew, that could lead to their capture. The hand of God.

He tossed a partly smoked cigarette into the rain that had started to fall gently but steadily, as it did every day in that season, at that time of the afternoon. Automobiles passed

and their tires made a sound on the wet concrete like meat
frying on a griddle. In the distance Amesquita could still
hear the octave wail of the ambulance, carrying the injured
couple away. He hoped they lived. Someone had said the
woman had a brutal laceration from ear to ear. The man's
skull was crushed, one of the officers told him, "*como una
caja de fresas.*" It did not look promising.

Linda sat in the front seat, dressed neatly in a blouse and
skirt and wrapped in a blanket. She appeared to be sleeping
peacefully. Amesquita leaned into the open car door and
wiped his finger across her smooth forehead. He examined
the tan powder on his fingertips.

"Make-up," the policeman behind him said. "They
thought of everything."

"Has anyone . . .?" Amesquita began.

"We looked. We did nothing else," the man said. "At
first we thought she was alive."

"Yes," Amesquita said. He turned back to the girl. He
carefully unlatched the shoulder belt and then unbuttoned
Linda's blouse. There was a tremor in his hand he had never
known before. He shook his head and straightened up and
out of the car. He looked away from the scene. The rain fell
around him and dripped from his nose and chin. He had
never seen his own hands shake like that. He had always
been so sure on the job. Now, as he reached back in and
pulled open the blouse, he felt for the first time in his career
that he was going to lose control, to be sick or cry or simply
walk away from there, perhaps just give up completely, thinking: Maybe there does come a point when you really have
seen too much and your poor old head just can't hold anything more. Part of him wanted to be tough enough to keep
on taking it, to have no emotional involvement, no reaction,
while another part knew that if he were that tough, he
would become a monster equal to the monstrosity of what
he now saw.

It was no wonder it had worked so well. Linda looked so
pretty and peaceful, the perfect picture of a five-year-old girl,
asleep on a long vacation. Customs would never have thought
to wake her; a quick finger to the lips would have stopped

the most cynical investigator. She was done up with regular surgical suture, an even, professional line of stitches from the base of her throat to the mound of her small, bald pubic bone. The police and coroner's photographers moved in and they, too, were aghast—even in Mexico they had never seen anything like this. Amesquita saw a hardened detective of twenty years' service cross himself at the sight. The paramedic clipped the stitches. It was up to Amesquita to reach into her to withdraw the first plastic bag, streaked with dried blood. He backed away from the Mercedes and held the bag out to be taken away so that the laboratory could analyze the brown crystals inside and check for fingerprints that would not be there.

Amesquita could not force himself to reach inside Linda for the next six bags; he could not even bring himself to look into the car again. He refused to believe that anyone could do this. So he turned away to the rain that fell now around them. He wanted to cry for her—he knew he should cry for her—but he was still too much in shock. He shook his head and looked off down the highway until one of his officers came to inform him that the ambulance had been ambushed by men with machine guns. The drivers and two paramedics had been gunned down, killed, along with the couple from New York.

Amesquita put his hand over his mouth and sucked in a long breath. He could feel tears forming in his eyes and ground his teeth together, determined to control himself. They were everywhere, he thought. What more could they do to us? The rain poured down the back of his shirt, but he didn't even notice until he was distracted by the sound of someone vomiting. Amesquita turned just in time to see Danny throwing up his breakfast onto his shoes. Amesquita flew into a rage.

"Who let this boy in here?" he screamed, going from man to man among the police. "I told you to keep this god-damned area sealed off. What in hell are you getting paid for? Get him out of here!" And whispered, "Now."

There was a great commotion as the police hustled Danny out of the perimeter and back to Amesquita's car, which sat in the rain, steaming from the heat it had collected on the ride out.

Amesquita turned back to the highway. He could see a white Chevrolet screaming toward them on the rain-slicked road ahead of a great rooster tail of mist, a rotating blue emergency beacon flashing on its roof. Amesquita pulled his jacket around him. He could hear the Chevrolet's siren. He found a dry cigarette in his pocket and lit it with a Zippo, sheltering the thick, wavering orange flame from the wind and water with his cupped hands. He absently wondered what the approaching American agents in their white Chevrolet would do if he calmly took one of their "foreign aid" M-10 submachine guns from a nearby Mexican government car (also bought with foreign aid money) and simply opened fire on them. What would they do? he wondered. They would die, that was the answer. And more would come behind them, like fire ants. For his money, they could close the Mexican-American border permanently, build a regular Berlin Wall there, for all the good U.S. "aid" was doing down here. In most cases it was difficult to tell which country produced the more corrupt officials. The bribery, gunrunning, shoot-outs, smuggling, double and triple cross at every turn were so common down there that it sometimes seemed America had declared war on Mexico. Amesquita saw the American press reports about operations in Mexico and knew most people would never understand that being in Mexico was like being on the moon for all the authority there was to protect you. And if you weren't part of the drug-running business, like most of the men sent from America and most of the in-country nationals on the narcotics force, you ran the daily risk of disappearing forever without a trace.

The car was approaching now at such a reckless speed that it slid sideways when the driver tried to stop it and a group of Mexican policemen scattered in fear for their safety. Fassnacht bolted out of the passenger side and stormed up to Amesquita. He wore a new-looking leather sport coat and a tie. He had shocking blond hair, eyes the color of overcast and white skin drawn tight across high cheekbones and caved-in cheeks. Before he had even reached

the scene, Amesquita said across the distance, "Go home."
He puffed on his cigarette, immobile except for the column
of smoke whipping into the wind.

"Don't tell *me* to go home," Fassnacht snapped, walking
toward him. "The bureau is going to want analysis. We'll
need reports on all this."

"I told you to go home," Amesquita said. "I'm not in the
mood to tell you again."

"You're way outta line, fella," Fassnacht began as he approached Amesquita. Fassnacht was speaking as if Amesquita
worked for him. It was his mistake not to have seen or read
the message on Amesquita's face, which was so plain that
even a few of the Mexican police officials had turned to
watch what would happen when Fassnacht began berating
the single toughest narcotics cop in all Mexico. Amesquita
reacted instantly. One moment Fassnacht was rambling on
in his nasal gringo twang; the next Amesquita was holding
him off the pavement with one hand and pushing a small
knife into his throat with the other. The knife appeared as
if it had been part of a magic act. The blade just penetrated
the skin. A small line of blood began to make its way down
toward Fassnacht's collar.

Now everyone at the scene stopped to watch. There were
two distinct reactions. The Mexicans seemed momentarily
distracted by something mildly amusing, as if an armadillo
had been run over by a passing car. The other American
agents, who had emerged from Fassnacht's Chevrolet, however, vibrated with anticipation. Amesquita paid no attention to any of them. His eyes were fixed on Fassnacht's as he
held the knife in the man's throat. Fassnacht stood on his
toes and the blood turned his tight white collar red and ran
in the rain that soaked them both.

"How do you know what was in that car?" Amesquita
demanded. "It wasn't broadcast on the radio. Only an auto
wreck was broadcast. What makes you think this is a drug
case? Or do you know something I don't know?" Amesquita
pushed the knife a little deeper. Fassnacht said nothing, his
face twisting in pain. "I told you nine months ago," Amesquita continued. "You may be fooling your State Depart-

ment, but you're not fooling me. You're not going to recover
Mendoza's investment that easily. The evidence stays here."

Fassnacht lifted his throat high to get a breath and
croaked out, "You're crazy." The other Americans were going
mad with a desire to do something, to be heroes, shifting
from foot to foot nervously, while the Mexican police simply
stood in the rain, obliviously smoking or spitting, holding
their automatic weapons casually, as if it were all a big joke.

"You're through, Fassnacht," Amesquita promised, pulling
him even closer—now they were almost kissing, like lovers in
the rain. Without another word, Amesquita released him as
suddenly as he had attacked. Fassnacht backed off as if something might explode at his feet and stood among his com-
panions.

He held his throat, his hands smeared with his own blood.
"I'm going—" He coughed and began again. "I'll . . ." He
looked at his hands and his face registered shock. "I'm going
to get you, spic," he said.

"*¡Ramón!*" Amesquita called, and a man with a selective
fire rifle stepped up beside him. "*Matalo.*" The policeman
pointed the rifle at Fassnacht, switched it to FULL and released the safety. Fassnacht and his agents stood in stunned
disbelief. At just that moment something took over in
Amesquita—he wouldn't know until years later whether to
be proud of it or to regret it—and as Ramón fired the little
weapon, Amesquita gently pushed the barrel toward the
ground and the hail of nine-millimeter bullets chattered before the men, harmlessly chewing up the concrete.

The group of Mexican *federales* laughed, high and tired,
as if it were the last joke in a long night of drinking.

"Go home," Amesquita said quietly as the Americans
scrambled toward the Chevrolet and screamed off in the
direction from which they had come. The rain stopped as
abruptly as it had begun, as if someone had simply neglected
to pay the water bill.

Amesquita drove for half an hour without speaking, with-
out even seeing the road before him. He had wanted to show
Danny how things were down in Mexico. Well, he thought.
If the boy had not had enough to convince him, it was hope-

less. Just at that moment Amesquita needed to believe in something. So he chose to believe that Danny had learned his lesson.

"So," Danny said, "he works for Mendoza."

Amesquita kept his eyes on the road, which turned to dirty, molten lead in the afternoon sun. "You came back," he said.

"Yes. I heard you say his name." When his uncle said nothing, Danny asked, "Mendoza did that? To that little girl?"

Amesquita nodded, his lips pressed together to form a thin pink line. "His men." Amesquita shrugged. "It would not surprise me to learn that Fassnacht himself did it."

"Why did you push the rifle down?"

Amesquita pressed his lips together again. "A failure of nerve at the critical moment."

"Where were they going?"

"Chicago," Amesquita answered.

"That's where Mendoza lives?"

Amesquita was so worn-out, so desperate to believe that Danny had the good sense to let it go, that all his defenses malfunctioned. He admitted that Mendoza lived in Chicago, which was fast becoming a major distribution point for heroin in America. He even rambled on a bit about the talk at high levels in several governments—of increased poppy growth in Mexico, which signaled a world-wide shift in heroin manufacture from the Middle East to North America.

The following morning Amesquita drove Danny to the airport. Before they parted, he embraced the boy, slapping him on the back. "*Acuérdate, sobrino,*" he told Danny. "*En el valle do los ciegos, el tuerto es rey.* Be sure and keep at least one eye open, huh?"

Then Amesquita turned Danny loose and drove back to the office, his air-conditioned automobile whipping along through the dry passing land, past the run-down shacks with corrugated metal roofs and worn-out truck tires stacked on top and the emaciated chickens and goats foraging in the dust, the wild juxtaposition of poverty and wealth like a warp between two dimensions, forever invisible to each other.

2

FORREST WAS in great demand on the Chicago social circuit. His work with Eisenhower in '56 and Nixon in '60, along with his experiences in the war and in the air, made him a perfect cocktail party guest. He had the right measure of romance and flash to adorn his solid foundation as a business lawyer. And of course, he was an unmarried man with money.

Aviation seemed the favorite topic; people of all sorts were drawn to the wholesome danger of flying machines. Forrest would inevitably find himself pinned in a corner by someone who wished to hold forth on the wicked stall-spin characteristics of the Gloster Meteor or the JU-87 Stuka. Those were the men—the judges and politicians—who piloted nothing more than a marble-topped desk.

At his own parties Forrest was able to hand off such guests to Danny. Forrest enjoyed seeing his son run the wheelchair generals to the ground with his superior knowledge of aviation, which Danny used in such an ingenuous fashion that he never seemed to be showing off.

It was during the period following Danny's return from Mexico that he took full advantage of this situation, prevailing upon assistant state's attorneys and stray federal judges to take him along on skeet shooting expeditions at the Lincoln Park Gun Club or the Northbrook Gun Club, where he sharpened his skill at handling a shotgun. At the parties

Danny would encourage them to tell him war stories about the bad, bad criminals being caught in those days in Chicago. He could back them into an information corner when it came to aviation, but he could also play the wide-eyed teen-ager. It was so natural. Young boys love to hear adventure stories; Monday-morning quarterbacks love to tell them.

At an early autumn barbecue Danny finally caught a big one. He spotted a man from the Justice Department lurching across the lawn, holding a bottle of Chivas Regal scotch. Danny brought him a fresh glass of ice. The man poured some scotch into it, thinking Danny wanted a drink. "No, sir," Danny told him, "it's for you."

"Oh, oh, thank you, Danny." He handed Danny the bottle and took the glass. He draped his arm across Danny's shoulder, burped loudly and blew alcohol all over the side of Danny's face.

"Boy," Danny said as they walked across the lawn under a thousand-mile sky, "I was reading about that big heroin bust. Who's that guy they're always trying to catch? Mendoza?"

"Thass 'im all right," the Justice man said.

"Must be tough to catch a man like that."

"M'possible," the Justice Department man said. "Fuckin' impossible, excuse my French, but you know what I mean. The man's got guards around him day and night. Greasers. It's just too much."

"Where does he live?"

"Lives above a nudie joint on Rush Street," he said, hanging onto Danny for balance, jingling the little spheres of ice in the crystal glass each time he lurched for his deteriorating equilibrium. "Place called the Flesh Pot. Terrible place. Just terrible."

Knowing what Rush Street was like, Danny asked why he would live in such a place.

"It's just his base of operations. Man's got houses everywhere under different names. But he stays at Rush Street." The man shrugged wildly. "Probably because he's a fuckin' greaser," he added, and laughed.

"You can't just go and arrest him?" Danny asked.

The man continued laughing in exhausted gasps. "It's not that simple, son. Can't get anything to stick."

"You guys must have him under surveillance day and night, huh?"

"Sometimes we do, sometimes we don't. We can't always spare the men."

"I guess a guy like that never goes out alone either."

"Sure he does."

"Why would he risk it?" Danny asked.

"Everybody's got a chink in his armor. Mendoza sometimes goes out to buy a six-pack of beer from his cousin's store down the street. He goes alone. I guess even Mendoza gets tired of greasers now and then." The man expelled a cloud of alcohol fumes at Danny.

By November Danny had spent many nights outside the Flesh Pot on Rush Street, watching for additional clues to Mendoza's habits. The very first time he saw him it was like being transported back to 1956. Just as clearly as if it were playing upon a screen, Danny saw Beto lying on the floor, the pistol skittering across the room, Mendoza's face as white as the moon.

Danny developed a distant, grudging respect for Mendoza as he watched him. He was clever. The apartment on Rush Street was inconspicuous. So were Mendoza's men. They drove older automobiles and wore very plain clothes, which made them look like lower-class Mexican workers. Only the steel pincers and his size made Mendoza stand out. He was big for a Mexican, six feet or more and easily over 250 pounds. Amesquita had called him El Cochiloco—The Crazed Pig.

In the suburb of Lincolnwood was a sporting goods store that sold firearms. Its front was made of two large display windows. One evening in November Danny drove by, threw a brick through the window and just kept driving. He went around the block and timed how long it took for the police to arrive. It took three minutes. A few nights later, when the window had been repaired, he did it again, only this time he took the Browning Superposed Magnum twelve-gauge from a display in the window. He was gone in thirty seconds.

Alone at home one afternoon, he sawed off the barrel and stock.

On November 20 Danny wiped the gun with oil and then put on his gloves. He loaded two three-inch shells into the gun and put it in a brown grocery sack. Leaving his car near the university, he took the elevated train to the Rush Street area and waited. Mendoza didn't appear that night and Danny returned home, frozen and tired. The following night he waited again, but still Mendoza didn't come out. On the twenty-second and twenty-third, he saw Mendoza three times, but he was with his troops. Danny was not discouraged. He was afraid, more afraid than he had ever been, but he was also patient and determined.

On November 24, 1964, Danny waited four hours in the snow until his feet became so numb that he realized he would have to give up once again.

At eight o'clock, just as he was about to leave, Mendoza came out of his apartment building alone. Looking once around him, Mendoza strolled away in the snow, leaving Danny paralyzed in the alleyway.

When Mendoza returned, he was carrying a six-pack of beer in a brown paper bag, cradled against his big belly as he waddled through the wet snow. The snow had stopped a few minutes before and a break in the cloud cover showed the moon, round and gray, bearing down. As Mendoza approached the alley, Danny put his hand inside the bag, released the safety and put his gloved finger into the trigger guard. He moved toward the sidewalk and took a deep, trembling breath. Mendoza didn't notice Danny until he spoke.

"*Señor*," Danny said sheepishly as Mendoza turned to see a young boy with a paper sack. Danny spoke in Spanish. "I'm only sixteen," he explained. "Can you buy me and my friends some beer?"

Mendoza smiled as Danny backed into the alley. Mendoza

grinned and stepped out of the light of the street to get a closer look. Their movement was like a dance. Danny's left foot moved backward, Mendoza's right forward. Mendoza emitted a low, derisive laugh. "Who are your friends?" he asked, holding the six-pack of beer before his massive abdomen, as if holding a partner.

He was in the moonlight, away from the action on Rush Street.

"Alberto de la O," Danny answered, and felt his entire body go numb with fear. He saw the expression cross Mendoza's face—he could hear it! The music was drifting through to him now, as he looked around the alleyway with surprise and recognition.

Danny felt a sudden collapse deep within his bowels. He inhaled, long and quivering, and his throat closed. Mendoza's dance had taken him back one step toward the street. "Remember?" Danny asked him. "I shot your hand off." Danny pulled the trigger twice in rapid succession.

The gun blew right through the sack, skipped out of his hands and over his shoulder into the darkness. Some of the pellets went through the bag Mendoza was carrying and the pressure inside the cans sprayed Danny with beer. Mendoza fell back in the moonlight and lay face up without moving, the six-pack still clutched to his great stomach as the beer spewed out in all directions. Mendoza had no neck. There was blood everywhere.

Danny dropped the torn remains of the bag out of which the gun had thrown itself. The police car pulled up just as he turned and began running through the alley. Someone on the street was screaming.

Danny disappeared into the subway station with one policeman running behind him. Danny entered the last car of the long train and began making his way forward from car to car. The policeman did the same. Danny had pulled the hood of his parka up so no one could see his face, but now he knew he was caught. Danny leaped from the train at the Foster Avenue stop, directly across from the middle of the campus, where he had hoped he could mix with the students.

By the time he was inside the library, security guards and police were pouring in. Danny ran down the narrow metal stairs into the stacks. During his research the previous summer he had noticed the rest room there. He headed for it now. The sign said MEN. As Danny put his hand against the push plate on the door, he suddenly noticed that it was only half of the sign. The left half of the sign had been cracked off. He heard footfalls pinging down the stairs. His options had run out. Danny pushed into the ladies' room.

MAGGIE CAME FROM ARKADELPHIA, Arkansas, one of the few in her graduating class to go on to college. She began at Northwestern University's Journalism School in 1963, obsessed with the notion that things could be understood in a world that seemed increasingly baffling.

By the fall of 1964 she was unsure. She had assumed college would precipitate an orgy of understanding. It had only left her confused and anxious.

The evening of November 24, 1964, she was in the library, working on a report at one of those uncomfortable desks put there as if to test how tough and determined a student really was. Each time Maggie finished with a load of books, she had to trudge down four flights of stairs to the lowest level of the stacks, only to return with another armload she knew would yield nothing. At about nine o'clock she decided to make one final trip before quitting.

The narrow stairs were constructed of metal lattice. Her boot heels made a pinging sound as she descended. At the first landing she stopped to use the rest room. It was tiled with old ceramic squares, yellowed with age and crazed with a reticulum of dirt. The room was lit with unflattering, relentless light from bare, faintly blue tubes. There were only two stalls, side by side, and one was occupied. Maggie closed herself into the other and stood for a moment with the oddest feeling that something was dreadfully wrong. She just stood there, unable to pinpoint the source of her anxiety. She had a sudden impulse to run for no reason. She unlocked the door just as the other woman began to leave. She smelled beer.

Seized by a sudden, inexplicable panic, Maggie barged out of the little metal enclosure and found herself face to face with Danny. She started to scream, but he had his hand over her mouth so quickly she didn't even see him move. One moment they were looking at each other—it was difficult to say who was more terrified—the next, Maggie was locked in his arms. And then in his life.

Danny's first words to Maggie: "Don't be afraid, I'm not a pervert."

Maggie laughed right through his hand—whether from relief or fear or the sheer idiocy of what he'd said, it was difficult for her to say. He sounded so sincere. "I'm hiding from the police," he added, as if that explained everything— sure, why not, that's absolutely fine, come right into the ladies' room and hide out from the police, young man, that's what it's here for.

For a moment Maggie thought he was a foreigner (*I'm going to be raped and cut to small bits by a foreigner*, as if that would somehow be worse than by an American). Danny took his hand from her mouth. He spoke directly into her face, close to her forehead, which came just to his lips. Maggie could smell his breath, like air from a winter seaside. She remarked to herself that it was odd: He smelled like beer but his breath did not. She had not yet completely dismissed the possibility that she was in grave danger of losing her virginity or her life or both (and she was not altogether certain in which order she would prefer to have lost them either) but even in that uncommon situation she noticed his eyes and they somehow deflected her worst fears. His eyes contained a mixture of colors, like flecks of stone, as if they'd been carefully assembled of layers of colored gems and had then been cruelly shattered. She watched them as Danny hastened to explain that he hadn't done anything really wrong but that the police could cause him a lot of trouble if they caught him. Maggie assumed the problem was due to a panty raid or some other prank for which college students get chased around by campus police now and then—a Keystone Kops movie in which the villains get run over by steam rollers and then pop back to life to continue running. Or if she didn't actually believe this, she at least gave enough credence to the logic of it that she allowed herself to relax—yes, that was a good enough explanation of his presence there; it was what she wanted to hear. Whatever the exact nature of her suspicions, she put them from her mind and chose to believe that Danny was fundamentally right and the police fundamentally wrong. By 1964 it had already begun to seem that the police were always wrong.

Maggie walked out of the rest room at the very moment the police were coming down the stairs into the stacks. She feigned interest in a hairbrush, which she was attempting to stuff into her overstuffed shoulder bag. A university security guard came down the stairs first, followed by Chicago detectives, who had been joined by the local police. Maggie thought the profusion of police odd, but not odd enough to displace the logic she already had.

The campus cop lunged at Maggie and demanded to know who was in the rest room. Maggie continued trying to fit the hairbrush into her purse. She looked up as if he'd asked her the time of day. "What?" she asked.

The security guard was flustered and in an obvious state of agitation. He looked at the wooden handle of her brush protruding obstinantly from her shoulder bag. Then he stammered something, touched his fingers to his brow in confusion and ran off in pursuit of the police, who had begun to fan out through the stacks. Maggie watched them with a mild, abstracted air until she could no longer hear their pinging footfalls. She opened the ladies' room door and signaled to Danny.

"We'd better get out of here," he said, taking her by the arm.

Although Maggie thought about it for another decade and more, she could never explain why she hadn't pulled away from him and demanded to know what on earth he meant by *we*. Even as she went with him, she wondered. She had no answer then, no answer ten years later, but it did not matter; the running was the point, running from the dread load of reference books she'd left beside the hand basin in the ladies' room, from the all-consuming frustration of her night's work, the vacuum of answers, the simple triteness of her student life.

They found Danny's car where he'd left it and drove far from the university to a forest preserve, where they parked beneath the intermittent moonlight. Maggie watched Danny, who sat at the wheel staring out the windshield, lost in thought. He looked quite young, she thought. Just a boy, really.

"You smell like beer. Are you drunk? Do you want me to drive?"

Danny looked down at his coat and brushed at the spots. "I'm fine. I just got some on me."

"Why were the police after you?"

"I gunned a man down," he said. Then he turned on her and laughed loudly.

Maggie laughed, too. "Then a posse will be after you soon."

"Tell me about yourself," Danny said, staring into his lap. He didn't feel like talking, but he knew he should.

"I'm in the School of Journalism," Maggie said. "And sometimes I don't know why. No, most of the time I don't know why."

"That's easy. You're an information freak. You want to know all the stories."

Maggie thought about that. She had never considered that elegantly simple possibility: that she simply wanted to know all the stories.

"Reporters just like to be there when something happens. Most people do," Danny said. "But reporters actually get there."

For the first time in months Maggie felt a surge of enthusiasm for all the work she had put in. For if, indeed, there was no understanding to be had, at least she would get the stories.

"What's *your* major?" she asked, assuming he was in college.

"Aerodynamics."

"Come *on.*"

"No, really." It might as well have been. Maggie could have listened to him all night, using terms such as El over Dee Max and angle of attack. She had been afraid that he would want to neck in the car like most boys, but he just kept talking, as she began to realize that he was certainly one of them, there was one in every class back in the sixties, Renaissance Man-berserk, bent on testing the limits of his own operating envelope. She was at once afraid of him and drawn to him. Those boys always attracted attention. The girls liked that close-to-the-flame illusion, and the boys wanted to be there when he finally burned himself down.

Many died along the way, while others simply wore out the posture and went straight, attaining only that sort of straightness old astronauts find, uneasy at peace and at home. True adventurers come home can be the saddest people on earth.

The night Danny fell into her life with all the delicacy of a garbage can falling down a fire escape, Maggie knew already something monumental had happened to her. She just didn't know what it was.

By the time Danny returned her to the dormitory it was snowing steadily. Big, wet flakes fell out of the dark and windless sky, illuminated in the old yellow streetlights of Evanston. Danny stopped the car on a street called Emerson near Sheridan Road beside the East Quad, a rectangular bit of earth circumscribed by squat buildings of ginger stone with heavy tile roofs, beneath which women lived in the mysterious golden incandescence of frosty nighttime windows.

When Maggie said she had to go in, Danny watched after her, wondering what had dropped this person into his life at such a moment. He knew he was supposed to feel something, but he could not figure what it should be. He had been going along the same path for so long that he was at a loss now that it had come to such an abrupt end.

And Maggie vanished into the snowy dark, up the long walk around the building called Hobart House, unaware of the path she was on, the one Danny had described: You don't get answers, but you sure get the stories, ones you can print and ones no editor would touch in a year of dead Sundays. What it's all about is you know a lot of stories you'd rather not know.

During the night the snow ended and the temperature jolted to just above zero, leaving a blinding clear sky when the sun rose. Danny waited for Maggie outside one of her classes and they walked through the town, talking. Maggie, of course, had read about the Mendoza "gangland-style" killing in the morning's newspaper, but she would no more have suspected Danny of being responsible for it than for the assassination of President Kennedy. She barely paid the story any attention, in fact. She was looking for the business section to complete an assignment that was due.

In downtown Evanston was a fountain, a round, soulless concrete casserole turned off for the season. They passed it going south, on their way toward Main Street, where they turned east toward an old frame hotel that had been used to house some of the victims of the Chicago Fire, when doctors and lawyers and other well-off folks, having been burned out of their homes, moved north as a temporary measure, discovered suburban living, and stayed.

They spoke of this and of Antoine Ouilmette, a French Canadian who was the first white settler near Chicago, having arrived there in July of 1790. During the massacre at Fort Dearborn he saved the lives of at least two whites and, for the next four years, was the only white man in the entire area. ("Like Rimbaud at Harrar," Maggie said.) In 1796 Ouilmette married a half Indian, half French squaw with the unlikely name Archange. The marriage in effect gave Ouilmette control of an enormous parcel of land, which was dotted with Potawatomi burial grounds and the remains of prehistoric tool-making shops. ("Some of the graves are right on campus," Danny explained. "Under Dearborn Observatory and Heck Hall. Deering Meadow.") Though Ouilmette himself lived like and was indistinguishable from the

Indians, in 1844 his children petitioned the President of the
United States to violate prior agreements that prohibited
the sale of Indian land. Presidential permission was granted
and 640 acres, 300 of which were in Evanston, were sold
for $1,000.

Danny returned the next day and the next. He was per-
sistent, but Maggie found it impossible to become irritated
by his attentions. Other boys, dressed up in suits and armed
with fake IDs so they could buy wine, had taken her to
fancy restaurants. They had kept her out at interminable
foreign movies with subtitles to prove that they could appreciate fine art. And they always ended the night with a
blundering attempt to pop all the catches on her clothes, as
if she were an oyster they could simply shuck out into the
open and slurp down with a late beer.

Danny took her to see Sleepy John Estes and Bob Dylan,
and she introduced him to the poetry of e. e. cummings. He
drove her to Bishop's Chili House on the South Side, where
construction workers gathered at nine in the morning for
boilermakers, "To get their buzz together," Danny explained,
"before going up on that high steel." He took her to the
basement of the Field Museum of Natural History to see
the mummies of cats and people and hawks.

When Maggie went home to Arkansas for Christmas,
Danny wrote to her every day. When she returned, he was
waiting at the train station and she was so tickled to see him
that she hugged him, never knowing what the proximity of
her breath and body was doing to him.

One winter morning they rode out west from the university, gradually passing out of the cramp of houses and stores
to winding lanes through silver woods under high, thin cirrus.
Danny turned north, then west and the woods gave way to
unilevel industrial parks, acre upon acre of static, septic
sprawl, deadly silent and motionless on a weekend morning.
They turned off Willow Road onto Milwaukee and rounded
the corner into another time—it was like driving into 1940.
Pal-Waukee Airport, named for the intersection of Palatine
Road and Milwaukee Avenue, had not changed significantly

in thirty years. The only clue that it was 1965 was a collection
of airplanes parked wing tip to wing tip along the ramp and
out across the snow.

Danny's plane was chained to three metal rings sunk into
a square of concrete in the heart of the field. Bolted to the
ground nearby was a red metal chest. Danny took from it a
small propane heater, which he attached to the airplane's
engine compartment.

"What are you doing?" Maggie asked. She had a special
way of looking at Danny with affection and reserve, as if
he were playing tricks on her and maybe—just maybe—she
was enjoying it.

"Gets lonely out here," Danny explained as he opened
the door to the plane. "I'm giving it warmth essential to
its growth." From the cockpit he removed the control lock
and a tube that had a plastic post sticking up from its center.

"What's that?" Maggie asked.

"It's a device for artificially inseminating cows," he said,
pushing the post up into a valve beneath the wing. The tube
filled with fluid.

"It's a fuel tester," Maggie said proudly. "And that's water
in the fuel." She pointed to the spheres at the bottom of the
tube, which looked like dirty pearls.

"Very good," Danny said, dumping the gasoline onto the
snow and draining more fuel into the tube. "How did you
know that?"

"Ever hear of books?" Maggie asked with a smirk. "They're
kind of rectangular-looking things and have all these funny
marks inside them?"

Danny walked along beneath the wing, checking its under-
surface. "Do you know what happens if we don't drain the
water out?" He wiggled the aileron and saw the yoke move
in the cockpit.

"Just about the time you get off the ground the water
reaches the engine, and about four days later there's a lot
of slow walking in your hometown."

"Outstanding," Danny said.

Maggie followed him as he squatted next to the cowling
to check the static port. "You're not the only one who knows

about airplanes," she told him. "I've been reading up on the subject."

"Why would you do a thing like that?" Danny squinted up at her.

"I'm just naturally curious, remember?" She turned away toward the field as if she weren't interested at all.

"Curious," Danny repeated.

"So how come you're preflighting the plane?" Maggie asked. "I read that, too. Preflight. It means to check all the things on the preflight checklist before you fly."

"Well?" Danny asked, as if that explained why he was preflighting the plane.

She looked at him and frowned, puzzled, then put her hands on her hips. "Oh, no," she said. "No, noooo. I'm not going up in *that.*"

"You couldn't pick a better day for it." He ran a finger over the propeller blades, checking for nicks.

"We'll *die,*" Maggie said.

Danny was at the nosewheel, checking the shimmy damper. He took a pen from his pocket and tapped the exhaust stack. It made a bell-like tone. "I'll tell you what." He squatted on his heels, squinting up at her in the bright sunlight. "We'll take off, and if you're afraid, I'll land right away. I'll have you back here in two minutes." He stood up, opened the inspection plate on the right side of the cowling and checked the oil. He continued around the plane.

"God, Danny, I've never been in an airplane before," Maggie said. She laughed, giddy with the almost tactile thrill of it, like someone who wants to go swimming but can't get beyond putting one toe into the icy water.

Danny was already putting away the heater. "She's warm," he said. "Let's hit it."

"Don't say hit," Maggie told him.

Danny opened the passenger door. "Up you go."

"I don't know . . ."

"It's cool," Danny assured her.

When Danny and Maggie were strapped in, he started the engine and tuned the radio. Maggie heard a recorded voice chattering very fast like a muttering tobacco auctioneer.

"What's *that?*" she shouted above the engine's roar.

"Listen." Danny pointed at the radio. The recording began again. The man spoke so fast Maggie could understand only one or two words, as if she were listening to a foreign language she had just begun to study. "Pal-Waukee Airport Information Romeo, the one-five-zero-zero Greenwich weather two-five-thousand thin scattered visibility unrestricted temperature two-one wind one-zero-zero variable at five altimeter three-zero-one-three ILS runway one-six circling approaching in use landing and departing runways one-two left one-two right and one-six IFR departures on runway one-six may be requested to complete a right turn to no less than three-two-zero degrees east of the O'Hare three-four-five-degree radial, if unable to comply please advise the ground controller. Advise on initial contact that you have received Information Romeo."

"Jesus Christ," Maggie said as Danny tuned the radio again.

He picked up the microphone. "Pal-Waukee Ground," he said, "Cessna seven-zero-five Kilo Romeo in area two southeast departure with Romeo."

They were then cleared to the active runway, short of which Danny ran through his final checklist, that all-important document that ensured that he hadn't forgotten the vital thing, the last thing he would ever want to forget, whatever it might be. In flight it could be anything—you could forget to turn on the fuel; you could leave the ignition on only one magneto and then lose it; you could neglect to retract the flaps and never even leave the ground as you slammed through the fence at the end of the airfield; or you could fail to secure your seat in its sliding track and find that as you rotated into flight, you slid back so far that you could no longer reach the controls. You could forget and leave one of your gas caps off or loose, discovering that when the plane reached about 100 knots, the slipstream hungrily sucked the tank dry in a minute or so—a most embarrassing occurrence.

Danny knew that there is more to the miracle of flight than just being aloft. It is a game in which the pilot is constantly pursued by demons bent on destroying him with his own hands. Although Danny said nothing of this to Maggie, she knew it instinctively and sat in silence, watching her fate take shape in the hands of this boy, as a cold, hard knot formed in her middle. When she heard him say, "Five Kilo Romeo is ready in sequence," she said, "Oh, Danny," but he paid no attention. This was his moment.

"Five Kilo Romeo," the radio said, "right turn approved, cleared to take off runway one-two left, wind is one-three-zero at six."

"Five Kilo Romeo will be straight outbound," Danny said.

"Roger, Five Kilo Romeo, approved as requested."

"Five Kilo Romeo is under way," Danny said, and advanced the throttle to the stop. As the plane began its take-off run, he checked the tachometer and listened to be sure the engine was developing full power.

"Oh, boy!" Maggie said. She sounded like a child on her first roller coaster ride, trying to decide whether it was going to be the most thrilling moment of her life or the gravest sort of error. "Oh, boy! Oh, boy!"

Danny let the nosewheel lift and the plane left the ground so gently it was difficult to tell they were flying. "Danny!" Maggie screamed. "DANNY!"

Suddenly she saw how hard he was concentrating. She stared at him for a moment, biting her lip and in awe of his fusion with the machine. She watched him control the plane's ascent, saw against the blinding blue sky the fine line of his nose, as if it had been lifted from a piece of statuary. His left hand was on the wheel, relaxed. Only his little finger and thumb were in play, urging the control yoke left or right as required.

The concentration she saw was due to the fact that Danny was watching the altimeter, waiting for it to read 1,150, which was the altitude he would need to execute a 180-degree turn and make it back to the runway if the engine decided to quit. As they passed through 1,300 feet, he relaxed, checked out the rear window once more to make sure they were flying the extended centerline of the runway and sighed. "Nothin' to it," he said, and patted Maggie on the knee. "Smooth as glass this morning."

"Danny!" Maggie shouted again. Every muscle in her body tensed with the unnatural state she was in. In a few seconds, she thought, we've gone higher than the tallest building in the world. She looked out the window as the airport pitched away behind them and abruptly her desire to speak fled. The day was absolutely clear. She looked out into the distance as they climbed. She could see a cluster of landmarks in the distance like the set of a science-fiction movie. Downtown Chicago. It was more beautiful than she could have imagined. She felt her muscles begin to relax and she sank back into the seat, noticing for the first time how comfortable it was. Below, she saw the trees, as stark and bare as if they had died suddenly in the night. The white landscape stretched beneath them, incandescent in the sun, with the tortured course of a river running through it.

"Danny," she said again, but there was no edge to her voice. "It's so beautiful."

"Want me to land?"

She shook her head and continued to gaze out the window. Danny made gentle turns left and right so he could see beneath the nose. The radio crackled to life. "Now, Five Kilo Romeo, call the Navy on one-twenty-six-two and have a good day."

"Five Kilo Romeo, *adios*," Danny said and switched to the frequency of Glenview Naval Air Base so that he could let them know he was overflying their field. "Glenview Tower, Cessna seven-oh-five Kilo Romeo," he said.

"Five Kilo Romeo, Glenview Tower."

"Just off Pal-Waukee out of fifteen hundred for two southeast bound, permission for flyby."

"Approved," the voice said without ceremony.

Maggie let her head roll back against the seat and smiled. "I love it!" she shouted.

"Maggie," Danny said, reaching across to squeeze her hand.

"I love it!" she hollered again, laughing and pressing her nose against the window to watch the air base pass below. "Danny," she whispered, "look at all those planes." They passed over a superhighway and Maggie said, "Look how small those cars are."

"Look at those ants," Danny said. "They look just like people."

Maggie turned to give him a dirty look. They flew over Northwestern and Danny circled Hobart House to show Maggie where she lived. He turned north and flew up the lakeshore over Wilmette, made two turns around the Baha'i House of Worship—an enormous, pallid concrete breast sticking unashamedly out of the ground—and continued northwest to Libertyville, where he once again called Pal-Waukee Tower and reported inbound.

When Danny had parked on the slab of concrete, he and Maggie sat listening to the gyros wind down, the engine ticking itself cool in the icy air, and their ears rang with the quiet. "I love it," Maggie said. "I want you to teach me. I just love it."

Danny leaned over and encircled her in his arms. She laughed softly into his shoulder. "I love *you*," he told her, and she swallowed her laughter. She did not pull away though.

She put her arms around his neck and whispered, "I mean it. I want to learn to fly."

"I mean it, too," Danny said.

As the weeks passed, Maggie begged him time and again to take her flying. Years later she would wonder if that was her way of sublimating; it was so erotic, hanging up there over the virgin white landscape, alone with Danny in the cocoon of warmth—such a precise little dance with gravity and wind. She handled the plane with deliberate, studied precision, doing everything exactly as Danny told her.

Maggie's schoolwork and even the deadening student schedule began to take on a new color and resonance. Her life seemed full of interesting things and each one of them vibrated with incipient revelation. She had the constant and delicious sense that not even the simplest gesture or incident was without momentous implications.

One night Danny and Maggie went to have dinner with Forrest. Forrest did have a way with women, Danny had to give him that. He charmed Maggie, telling jokes and (to Danny's surprise) outrageous anecdotes about the White House press corps from his days with Eisenhower and Nixon.

After dinner Forrest left, saying he had to go into Chicago and would not be back until at least 1:00 A.M. Danny knew it was for his sake that Forrest left. Maggie was not ready for such an evening, though, not yet, not there, and certainly not to be handed over so transparently from father to son. It didn't come as a surprise, then, that Maggie declined the invitation when he made no more than a pro forma pass at her. Even Danny could not have gone through with it.

So they drifted through the weeks together, to kiss and move away and kiss again, talking and listening to Joan Baez or Bob Dylan or one of the really forgotten names now.

Maggie refused him and Danny's hands won the precious territory by inches, as Maggie's lines of defense were pushed back before the steady, patient pressure. *The hands, Maggie thought years later, it was the hands that did it, that could hold an airplane so steady and yet were so gentle I could never fear them. The hands I saw launch a sleek paper airplane out between the gargoyles atop the theological seminary one icy, windy day. I had dared him. He said he could sail a paper airplane from Garrett Seminary all the way to the lake, and I dared him to do it. His thin fingers folded the paper with such precision, creasing with the hard, white half-moon of his thumbnail and all the while talking clean configuration, mean dynamic chord, form drag. . . . He aligned it with his happy eyes, laughing as we climbed the narrow stone steps to the tower. Without warning, he launched it into the wind and it did, it sailed all the way to the lake, Danny was so proud, those were the hands I longed for to read me in the blind, Braille darkness.*

Maggie did not give up her virginity easily, even to Danny. For six months he spoon-fed her affection, six months he played along until—after a four-hour telephone conversation during which he broke through the last barriers of maximum-security, escape-proof logic she had erected—Maggie went upon his instructions to the Library Plaza Hotel and waited. It was June 9, 1965.

She lay on the double bed. A steady blast of icy air roared from a window air conditioner. To Maggie the room appeared to be decorated for octogenarian virgins, a place to sit and fade and pass along in the lengthening sunlight of history. Maggie wore a cotton summer dress, which Danny said made her look like Botticelli's *Primavera*. She grew colder and colder each time the compressor kicked in or went off with a thunk.

Maggie had taken two baths. She was clean inside and out, clean underneath her fingernails, clean in every fold and crevice, from the tips of her eyelids to the auburn rose below. She had no doubts, Danny had convinced her and she shivered remembering the many nights they had spent in a car or standing in the blowing snow, after touching each other until they could no longer touch without *becoming* one another. And now she wondered how he had waited—indeed, *why* he had waited. Such stamina. Had the positions been reversed—had Maggie wanted something so much and been refused so consistently—she would have been long gone. Long, long, long.

By the time Danny arrived Maggie was freezing. He was precisely on time. Maggie had been a few minutes early— something like ninety of them. Danny burst into the room, smiling and nervous, flushed from the heat of the day or from embarrassment. Maggie lay chilled to the core beside the clunking, thunking air conditioner in her Botticelli dress, lying on her back, as stiff as a stick. Danny undressed. *He took off all his clothes right in front of me, I watched him do it, standing on one foot to remove his shoes, socks, pants, balancing with the exact unawareness of a wild animal. He moved as if he weighed nothing at all, as if he might just leave the earth at any moment and rise away. I thought of him as an aviator. He preferred the term* airman.

It seemed to take him hours to get undressed, he never even knew what he was doing to me (neither did I, I was so green he could have rolled me up and smoked me) for he'd

never had a woman before, and when he came to me, finally,
my stick of bones on the hard bed, his skin was so smooth
and tight, if you'd dropped a silver dollar onto his stomach,
the coin would have bounced a foot in the air, we didn't
know what to do with each other, neither one of us had ever
made love, but it was so easy, so simple—no one had ever
said it would be simple—I wasn't even cold anymore when
he got into the bed, our skin hot together, holding each other
for a long time, just holding, arms and legs entangled like
children absently napping in the afternoon. And then it was
quiet and brief, with Danny saying, "Maggie, Maggie, Maggie," drawing it out to fourteen syllables each time, over
and over, it was brief and twice, then three times. Then
four for a long, long time. He had found what he had been
after for so long and he liked it so much it made me laugh
out loud, it was so much fun, we were giddy and high and
silly with it, success, success—Danny positively glowed with
achievement, I loved him so that afternoon, it's difficult to
believe it was ten years ago, Lord, and it's an odd, double
feeling, like paying to see a sleight of hand trick so clever
that even after you've lost the money, you shake your head
and wonder, was it worth it? You know you've been tricked
and you think: Well, I wanted to be tricked (I even paid
for it!) and it certainly was a good trick. . . . Six months
after I left Danny, I thought I'd gotten over him. Now I
realize I haven't even begun to sort it out. When I think
about that, it can be the coldest joke in the world. Sometimes I laugh out loud. And sometimes I just sit down and
cry. Sometimes I come apart at the seams, but that's okay.
Danny used to say, "If you're gonna come apart, just make
sure it's at the seams, where we can put you back together
again."

Calculated
Risks

3

THAT FALL Chip and Danny enrolled at Northwestern University, and while Chip seemed to disappear into it with the skill and confidence of long practice, Danny immediately began looking for ways out. Two great changes occurred for Danny that season. He and Maggie took an apartment together, a small place on Chicago Avenue across from the commuter train station, but the apartment was not the point. It was the first time in memory that Danny had ever lived with a woman—sister, mother, lover—any woman.

Danny also met Michael that autumn, a rail-thin graduate student in the chemistry department who had a wild Jewish Afro, which he called an Isro. At first Danny thought he was just another hippie, a love child full of vague concepts, misdirected energy and morning glory seeds. It wasn't long before Danny realized that Michael's appearance amounted to nothing more than protective coloration. Danny saw it first in Michael's eyes. Their clarity, the way they seemed to take in his surroundings with restraint and calculation, in contradiction of everything else Michael appeared to be. Danny didn't know what Michael's game was, but he knew it was not played with a softball.

A couple of weeks after they had met, Danny and Michael were in someone's apartment, smoking grass—flowers so aromatic and potent that Danny sat in blunt, astonished silence, trying to keep from falling off the wall-to-wall carpet, while Michael talked and giggled. Danny was amazed that

no one else could see through Michael's hippie pose. He was
also amazed that no one else noticed that although Michael
smoked as much as anyone in the room, he might as well
have been smoking Winstons for all the dislocation he
seemed to be suffering.

"Totally like this leaf," Michael said, "is the apex of the
phenomenon. This leaf has *traction*, can you feel it?" He
looked at Danny. Michael pretended he was talking to everyone in the room, but Danny knew it was between him and
Michael. "Totally like torques you out, you know?" His accent was Palos Verdes. He said the word *totally* as if it were
two syllables, *toad-ly*.

Danny, for one, could not understand, no matter who
Michael was beneath his disguise, how he could even talk
behind the grass they'd smoked. Danny watched the room
spin and spin. At one point he had the illusion that the room
was trying to digest him, and a flutter of electric panic raced
through him, bringing heat to his face. His extremities were
cold and tingling. He felt as if a moose were kneeling on his
chest.

Danny had never smoked grass before and found it difficult
to believe how high he was. He had stopped puffing on the
joint that was being passed around but he just seemed to get
higher and higher. He could not talk. Each sentence he
began unraveled halfway through and the words lay like a
hopelessly knotted mass of yarn about him. His own voice
was frightening to hear, as if he were in a deadened chamber
hearing it transmitted solely through the bones of his head.
The people and objects around him seemed of another
world, as if he were merely peering into it from afar, through
a lens or even a microscope. He was disassociated, nearly
catatonic and fluctuating wildly between the edge of gripping
terror and hysterical euphoria. He was, as Michael put it,
"ripped to the tits."

About three hours later, when Danny had begun to come
down, Michael mentioned in the most offhanded way that
he had heard Danny and Chip were excellent pilots. Without thinking—which was a task that required a good deal of

effort just then—Danny informed Michael that together he and Chip could fly any type of aircraft better than anyone. One thing Stew and Forrest had not taught them was modesty. Michael fixed Danny with his eyes at that moment in a way that Danny knew carried an alarming freight of significance, but he did not know what it was. A few minutes later Michael looked at Danny again and said, "You look like you need some air. Let's take a walk."

Outside, Danny began to feel some relief. He was still high and was glad to be moving around, out of the room that had been trying to digest him. Michael put his arm around Danny's shoulder and spoke like a hypnotist, softly, steadily. Later Danny was unable to remember exactly what Michael had said. But as he spoke, Danny gradually began to see, if not how he had known that Michael's hippie appearance was a fake, at least what the pose was covering.

"You're a dope dealer?" Danny asked.

"No, no," Michael said, patting him on the back. "I'm a broker."

"A broker?" Danny asked with a laugh. "You make it sound like some kind of Wall Street business."

"That's right, man. I know that everybody thinks I'm just the greatest little hippie that ever hit the campus. And I am, of course, totally like for sure." He laughed. "But there's more to it, as I think you can see. When I was seventeen, I saved up a little money. I was just out of high school and got on a plane to Amsterdam. I bought eight kilos of hashish and eight cheeses, you know, those big round ones they import here? I threw away the cheese, wrapped the hash up in wax so it wouldn't smell, then in the cheese wrappings and just flew back with it. I looked like an all-American kid, coming home from vacation. They didn't even ask me to open my bag."

Danny looked at Michael in disbelief. Michael smiled and dug into his pocket. "Here," Michael said, "I brought these along just to show you." There were two passports, both of them black and blue from the beating they'd taken beneath the stamps of countries all over the world.

"Nepal?" Danny asked.

"I went halfway up Shisha Pangama with Sherpa guides when I was eighteen, just to see the town where they make temple balls of royal Nepalese hashish. Look here," he said, pointing out the stamps on one of the passports. "Vietnam, Morocco, India, Thailand, Colombia, Perú, Turkey."

"Apart from that, have you done any traveling?"

Michael laughed. "I like you, Danny. I want you and Chip to work for me."

"Dope dealers are bad news," Danny said, shaking his head.

"First of all," Michael explained, "you're thinking of smack dealers. This is a completely different business. Secondly, I'm not asking you to deal. You have to understand, there is a difference. You're a pilot. I'm asking you to fly for me. Look, you smoke grass. I smoke grass. Half the kids on campus smoke grass."

"J. Edgar Hoover doesn't smoke grass," Danny said.

"Then we won't deliver him any," Michael offered with a smile. "Look. Grass is something people want, something that is not hurting them."

"Something that is illegal."

"It's not like you think. The people who grow grass are Indians. Dirt farmers just trying to scratch out a living, man. We buy their crop. It's all they have. A single good crop bought by us can keep hundreds of families going for a year. Hundreds."

If Michael had not gotten Danny's agreement that day, he had at least started him thinking. He could see through Michael's obvious attempt to con him with geopolitical nonsense. Even the dirt farmers and hundreds of families, though something to consider, were part of the con. On the other hand, Danny could not help hearing a voice in his head, saying: Go ahead, man. Put it to the wall. If you're such a hotshot pilot, why couldn't you pull it off? Maybe that *is* where the true adventurers are these days. And, thinking back to the night he met Maggie: That's a very hard act to follow.

Danny had visited Michael several times during those

weeks, one side of him saying he wasn't interested, the other saying tell me more. Michael told him as much as he wanted to hear. "Shit," Michael said one afternoon, "we've got airline pilots who do it on their days off. And they're straight as the day is long, Danny. Even with their salaries, though, they find it difficult to resist a gig that takes twenty-four hours and makes them twenty thousand tax-free dollars."

"Twenty thousand dollars?" Danny asked.

"Each," Michael said.

"No." Danny shook his head. "No, I'm afraid not."

"Whatever," Michael said. He knew, even if Danny didn't, that he had him, pinned and wriggling in a box like a butterfly. If it wasn't the money, it was the noble Indian families, working and slaving their lives away, growing their simple crop. If it wasn't the Indians, then it was the adventure—Michael didn't know what kind of adventure Danny had been through, but he could see it in his eyes. He knew Danny had come home to a vacancy and flatness that ate at him, and Michael had presented him with a clear alternative. Pirates with knives in their teeth. Smugglers.

Danny told Chip, of course, and when Chip heard about the rate of pay, he said, "Well, I don't know about you, but I'd do it tomorrow, man. In a superheated second I'd do it. Are you kidding me? Twenty thousand dollars?"

"I don't know," Danny said. But he was already lying to himself by that time. He knew. "It's awfully illegal."

"Just think what you could do with twenty thousand dollars," Chip said.

"Hire a lot of lawyers," Danny said.

Michael's contact in Tucson had picked up a DC-6 Executive Freighter with new engines. At $195,000, it was a steal. Danny told Maggie that he and Chip had a rare opportunity to get type-rated in a DC-6 if they flew out to Tucson. This was true, of course, and Maggie thought it was a great opportunity for them. Danny and Chip did fly out there and they did meet an instructor—chief pilot for a major airline—who taught them how to fly the DC-6. They didn't ask a lot of questions, other than those that had to do with the opera-

tion of the aircraft. It was apparent that very powerful
people were involved. How else could they get the chief
pilot of one of the nation's largest airlines? How else could
he get permission to do touch-and-go landings on a military
airstrip?

After their check-out training Danny and Chip flew the
plane to Mexico, following a regular airline schedule. They
took off just ahead of a flight for Mexico City. When the
passenger plane was airborne and out of sight of the airport,
Danny and Chip flew their DC-6 right in on top of and
just behind it, where neither the crew nor the passengers
could see them and where they would be above the airliner's
wake. The reason for flying piggyback was that it would
result in only one radar picture on the scopes. Since that
picture was identified as a scheduled flight, no one would be
suspicious.

When they were safely airborne, cruising along peacefully,
Danny looked over at Chip and said, "You know, we don't
have nearly enough training to be flying this thing alone."

"I'm counting on your remarkable ability to land anything
anywhere," Chip told him.

"You may wind up counting on your toes."

"You're not having second thoughts, are you?" Chip asked.

"Naw, shit," Danny said with mock disdain, "I had those
weeks ago. I'm having deep regrets now."

Once they crossed the Mexican ADIZ, they peeled off and
disappeared to a lower altitude, where radar could not paint
them or where, if they did show up, it would be as ground
clutter or low-flying local traffic.

They landed at night in what appeared to be jungle. Fire
pots had been lit in a straight line to indicate a landing strip.
At that moment they knew the full value of Stew's grueling
and unorthodox training methods.

"Short-field, soft-field night landings in a DC-6," Danny
said, hogging the great aircraft around into a turn to line up
with the lights. "God, I hope there's really a landing strip
down there. We must be crazy. Gimme forty degrees."

"Forty degrees," Chip said, putting out full flaps. "I don't
think there's much doubt about it."

"About there being a landing strip?"

"No, about us being crazy."

"Gimme spoilers on the flare," Danny said.

The strip turned out to be nothing more than a dry mud path hacked out of rain forest. They never even shut down the engines. In the strange, flickering firelight they could see men in military uniforms with what appeared to be machine guns. About forty Indian-looking men loaded bales into the plane while others fueled it.

"Chip."

"Yeah."

"Are those army guys?"

"Maybe they're extras from a movie somebody's shooting around here."

"And do you see machine guns?"

"I see fire sticks," Chip said. "What do you make of it?"

"*Beaucoup* strange," Danny said.

"*Beau*-fucking-*coup*," Chip agreed. "Let's switch these engines to rock-and-roll."

"A-firm."

As the men secured the loading door and waved them off, Danny and Chip were reading their final checklist, chattering off the items as fast as they could. Danny made his shortest short-field takeoff and breathed a sigh of relief as he crossed over the black expanse of trees below.

They landed at dawn in the Arizona desert, where they were met by men with trucks and firearms. They were put in a Jeep and driven to a road. There they were given a car and told to leave it at the Tucson airport with the keys in it. From there they took a commercial flight home.

A few days later Michael gave them each a bankbook that said in neatly engraved script:

CASTLE BANK & TRUST
(BAHAMAS)
LIMITED
[PRIVATE BANKERS]

Inside each book there were printed numbers indicating that their accounts had been credited $20,000 each. A dollar a pound, just as Michael had promised. They had been gone less than a week. Michael had told them that the rate at which they were being paid was low, because it was their first trip. Danny and Chip didn't mind. It was more money than they had ever made or were ever likely to make in a year on any job. Danny felt a deep sense of accomplishment—a kind of relief and release, as if he'd worked some poison out of his system. He understood why people do such things as diving to the bottom of the ocean or walking across the Kailas Range. The only problem was that home, afterward, seemed so dull and attenuated, like watching a movie that is never quite in focus. Out there, in the danger zone, everything seemed sharp and clearly defined. Back in his little suburban apartment, he felt adrift and vaguely anxious. Only the newness of living with Maggie deflected these feelings.

"You didn't get any sun," Maggie observed when Danny returned from Tucson.

"They don't have sun lamps in DC-6 cockpits," was all Danny offered by way of explanation. And if he sensed any suspicion on her part that there had been something more to his trip than what he had told her, Danny did not dwell upon it.

It was his mistake. Watch your six, Forrest used to tell him, meaning watch your six o'clock position, meaning watch your ass. Danny still had a long way to go in fully appreciating that dictum. For if he correctly read the adventure in Mexico as some pinnacle of experience—and it was, at that point, nothing more than an adventure—he still hadn't developed a sophisticated enough sensor for what Maggie knew instinctively in her farm girl heart. Fat, dumb and happy, was what Stew had called it, when you're most relaxed, completely secure, enjoying the view and merrily running out of gas.

⌒

ONE MORNING Danny and Maggie went out in the plane, departing north-northwest over the VOR. The ride to Grayslake took only a few minutes, and Danny directed Maggie to land on the uncontrolled airstrip they could see below. He picked up the radio and called Campbell Unicom to learn that Runway 27 was in use. The wind was calm and Maggie made a perfect landing, as she had been doing for some time now. They parked by the little building and went inside.

It was a combination café and fixed-base operation. There were several telephones for calling flight service, and on one wall a dozen shirttails had been pinned, with names and dates lettered crudely on each. It was customary for older pilots to rip off a student pilot's shirt the day he made his first solo flight.

A withered old man sat at the counter drinking coffee. Danny and Maggie sat next to him and a line boy brought them coffee. He couldn't have been more than fifteen.

"Run back there and get me some prop wash," the old man told him.

"Yes, sir," the boy said, and ambled into the back room.

The old man wheezed and laughed until Danny thought he'd fall off his stool. A moment later the boy came back out, red-faced and eyeing the old man with growing suspicion.

"Go back there," the old man continued, "and ask him if he's got a sky hook." When the boy didn't respond, the old man laughed and laughed and fell into a coughing fit.

"Let's go flying," Danny told Maggie. He dropped a dollar on the counter and they went out to get into the plane. He had Maggie take off, turn around the pattern and then land again. He directed her to pull over to one side. Then he opened the door and got out. "See you later," he said.

"Danny," Maggie insisted, "stop playing around."

"I'm not," he said, holding the door. "I'll be down here, watching you. Do three touch and gos and then make a landing to full stop."

"Danny, I can't do that."

"Sure you can. Just do it like you've been doing it. It's time now."

"Oh, Jesus," she said, but Danny had shut the door. She

reached the throttle and gunned the little plane. It rolled forward and she guided it toward the arrival end of the runway. Of course, she could. She had landed the plane hundreds of times. Her logbook said so. She knew everything to do. She could do it in her sleep. Well. She sighed. Well.

She looked left and right and up and down. The sky was clear. She wished the engine would just stop, right now on the ground. But it wouldn't. It was a Teledyne Continental normally aspirated, direct-drive, air-cooled, horizontally opposed, carburetor-equipped, four-cylinder engine with 201 cubic inches displacement. Oh, my God, she thought, I know everything I'm supposed to know; there are no more excuses.

She pushed the throttle to its stop and screwed in the friction lock. The little Teledyne engine roared and the sixty-nine-inch propeller spun into a translucent disc. She was rolling down the old asphalt runway. She refused to allow herself to look to one side, where she knew Danny would be standing. He loves me, she thought, he loves me, and he would not be sending me up here alone unless he's certain I'm ready.

The plane broke ground, as light as a moth—no, lighter. It lifted into the air and Maggie felt something shift in her, a feeling as profound as a bowling ball dropping through whipped cream. Straight out, she thought, glancing back to see that she was flying the extended centerline of the runway, straight out to 1,000 feet, then turn left. Always turn left in the pattern unless instructed otherwise. Notice: Continental Motors Specification MHS-24A, Ashless Dispersant Oil: This oil *must be used* for first 50 hours or until oil consumption has stabilized! She knew it. She knew it all.

The earth below was beautiful. More beautiful, Maggie had to admit, than it had been even while flying with Danny. She was alone now; for the first time in her life she was truly alone, her destiny quite literally in her hands. It was a stunning revelation. She could pick up the radio and scream for help. She could call her mother or her lover, she could call God or the federal government, but only she could bring herself safely back to earth again. It was either competence or death. It was the most remarkable thing she had ever experienced. It changed her life in a few seconds, for she knew that she had learned everything she needed to know to make the flight successful. She was alone, on her own, and she would survive to do it again (demonstrated crosswind velocity is the velocity of the crosswind component for which adequate control of the airplane during takeoff and landing was actually demonstrated during certifications tests. The value shown is not considered to be limiting). She had her life in her hands and it felt good.

Maggie turned left and this time could not help seeing Danny below. She was only 1,000 feet off the ground, less than one-fifth of a mile, but he looked like nothing more than a speck. She screamed, "I love it! I love it!" and laughed. The plane flew itself downwind and she rolled left again (the design load factors are 150 percent of the above, and in all cases, the structure meets or exceeds design loads) and again, chopping the power and letting the plane down toward the old airfield. When her wheels kissed the asphalt, she gunned the engine and was airborne again.

Later, when she had made her full stop and Danny came over to congratulate her, she cried with joy. He took a pair of scissors from his flight bag and carefully clipped the tail of her blouse off and brought it to the old man at the bar inside, who lettered Maggie's name and the date and hung it on the wall.

During the following months, when they weren't out flying, or when Maggie wasn't in school, Danny and Maggie spent their time in that suspended state living together can be when it is new. They painted their apartment together and made it their own, hanging Maggie's copy of *The Old King* by Rouault, Danny's poster of *The Old Guitarist*. As winter set in, they would sit and watch the snow fall on the roof of the auto mechanic's garage below their window and sometimes, early in the morning, they would drink coffee and stare at the people waiting for the commuter train at the station across the street, speculating on what each one would be forced to do that day.

"That one there," Danny would say, pointing. "With the

camel coat. He's gonna kiss a whole *gang* of ass today, I'll bet."

For Danny just being with another person was a new and mysterious experience. Some evenings he would make Maggie lie still on her back so he could rest his head on her chest and listen to her heart beat. Sometimes, when he'd see her walk across the room, naked from bed in the morning, he would tell her to stop, just so he could look at her and attempt to fathom such an image as he had never seen.

"Oh, go on," she would say, embarrassed. "You don't want to look at me." And she would disappear into the bathroom. But she was wrong; he did, he did want to look at her.

Living with Maggie for Danny, could sometimes be like visiting another planet, and when it was, he never wanted to leave home.

Danny had enrolled in the fall quarter at Northwestern, but after four weeks of it, he stopped going to classes. It was not difficult in those years to be out of school, out of work, to be idle and attract no attention. All over the country boys and girls had begun to do just that; soon an entire generation would rise up and promptly sit back down. Maggie was too busy with her journalism career to be overly concerned that Danny was not continually busy.

She credited Danny with helping her through the period of her worst doubts about journalism, though he teased her mercilessly about reporting now that she could take the teasing.

"What a lovely way to make a living," he would say. "Talking on the telephone to hostile strangers, pounding on doors to ask angry, secretive people questions they don't want to answer about things that probably aren't even your business."

Maggie would laugh. "Yes, true enough. But I have all the stories." Maggie knew. She was there because she was an information freak. *She* wanted to know what was going on. "I," she told him, "can pick up the *New York Times* and laugh. That's not the way it came down. I know. I was there."

In the spring she had an assignment to report on what had

come to be called a love-in, which was taking place on the campus. Michael staged the event, of course, the supreme hippie orchestrating the loud, sprawling festival for the delight of anyone who cared to come. The winter air that had made the very act of breathing painful only weeks before now tasted fresh and balmy. Strung out in Deering Meadow in front of the very library where Danny and Maggie had met were a hundred or more students and hangers-on, tripping, smoking grass, kissing, listening to the loud rock-and-roll music that blared from giant speaker columns set up beneath the trees. Deering Meadow was bordered, west and east, by Sheridan Road and Deering Library, a stone block of a building that Frank Lloyd Wright had once said looked like a dead pig on its back. North and south were remnants of what had once been forest, and neither the builders that built nor the dancers that danced had the dimmest inkling that the ground beneath their feet was a sacred Indian burial site.

Danny and Maggie held hands as they walked toward the scene. They spotted Michael in the crowd and waved. Michael began to make his way toward them through the giddy, agog disciples. Four police prowl cars idled on Sheridan Road between the fraternity houses and the love-in. People were dancing with their shirts off, boys and girls alike, but the police would not interfere unless someone filed a complaint or the crowd threatened property or life. The university wanted to maintain a low profile in those tense times. The police wanted to see teen-age tits.

Danny and Michael hugged each other. Over Michael's shoulder Danny watched brightly painted breasts of every size and shape bounce in the sunlight, some of them painted up to resemble Easter eggs—ostrich Easter eggs or, in one case, perhaps dinosaur Easter eggs.

"Michael," Danny said. "Goddamn, boy, what's this you've got going here? You gettin' all these innocent children hooked on drugs? I bet some of them have already shot up that marijuana stuff and smoked some Coca-Cola."

Michael giggled. "Far out," he said. His face was painted. "Come on," he told them, getting between Maggie and

Danny to interlock arms with them. "Virginia and I are about to *drop*. Why don't the four of us drop together?"

"Drop to where?" Maggie asked.

"Drop acid," Danny explained. "LSD."

"Oh," Maggie said in a falling voice, as if she'd just forced Danny to reveal something she had not really wanted to know.

"Really," Michael said, "you ought to try it. It's pure Owsley White Lightning. Reagent-grade Mindfuck."

"What's Owsley White Lightning?" Danny asked.

"Augustus Owsley Stanley the Third," Michael explained. "Dude on the left coast. Best acid this side of Sandoz."

"If you think so," Danny said. "I think we'd probably like more of a controlled environment." Danny gestured at the screaming, lurching crowd. The breasts.

"Whatever." Michael rummaged in his freaky Isro hair and found a joint behind his ear. They sat on the grass and Michael lit the slim wheatstraw cigarette by holding the tip over a burning match. He sucked on it noisily before passing it to Maggie.

"The police," she said, gesturing toward Sheridan Road.

"No sweat," Michael said.

Maggie puffed on the joint, then lost all the smoke in a coughing fit. She took another hit and held it with a frown, as if it were certainly a silly thing to do, probably a waste of money, possibly bad for you or even immoral, but she was damned if she'd be left out.

"You two are really beautiful," Michael said. "Totally like beautiful together. Like children."

"May I quote you?" Maggie asked.

Michael took a small box from his pocket. In it were a dozen white pills. "I want you two to have this for a special occasion," he said.

"What is it?" Maggie asked.

"White Lightning. Good, pure Dreamfuck LSD." He wrapped two tablets in a bit of tinfoil. "These are nominally four hundred mikes. You might want to split one the first time." Michael sighed and stood up. "Well, I'd better find Virginia. We've got to drop before the day gets too far along.

My moon is in Taurus and right now is the perfect time."
Just as he was turning to leave, he added casually, as an
afterthought, "Say, Dan, we've got to talk."

"Sure thing," Danny said. "We'll see you later on. Maggie
and I are going to drop some lunch now."

Michael giggled and wandered off into the loud, swaying
crowd. Wild electronic music screamed its hollow howl
across the green meadow and the breasts jiggled in the sunlight. Across the road one of the policemen had field glasses
pressed against his face.

When Michael was out of earshot, Maggie said, "Boy, he's
a caution, isn't he?"

"A-firmative."

"What did he mean about talking to you?" Maggie asked.

"Beats me."

If Maggie did not believe that he was telling her the
entire truth, she showed no sign of it.

Michael and Virginia were sitting in the living room of their
house when Danny arrived. Virginia was only four feet ten
inches tall and had a small, perfect nose. Her mouth was
too wide, but it gave her a startling sexuality, which she
seemed to enjoy. Her expression seemed to convey that she
was continuously on the edge of pain or ecstasy. When
Danny walked in, Virginia was rolling a small black ball of
opium between her thumb and forefinger, staring at it as if
in a trance. She had the tiniest fingers Danny had ever seen.
She sat cross-legged in her chair, her little muscular thighs
tight against her short skirt. Danny had to concentrate to
keep from staring up her dress at the little banner of white
cotton that curtained her deepest mystery.

"Daaany," Virginia sang as he came in, "you want some
opium?"

"Dopium?" Danny asked. "Maybe some other time."

"Outta sight," Virginia said.

"We're going to talk," Michael told Virginia.

"Far out," she said, as if Michael had just explained to
her some basic law of nature. She stood and left the room.

"What's going on?" Danny asked.

"I have another trip for you and Chip if you want it."

"No, I don't think so. That was sufficiently spooky the last time. Many firearms. Many weird people."

"The firearms were there to protect *you*. These people are our friends."

"Your friends," Danny corrected.

"This trip will be in the daytime. A very easy trip. In and out. Five dollars a pound. Forty thousand pounds."

"*Five* dollars a pound? That's a hundred thousand dollars apiece."

Michael smiled. "I told you last time the rate was low."

"Jesus, I don't know."

"Danny, we're like the Coca-Cola Company. Success is based on the principle that everyone at every step along the line makes money. If everybody's happy, it reduces the risk of fuck-ups, rip-offs. Whatever."

"Another six?"

"Nice airplane," Michael said. "In addition, you'll have the rare honor of meeting Manolete."

"The bullfighter?"

"No, but I understand he was named after the bullfighter. Manolete is the *man*." Michael made a fist and held it up, fingers forward, giving it a single shake to signify power. "Beautiful cat."

Danny sighed, clearly torn, telling himself that it is all right to do something like this if your motives are pure. No, that rationalization didn't cover it. Pure what? Greed? It's just flying, he told himself, but he knew that was a lie as well. Well, what then? "I'll have to talk to Chip," Danny said, and immediately knew that was a cop-out. He knew what Chip would say.

Michael stood up and put his hand on Danny's shoulder. "Whatever you say, Dan."

Danny and Maggie sat at the little table in the dining area of their apartment. It was midmorning. They had eaten a big breakfast and were drinking orange juice and coffee.

Danny took one of the Owsley White Lightning tablets and cut it in half with a folding knife. They each swallowed half with orange juice. They cleared the table and then went back to the living room, where Maggie sat on the couch, her legs crossed Indian style. Danny sat in an overstuffed armchair. They faced each other across the room and waited. They smiled at each other. There was silence until someone in another apartment flushed a toilet. Then there was silence again. Nothing happened.

Out the window was the fire escape, the auto mechanic's garage below, the sunlight. Pigeons came and went on the mechanic's roof, emitting notes of tender surprise, *Ooo! Ooo!* Beyond the garage were the tracks for the elevated commuter train, which clattered to a halt at the Dempster Street Station every ten minutes or so and then rattled away again, a single car at this time of day, riding its electric rails. The day was clear and warm—truly beautiful. More beautiful, in fact, than Danny had ever seen it. It hurt his heart to look. The way the sunlight came through the burlap curtains, brilliant, crystal-clear spokes of sun, shooting through the room like sabers of light. He could almost hear them clashing. It was astonishing.

He took a deep breath. It was like inhaling a powerful stimulant. That must be oxygen, he thought. He couldn't stop himself from smiling. The air was exceptionally clear. Danny breathed again. It was so good. He did it again, gulping voraciously. He watched the sunlight. He was stunned by the beauty of the garage below, the wrought iron of the fire escape, the fat pigeons; it almost made him want to cry out with joy. Suddenly all the pigeons took off at once, turned around just twenty feet above the garage, as if they were all attached to the same central projector in a planetarium below, mere artificial images of themselves on the screen of the sky. When they landed, Danny remembered the first time he'd seen the miracle of flight, centuries ago now, on the floor of the Rio Grande Valley after a hurricane. He felt the very walls of the cells in his body straining from the pressure, as if from some internal radiation, as if he were going to burst with ecstasy.

Still, the question remained: Why wasn't this super White Lightning Owsley the Third Acid of Michael's working? Nothing was happening. Zero, he thought. Zip. A page from the dictionary appeared in front of his eyes, just floating there in the air. He read from it. *Ziti*, it said, *zizith, zloty, zoan, zodiac, Zoroaster, zoon*—wait, that's out of place: *Zounds! Zoysia*, any of several creeping grasses of the genus *Zoysia* native to Asia and—you know—ordinary lawn grass, naked in Asia . . . Wow.

Danny looked up at Maggie to see if she had seen the page. She was smiling. She had obviously seen it, too. Danny had never fully realized how breath-takingly beautiful Maggie was until this very moment. How could he have missed such a thing? He stood up to go to her, to touch her. It was about fifteen feet across the room, but he must have slipped because he floated into the air and crossed the distance in a single step. Wow, wow, what was that? They were face-to-face and he could feel the oxygen molecules entering him through his nose and mouth. Their faces were very close. Danny touched Maggie and felt the energy pass from her body into his. It was intensely sexual. They both giggled. Maggie felt it, too.

Without a word, they took off all their clothes and their eyes stayed together the whole time, locked onto each other. They got onto the sleigh bed. They both understood in that moment that they had never made love before. It had all been a dress rehearsal for this moment—they were virgins, always had been. Danny eased Maggie's legs apart, lifted her knees up and just lay there with his head between her legs, looking into the mystery. Orchid, he thought.

When she could wait no longer, Maggie pulled him to her and they stared at each other, Danny lying on top of her until she pulled him up just so and he slipped inside her. Maggie drew a breath of the same oxygen molecules into her body. Danny moved slightly, gently within her, and the energy passed back and forth between them like alternating current, switching direction so rapidly that it made him want to scream. Maggie and Danny came together for the first time then, and the wall behind the sleigh bed exploded outward, revealing a grotto beyond, shimmering with jewels and colors and little riptides running silver and iridescent green, blue, gold . . . *Dreamfuck.*

They got up, still naked, and climbed out the window onto the fire escape, naked in the warm brightness, giggling to each other. They climbed the flight of stairs to the third floor, outside the building. Danny looked down through the lattice of iron to the concrete walk by the mechanic's garage below. It was a long way down. A pigeon took to the air nearby. I can do that, Danny thought, and moved toward the rail. I'm an airman. He was naked and he could fly. Maggie had begun to climb the ladder to the roof and she turned around to see where Danny was. He was halfway over the railing.

"Danny," she said, giggling. "What are you doing? Come on up."

"I'm going to fly."

"Look at me. I'm going up to the sun. Come with me. You can fly later."

Danny was almost ready to fly, but he turned around to see. He looked up and saw Maggie's cheeks, spread as she hooked one bare foot on a higher rung, the orchid mystery there. He let himself back onto the fire escape. He could fly any old time.

They lay on the roof, lightly touching each other, feeling the sun's energy—all the wavelengths of ultraviolet, gamma, alpha, the heat of infrared. They felt greens and oranges cover them like leaves and cool liquid copper. Little cells beneath the skin took certain wavelengths and turned them into umbrellas of color.

At some point they noticed they were being watched.

At first it was merely a flash of light, a signal mirror from a far building. They searched until they saw the little figure with binoculars. They laughed and made love for whoever watched, and when they came, it was together again and the roof exploded. They fell through, waving at their audience, fell all the way down to the apartment again.

They dressed slowly, feeling their clothes, marveling at how strange it was to put oneself into those tubes of cloth, to wrap one's body about.

Maggie and Danny walked down to the lake at the end of Greenwood Street. Miles out, near the horizon, sea serpents leaped a hundred feet out of the inland sea. Danny had never noticed that there were sea serpents in Lake Michigan. It was something to remember. Sea serpents.

~

MANOLETE WALKED AMONG the tall, healthy weeds that grew in rows inside the volcano, spaced between similarly healthy rows of corn to disguise them from the over-zealous American helicopter crews that might be flying over, unaware of arrangements that had been made on the ground.

A small platoon of Zapotec Indians followed Manolete on his rounds and he occasionally muttered instructions to them in their clipped dialect as he examined the leaves of plants, which glistened with a moist amber resin in the steady sunlight.

Manolete's white clothes were accented only by the thick black leather belt from which a holstered revolver hung. The need for it was unclear. Scattered throughout the fields and ringing the perimeter were *federales*, sweating in the morning air, their light automatic weapons propped against their knees or strapped over their shoulders. The guards looked as if they hung halfway between this scene and a dream of it. It was deceptive, though, like the sleep of gunpowder.

A small group of Indians huddled in a circle, laughing. They had placed a lizard in a thick black river of ants and were making bets. The ants ate the lizard's eyes first so that it could not see to fight back. Then they systematically ate the lizard alive.

Manolete cocked his ear to the sound of the approaching aircraft and checked a heavy silver Rolex chronometer. He made his way through the plants toward the airstrip cut into the forest that surrounded the fields. As he approached, he could hear the tinny sound of a transistorized radio one of the Indians carried around his neck. Manolete hollered at the group surrounding the lizard. The Indians stirred and moved off in the trembling heat toward a caravan of burros, which they began to lead toward the landing strip. Each burro labored under the mass of two oil drums.

Beside the runway were the bales, wrapped in black plastic, baking in the sun.

The plane exploded into the air above the crater, full throttle, both engines whining, and squatted on the airstrip, kicking a great plume of dust into the thin morning air. It skidded to a stop, turned around and taxied back into the takeoff position. Manolete dusted his white clothes with both hands.

Near the bales two *federales* sat sweating, oblivious to the new layer of dust that settled on them and the wind from the propellers that whipped the straps of their rifles. Manolete hollered and they stood, as a group of Zapotecs shuffled toward the bales and began lifting them with grudging, implacable indolence.

The dust hung in the air with the smell of grass and kerosene in a silence as profound as if a cannon had just been fired.

As Danny and Chip hopped to the ground, Manolete hurried over, grinning. When he reached them, he threw his arms around Chip, who reacted to the little brown man's gesture of friendship with such mute baffled outrage that Danny had to laugh. Manolete didn't know why Danny was laughing, but he joined in the laughter, giving Danny the same vigorous *abrazo* he had given Chip, slapping him loudly on the back.

"You are Cheep?" he asked Danny.

"No, Daniel," he said.

"Ahhh," Manolete said, then turned to Chip, who smiled uncertainly, as if Manolete might try to kiss him next. "Come inside where it's cool," Manolete told them with exaggerated good humor.

As they followed Manolete into the building with its corrugated steel roof, Danny and Chip were hit with a tremendous asphyxiating blast of heat from within the dark building. At the end of the warehouse was an office of sorts, a corner enclosed by flimsy walls and furnished with an old metal desk, a filing cabinet and a couch. In one corner a propane refrigerator vibrated on its rotted rubber mounts. One wall was pegboard fitted with hooks on which hung several revolvers in leather holsters, some bandoliers of shotgun shells, three pump shotguns, four M-16s and three Swedish K selective fire rifles.

Danny whistled when he saw this. "The goddamned War Room," he said.

"What?" Manolete asked with a mild, abstracted smile. He bent to the refrigerator and brought out three six-ounce bottles of Coca-Cola.

"Swedish Ks," Chip said, accepting the Coke from Manolete.

"These are berry nice weapon, no?" Manolete asked with a smile. "Just like your CIA use."

"None of my business," Danny said, "but did you get them from the CIA?"

"No, no," Manolete said. He put his little finger into the neck of his Coke bottle and loosened a plug of ice. Then he drained the entire bottle without removing it from his lips. He set it down, cut loose with a loud blast of air from deep within his throat and shook his head. "I get these from the *cubanos.*"

"*Cubanos,*" Danny whispered.

"*Sí, cubanos.*" Manolete sat at his desk and motioned for Danny and Chip to sit on the gutted leather couch. "They bring strange things here," he added. Danny watched as Manolete extracted a package of cigarettes from his pockets and shook the tips of three or four into the open. He held out the package to Danny and Chip, who declined the offer with a wave. Manolete lit his cigarette and Danny noticed his watch. "Last week," Manolete continued, "the *cubanos* offer to pay us with rocket launchers from Russia." He laughed as if that were the funniest thing he had ever heard. "What do we want with rockets?" He took a puff from his cigarette, holding it between his thumb and forefinger in such a way that he had to turn the heel of his hand toward his chin. "We have no enemies," he said, blowing a brown-tinted cloud of smoke, which hung in the dead, unmoving air. "You see the *federales?* Who would attack us?"

"Do you know why they're here?" Chip asked.

"The *cubanos?* I don't ask. They are good for business. They pay us in gold. That is good. They pay according to the morning fix in London. They have strange toys, these *cubanos*. They have radios, little black ones"—he made a phantom shape in the air with his hands, half the size of a shoebox—"and they get the gold prices each morning direct from London on these. They can talk to Paris, Moscow, Bangkok and"—he smiled—"*cómo no*, Havana. Once they let me call my sister in Chicago on their radio. It rings in her phone, just like I am next door."

Danny and Chip exchanged looks but asked no more questions.

"You will be doing much business with us?" Manolete asked.

"I think this is our last deal," Danny said.

"Too bad. We need people like you." Manolete paused in thought. "When you are done flying this plane, you go to Cuernavaca to the hotel called La Manzana. Werner is the owner. A very good friend. Anytime you are in Mexico, if you need anything, you go there and he will help you." Manolete smiled, leaving to their imagination what he might mean by "anything."

"Sure," Chip said. "Sure thing."

They finished their Cokes and went back into the sun. Inside, outside, it made little difference, the heat was bad either way. When Danny's eyes adjusted to the light, he could see the Indians refueling the aircraft from the drums on the backs of the burros.

"*Estas hecho una cuba.*"

"I hope they're straining that fuel through a chamois," Chip said.

"They know," Manolete said. Then he barked orders at them in their Indian dialect as if to demonstrate to Danny and Chip that he was, indeed, on top of things.

"Have you worked a weight and balance?" Chip asked.

"You want to check the load?" Manolete asked. He reached into his pocket and took out a few pieces of paper to show him. They were photocopies of pages from the operating manual for the DC-6 freighter, graphs showing the limits of the center of gravity, the maximum certificated weight for takeoff, engine-out climb profile and so on. Danny and Chip had heard that many pilots who flew such commodities never bothered with these details. They had also heard that pilots who ran their operations that way sooner or later punched a very expensive hole in the jungle.

Chip pushed the papers back at Manolete. "I have your word," he said. "That's good enough for me." What Chip really meant was that he had seen the graphs and they were correct. He was simply observing the etiquette of the business: Complete trust stated, profound suspicion implied.

Manolete was a pro. He didn't mind. *"Diós te lleve,"* he said, hugging Danny.

"Y tú," Danny said.

Danny and Chip climbed into the ship and situated themselves in the cockpit as Manolete watched. The Indians drifted away from the landing strip, some of them leading burros, which walked more easily now that the drums were empty. Manolete could see Danny and Chip talking. Chip turned and put his thumb up in the air. Manolete signaled thumbs-up in return.

The engines began to fire, filling the air with the smell of burning kerosene. The aircraft stood at the arrival end of the runway and Danny held the brakes while putting the throttles to full takeoff power. When it began to roll, it appeared the plane would never gain enough speed to leave the ground. But as it passed the last stand of trees before the forest closed in, the nose lifted and the craft labored into the air.

Danny made a low-level shallow turn upwind to gain altitude without covering much ground, and the plane slipped over the dead mountain's ragged green lip and was gone.

They left the plane in Arizona, and boarded a commercial flight to Cuernavaca. Once they were settled in their seats and the airliner had begun its climb, Chip said, "Now this wasn't really the last deal like you told Manolete, was it?"

Danny looked at him oddly. "What do you mean?"

"Well, I was doing some figuring. If we could do just one trip a week for ten weeks, we'd have a million dollars apiece."

"If you think so, Charles," Danny said, and turned to rest his head against the window, watching the earth below. Danny wondered, as he dozed, why Chip would want to make more trips. Danny felt he'd had enough adventure for a while. He certainly had enough money.

At La Manzana they met Werner. They didn't know what Manolete had told the man, but it had clearly been the right thing. Werner treated them like royalty. For several days they ate and drank and swam. They even managed to acquire suntans. When they returned home, though, it was as if nothing at all had happened. That's the way it was when a deal came off properly: Nothing happened, nothing at all.

WHEN SHE AND DANNY gave themselves to each other, Maggie had no idea what her expectations were. They had fallen together in such a haphazard way that she'd never had the time most girls have to think. About monogamy, for example. She had never stopped to wonder if it came by the pound or quart or whether it simply covered everything like a blizzard.

By the time she was forced to consider all this she knew that like justice, monogamy was just another paradox. That realization did not make any more palatable the jealousy, bitterness, injured pride not even her own rage. Not any more than embracing the concept of illness will heal the sick.

When Maggie realized that she had begun to suspect Danny, she felt terribly guilty. When Danny disappeared for several days, she suspected him of running off with another woman and fought her feelings, embarrassed by them. But one evening Danny didn't come home until well after midnight, and when he did, he looked like a dog who had been left out in a hailstorm. He did not throw his arms around her and kiss her as he normally would have. In fact, he maintained a distance from her that was so obvious it was almost painful to watch, especially since she could smell—even across the room—another woman's perfume.

Danny tried to act cheerful, but it fell miserably flat. Still, Maggie said nothing, not even when Danny decided to take a shower, which he never did at night.

Maggie even fixed dinner. In fact, she went out of her way to be civil, went overboard, really, opening a bottle of wine and putting music on the stereo set.

Maggie did not ask any questions. Somehow she knew she would not have to. After dinner she cleared the table and they lay quietly on top of the sleigh bed, which remained neatly made. They did not undress; they simply lay there. Bob Dylan sang. *When your mother sends back all your invitations . . .*

It was a strange evening—a strange time all around. "Things," as people had got into the habit of saying, had begun to "get heavy." The world appeared to be reaching critical mass. Students were in revolt. Bobby Kennedy was alive. He was vital. Detroit, Washington, Baltimore, Berkeley, Watts, Chicago were in for heavy weather. The greatest leader in the world bombed Vietnam again and again. Boys were getting their faces shot off. Dylan, the Beatles, Mick Jagger sang and sang. Hendrix and Joplin and Morrison, too, sang for a time. A strange evening, a strange time, as Maggie lay on the sleigh bed with her man, though he might have been a stranger at that moment.

"I've got to tell you something," Danny said.

"I know," Maggie said. She wasn't angry. She wasn't anything at all. She just knew. "I know," she repeated. She stared at the ceiling of the little apartment where they were supposed to live happily ever after.

The ceiling danced with the candlelight, crescents of shadow overlapping to form darker patches where they crossed. Dylan sang the sad electronic song, *you're tired of yourself and all of your creations.* "Tell me," Maggie said. She could not stop staring at the ceiling. "Go ahead and tell me."

"How do you know?"

Maggie stared at the ceiling and at first said nothing. Danny thought she was angry, but he was wrong. "I just know," she said. "Tell me now. Tell me exactly how you did it." *Now when all of the flower ladies want back what they have lent you . . .*

"It was nothing, really," Danny began, already lying with-

out exactly meaning to, putting it in a passive form—it was
nothing, as if he had taken no part in it, as if it were something that simply happened, like an earthquake or a hurricane, anthrax or leukemia. "I met this girl," he continued,
and Maggie wondered if he were going to say that she put
a gun to his head and forced him to disrobe, but she said
nothing. "It was really stupid," Danny said, which Maggie
knew meant that it was really smart—or smart-assed, *and
all of your children start to resent you* . . . "You know,
everybody on campus is making films; everybody's a film
maker these days," Danny said. "So I ran into Howard, met
him on campus."

Maggie stared at the dancing light on the ceiling and everything seemed to move away from her, as if the world had
taken a small step back from her field of vision. Nothing
could touch her. She didn't even know the man who was
talking to her. It was a stranger's voice and it made no
difference what he said or did. It would take her years to
realize that that was one of the mechanisms by which men
and women drift apart during those impossibly close rela-
tionships. The man does things that kill the woman inside,
little by little. The woman, out of sheer survival instinct,
begins to insulate herself, to back off, to drift into other
worlds of anesthetic remoteness. It's either that or end it,
because some things are too painful to take full strength.

Danny could not see this, for Maggie gave no outward
sign, so he continued to talk, oblivious to the fact that
Maggie was drifting into deep space. "Howard said he
wanted me to be in one of his films," *and you're sick of all
this repetition* . . . "Well, we talked about it. He introduced
me to the girl who was going to be in the picture. You know.
It seemed like an interesting idea." Danny stopped and
watched Maggie. She was only vaguely aware of someone
watching her from a long way away. She continued to stare
at the ceiling. Danny took a drink of wine. The ceiling
danced and danced. Dylan sang. "Anyway," Danny continued, "it turned out there were nude scenes in the movie,"
*trying to prove that your conclusions should be more
drastic* . . .

"Nude scenes," Maggie repeated dreamily. The ceiling danced and danced. They offered you a million dollars and you had to do it for your country, she thought.

"Both of us, yes. Naked. The girl wanted to do it. I wanted to think it over. So Howard went away. Left me and the girl to talk it over."

"You were considering it then?"

"Yes, and—"

"And you screwed her," Maggie said. She felt no malice. It was a simple statement of fact. She lay there like a sack of sticks, her own protective circuitry working so well she was not even there. She wasn't the first woman who had ended up running on no current at all. She would learn, she would learn how easily it could get to the point where you didn't hate him or love him anymore; you just endured him. She never wanted that to happen between her and Danny. She would leave him before she'd allow that.

"It just happened," Danny said, but Maggie wouldn't look at him. It was an outright lie and both of them knew it. Copulation doesn't just happen. Yet he pressed on in the face of it. "It had no significance," he protested.

"How was she?" Maggie asked.

"Aw, come on . . ." Danny began. He knew he was caught, wrapped and tied in his own ribbon. He looked away and said, "I don't know why I do these things," admitting for the first time that he had done it, that it hadn't just fallen on him like a safe.

"These things?" Maggie asked. She sat up and looked directly at him. "*These* things?"

Danny stood up. Maggie lay back as if nothing at all had happened. The ceiling danced. Dylan sang.

In a safe-deposit box at his bank near the university, Danny had $120,000 in cash he had withdrawn from his Castle Bank account in the Bahamas. There was not much he could do with it, other than to pick out a few bills from time to time to pay the rent or buy a bottle of wine, go to a movie or occasionally pay for repairs on Kilo Romeo. Those pilferings did not put a noticeable dent in the stacks of money, though. He had to admit, he hadn't made those deals for the money.

For Chip it was different from the outset. "It's good," he had told Danny. "Money. It's pure, like the calculus. Like computer power."

"We don't need more money. Do you realize how long a hundred and twenty K would last?"

"It's not how long the money will last," Chip said in that calm, studied tone of voice he used when he was speaking of the physics he studied or the mathematics. "Money is its own end."

"Chip, don't give me more of your nihilistic, cerebral bullshit. If we're gonna make the trip, hey, it's fine with me, but let's admit that we're doing it because it's great fun to be deep in like that. Let's say we move marijuana because it's there."

"Then you have your reasons, I have mine. Amounts to the same thing in the end. If you're so overcome with the adventure, I'll take your share of the money."

"Now wait a minute," Danny said, "I'm not a communist."

"See?"

Each trip was made with a newly purchased airplane—that was considered simple overhead. Michael bought another DC-6, which was about the best all-around workhorse airplane for hauling heavy loads in those days. With 40,000 pounds on board, the DC-6 was technically overgrossed, but it handled it beautifully. Also, the plane was cheap. Michael picked up a fine used DC-6 with zero-time engines for under $200,000. When the deals were done and the aircraft abandoned, the feds or customs would find the plane out on some southern airstrip and wrap it in plastic tape that said EVIDENCE—DO NOT OPEN. They would search for the culprits, who would be long gone by that time. The only way to find them was if they happened to crash. Occasionally they could catch a smuggler crossing the ADIZ and scramble a chase plane, which would try to take movies of the dope plane. When possible, the smugglers would throw the dope out as they flew an evasion pattern. Even then it was difficult to make a case based on "large bundles of what appeared to be vegetable matter" being tossed from an airplane.

Since you can't put sirens and lights on top of a chase plane, why should anyone be expected to land and give up? By the time the airplane being pursued actually did land (and if the chase plane hadn't run out of fuel—smugglers tend to carry auxiliary fuel tanks to extend the range of their planes) what could the police do? They could search the plane, perhaps pick up a few seeds and stems if the wrapping on any of the bales had broken. Occasionally there would be some money, though that wasn't illegal and most pilots knew the cardinal rule: Never put your dope and your money in the same place. That was like asking to get ripped off.

So the planes impounded were generally without crew or cargo and were eventually put on the auction block. Unlike captured boats, which would have rotted from sitting for months in a slip somewhere, the planes were generally as good as new, if not legally certifiable as airworthy, because of unauthorized fuel tanks that might have been installed. Agents of the importers simply bought back the planes at the auctions. The paper work on airplanes was a joke anyway. It wasn't like having an automobile. Who was going to pull you over to check your registration? Superman? Besides, smugglers get paid infinitely more than policemen, are better equipped and certainly more numerous. Getting caught was just bad luck, about as likely as getting killed in a civilian air crash.

It was therefore with an air of relative calm that Danny and Chip took off for their next trip to Mexico. When they landed the freighter in the volcano, however, Manolete was nervous and it showed. There appeared to be more guards there than before and they, too, seemed nervous—certainly not the sleepy *federales* Danny and Chip had seen before. These men were ready for something.

"We must hurry," Manolete cautioned as he led them into his office beneath the steel roof in the heat of the warehouse.

"What is going on here?" Danny asked.

"We have friends among the *cubanos*," Manolete said. "People who tell us things. They say we are no longer safe here."

"I don't understand," Danny said. "You said you were so well protected."

"They don't tell us more than this. I don't know. I only know one of our people has brought word that we are no longer safe here. We are shipping everything out now. Your load and then three more today and then we all go into the hiding. You saw the fields. They are cut down. Nothing but the corn remains. We have planted no new crop, too. I'm afraid, my friends, this really is the last deal for us."

"Where will you go?" Danny asked.

"The Indians they will go back to their homes in the hills, where they have always been. I go to the city. Maybe I go to Chicago and stay with my sister." With a smile he added, "Maybe I go to Acapulco and sit on my ass."

"What then?" Chip asked.

Manolete shrugged. "They will come and tell me when this place is safe. Or maybe I find another place."

"They? Who in hell is they?"

"I've been in this business for many, many years," Manolete said. He seemed tired and not altogether disappointed that he was leaving. "I never ask questions. I grow the best leaf in Mexico. But the business is moving out, I can see it. The heroin is coming in. All the fields are turning to poppies. All the leaf is coming from Colombia now. In boats." He arched his eyebrows and gave Danny a long look. Then he did the same to Chip. "You know about boats?"

"We've heard," Chip said.

"You boys are good. You don't show off. Many people who come here think they are beeg criminals. But they are only beeg fools. You be careful, my friends. Just do your work and say nothing, eh?" He poked himself in the chest and laughed. "And you grow old like Manolete."

"What are you getting at?" Chip asked.

"Marijuana in Mexico is through," he said. He drew his thumbnail across his neck. "Some will come out, sure, but prices in Colombia, the government in Colombia, the *quality* in Colombia—they are all more favorable to trade. The entire business is going down there, and if you want to stay in this business, you go down there, too."

"I see," Danny said.

"Anyway," Manolete said, "hey, on a ship you can move fifty tons, eighty tons—there's no limit, all you have to do is find where the leaf is."

Chip whistled. "Sweet Jesus, eighty tons."

"*Sí*," Manolete agreed, "this is a lot of leaf, no?"

"There is definitely that, *mano*," Danny agreed. "But I'm afraid this is going to be the last deal for us."

"Okay, *manito*." He slapped Danny on the shoulder. "You must go now. Another plane will come soon."

The Indians had finished refueling the airplane and were leading the burros away. The three men stood before the plane for a moment, looking at one another.

Manolete said, "So maybe I see you in Barranquilla."

"You be real fussy now, *mano*," Danny told him.

"*Y tú*," Manolete answered. "*Tened quidado, hermanitos.*"

Manolete hugged them. Danny and Chip got into the plane and roared down the strip. But as they passed the last stand of trees, they already knew something was wrong. The nosewheel had not lifted and the runway was used up.

Danny forced the plane off the ground prematurely, the stall warning horn blaring, telling him he was critically slow —it was either that or slam through the wall of trees ahead of them. There was no verbal communication between Danny and Chip in that century of seconds, but each of their minds was screaming and their synchrony was nearly telepathic. Chip hit the switch that retracted the landing gear just as the plane exploded through the tops of the trees at the edge of the forest. The plane shuddered in sickening sonic waves of its aluminum gong as both Danny and Chip looked ahead for a place to set the plane down. Yet for all their emergency training, there was no cure for a million unbroken acres of jungle when what they needed desperately was something flat and vacant. They were taking off from a mountaintop airstrip and not nearly high or fast enough to turn back and land. As Danny held the plane, as if by a thread, in roaring, quivering flight, it finally slipped over the dead lip of the volcano and they began to descend down the slope toward denser air, still clearing the trees by a scant hundred feet, but alive.

"Overloaded," Chip said through his teeth.

"What was your first clue?" Danny asked, holding the throttles forward with so much pressure that the back of his hand turned white.

"Something about our rate of climb . . ."

Danny hit the elevator trim. "Flaps fifteen," he said.

"Fifteen," Chip said, hitting the switch. "You got El over Dee Max, looks like. As we descend," Chip went on, calculating in his head, "we should go from roughly twelve thousand MSL to three. That'll help. We burn off enough fuel, we might be able to climb back up to altitude and return to the strip."

Danny's face turned red with outrage. "Well, that's fucking wonderful!" he screamed.

Chip shrugged. "I'm open to suggestions."

"Okay, how about you crawl back there and throw some of that pot out."

"Number one," Chip said, "I can't get to the cargo door. Number two, it took forty men quite a long time to load that grass. Imagine how long it would take me. Number three," Chip said. Then he tapped a placard above the cargo hatch unlocking mechanism. It read: CAUTION! DO NOT OPEN IN FLIGHT.

"You know . . ." Danny began, but Chip cut him off.

"Watch that hill!" Chip hollered.

Danny glanced up and threw the plane into a shuddering turn.

Chip whispered, almost to himself, "No accelerated stalls, please."

"What're you, my fucking instructor?" Danny shouted, the aircraft barely under control as the small hill whipped by them.

"That little landmark is not on these charts," Chip said, tapping the map in front of him.

Danny sighed as they returned to level flight. "My people."
Chip said nothing. Danny checked his instruments again.
He could feel himself shaking inside. "Have you ever heard
of the Mexican Space Program, Charles?" He laughed without humor. "Do you know *why* you've never heard of the
Mexican Space Program, Charles?" He jammed the throttles
forward as if there might just be a tiny bit more horsepower
hiding in there somewhere. "We lost fifty feet in that turn."

"Positively El over Dee Max," Chip said.

"We lose ten feet here and ten feet there, we're gonna
nickel and dime ourselves right into the forest."

Chip checked the instruments before him. "Our fuel flow
is very high," he said. "Just fly around here a little. Then
let's see if we can climb."

Gingerly, Danny began a shallow 720-degree turn, grum-
bling to himself, "Boy, I hate like hell trying to land this
thing there with twenty tons of pot strapped to my ass."

Half an hour later they tried climbing again and the plane
slowly crept up until they had adequate altitude to clear the
rim of the volcano. When Chip indicated that they had
burned off sufficient fuel to attempt a landing with all that
grass on the high-altitude airstrip, Danny rolled out on a
return heading. They rode toward Manolete's without speaking. They both knew what they feared, but there was no
point in discussing it. Since there was no radio communication with the people on the ground, there was no way to tell
them they were returning. If another airplane had parked
on the strip . . . Well, there really was no point in discussing it.

Ten miles from the mountain they saw the greasy plumes
of smoke pouring into the sky.

"What in hell do you make of that?" Danny asked.

"Mount Vesuvius?"

"What Manolete said. Jesus shit. I hope he got out."

Chip said, "I don't know." The volcano, indeed, seemed
to have come alive, and as they approached it, they could
see flames licking the lip of the mountain. "Guess what."

"I think I've already guessed. I believe we've gotten close
enough."

"I'll take it," Chip told him, putting his hands on the yoke. "You look on that chart for someplace to go."

"Roger," Danny said as Chip began a delicate 180-degree turn back the way they'd come. Danny rustled the charts, scanning the hundreds of miles of open space for something— anything. He banged the top of the instrument panel, shout- ing, "Goddammit!"

"Hey, hey," Chip said in a calm voice, "easy on the avionics there, Airman Paine."

"We burned up all that goddamned fuel, Charles," Danny said, "and we're burning options just as fast."

"What do you make of that mess back there?"

"What do *you* make of it?"

"Cuban rockets."

"Cuban rockets," Danny whispered. Then he slapped the map he had been studying. "Here! We just might be able to set this thing down without killing ourselves. Do you think we can make it on the fuel we have?"

Danny fed Chip the figures and Chip did the calculations in his head to determine whether the amount of fuel they had left and the rate at which they were burning it would allow them to get to the road depicted on the charts. It was just outside a town and near enough to the jungle so that they might escape without being detected. It appeared to be a big highway. They would have to deal with the problem of undelivered goods later on.

They flew toward the road, watching intently for any signs of the town ahead of them. Half an hour passed. Then another ten minutes.

"Technically, according to my calculations," Chip in- formed Danny, "we are already out of fuel."

"Come on, come *on*," Danny said, craning his neck, look- ing down at the jungle.

"We are fuel critical," Chip said.

"We've been fuel critical this whole flight." Danny straightened and pointed. "Contact. Eleven o'clock."

"Where? Where?"

"There."

"Where?"

"There!"

"Holy shit."

"And there's the road."

"Oh, no." Chip's voice sank.

"It do look tight," Danny said. "You want me to take it?"

"Better had," Chip said. "We just lost number one." He began shutting down the mixture on that engine as Danny took over the controls, trimming for glide, feeding in rudder and putting the nose down to compensate for asymmetrical thrust.

"Say, Chip, why don't you put something in front of your face? This might be a little bit rough."

"Go ahead. I've never seen you make a bad landing yet."

Before Danny could respond, number two died and then they were out of gas altogether, as Danny released the rudder and retrimmed, putting the nose toward the earth. The silence was astonishing after so long with those enormous engines roaring around them. "Fifteen degrees," Danny whispered. It was amazing. They could hear each other in the silence.

"Fifteen degrees," Chip said softly. "Looking good, Dan."

"Spoilers on the flare," Danny said as the plane nosed over and the glide path steepened. "Twenty-five degrees."

"Twennie-five," Chip said, and actuated the flap motor. The nose pitched forward a little more. They were headed right for the edge of the road. "You've got it dicked."

"Not yet. Get set to shut down electrical," Danny said. "Now forty degrees."

"Forty," Chip said, and they listened in the eerie quiet as the flap motors whirred and then stopped.

"Electrical systems off," Danny ordered.

"Number one electrical system off," Chip said, throwing switches. "Number two electrical system. Off. AC and DC buses. Disengaged. Standby power. Off."

"Ready, here goes," Danny said, and began his flare. Chip fired the spoilers when the plane made ground contact. Danny locked the brakes, burning up the pads and the main tires blew. As the plane slid along the highway, the right wing tip caught an overhanging tree branch, tearing aluminum and flinging ribs into the air, and the aircraft began a slow, howling pirouette. The left wing dipped low, touching the ground and sending a shower of sparks into the still air until the plane finally came to rest.

They both sat in silence, breathing hard. "Goddamn," Danny said. "Goddamn. God. *Damn.*"

"Fucking A-firmative," Chip said. "Beautiful."

Danny grinned over at him. He laughed nervously, as if he could not quite believe they were alive. "That was really something, wuddnit?"

"Let's get out of here. And tell your ego that it just rolled a quarter-million-dollar aircraft into a ball on a Mexican highway."

The blank wall had a weathered wooden door in it. Next to the door was a sign that said La Manzana. It was impossible to tell what might lie behind that door. The street itself was loud and dirty. The people looked hungry or injured, criminal, poverty-stricken or slightly mad.

When Danny and Chip stepped through the door, the scene was silent, except for the honk of a lone white peacock, which stood in the garden displaying its tail fan. Wooden tables had been arranged on the lawn at discreet intervals. People of various nationalities sat, sipping and talking intimately with all the confidence and theatrics of spies exchanging state secrets in deepest woods. Appearing and disappearing in patches of light and shadow, carrying trays in a graceful, urgent ballet of entreaty, waiters in white jackets and black bow ties glided across the lawn as if being propelled on frictionless castors.

Although a wall with broken glass embedded in its topmost surface ran the perimeter, it was not visible to the guests, so clever was the landscaping inside La Manzana. Banana, avocado, pineapple and royal palm with bark like poured concrete shielded the eye from any sense of being caged in that wild, loud city.

At La Manzana the casual observer would see macaws, parrots, monkeys and exotic birds with no names except those given them by the Indians. The tourist would see people doing nothing more mysterious than drinking, eating and watching the menagerie. Yet there was more.

Danny and Chip were seated at one of the wooden tables. At the next table two men were speaking in German.

"Did you get anywhere in that German course you started?" Chip asked.

"Negative, why?"

"Shh," he said, cocking his ear.

"What is it?" Danny asked.

"They're discussing plutonium futures."

"You're making that up."

"No, they are. Don't ask me why."

A waiter brought drinks and set up an easel, on which he placed a wood-framed blackboard with the menu neatly lettered in white chalk. Theirs was in English. At other tables the menu had been printed in Spanish, French, German, Japanese and even Russian.

Danny signaled the waiter and addressed him in Spanish. He asked if Werner was free. The man said he would ask, then bowed and moved back across the grass. A few minutes later Werner came bounding into the open, a Germanic monolith, smiling and flushed as if he'd had his face too close to a stove all day. He smelled of garlic and beer, and when he spoke, a jubilant haze of spittle hung continuously about his moist and shiny lips.

"What a surprise!" he blurted out, planting his vast rump on the small folding chair beside their table. His reddish brown eyebrows were as thick as pig bristle and grew untrimmed in wild profusion. They moved up and down, as if clicking between two positions of detent—either crushed down over his moist eyes in severe concentration or lifted almost to his scalp in an expression of mute and utter bafflement. "If I had known you were coming, I would have prepared something extra-special," he said, his fricatives producing an explosive cloudburst of saliva over the pair.

"How are you, Werner?" Danny asked.

"Well," Werner began, as if he were going to make an announcement. But there was nothing more to say. "What is it then? Business? Pleasure? Do you need entertainment?"

"We need a room. I'm sorry we couldn't give you some notice. I know it's tight getting a room here. We, um, dropped in rather unexpectedly."

Chip said, "Rather."

"It happens," Werner said gravely. "It happens." His eyebrows dropped to lower detent as he considered the problem for a moment; then they rose to the rim of his flushed scalp. "We have," he said, "by a great stroke of luck, your favorite suite open. A couple from Alaska was coming to take it tonight, but by the same stroke of luck—not so great for them—it will be nonexistent when they arrive." Werner smiled at the crystal blue sky, as if he'd just had it painted that color that very morning. He stared at Danny. "If that's all right with you."

"We'll take it, Werner. We don't need anything else right now except lunch and a few beers. But"—he put his hand on Werner's arm—"we are not here."

"You are not here," Werner repeated solemnly.

"We're not here at all," Chip added. "We have never been here either."

"You have never, ever been here," Werner said emphatically, nodding.

"You've never met us," Danny suggested.

"Never in my life." Werner shook his head.

"Ever," Chip added.

"No," Werner said with grave significance. "I understand completely. Our hospitality is matched only by our discretion." He put his huge hands on his knees and pressed himself into a standing position, expelling a volume of air. "I'm sending over the special. It is on the house, of course."

"No, no," Danny said. "We are customers."

"For customers like you," Werner sputtered grandly, atomizing a cloud of saliva between them, "lunch is merely an olive in the martini. Your suite will be ready when you're finished eating. Would you like *two* suites?"

"One is fine," Chip told him.

"One last thing," Danny said, touching Werner's arm.

"Name it."

"There is a federal officer with the narcotics detail. His name is Santiago Amesquita Garza. Do you know him?"

"Quite well."

"Call him—no. If you could go see him. It would be better not to use the telephone. Bring him here to my room. Right after lunch if you can."

"It is done," Werner said, and straightened up to leave. He gave Danny and Chip a puzzled look and then bounded off across the lawn. It would not have seemed possible that a man of such mass could move like a gazelle.

"Goddamn," Chip said.

"Goddamn what?"

"I just can't help thinking about all that money we lost."

"You are fucking incredible, Charles. That is the very least of our problems. Sometimes I think you are completely out of touch with reality."

Danny and Chip drank beer in the shade, watching the guests of La Manzana.

Their meal was brought. The waiter took their beer bottles and served wine. At the next table a man with a heavy Peruvian accent engaged an American in an intense conversation.

"These is one of a kind," the Peruvian said. "You haff to want it or there is no point in talking. It is the forst book ever print in the South American continent. There is only one forst book print in that continent, Señor Butera, there will never be another."

"I see," said the American, "but the price is too high."

"Ninety thousands dollars ees not too high for these one of a kind item."

After twenty minutes of pressure from the Peruvian the American became so uncomfortable that he got up and left the man holding his rare book and staring at his plate of fish. Danny and Chip laughed into their napkins and continued eating. When they finished their meal, busboys cleared the table. After coffee the headwaiter came over and said that Werner would like to see them inside whenever they were finished. In the lobby Werner gave them two keys.

"Amesquita has already gone up," he told them. "He's eager to see you."

"Thanks," Danny said, and they climbed the polished wooden stairs. Amesquita was standing across the room with his back toward the door, watching the garden from the window of their suite.

"It's beautiful at night," he said without turning around to see who had entered. "They light candles in little glass chimneys on wrought-iron stands and in between are fresh-cut flowers." He spoke as if he were lying in bed with a lover. "The entire garden is filled with an orange glow, but the sky is still very blue at this time of year."

Amesquita turned around to face them. He looked older and smaller than Danny remembered, as if he had been living in an atmosphere at far greater pressure than most and was gradually being crushed by it.

Danny said, "This is Chip."

"Yes, I know about Chip," Amesquita said. He crossed the room as if to examine Chip more closely. "Brilliant student of physics."

"How do you know?" Danny asked. Then he quickly added, "Never mind."

"Information is power," Amesquita explained. He smiled his crooked smile, but it did not come off, as if nerves critical to the formation of a smile had been severed by a surgeon. "They say knowledge is power, but there is no knowledge. There is only information, and it changes from day to day." Danny and Chip said nothing. Amesquita continued. "So, you have gotten yourselves in trouble and you want me to get you out."

"You really do know everything, is that it?" Danny asked.

Amesquita tapped the side of his head and sat heavily on the couch. "Let's see," he said, putting his thumb and forefinger against his temples. "It began with one DC-6 Executive Freighter, United States N-number one-zero-one-three Uniform."

Danny and Chip looked at each other.

Amesquita stood again and went to the window. Lunch had been over for some time now and only a few people remained on the lawn. Amesquita turned back to face Danny and Chip. "Look, you may think you're salty, experienced smugglers. But there are still a lot of things about this business you don't understand. Being in this business is like having a very rare disease. There are no symptoms. You can do anything a normally healthy person can do. Except that you may drop dead at any moment. I don't care if you run marijuana—no, that's not true. I *do* care. I just can't do anything about it. I don't have the time and I don't have the manpower. But if you are going to do this thing, I don't want to be the one to find your bodies. I don't want you getting yourselves killed in Mexico. All that's left are a few Zapotecs and rednecks running a few hundred pounds a week over the border in trucks. Trucks," he said, dismayed. "The marijuana business isn't even in Mexico anymore, boys, where have you been? The trade is being run out of Mexico by the heroin business."

"Manolete said the grass was coming from Colombia now," Danny said.

"Manolete is dead," Amesquita said.

Again Danny and Chip looked at each other.

"His fields rocketed," Amesquita continued. "Bigger concerns are taking over that land. In a month it will be planted in poppies. And if I take one of your American helicopters over it to spray the plants, I'll get shot down with American weapons. Or German or Russian weapons. It's war down here. Manolete never told you *that*, did he? Oh, yeah, Manolete," he said with disgust. "Big savior of the Zapotec Indians. He bought up that whole goddamned mountain—he owned it. Hired those *indios* for pennies. Big savior. Those Indians trusted him, too. They didn't know what was happening. They didn't know how to load a ship or protect themselves when things came apart."

"The ones who overloaded us," Chip said.

"Is that what your plane is doing in the jungle?" Amesquita asked. "Overloaded?"

"Out of gas," Danny said.

"Those men," Amesquita said. "They didn't do it on purpose. They're dirt farmers. How would they know to work a weight and balance on a complex transport-category aircraft? You're lucky you weren't killed, you two."

"Did you see where we landed?" Danny asked. At first Amesquita didn't answer. He detected in Danny's question, in his tone, a note of pride, a glimmer of pleasure, which disturbed him greatly. This boy was not learning. This, Amesquita thought, this near disaster is just what brings him down here, as if Danny were asking, *Did you see where we fucking landed that mother? Wasn't that the tightest damned landing you've ever seen?*

"Look," Amesquita said, "if you're going to do this, go straight to South America and buy a boat." He waved his hand. "Get off this continent and do whatever you want with your grass."

"*Mire, tío,*" Danny said, his tone subdued. "*No quiero queso; quiero salir de la ratonera.*"

"You're a funny boy, Daniel, but I can't help you. I ought to take you in. Not just because I'm a lawman, but because it might save your lives. If you keep fooling around down here, you're going to get killed, either because you get involved in heroin and don't know what you're doing or because you keep moving large loads of marijuana and the other growers don't want you here." He sighed and shook his head. "China White. Cambodia, Laos, Turkey—they're going to dry up. Mexico is becoming the new center for the West. Don't you know about the *cubanos?*"

"*Cubanos,*" Danny said. "Sure I do."

"What do you think they've been doing here?"

"I thought it was political."

"Heroin *is* politics."

Danny went to the window to watch the garden. He saw Werner grinning, waving his arms and showering someone with saliva. The peacock pecked along the perimeter, its fan closed.

"Why do you do it, *sobrino?*"

Danny watched an Indian worker carry a macaw across

the lawn and put it on its perch. Danny turned back to face his uncle. "Why do *you* do it?"

"It's my job."

"Oh, bullshit."

"I'm in it for the money," Chip said.

"That's bullshit, too," Amesquita said. "You two think you're having a great adventure. Well, I'll tell you what, this is a very good way to die."

Danny remembered something he had heard a long, long time ago. He wondered why, indeed, Amesquita did what he did, against impossible odds. Why Beto had done what he had done when he knew how dangerous it was.

"Well," Danny said, "if it's as good a way to die as any, it's as good a way to live as any."

"Well, do me a favor and get yourself killed in another country," Amesquita said.

"Just do *us* a favor," Danny said. "We need your help to get out of Mexico."

"No," Amesquita told him. "No way."

"We *need* your help," Danny said.

"If you think I'm going to get you out of this one, you're crazy," Amesquita said. "There are a lot of people around here who would love to nail me on something. All I'd have to do is help a dope smuggler out of the country and they would put me away where my wife and kids would never see me again."

Danny turned back to the window. He watched a woman in a bathing suit cross the lawn on her way to the pool. He was beginning to see that information, as Amesquita had said, was the only real power. He had vowed he would never tell anyone. Still, under these circumstances it might mean his only chance to get out of Mexico.

"*Tío*," Danny said, making one last attempt, "if you get us out of Mexico, I give you my word, we'll never set foot back here again."

"I don't care," Amesquita said. "You come back all you want. Just don't come back for marijuana and don't get caught because I cannot help you."

Danny turned to face him. He could see Amesquita's

determination. Danny had backed the man up against his family and Amesquita was not going to change his mind unless forced to. Danny hesitated. Amesquita moved toward the door. He shook out a pair of sunglasses and put them on.

"You owe me," Danny told him.

"I don't owe you nothing," Amesquita said angrily.

"Mendoza."

Amesquita waved his hand as if to dismiss him. "He's been dead for years." He turned with a puzzled look. "Didn't you know that?"

"That's exactly what I'm talking about."

"What's exactly what you're talking about? What?"

"How many people know exactly how Mendoza died?" Danny asked. Amesquita said nothing. "I'll tell you. He was returning from the grocery store with a six-pack of beer. He was shot at close range with a sawed-off Browning Superposed Magnum twelve-gauge. The gun was left at the scene. In it were two three-inch, double-aught buckshot shells. Winchester brand. The gun was stolen from Lincolnwood Sporting Goods November fifteenth, 1964. A brick was thrown through the window a week before, and then another thrown through the same window the night of the burglary. Mendoza's wounds were caused by the blast through the chest and abdomen. He was nearly decapitated by one of the shots. He was lying on his back, still holding the six-pack. The cans were punctured. The police chased somebody as far as Northwestern University. They lost him in the library." Danny stopped. His hands felt icy, his breathing shallow and quick. "Did I miss anything?"

Amesquita walked unsteadily to the couch and sat. He put his head between his knees as if he were going to faint. He straightened and removed his sunglasses.

"Danny," Chip said, but neither Amesquita nor Danny responded.

"You?" Amesquita asked. "You?"

Danny nodded. "I didn't want to tell you, *tío*, I really did not want to tell you."

"Mother of God," Amesquita said. "We thought it was professionals. The *cubanos* maybe."

"No one knows," Danny said, suddenly frightened by what he had let out in the open. "No one."

"Why?" Amesquita asked. "Why?"

"How many reasons did I need?"

"*Hijo*, you were just a child."

Danny watched Amesquita nod almost imperceptibly and was unsure if he'd done the man a service or in some mysterious and complex way had betrayed him. "Let's go," Danny said.

"Yes," Amesquita agreed. "You must go now."

"That's all I can do for you," Amesquita said. "I have to protect my family."

"It's enough." Danny extended his hand, but Amesquita just looked at it.

"*Sobrino*, you're going to get yourself killed one day. Stay out of this business."

"Thanks, *tío*." Danny turned away and Chip followed him along the dark, deserted airstrip among the planes parked in rows. A light rain had begun to fall. Amesquita had told them the Bonanza was the most recent confiscation. It was wrapped in white plastic tape printed in red letters that said PRUEBA—NO TOCAR. Danny and Chip stripped it off and checked the systems. In a few minutes they were airborne, flying without lights and hoping they didn't meet anyone coming the other way. Just after takeoff they saw the purple tower of a thunderstorm cell in the mature stage, its anvil ignited from time to time by flashes of electricity. The rain beat against the windshield, blowing at them from more than ten miles away, as they cruised along in the clear but gusty air.

During the flight Danny explained to Chip what he had never explained to anyone before. He told him of Beto and the union organizing in Harlingen, about Mendoza, who was a young Mexican hood back then. He told him of a hot night in the shack when the air was merciless and still and about Mendoza, standing in the moonlight with one hand gone. He told Chip how he had vowed to hunt the man

down and had done it. He even told Chip how he and
Maggie met.

Chip sat in silence, thinking it over for a long time. He
watched the VOR needle flop back and forth wildly, watched
the TO/FROM indicator flag flash off and on as they crossed
the navigational facility along the coastline.

"Well?" Danny asked.

"It's done, Dan, what can I say? I could get pissed. You
bringing me down here, risking my life without telling me
everything. I could even envy you, I suppose. People want
to kill each other. Not too many of us ever get the chance.
I don't know what to think. Maybe you did a good thing.
Mendoza was a monster the way you tell it. The question
isn't how I feel about it, it's how you feel about it."

Danny said nothing. That was the question, always would
be, for that matter. People are taught that everything can
be lined up neatly on one side or the other, the good over
here, the bad over there, but it didn't work out that way.
Danny knew there would never be an answer, only the question. One either learns to embrace the question, to love it, or
one goes mad. Chip commented later in the flight, "Looks
sort of like you're between the muscle and the bone now."

↤

IMMEDIATELY AFTER her graduation in June 1967,
Maggie had taken a job with the *Chicago Daily News*. Soon
after she began, they had assigned her to the night shift,
which was a step up inasmuch as the night just seemed to
generate its own news.

When Danny returned home, it was afternoon and he was
hoping she'd be on her way to work. He wanted some time
to collect himself before he had to answer any questions.
He knew she could easily suspect that his absence had been
due to another woman, and while that was better than her
knowing what he'd really been up to, he wanted to convince her it had been neither infidelity nor criminality that
had kept him out those few days.

She was there, however, sitting at the breakfast table, reading the paper in the light from the windows. As he came in, she stared at him without saying a word. Then she stood up and took a long sheet of paper from a drawer. The paper had sprocket holes up and down either side.

"I saved this for you," she told him flatly.

"You're not at work."

"It's my day off. I guess you wouldn't remember my schedule, though."

Danny knew it was bad, whatever it was—certainly worse than the night he had told her about going to bed with that other woman. "What is it?" he asked, taking the paper.

"Read it," Maggie ordered, turning from him to sit at the table again. She shook out her newspaper with such agitation that it ripped and then, in a flurry of anger, she crumpled it up and threw it down.

Danny looked at the sheet in his hands. It had been torn from an Associated Press teletype machine and was printed in faint ink. The dateline was Cuernavaca and it was a story about a DC-6 that had crash-landed in central Mexico with twenty tons of marijuana on board, "valued at $12 million," it said. Danny wondered where they got that figure. "The police are searching for suspects," it concluded. Danny folded the paper along its perforations and placed it on the table across from Maggie.

"You know," Maggie said, shaking her head as if remembering something long ago, "when you first went out west to get type-rated in that DC-6, I thought: Oh, that's great! What a wonderful opportunity for Danny. He loves flying so much." Her tone was so bitterly sarcastic that Danny hung his head in shame. "Then a thought occurred to me. I was ashamed of myself for even thinking it. I thought: Now what an awful thing to think about him. You know what that thought was?" she paused, but she knew Danny wasn't going to respond. "It was that just maybe, somewhere in your deranged, renegade heart, the notion had developed that being such a hotshot pilot and all, you just might run a load of dope across the border." She stopped again, but

Danny didn't even look up. "I really felt awful about thinking that. I felt small and paranoid and petty for thinking
such a thing."

She looked at Danny and shook her head in disgust. "Because, you know, all this time, I've really wondered about
the money you have. Did that ever occur to you?" When
Danny didn't answer, Maggie jumped up and slammed her
fists into the tabletop, shouting, "Well, did it?"

Danny started to say something, then stopped.

"Well, I really wondered, and of course I just assumed
it was from your father or something. I mean, what else
could I assume, right? Unless I wanted to be a screaming
paranoid and think you were running dope." Maggie sat
back down, breathing hard. "You know, the worst part is
something you probably didn't even think of. Because running dope is one thing. Maybe I could even tolerate that—
I don't know, but maybe. But you think I'm a fool. That's
the worst part. You think I'm an idiot. You've kept me in
the dark like a child, kept me out of a part of your life that
is so important you could have turned up dead down there
and I would have gotten it over the goddamned wire!"
Maggie was shaking with rage. She stood up and walked
away from the table, then walked back and placed the flat
of her hands on it, leaning over Danny and shouting, "You
never thought of that, did you? You kept *that* part a secret.
From *me*. And that is unforgivable. Do you see?" With
that, she went straight to the front door and walked out.
Danny ran out into the hall to stop her, but she turned on
him so violently that he let her go.

It was three in the morning. Danny sat at the table, drinking beer. The stereo set had been playing, but now the tone
arm went around and around the center of an album, making
a complicated series of clicks and hisses at each revolution.
Danny heard the key hit the lock, heard it cleave to the
tumblers with the familiarity of long use, then heard the
mechanism rotate and watched Maggie come in. She didn't
look at him at first. She turned her back as she closed, then

chained the door. She stood like that for a moment, then faced him, holding the doorknob behind her back, her eyes cast down at her feet. She slowly looked up.

Danny crossed the room and put his arms around her. She did not react. "I owe you an apology," he said quietly. "I'm not sure that's going to be enough, though." Maggie put her head against his chest. She dropped her purse at her side and enclosed him with her arms, tentatively at first, then with more and more pressure. "I mean it, Maggie."

She pushed him away. "I mean it, too, Danny. I'm not going to cry over you. I've made up my mind. I'm not going to see you dead and I'm not going to cry over you. I want to know exactly what you intend to do."

"It's over," he said. "That was the last deal."

"Because you don't seem to realize how much I love you."

"It's over," Danny repeated.

"Because I swear, I'll leave you."

"I mean it," Danny said, "I really—"

He stopped, thinking: What do I mean? What if she had known from the first—what if Maggie had known everything? It made him realize that he had been living a cover story from the moment they met. His first words to her had been a lie, and every day he had had to lie just a little bit more. Now what would happen when Maggie found out everything? He could not let her find out as she had found out about the crash in the jungle. He would have to tell her himself, tell her the whole truth. The only problem was that he didn't know what that was.

5

WHEN MICHAEL TOLD Danny and Chip what they could do to set the accounts straight after crash-landing one-three Uniform and losing its load, Danny refused. He paced the room, insisting that he had just promised Maggie he was out of the business and he couldn't go back on his word that soon—no, not ever. He did not want to lose her over something as stupid as marijuana.

"You'll lose your life," Michael said. He sat in his chair, shaking his Isro sadly from side to side and looking morose. "Danny, if it were me, I'd say it was totally like a shared risk. It wasn't your fault they overloaded you. It wasn't your fault that when you tried to turn back, Manolete had come up short." That's what Michael called getting killed: coming up short. "But it's out of my hands and it's a real bummer for me, too. Don't you understand? These people sell this stuff for seventy-five dollars a pound. What you guys left in the trees represents three million dollars to them."

"Holy shit," Chip said. "You mean we've been taking slave wages for running this stuff?"

"It's not slave wages, Charles," Michael said, annoyed. "You have no investment in this. You just fly airplanes. Anyway, I've already worked out a way for you two to pay off your debt. It's painless and simple. One trip, a one-day turn-around. In a Learjet."

Danny was firm. "Michael, there has to be another way."

"You could run."

"Yeah, but for how long?" Chip asked.

Michael thought for a moment. "I'd say the average length of time would be about a month, give or take. Some they get inside the first week the contract is issued."

Danny stopped pacing and stared at Michael. "Contract?"

"Your relationship can survive this, Dan," Michael told him. "Maggie would rather have you alive, wouldn't she?"

"Danny, I'll go alone," Chip said. "You don't have to make the trip."

"You can't fly a Learjet alone," Danny objected.

"We'll get another pilot then. There have to be other pilots."

"It's a thought," Michael said.

"I couldn't let you go do this alone," Danny said.

"You don't have a lot of selection," Chip said. "If you won't go, somebody has to."

Danny thought about it for a moment. "Who's the other pilot?"

Michael shrugged. "We'd have to pay somebody. Unless . . . There's one guy I know, FE with one of the big airlines. He's new, but he has a lot of jet time."

"I'll check him out," Danny said. "I want to take a ride with the guy before he goes with Chip."

"It's all right with me," Chip said.

Two days later Danny was at an airport, standing beside a Learjet, when the airline pilot showed up. His uniform looked as if he'd slept in it. He was only in his twenties but appeared well on his way to a heart attack.

"Whatcha got in the bag?" Danny asked as the man approached.

"It's a snack. I didn't have time to eat breakfast." The man looked nervous. He was sweating.

"You're half an hour late."

"I had car trouble."

Danny didn't believe that, but he said nothing. "Let's blast off."

As the pilot took off in the small twin jet, Danny tuned

in the ILS localizer and noted that they had already drifted four degrees off the extended runway centerline before they reached 1,000 feet. Seeing Danny manipulating the avionics, the pilot asked what he was doing. "Nothing," Danny said. "Go ahead, you're doing fine."

Danny had the man shoot some practice ILS approaches under a hood that restricted his vision, simulating a situation in which they were flying in clouds. The approaches were so sloppy that had they really intended to land, they would not have made it. During one of the approaches Danny opened the lunch bag and saw two oranges. He told the pilot to land. When the airplane touched down, it was traveling approximately fifteen knots over the target speed for landing, an extremely dangerous practice, especially on short airstrips. The pilot had to stand on the brakes.

"How'd I do?" the man asked when they were parked.

"Fine," Danny said. He had a thought. It had been in the back of his mind and just came forward as he was staring at the pilot in full sunlight, seeing the little blue veins on the surface of his nose. "Mind if I have one of your oranges?" Danny asked.

The pilot turned red and began to stutter. He said something about having to have extra vitamin C. He was clearly lying.

Danny grabbed the sack. The pilot struggled for a moment to get it back, then just hung there in silence like a defeated child. Danny put his teeth into one of the oranges.

"Vodka," he said. "Nice snack." He had heard of those airline pilots who get themselves so backed up against it that they start drinking on the job. One of the ways to get away with it was to inject an orange with vodka. Danny dropped the torn orange back into the sack and got out of the plane.

Chip and Danny met at a campus cafeteria called the Grill, which had wooden booths around the perimeter of a room half the size of a football field. The place always smelled of frying cheeseburgers. They sat in a booth drinking coffee.

Danny said, "I flew with that pilot."

Chip asked, "How are the paying airline passengers of the world being treated these days?"

"Oh, great, just great. He was absolutely wonderful. Landed fifteen knots over the bug, flew outbound anywhere between four and eight degrees off, did a missed approach in the wrong direction, busted his MDA on five practice ILSs—I'm telling you, this dude is just what you need for that kind of trip."

Chip said nothing. He put his chin in his hand.

"Oh," Danny continued, "one other thing."

"More?"

"Remember that little trick with the hypodermic and the grapefruit Stew told us about?"

"He *didn't*."

Danny nodded. "Oranges."

"Well," Chip said, "I guess I'll fly this one alone."

"No, I'm going with you."

"You swore you wouldn't go."

"I don't have any choice. I'll talk to Maggie. She'll have to understand."

"Look, I'm going to have to find another pilot anyway if you're quitting. I might as well find him now."

"You're going to keep flying these trips? What for?"

"Money."

"Bullshit."

"Adventure. Money. I don't know. I've lived in my head for too long. Out there—you know what it's like out there. You can *feel* it. It's sex."

"I know," Danny admitted, looking down into his coffee cup. He sighed and shook his head. "So when I tell Maggie that I'm making this one last trip to settle accounts, I'll be half lying anyway."

"Don't bother. I'll find somebody else."

"Hey, look," Danny said angrily, "just fucking quit with the other pilot crap, all right? I'm going. Period. Then we'll talk about the rest. This trip, I'm going."

"Take it easy. You want to go, I'm not going to stop you. I just thought you said you weren't going to go."

"If you don't want me along, just say so."

"Don't play prima donna with me, Paine. You want to go, you go. You don't want to go, that's fine, too."

When Danny attempted to explain to Maggie what was going on, she cut him off, saying, "You don't think I'm naïve, do you?"

"What do you mean?" He was shocked. He was trying to tell her the truth, the whole truth for once.

"I mean that I knew you would have to pay for that airplane you and Chip crashed. I assumed you were responsible for the grass in it. I just guessed that you didn't have enough money to pay for everything out of pocket since you haven't told me how much money you really have. So—" She shrugged her shoulders and held out her hands as if it all added up to the same thing no matter which way you sliced it.

Danny nodded. He sat down on the bed. Maggie turned around and began undressing. It was night and the music played softly from the other room. Danny felt like an amateur next to Maggie.

↤

DANNY AND CHIP went to see a man known to them only as Eddie, who lived in a run-down neighborhood near Irving Park and Broadway in Chicago. From the outside his house looked as if it had been condemned. On the street were cars suspended on cinder blocks, their hoods sprung, windows broken. The house next door had been gutted by fire.

Eddie's place, in contrast, turned out to be a little mansion —all natural wood and Chinese razor-cut rugs, Iranian carpets from Nain and Kashan with warp and highlights of silk. There were four Miró lithographs on the walls of the living room, and a Steinway dominated one quadrant. Eddie himself looked as if he belonged on the street rather than in the house, as if, perhaps, he had broken into it for the evening. His face was a tortured landscape of pocks, scars and lines, and his eyes seemed to be taking turns doing the job of moving left and right and of focusing.

"These are the keys," Eddie said with an oleaginous smile, dropping them into Danny's hand. "Drive carefully now." He laughed. Danny and Chip smiled warily. "You're to file instruments for Lauderdale, flight level three-niner-zero, then request VFR on top, descend to thirteen thousand somewhere over Georgia, assuming there is a top. Be sure you cancel before you get to the coastline. Monitor Mirimar TRACON on three-sixty-three-point-one; that's the federal narcs' communication channel in case you didn't know. Tune in the Jacksonville VOR—they have an SWB that'll give you weather and an altimeter setting at quarter past the hour. Then go down to two hundred feet MSL. You'll be burning a hell of a lot of fuel, but the Loran C and Omega they've got out there can't paint you that low. That should put you a safe distance over the water, too. If anything happens to go haywire at that point, by the way, don't try to fly in ground effect over the water. Unless you've got an awful lot of hours in small jets, the Lear has some funny characteristics at low speeds. Also, if the water is choppy, the ground effect won't work."

"Does this one have the vortex generators installed?" Chip asked.

"We took 'em off," Eddie said, "but if you fly anywhere above about Mach point-eight-three, you'll start to get aileron buzz. That's your first indication of Mach buffet and you've got to back off. There was a stick puller on it, but some joker had it disabled. If you push the speed now, the only warning is that aileron buzz. Next thing you know you've got Mach tuck." Eddie made his hand like an airplane going into a steep dive. "Then it's a quick trip all the way down."

"Good to know," Danny said.

"Yeah," Eddie said as if he hadn't heard or didn't care. "Anyway, what you want to do is go straight south, using the Key Biscayne VORTAC and refuel at Cay Sal. You'll be right next to Cuba, but it's all our people there. Just soldiers, spooks and us."

"Spooks?" Chip asked.

"Spooks," Eddie repeated. "They do some training there. We ignore them, they ignore us, get it?"

"Whatever you say," Danny told him.

"Now you're on your own as far as getting around Cuba. I personally would take the Yucatán Channel. I assume you're smart enough not to try to overfly Cuba, so take your pick. If you intercept the Aruba two-seven-zero degree radial and track it in toward Colombia, you should hit the airstrip dead on. They'll have you four thousand five hundred feet, lit by fires. You stop, take off, that's it. Use Cay Sal again on the way back."

"Sounds elementary," Chip said.

"Happens every day. Anything else, fellas?"

"No," Danny said. He and Chip turned to leave. "Keep it in your boots, Eddie."

Eddie had the top of his head shot off. Someone forced his mouth open and put a scatter-gun into it and blew his brains all over the ceiling of his little uptown mansion. Danny and Chip took a long drive when they got the news. They drove up Michigan Avenue, looking at every car that passed as if it might contain some torpedo-headed extra from a Steve McQueen film. When they crossed the Chicago River, Chip rolled down the passenger side window and tossed out the Learjet keys, watching them twinkle in the bright December sunlight and disappear into the oily brown water that was gradually freezing in a rippled froth. "What's Michael going to do?"

"Find himself another comedy team," Danny said.

"Does Maggie know?"

"Yeah, I told her. That's it, man. No more cocaine deals. No more gangsters."

"What'd she say?"

"She said that if I wanted to hide, she could put us underground in Arkansas where they'd never find us. She said disappearing into Arkansas was like disappearing off the edge of the world."

"Exceptional woman, Danny. Don't fuck up."

"The best. I think she may be too good for me."

It was an interesting time, interesting all around. Dylan had nearly killed himself in a motorcycle accident, and after rumor and silence, a strange, skinny Dylan had appeared smiling on the cover of *John Wesley Harding*. Smiling! An odd time. Martin Luther King was alive with his dream that the lion would lie down with the lamb. Bobby Kennedy was a contender. Maggie spent a lot of time in those days reading wire service dispatches and in the coming years she could not remember a more charged chunk of time. Peace symbols and riots, heart transplants and atom bombs going off here and there, while the greatest leader in the world peed in the tumbleweed on a ranch in Texas as reporters looked on in shock ("Mr. President," one intrepid journalist is said to have asked, "aren't you afraid it might get bitten by a rattlesnake?" The greatest leader in the world had smiled understandingly at the miserable pissant who had dared to address him with such a question. "It *is* part rattlesnake, son," he is said to have answered).

It was a time of limitless possibilities and the only time that Danny would ever be called to serve his country.

It was the day after they had thrown the keys to the Lear-jet into the river. There was good news and bad news. Michael called and said, "Don't worry. You're in no danger."

"What the fuck do you mean, no danger?" Danny demanded.

"Take it easy, take it easy, I can't explain right now. I'll see you when I see you. You and Chip are in no danger."

"What are we supposed to . . ." Danny began, but Michael had broken the connection.

That was the good news. The bad news came early the next morning while Maggie was still asleep. She stirred at the sound of Danny's laughter. She yawned, rolled over in bed and opened her eyes. Danny sat in a chair, holding a piece of paper and a blue number ten envelope.

"I think the Lady Days have begun," Maggie said. She

looked at the clock and groaned. "Oh, God, I've got to interview a politician today. Why do I always get my period when I have to deal with assholes?" She squinted at Danny. "What are you doing there?"

Danny reached over and handed her the letter. Maggie looked puzzled. "Greetings," it said. Then it instructed Danny to report to his local draft board for a preinduction physical examination. Maggie read the letter again, as if it might contain some deeper meaning, but that was all there was: Danny had been called. Maggie's radio alarm clock went off just then. The song was "Good Vibrations."

Danny laughed and slapped his knee. "Good fucking vibrations."

"Oh, Danny."

Both Maggie and Chip expected him to react, but he just joked about it through the next few days. Late one night they all sat up in the apartment, drinking wine and talking. Maggie and Chip had been trying to convince Danny to face the problem—to do something about it—but he just shrugged it off.

"I know this may be a strain on your mental powers," Chip told him, "but this happens to be one of those problems that you have to face. It requires action on your part. I think you'd do well over there, frankly. I've got nothing against war. I might even like to try it myself sometime. But what they're doing in Vietnam is not smart. That is not a well-conducted war. They're just feeding meat to the machine. And I'm not so sure I like that."

"Chip," Maggie said between her teeth, "what are you saying?"

"I'm just saying that he should decide to go over there or not to go over there. Going over is fine, except for one thing. This particular war is crazy."

"All war is crazy."

"Not really."

Danny stood up. "We've got the Selective Service trying to decide what to do with me. Now I've got you two arguing over what to do with me. It's my ass, don't forget that."

"No, it's not," Maggie said. "That's just the problem, Danny. It's not your ass. If you go over there just because you're stubborn and then you get your fucking face shot off, you owe me and you owe Chip and you owe Forrest." Danny said nothing to contradict her. "If you don't watch out for yourself, it's just like telling me and Chip to go fuck ourselves." She looked to see if he would react, but he just sat there. "And nobody tells me to go fuck myself."

It was just after dawn when Danny left the apartment. Maggie followed him down the stairs to the front hall. The sky had been whipped into a dark froth. It was one of those days when you know your body is generating heat—it has to be—but you can't figure out where it's all going, the weather just sucks it out of you and leaves the shuddering husk.

"I guess I'll be back in a few hours," Danny said.

"I trust you."

Maggie stood watching him disappear down the street and wondered: Well, it's easy enough for me to holler and rant, but what would I do? What would I do, faced with the choices? Or faced with a red-faced sergeant screaming for me to strip down to my shorts for a physical?

Maggie did not know the answer. She went back upstairs and poured the last of the coffee they had made into a mug and sat by the window, watching the commuter train rattle to its stop. Large flakes began to fall, then turned and went straight up outside the windowpane. It was such a violent display it seemed wrong that it made no sound.

An hour passed and the coffee went cold in her cup, untouched. Snow began to accumulate, banked in the corners of the garage roof below. Maggie moved to the couch and put her feet up. It seemed as if fifteen, maybe twenty seconds passed. She felt a hand on her arm and jerked to a sitting position.

"Wake up," Danny said.

"What? Did you go? How come you're back?" Maggie looked around. The light had changed.

"Yes, you fell asleep. It's noon."

Maggie stretched. "Noon?"

"Noon."

"What happened? What are they going to do?"

"They said I'm unfit for military service," Danny told her. He looked stunned, as if he could not believe it.

"Danny!" Maggie shouted. "What did you do?"

"Nothing. I told them I couldn't talk on the telephone."

Maggie looked puzzled. "You what?"

"I told them I couldn't talk on the telephone. That's all. And they kept sending me around to more psychiatrists and each one would ask the same questions. I just kept saying I couldn't talk on the telephone. Then they told me I was unfit for military service. They said, 'Go home.' "

"Telephones?" Maggie asked. "Telephones? They don't kill 'em with telephones."

"No, they don't. No one even asked me if I had a telephone."

"Telephones!" Maggie shouted, hugging Danny.

"Mothering telephones."

There was a celebration, during which Danny and Chip drank so much beer that Maggie suggested they simply open the cans and pour them down the toilet, eliminate the middleman, so to speak. Chip became intoxicated and wandered around the apartment, saying, "Dan, Dan, I'm intoxicated," over and over until he fell down, lay in one spot and recited the Lorentz transformation several times, insisting that it was the basic tool of relativity because it allowed one to see an event from two points of view.

"Enough!" Maggie shouted, the fourth time Chip went over it. "Everybody go to bed."

"I can't go to bed with you," Chip complained. "People will talk."

It was one in the morning when Maggie finally called a taxi for Chip and dragged Danny to bed. Danny and Maggie liked to sleep skin on skin, naked under heavy covers, so they kept the window open a few inches even in the coldest weather.

The world was quiet, utterly quiet, as they lay unconscious, their shell of warmth surrounding them, their hot skins laminated together, arms and legs intertwined. Pigeons slept on the auto mechanic's roof. A chill breeze sighed into the room, pushing the curtains back and to.

It was just before dawn when the sledge hammer tore the door from its hinges. Men in leather jackets swarmed into the apartment, shouting.

"Freeze, motherfucker!"

"Freeze!"

"FREEZE!"

Danny wanted to tell them he had frozen years earlier. Then he realized that they were the men who had put the shotgun into Eddie's mouth, the ones who were coming after him now for the dope he had lost in his jungle escapade.

"Take me," he said. "Leave her out of it."

"Shut up," a man said. "Get up and keep your mouth shut."

Danny slid from the bed and stood in the center of the room. He looked at the man, who wore a leather sport coat over a shirt and tie. He walked slowly over to Danny, who stood as naked as a sculpture. Maggie sat in the bed, the covers pulled to her chin. She looked as if she wanted to scream but had been struck dumb.

The man had shocking blond hair and eyes the color of overcast. His skin was white and tight and bloodless and had all the vitality of a snowbank. Even before he held up his leather folder with the badge, Danny knew who he was and suddenly wished these had in reality been the men who owned the lost dope.

Fassnacht walked around Danny as if inspecting a piece of property. "Federal agents," he said. He motioned to one of the men, who took a laminated yellow card from his wallet and began to read the *Miranda* rights.

Then the men tore the place apart. They didn't hurt Danny or Maggie. They put cuffs on them and wrapped them in blankets and then tore the apartment into small, unidentifiable bits with a single-mindedness of purpose that would have been fascinating if it had not been so horrifying. They ripped and pillaged their home—Maggie's home— where she had lived so neatly, ruining everything that was precious to her, digging into her personal secrets, her life, letters, underclothes, with no apparent notion of what they were touching.

Maggie knew, then, what it was to be raped—the primary, internal violation of it—and knew in that instant of revelation and indignity that she had no choice but to leave Danny.

She protested at one point that there were no drugs in the apartment. Maggie also said that she was going to sue them for false arrest and a whole list of other things, at which point Fassnacht came over and looked at her for a long time without saying anything. Then he told her, "I don't think so. We've never been here. You never even set eyes on us."

If Maggie did not fully understand that what these men were doing was off the record, Danny certainly knew what it meant.

At one point Fassnacht stormed up to Danny, enraged that he could find nothing with which to hang him. He said, "You slipped out of that draft thing. You thought that was pretty clever, didn't you?" Danny said nothing. "I gave them your name, in case you were wondering. Extremely selective service. Well, you're not going to get away. And incidentally, your uncle, Amesquita. He's a dead man."

"I don't have any idea what you're talking about," Danny told him.

"Then don't let it put you uptight."

Fassnacht rounded up his men and they left as suddenly as they had arrived. The last one out the door removed the handcuffs. Danny didn't move. Maggie got up, naked in the icy, devastated room, and picked her barefooted way through the rubble on the floor.

The only pair of underpants she could find had a fist-size hole ripped in the crotch. She dressed deliberately, looking around with the kind of awestruck, sleepwalking shock of someone who has been in a bad automobile accident.

The sleigh bed was destroyed. There was nothing left but the wooden frame. The cotton stuffing was all over the apartment. It floated in the toilet bowl, where one of the agents had put out a cigarette, which had colored the water brown. And where another had left the ultimate insult.

The paintings and prints and photos Maggie had matted and framed with such care were ripped to bits, scattered. Danny's old easy chair was just a cloud of stuffing now, a wooden skeleton, a handful of tacks. The drawers of their antique dresser lay around the room, one of them crushed flat, its sides splayed out, the nails sticking up. The dresser itself was tipped over on its face, the back ripped out. Their clothes were everywhere.

Food lay strewn across the kitchen floor, a jar of raspberry jam broken and smeared on the linoleum, half a loaf of bread in a corner, blue-edged with incipient mold.

A tiny bit of tinfoil was tossed in a corner. Maggie picked it up and worried it open. Inside was the single remaining tablet of LSD that Michael had given them so long ago. She dropped it to the floor. All that destruction and they'd missed the only drug in the apartment.

She picked her way among the books and records, notes to each other, blown through the rooms, stepped on, mocked. Danny sat on the floor in a pile of their belongings, his back to the wall, the windows, the fire escape where they had climbed naked into heaven. I'm going up to the sun. Come with me.

"Maggie," he said. She did not answer. She continued to roam the apartment. "Maggie," Danny said again. "Please don't leave."

Maggie watched the pigeons behind him as they flashed across the sunlight in a great wheel of natural flight, like the display on a planetarium ceiling. The sunlight traced designs through the wreckage at her feet as she scanned it, taking in Danny, crumpled in a heap on the floor, wrapped in a sheet.

"Don't ever beg," she told him. And then she walked out the door.

He telephoned her at the newspaper several times and she spoke to him at first, as if she were very, very tired, saying only, "Danny, please don't make this more difficult for me than it already is. Please don't call me here. Don't call me at all. We have nothing to say to each other now."

"Maggie, please."

"No, Danny. Forget it. Leave me alone."

The last time he called her, she simply replaced the receiver without saying a word. By that time Danny had paid the landlord and left the apartment. A crew had been hired to haul away everything he and Maggie had owned. The door had been repaired. Danny moved in with Chip while he looked for a new place to live.

That he knew it had been his own doing from start to finish did not give Danny any comfort. From the moment he met her until the moment she walked out the door, he had led her to their inevitable separation. The only problem was that in the interim he had fallen desperately in love with her. He had made no allowances for that when he played fast and loose with his life and hers. Now it just didn't matter what he did. So he tried to destroy himself.

The drugs in common usage at that time were grass, amphetamines and psychedelics. There were also sedatives, minor and major tranquilizers and mood elevators, none of which were in very great demand on the street.

During the period following Maggie's departure, Danny tried them all with the thoroughness of a scientist obsessed. Some stronger, more sensible part of his character emerged from the experience, for he neither destroyed himself nor became enamored of any of the drugs he tried. By far the worst, he thought, was cocaine. It reminded him of an old Mexican trick for catching a mountain lion. Beto had told him about it. You must make your knife sharp enough for shaving. Wedge it, blade upright, in a rock or tree stump.

Smear animal fat on it. The lion, scenting the grease, will come and lick the knife. If you have sharpened it perfectly, the lion will not feel the cut. He will only taste blood, which will make him lick more, which will cut him more, which will make him lick more, until he bleeds to death.

When Danny came out of his sojourn inside the American pharmacopoeia, Chip said something like: "I've never seen a man go through two months so fast in all my life."

Michael called. He said they were safe and should now settle accounts for the airplane they had crashed. When Chip and Danny arrived at Michael's house, Virginia was sitting in her chair, preparing some opium to smoke. Michael was laughing as they entered. "You guys," he said. "I can't believe how lucky you are."

"I'm so lucky I could just die," Chip said.

"Michael, what are you talking about?"

Chip watched Virginia rolling the opium. She held it out to him and he shook his head.

Michael said, "Eddie."

"Eddie?" Chip asked.

"Eddie. That's what I was trying to tell you on the phone. That is why you two are safe. There is no one to come after you now because Eddie is dead."

"They killed Eddie over the grass?" Danny asked.

"No, they killed him over a cocaine deal."

"Shot?" Chip asked. "Over some cocaine?"

"*Some* cocaine," Michael said. "He got shot because when you move that much cocaine into this country, you have to coordinate it with others in that business. Eddie was too independent for his own good. I mean, when some chap who looks like a major appliance wearing a polyester suit comes by and offers to sell you life insurance just before a major cocaine deal, you have to be pretty dense not to get the picture, right? He had promised to do business with them and then, I guess, just decided to sneak that load in on his own. It's so simple and so many people can't see it. In this business you're no better than your word. All you have to do is exactly what you say you're going to do. This business is too serious for liars. You have to be completely honest to be in this business. Otherwise, you don't last long."

"What's expected of us now?" Chip asked.

"Well," Michael said, "that airplane *was* my own investment. I could give a shit about the pot."

"We'll split it with you," Danny offered. "A hundred thousand from us, a hundred thousand from you."

Michael frowned, thinking it over. "A thousand bones each?" he asked.

"Why not?" Chip asked.

"Okay," Michael said. "Okay. I said I would share your risk if I could. That's fair. And there's a very easy way for you to earn your share, too."

"South America, I presume," Chip suggested.

"A very easy trip," Michael told them. "South America."

"South America."

6

THE SOUTH AMERICAN CONTINENT ROSE before them above the choppy, leaden ocean, raw, voracious, mute and tremendous, like the back of a sleeping beast. It was a sight that held Danny's attention right up until the moment he saw the chase plane, a dot on the horizon that grew rapidly blacker and larger and then screamed past them, canopy to canopy, rolling nearly ninety degrees wingover as it passed.

"What in the hell was *that?*" Chip shouted.

Danny was staring wide-eyed at the ground. "Do you see the strip? That motherfucker's crazy."

"Twelve o'clock."

"Well, get this thing on the ground." Danny looked out the side window, searching for the chase plane. There was little aft visibility and he only saw it as a monstrous apparition as it fired past them going in the same direction. "He's trying to kill us."

"Gimme forty degrees," Chip ordered, chopping all the power.

"Forty degrees," Danny said, throwing the flap lever. The plane began to drop like an elevator.

"Easy, easy," Danny cautioned. "Goddamn, here he comes again."

"We're on the ground," Chip said, pulling back the yoke as they slammed into the ground and went shooting along the runway. He stood on the brakes and then allowed the plane to turn 180 degrees at the end.

In utter astonishment they watched as the chase plane lined up to land right where they had just landed.

"We should run," Chip said.

Danny looked out his side window. All along the airfield were soldiers with rifles. "Wait, wait."

"What the hell is this guy doing?" Chip asked.

The plane was just flaring out to land when a black line appeared between them and the aircraft. The plane's wheels touched the ground.

"What the—"

"Arresting cable," Chip told him. "Jesus."

Danny could now see the steel towers on either side of the runway from which the arresting cable had sprung so suddenly. The aircraft seemed to lift for a second, as if the pilot had applied power to go around; then it hit the cable, broke into several large pieces and exploded into an orange fireball fifty feet around, scattering flaming fuel and metal in every direction. The mass of flame and wreckage seemed to be dancing drunkenly toward them, cartwheeling as it went. Danny and Chip put up their hands to cover their faces.

Half an hour later they sat in respectful silence before Moishe Shurtzer, a sixty-eight-year-old man dressed in khaki safari clothes that looked as if they'd been purchased that morning at Abercrombie and Fitch. His office looked like that of a suburban physician. On the polished wooden desk was a gold-filled triptych frame with studio portraits of two hawk-nosed girls with bad teeth and one young man who looked like their brother. Danny and Chip sat on a couch that was made of expensive-looking fabric but had been covered with heavy clear plastic, as if for shipping. In a corner of the room a television set flickered silently.

"Sometimes your government agents get overzealous," Moishe told them. "I'm sorry you had to arrive under such harrowing circumstances. And on your first trip yet." He clicked his tongue. "They chase people around in their fancy planes. They're a hazard to life and property. What can I say? Our government here wouldn't be so reckless."

Danny and Chip didn't know what to say either. Moishe looked like somebody's grandfather. Yet he'd just had a planeload of people killed and was discussing it as if it had been nothing more than a mild embarrassment.

"This is quite a place you've got here," Chip said.

"Out there," Moishe said, "you could die of a heat stroke." He stood up and went to a cabinet. He took out a green bottle of sparkling water and poured three glasses of it over ice. "See this?" he asked, holding up the bottle. "You want to know from livings. My dearest friend in the world, who is only like a brother to me is right now in New York with this stuff, which only comes out of the ground in some nowhere town in France. France. It could be out of the tap, what do they know? Soon you'll see this for a dollar a bottle in the swankiest restaurants. Now, are we talking livings? Selling water in restaurants?" He shook his head.

Moishe sat down and sipped his water. "Michael tells me you two are the best. How is Michael?"

"Never better," Danny said. "He sends his best."

"Since I only taught him everything he knows, I don't suppose he would mind if you two began dealing directly with me. I think he might spare two pilots for his oldest and dearest friend, especially now that his business is changing."

"Changing?" Chip asked.

Moishe shrugged. Abruptly he seemed to change the subject. "I worked up in Mexico a few years back." He spoke dreamily, as if he could just see it. "I used to be a respectable businessman before your IRS ruined me. I know the Caribbean like the back of my hand. We saw the Cubans coming in." Moishe shook his head sadly. "I was in Cuba in the fifties, when it was a place to be. Talk about swanky." He crossed his middle finger over his index finger and held up his hand. "Lansky and I were like this. I saw the Cubans in the hills. We went up to talk to them once. They wouldn't listen. I knew they couldn't fail. I left a month before Castro came to power. Then in Mexico I saw the Cubans again. I knew what they were doing there." He held up a finger in warning. "Don't forget, I have friends, family, still in Israel. I was born there, don't forget." He shot

Danny and Chip—who were completely mystified by his monologue—a signifying look, sticking out his lower lip. "That's only three hundred miles from Turkey. And what do they grow in Turkey?"

"Cranberry sauce," Chip said.

Danny glanced at his partner, annoyed.

"You're a very funny boy," Moishe said without laughing. "But you know what I mean, eh?" I can tell you two are smart boys. The Russians are sending the Cubans to Mexico to grow opium poppies to flood the United States with heroin. You see the *shvartzehs* rioting? Burning the cities? Revolting? What do you think makes them crazy? Here, so far, we've been lucky, *kineahora*."

Danny nodded. He wondered if Moishe maybe had a few circuit cards that needed replacing, but he didn't contradict him. He had resigned himself to the fact that he would probably never know what was really going on, just as Amesquita had said.

"Ah," Chip began, "were you saying Michael was retiring?"

"No, not retiring. Changing." Moishe stood up and looked down at the papers on his desk, then held up several in succession. "Blind trusts. Retirement homes in Arizona. Fast foods. Pop music concert tours." He put the last paper down. "You two, you're making good money. What are you going to do with it? Are you going to buy a yacht? A house? A race horse?"

Danny shrugged.

"We should talk about this, you see. You need estate planning. Don't laugh. Wait until you have a million dollars cash and can't find a place to put it, forget about spending it. I met a kid the other day. He was about your age. He had four million dollars and change in foot lockers in his mother's basement, where he still lives. A nice Jewish boy, but do you call that planning? Maybe you want to buy something nice. A trinket for your girl friend that maybe has diamonds in it. Try it and watch the IRS come down on you like a pack of thieves." Moishe moved away from his desk. "But right now we have to work. Next time you come here, we will make more time to talk."

"Yeah, well," Danny said, "I think this is the last deal."

"Yes, of course," Moishe said. "So." He shrugged. "If you change your mind"—he smiled—"or you happen to be in the neighborhood . . . drop in."

"Yeah," Chip said, "but watch that last step."

When the job was done, Danny and Chip made their way into Mexico—as tourists—and checked into La Manzana. Werner, having been forewarned, had prepared an elaborate feast, beginning with little slices of sweet orange sprinkled with red pepper and ending with grilled red snapper with *salsa borracha.* Near the end of the meal a third place was set for Amesquita, who joined them in midafternoon.

Danny told him everything he could about his encounter with Fassnacht, his concerns for Amesquita's safety. While they talked, the white peacock spread its fan and screamed at the cloudless sky. A talking bird repeated the same German word over and over.

"It's an old feud," Amesquita explained. "Fassnacht is convinced that somehow I had Mendoza killed. He has always been convinced. At the time the repercussions were bad for him. Very bad."

"Why don't you just tell him that I did it?" Danny suggested.

"Because I don't sign your death warrant that easily, *sobrino*, even if you are weak in the head."

"Well, how come they haven't killed you if they'd kill Danny?" Chip asked.

"I'm lucky," Amesquita said. He laughed softly. "They've tried." He touched his chest with his finger. "Three bullets. I was in the hospital for months. Another time they bombed my car. I wouldn't be surprised if one of my own men was responsible. They're all corrupt."

"Jesus," Danny said. "Did it go off?"

"It went off," Amesquita said, and crossed himself as if

he were in church. "Killed the boy who fuels the cars. Very stupid. Anyway, Mendoza was king of that business when you shot him. When his death became known, there was a terrific scramble for his power. What you did, you have no idea."

Danny looked away across the lawn but said nothing.

"Oh, someone would have done it sooner or later," Amesquita assured him. "And Fassnacht was always considered the likely successor, which almost got him killed, too. Now he has Mendoza's position, of course, but the lines of power are obscure. No one really knows who is in control. It's all very confusing. Does Fassnacht work for the *cubanos*? Do they work for him? Are they doing here in Mexico what they did in Cuba and tried to do in Bolivia until your government people got Che shot?" Amesquita intertwined his fingers and shrugged. "I've been working on this for so many years now and even I do not know how it works. One thing you learn in this racket, you are hopelessly outnumbered and you can't win. You pick off one here, another there, but the war goes on. People get killed, blown away, disappear, reappear, get rich, go to jail—there is no reason or pattern. If you think about it too much, it will make you paranoid and in this business, if you're not paranoid, you're crazy. And the only cure for paranoia in this business is death."

"You're just trying to cheer us up," Chip said.

Amesquita waved his hand in a semicircle. "The whole land, as we sit here, is planted in poppies. We have word from your CIA that the United States is going to try to make arrangements with Turkey to stop growing the opium poppy. That will put the whole business right here," he said, tapping the table. "Now. Why do you think the United States would do such a thing?" He held up his hand in protest to anything they might say. "Oh, I'm not suggesting a conspiracy, no, no. But if paranoia makes sense, and if it is my job to speculate on these things, I ask, simply why? Why would your country deal with a heroin problem by negotiating with Turkey to stop growing poppies so that all the poppies will be grown right in your backyard?" Amesquita stuck out his lower lip and nodded. He didn't offer an answer; he just let them think it over.

"Fellow we know said the Russians had the Cubans growing opium to flood the U.S. market," Chip told Amesquita. "He sounded like a certifiable wall bouncer to me."

Amesquita shrugged. "I don't discuss such things. What's the point? Your country does a lot of strange things in other countries, right? United States 'advisers' are everywhere, stirring up trouble. So why not Russians hiring Cubans to grow opium? I don't know, but it's possible."

"Well, why would the Cubans do it?" Chip asked.

"Money, power, same reason anyone would grow opium."

"You're certainly right about one point."

"Which?" Amesquita asked.

"It doesn't make any sense."

"Yes, it never does."

"What will happen to you?" Danny asked his uncle.

"Me?' Amesquita pointed to himself as if it were a joke. "I will lose more battles than I win. If Fassnacht is the visible member of your government doing all this, how high up do you think the invisible part goes? If I am smart, I will retire. If I am not so smart, I will get myself killed." He attempted to arrange a smile on his face. "At Division HQ there is a sign posted that is our motto. It says, May I Die in My Sleep."

Danny almost asked him why he bothered to fight such a hopeless battle, but he stopped himself. If he wasn't prepared to answer the same question about himself, he couldn't ask it of his uncle. Just as Danny had known the night he killed Mendoza that he had somehow left the gravitational pull of ordinary existence, he knew that Amesquita had left it long ago—how and where and why were not important. It was with a sense of inner warmth that he realized that Amesquita, therefore, was probably closer to Danny than almost anyone else—by blood for sure, but also by some deeper tie.

"What does Fassnacht want with me?" Danny asked.

"We've won a few battles lately," Amesquita explained.

"We cut him deep two or three times. It's expensive and demoralizing for him when this happens. He thinks somehow you are helping me. You are in Chicago. The center of the business is there. Mendoza was in Chicago. You and I are relatives." Amesquita shrugged. "You try to figure these things out, you'll just confuse yourself."

"Do you think he suspects that I had something to do with Mendoza's death?"

"You were just a kid," Chip protested.

"Not so fast," Amesquita said. "Read your own papers. The local gangs in Chicago use children for assassinations. Do you know why? Because children can't be prosecuted. They're juveniles. They don't go to jail. They don't testify."

"So you do think he suspects me."

"I don't think it, I don't not think it."

"Why would he bother anymore? He's in control. In a sense, I did him a favor."

"No, you didn't," Amesquita said. "Anyway, that's not the point." Amesquita seemed to be getting frustrated, as if he couldn't get through to Danny. "Look," he said, "Fassnacht doesn't need reasons. Don't you remember that little girl? Don't look for logic; just look out."

A waiter brought more coffee. Amesquita asked for a pudding, and when the man had glided back across the lawn, he changed the subject. "So, you boys are working out of Colombia now." He withdrew a cigarette from his shirt pocket and lit it with a Zippo.

"What makes you think that?" Danny asked.

"Danny, Danny, Danny, you know better than to tell me a fib anymore."

"Well, how the hell do you find out all this shit? Goddamn, *tío*, sometimes I feel like I'm living in a fishbowl."

"You are, *sobrino*, you are." Amesquita laughed his first real laugh that day, thoroughly enjoying Danny's discomfort. A monkey screamed from across the lawn, and Amesquita pointed at him. "See him? He thinks we don't know what he's doing. He thinks he has a big secret from us. I go up to him and I say, 'Señor Mono, I see you have been eating bananas.' And he'll say to me, '*No me diga*, how did you know?' " Amesquita cackled loudly at this and Danny squirmed in his chair.

"So we made one last deal," Chip said. "To straighten out that problem with the plane we lost."

"You know," Amesquita said, "I don't know whether the dope is more addictive if you use it or if you transport it. Just one taste," he mocked, "and then just one more. One deal, then just one last deal."

"I'm tired of defending it," Danny said seriously. "It's a good business. We're pilots. Good pilots. We don't carry any cocaine or heroin. The grass isn't hurting anybody. We make good money."

Amesquita's laughter stopped and he said, "Damn it. You're not pilots, Danny. Don't lie to yourself at least. You're drug smugglers and you know it. Even in your country they would put you away for it. You're common criminals. In this country, if they caught you, they'd probably just starve you to death. In Colombia, they'd slit your throat. You know my position on marijuana, *sobrino*. I've never fought the trade down here because it didn't matter. First, it's as you say: It probably isn't hurting anyone. I don't know. Second, there's no way to stop it with the border the way it is. Third, there was the more important job of heroin. I don't care about the marijuana. I care that you are in over your head. You say you're just pilots. I keep telling you, if you like flying so much, go to Vietnam. Or get a job with the circus."

"That really was the last deal," Danny said.

"No, it wasn't." Amesquita threw his cigarette down. "It's too late for that and you know it."

Danny returned to Chicago in the season of heavy weather, when island-sized masses of warm air would come sweeping through town, bringing towering cumulus from the surface to 45,000 feet and fifty-knot winds that would take airliners and spin them around on the taxiways.

It was on one such day, shortly after Martin Luther King had been shot, when the weather seemed to imitate the frantic mood of the world, that Danny found himself driving

by the offices of the *Chicago Daily News*. The rain came
down so hard that it turned the car windows into a raging
dazzle of mercury. Outside, lightning exploded as if the town
were being shelled.

As Danny let his car creep along, he saw Maggie dash out
the front door of the building. Her yellow umbrella was
immediately turned inside out by the force of the wind as
she sprinted for a bus that had just stopped. Danny felt his
heart cease, then begin again. He began honking his horn
to attract her attention, but she could not hear. The bus
roared and pulled away from the curb, carrying Maggie. The
rain obscured Danny's view as he pushed on, running his tires
up onto the sidewalk in order to clear the car ahead of him.
The bus stopped at another corner, but he could not get
alongside it on the narrow street. He fired the shift lever
into park and sprang out the door into the rain. He was
soaked before he reached the bus, which was already pulling
away, and he ran back to his car, behind which a line of cars
had taken up honking in steady dissonance.

He followed the bus up Wabash and felt his heart pump
and drain so fast that he touched his chest in pain. The
entire front seat of his car was wet. As he jockeyed for position on the crowded street, his side mirror came off with a
crunch and a strip of chrome from a parked car went sailing
end over end into the street. My God, he thought, what are
you doing? Have you lost your mind? You're going to wreck
the car. You'll get someone killed. But he could not stop
himself. The bus turned onto Chicago Avenue, then onto
Michigan Avenue with Danny right on its bumper. He
could feel the electric trill of panic each time the bus stopped
and he leaned out to see if Maggie was getting off. Each
time she did not appear, he had to race ahead to catch the
bus again. It was a feeling of urgency and desperation he
had never known and it frightened him, knowing that he
would either catch her or die trying. It didn't seem to matter
which.

At one point an aggressive taxi driver got between him
and the bus and Danny simply ran him off the street. A
blast of thunder shook his car as lightning danced in branched

incandescence across the buildings, illuminating everything as if by an underwater explosion.

Finally the bus entered Lake Shore Drive and Danny was able to pull alongside, where he attempted to look into the windows, which were polished to wavering mirrors by relentless sheets of water. The storm seemed to gather, then unleash its full fury. The traffic on the drive slowed suddenly as drivers realized they could not go on. The buildings to the west disappeared altogether into a darkness that grew so benthonic that the automatic streetlights went on. Cars began to stall from ingesting water, while others simply pulled off the road.

Danny drove on, hard by the bus. Waves from Lake Michigan burst across the highway in places where it dipped too close to the beach. Finally, only a dozen feet away, he was able to see Maggie. Her head was down, buried in a newspaper. In her hair Danny saw the little barrette he had once given her on her birthday. "Maggie!" he hollered, but of course, she could not hear. He hammered on the steering wheel in outrage and impotence, then slammed on the brakes, skidding nearly out of control, as another car slowed suddenly before him.

The rain slackened a bit, losing some of its apocalyptic fury. The bus took the Foster Avenue exit and then followed Sheridan Road north to Bryn Mawr. He slid to a stop behind it in time to see Maggie step down, her yellow umbrella once again intact as the rain lashed around her.

Danny put the car in park by the curb and leaped out, slipping, righting himself and bolting across the street in front of the oncoming traffic.

Maggie was hurrying along in the rain and he had to run to catch her. When he finally reached her, he moved around in front and turned to block her path.

"What are you doing?" the woman asked.

The rain was pouring around them, and her umbrella was not doing much in the way of keeping her dry. Danny's face went through a series of contortions; he even looked over the woman's shoulder to see if somehow Maggie were behind her. The little barrette the woman wore was nothing like the one he had given Maggie for her birthday, and the woman did not even resemble her. She just had the same color hair, the same build. A yellow umbrella.

Danny had rented an unfurnished apartment near the lake. That afternoon he sat on a radiator in the bay window, watching the lake heave and spray. At four his father called to remind him that he was expected for dinner that evening. When Danny arrived, he was surprised to find that Forrest had a woman with him, a young, pretty woman.

Her name was Faye, and when she shook Danny's hand, she smiled in a way that seemed to carry so much freight Danny was unable to tell if he was imagining things or if perhaps Faye knew something deeply personal about him.

"What are you drinking?" Forrest asked. "Or does your generation drink?"

"We shoot drugs," Danny said.

"Well, there's plenty of that in the medicine cabinet," Forrest told him. "Help yourself."

Faye laughed and brought Danny a scotch. He didn't want to be impolite and tell her he didn't like scotch, so he took it. He found himself unable to keep his eyes off her. She wore a fashionably short skirt and had a model's legs.

"I want you to come to Washington with me," Forrest said. "Meet some friends of mine. Most of them are attorneys. One is even an aviator. And one of them," Forrest added with a smile, "may be our next president."

"You know Bobby Kennedy?" Danny asked. He heard Faye laugh.

Forrest walked to the bar where Danny stood. "You know damned well I'm not talking about Kennedy."

"E.," Danny said, "I'm not going to Washington to meet Richard Nixon, if that's what you mean. I'd never be able to face my friends again."

"E.," Forrest said with disgust, turning away as if his son were hopeless.

"What's E.?" Faye asked.

"If you get to know him real well, he let's you call him by his first initial."

Forrest said, "If your first name were Edmund, you'd keep it under your hat, too. Anyway, I insist you come to Washington."

"Do we have to go through the same old bullshit every time I come over here?"

"Watch it," Forrest snapped.

Faye looked worried.

"If you're *not* going to finish college or get some regular sort of work, would you mind telling me what you intend to do?" His voice no longer carried the wink at the end of each sentence. Instead, it spoke of frustration, of confusion and the helplessness of knowing that he could not control Danny or understand him.

Faye wanted to jump in somehow and give new direction to the conversation, but she said nothing. Danny could not help her or his father. He certainly could not brag about what he did for a living or recount his adventures the way people do to justify their jobs. In a world where people are defined by what they do rather than who they are, it made for uneasy social contact.

Eventually they sat down to eat dinner and Danny announced, "I brought you a bottle of wine."

"Good deal," Forrest said, signaling that he had accepted the truce. Knowing that Forrest had no appreciation of wines, he didn't bother to show him the label. Faye, however, turned the bottle around and gasped when she saw it.

"Something wrong?" Forrest asked.

Faye and Danny exchanged a quick look.

"No," Faye said casually. "It's just a good wine."

Danny said nothing. Forrest wouldn't have known a Château Giscours if a case of it fell on his foot. If Danny paused to wonder about Faye's reaction, it was only for a second, to remark that in her nature there was something naturally conspiratorial, to have read him that quickly and cooperated in keeping a secret from Forrest, even such an inconsequential one.

Throughout dinner Danny tried to say what seemed appropriate. Faye tried to keep the conversation going without touching on any difficult subjects. Still, the atmosphere was so unbearably stiff and distant that they all drank too much. After eating, Danny bolted a cognac, watched his father light a cigar and wished he were somewhere else.

"What would you think?" Forrest asked, "if I told you that Faye and I were going to get married?"

"Jesus Christ," Danny said involuntarily.

Forrest laughed. Faye glanced back and forth from father to son, expectant. Danny suddenly understood why he had been invited to dinner. For the first time he marveled that Forrest hadn't married in all those years since his wife died. In fact, Danny had never seen him with a woman, though there certainly must have been women in his life.

He thought of Nancy Paine, dead now all these years. Forrest had told him, when Danny first came from Texas, how beautiful she had been, what a wonderful woman she was. How brave she had been through her illness and how there would never be anyone else like her. Forrest had said he would go to his grave loving her.

As a child Danny had not thought to ask Forrest the obvious question about Nancy: whether or not she had known about him.

In the following years Danny never quite got around to bringing it up. It wouldn't have dropped very neatly into the middle of a conversation, like, Oh, by the way, Dad, did you betray your wife before she died or did you father me with her consent or what? And while we're on the subject, did you know my mother died of a fever that might have been cured if you'd sent American doctors to treat her? Did it ever occur to you that I might have wanted to get to know the woman who to you was nothing more than a casual fuck?

"It's great," Danny heard himself say.

"It's really important to us that you approve," Faye was saying. "I love your father very much, I hope you can see that."

It was as if she were speaking through a tube from a great distance. Danny could hear her, but she wasn't really there.

He could not remember exactly how he got out of the house. He was drunk when he left. Somehow he made it to his car and managed to get it started and rolling down the winding, tree-lined lane to the edge of the property, where he stopped and leaned on the steering wheel and let it all settle through him.

The next afternoon Danny sat again in his unfurnished apartment, staring at the lake. The storm had moved off and the water, as still as if it had jelled, was brown from the previous day's stirring. Danny drank Spanish brandy from a paper cup until he managed to get himself roughed up enough inside to call the *Chicago Daily News*. When the man who answered told him Maggie had taken a leave of absence, he felt a part of himself die. She was gone, the man said, no longer in Chicago.

Danny watched the triangle of a white sail far out on the lake in the failing sunlight. It seemed that each time he made a motion toward Maggie, their separation took a deeper bite out of him. It reminded him of what Maggie had called the Tar Baby Syndrome. You put in one finger and it comes away all covered with tar. You try to wipe it off and both hands become covered with tar. Put in a toe and your foot is coated with tar. Pretty soon you're drowning in it. The Tar Baby Syndrome.

Danny picked up the telephone and called Maggie's best friend. Half an hour later he was sitting in her studio apartment. Although Elaine could have afforded something much nicer, she just didn't seem to care. She had married early, but all she had left from the collision was a king-size bed and a stack of letters from I Corps. The experience seemed to have left her permanently disenchanted with men, for Danny could not remember ever having known her to consort with them in the four years since he'd met her.

Danny sat on the couch drinking a beer. Elaine sat cross-legged on the floor, staring down at a squat glass of vodka. She wore jeans and a sweat shirt. From a corner of the room a radio played folk music.

"You don't know any . . ." Danny began.

"Any other men?" Elaine asked. "No, I don't think so. I mean, no one I know of before you and Maggie broke up." Elaine looked up at him. "Listen, Danny, don't *care* so much." She had a strange voice with a slightly gravellike quality to it and the mildest hint of a southern accent left over from Arkansas, where she and Maggie had grown up together. Maggie had watched Elaine grow from a thin, abstracted, shy child into a thin, abstracted, shy woman. She hadn't seemed to change at all. She simply got taller, her voice got deeper and she grew slim breasts. She had been every bit as unhumorous as a child as she was now.

"I just wish I lived better," Danny said.

"She's not coming back. You've got to face that."

"Where did she go?" He hadn't wanted to ask—he had promised himself he wouldn't—but he could not control his desire. It wasn't a desire to have her back, but only to pinpoint the spot on earth where she could be found.

"You know I can't tell you that. It wouldn't be fair to Maggie."

"You know then."

"I do know. And it's not anywhere where you can reach her, so please don't ask me again."

Elaine got up, put a record on the stereo and brought Danny another beer. She poured herself more vodka and sat back on the floor, turning her back to Danny and leaning against his legs. "You're luxuriating in the torture, Danny. Whatever kind of stupid male chauvinist things you've done, torturing yourself isn't going to make it any better."

Danny put his hands on her shoulders. "I promised myself I wouldn't ask you where Maggie was. It just came out."

"Men have no control. They're all infants." She reached up and moved Danny's hand to another spot on her shoulders. "There," she said. "Make yourself useful. Rub my neck."

"Got writer's neck?"

"I've got writer's enigma," she said. "Mm, there. Right there. That feels good."

Danny walked his fingers down her back, kneading as he went. "I suppose if she had acted the way I acted, I would have been long gone myself."

"You were so awful?" Elaine leaned forward and sprawled face down on the carpet. "It'll be easier if I lie down," she told Danny.

He knelt, straddling her hips, and continued to massage her back. "I don't have a very stable pattern of behavior," he explained. His hands walked up and down her spine. Elaine was quite skinny. He could feel her bones with his hands and her slim hips wedged between his thighs.

"What did you do, beat her?"

"No, nothing like that. I treated her well when I was there. I was gone a lot. I was out of school. I didn't have a job."

"She always did like the straight life."

Danny leaned into Elaine's back with his fists. As he worked her back harder and harder, she fell silent for a time, except for an occasional toneless syllable, pushed out of her by Danny's hands.

"Do you like Maria Muldaur?" she asked casually, her voice reacting to the pressure of Danny's hands.

"Who's that?"

"Her." Elaine gestured with her chin in the direction of the stereo set.

"Yeah," Danny said. He hadn't really been paying attention to the music. His hands worked their way down across the waistband of Elaine's jeans and he slid back, straddling her knees so that he could knead her hips through the worn denim. She had the hips of a ten-year-old boy. Danny felt the stirring inside him, thinking: This is crazy. I should not be down here doing this. The Tar Baby Syndrome. He had one of her buttocks in each fist, crushing the resilient flesh over and over. He kneaded deeper and deeper into the crevice there, and when Elaine made no protest, he forced himself to move his hands back up her spine, all the way to her shoulders, before allowing them to return on their own to the gentle denim mound. The next time his hands traveled toward her neck, they did so beneath her sweat shirt and still Elaine said nothing, as Danny's interior dialogue continued: The back you have beneath your hands belongs to Maggie's best friend. What do you think you're going to do? Any minute she's going to protest quietly that you are getting too familiar with her and that maybe you should be giving her a back rub, first of all, on top of the clothing and, secondly, by confining the territory covered by your hands to the actual back and not the buttocks. Danny's hands, however, continued on their own as the excitement rose within him.

When his hands came down again, they slipped around her pointed hipbones and underneath her. To Danny's surprise, Elaine arched her hips off the carpet while his fingers found, then identified, the brass button and slipped it out of its buttonhole with a soundless pop against the pressure of her lean belly. She held her arch as he let the zipper down. She even lifted herself higher when Danny pulled her jeans halfway down her legs, taking her underpants with them.

Danny felt a tremendous rush of blood to his face. His lower abdomen seemed to collapse as he stared at her bare pale cheeks, her jeans down around her knees, her pink underpants crumpled inside them. He touched Elaine with the flat of his hands, then with his fingers. Her skin was so smooth Danny wanted to put his face against it, so white and perfect. He kneaded the muscles there and his hands slid between Elaine's cheeks, then gently eased them apart, revealing the auburn starburst, and further, ringlets of beige hair covering a vertical line bordered on either side by delicate leaves of skin that disappeared between her legs. His hands moved between her thighs, slipping lower and lower into the recess, until one of his thin fingers came away moist and fragrant, straightening ringlets of hair that clung to it as it emerged from the heat inside her.

Elaine arched her back against his fingers, but when she

spoke, her voice sounded as if she were addressing a lecture group. "That's the best one on the album," she said.

Danny did not answer—he wasn't sure he could—as he slipped two fingers completely inside her, leaning onto one knee to reach that far and lowering his elbow almost to the floor, as if searching for something that was just out of reach. He drew them out slowly, curling his fingers.

Elaine inhaled sharply and said, "Oh!" with the inrushing breath.

Danny moved off her and she lifted her legs so that he could pull the jeans over her ankles and bare feet. He threw them against the king-size bed, and as he did so, some remote part of his mind speculated on what a lieutenant in the United States Marines would do if, returning home unexpectedly from killing Orientals in Vietnam, he discovered his young wife sprawled naked on the floor with a half-Mexican dope smuggler mounting her from behind.

When he turned back to Elaine, she was already taking off her sweat shirt. He helped her, then fumbled out of his own clothes and knelt over her again.

"Listen to this harmonica solo," Elaine began to say, but Danny leaned forward to move her legs apart and she stopped speaking. He entered her from behind with a kind of brutality, almost as if he intended to hurt her, but she was so wet already that he slipped right inside her.

"Mm," Elaine said, "that feels good." She spoke in exactly the same tone of voice she had used when he had rubbed her back. It seemed he could not give her pain and could not give her pleasure. He couldn't reach her at all and this realization made him angry. He was unsure whether he was angry at himself for the failure or angry with her for being so remote when exactly what he wanted was a connection as solid as two railroad cars coupling. As his anger grew, his movements became that much more vigorous, his hipbones slamming against Elaine's narrow rear.

"Don't come inside me," she said. "I'm off the pill."

Danny felt the heat rise to his face when she spoke. He could not explain why it infuriated him for her to say that, but suddenly he knew that he could just as easily strangle

this woman as fuck her—for what he was doing to her was
not making love. It was, in fact, what the word *fuck* had
always suggested to him, this kind of blind, violent batter-
ing of someone with his sexual apparatus.

Danny grabbed Elaine's hips and held her with all his
strength as he came inside her, trying his best not to give
any outward sign that he was filling her with his semen.

He moved more slowly after that, waiting to see if she
could tell what he had done, but she simply lay there and
said nothing more. He continued to move until he came
again. The second time, however, he slid out of her and
pressed himself between her buttocks as he came.

"Thank you," she said, and stood up to put her clothes on.

ON TELEVISION DANNY ONCE SAW a movie about
a kidnapping. The ransom was $1 million and it was delivered
in a black briefcase, which was opened for the camera, showing neat stacks of bills.

In a Chicago bank Danny locked himself into a small room
and opened a safe-deposit box, stacked nearly a foot deep
with bills. It was not even $100,000. He had other safe-
deposit boxes just like it in other banks, packed just as full.

The truth, Danny had learned, is that money is very
unwieldy. He had come to the bank not to contemplate his
money, but to retrieve some of it in order to furnish his
bare apartment. He put a few thousand dollars into a knapsack and returned the box to the vault. He worried about the
money. It wasn't earning interest. It just sat. His concern
compounded itself, because it made him think he was like
his father—a businessman.

Chip was waiting in the car outside the bank. Together
they drove to four furniture stores to avoid spending too
much cash in any one place, which might attract attention.

"This is shit," Chip said as they drove away from the
last store.

"What's shit?" He was in a good mood. It pleased him to
spend some of the money.

"All that hassle just to buy furniture. It took us nearly a full day. We should be able to pay like ordinary people. You know, walk into Field's and plunk down a credit card."

"Poor little fucker," Danny said.

"You know what I mean."

"I don't think it's so awful having all this money."

Chip drove, turning onto Lake Shore Drive near the Oak Street Beach. "Danny, we don't have a lot of money. Do you realize how much money real wealth amounts to? Look at Howard Hughes. Now *that* is wealth. We have some money, but we're not anywhere near rich."

"I'm rich as I need to be."

"And not only that," Chip continued, ignoring Danny's comment, "but the little money we *do* have is just sitting in boxes and rotting."

"Is yours rotting? I'd certainly get a dehumidifier if I were you, Chipper. I've seen what mildew can do to money."

"Go screw yourself, Paine."

Chip drove in silence for a time, watching the people on the beach.

"What the hell are they all doing out there?" Danny asked. Then he shouted, "Hey! Get back in your offices, you squirrels!"

When they pulled up in front of Danny's apartment, Chip turned from the wheel as Danny was getting out.

"Well?" Danny asked.

"Well, what?"

"What're you grinning about, you bourgeois son of a bitch dupe of the imperialist running dogs?"

"I'm gonna do one last deal."

"You have got to be kidding me."

"I'm gonna do it," Chip warned.

"And you want a copilot."

"I don't care which seat you sit in."

"You are incredible," Danny told him. "Here we are, safe and sound—"

"And bored. Danny, I'm going stir crazy. I've spent my life inside books. The only real thing I've ever done was out there." He pointed south. "I think it's gotten the better

of me, too. I've had this craving to put it to the wall. Do
you know what I mean?" Danny smiled at him but said
nothing. "I don't know. You come home, but you always feel
it out there, waiting, whenever you want it. Adrenaline, man,
it's the best drug in the world and it's not for sale. Every
time you want a hit you've got to go out and take it."

Chip stopped and the two men stared at each other in
silence for a moment. Then Danny laughed. He got back
into the car and leaned his head against the seat, smiling.
Chip put the car in gear.

The flight went without incident and only left them back
in Evanston once more. The glowing romantic picture Chip
had painted had in reality been a very fast turnaround. There
was not even any adrenaline to be taken. When Danny
entered his apartment, there was a note, which said, "See
me pls—Michael."

When Danny knocked on the door, a man in a sport coat
and slacks opened it. He had a short haircut and looked like
an undercover cop. That was when Danny got his hit of
adrenaline, right there in his quiet suburban community.
When the man smiled, Danny suddenly recognized him as
Michael and whispered, "Far fucking out."

"Don't just stand there," Michael said, waving him inside.

Danny couldn't take his eyes off Michael. "I've got to hand
it to you, Mike, that is the freakiest thing I've ever seen.
What's going *on?*" He looked around the living room. There
were transfer cases and trunks. The Oriental carpets had
been rolled and bound with twine. "Where's Virginia?"

"That's all over. My hippie days are finished. I'm on my
way to Tucson."

"What? What about Virginia? Did she leave you or something?"

"She was just part of the image, Dan. I thought you knew
that."

"I thought she was your girl friend."

"Well, she sort of was, but you know." Michael shrugged.
"I've got to move on."

Danny laughed. "This is crazy. This is really crazy."

"The sixties are almost over, Dan. Everything has got to change. *We* have to change. All is flux."

Danny said, "Of course!" as if he'd just understood it all. "Of course. The hippie routine doesn't wash anymore. So this is the new disguise."

"Don't forget this," Michael said, touching his sport coat. "You may need it someday. Just a haircut and some clothes and you almost didn't recognize me. I think the authorities will be a little confused at first, too."

"What are you going to be doing in Tucson?"

"I'll be working with a think tank. Doing research in chemistry."

"What on earth is a think tank?"

"Just what it sounds like. It's a new concept. Great minds go to a quiet place to solve problems, invent things, devise strategies, worry little molecules to death."

"They pay people for *that?*"

Michael smiled and nodded. "And of course, I'll make occasional trips to Vegas and return unexpectedly with loads of money."

"Not a bad idea. I was wondering how to get some of my money out into the open without setting off all sorts of alarms. You should have seen me and Chip trying to buy furniture with a knapsack full of cash."

"Well, most of my money is laundered through other channels. The Vegas thing will just be for local cover."

"Laundered? I like that. Laundered money. Do you have 'em do like light starch or something?"

Michael smiled. "You can't just keep your money in a shoebox. It's not only a waste, it's dangerous. You talk to Moishe next time you're down there. He'll square you away." Michael put his arm around Danny's shoulder. "He is the guru, man. Just talk to Moishe."

"You know, we keep saying we're going to do just one last deal. Then Chip wants to make another run. He's getting weird about money, Mike. I'm beginning to think there's no such thing as a last deal for him."

"Perhaps not. There's only one last deal I know of, and

you don't want to make that deal until you absolutely
have to."

"You'll still have your hand in out there?"

"Michael nodded. "One of Moishe's main channels into
this country operates out of Tucson. A big broker. If you
work with Moishe, we'll be seeing you in Tucson after a
time."

"Sure," Danny said. "Sure." He paused. "Them, Michael.
They, the ever-present they of the steel château. How do you
know when they are onto you?"

Michael winked. "People tell me things. You keep your
ears open. Little birds whistle."

Danny remembered what Amesquita had said about paranoia. And about information. And insanity.

"Come visit," Michael said. "You and Chip. We'll party
forcefully."

"Yeah."

They walked to the door and Michael held it open.

"Tell Chip to stop by here before I leave. I want to say
good-bye."

"Keep it in your boots, Michael."

Danny walked out into the sunlight. Barn swallows dove
at him and screeched. The sun was high, the sky as clear
as it ever was. Danny felt it was going to be a good summer.
He felt he had shed a lot of venom and he was due for some
slack. It had been an explosive year, but now he felt vital, as
if maybe, just maybe, things were going to turn out all right.

Flying. Night flying. Enclosed in the drone of the jet
engines, the slipstream, the warmth of the cabin, the dim
orange and green and blue enunciator lights in the instrument panel, with the cryptic symbology and such labels as
MACH TRIM, Global Navigation, VLF Omega, XTK/SX,
DIS/ETE, PITCH TRIM, against the formal, flat gray dash,
behind which all the signals raced through monitored sensors,
voting and monitoring—the entire found-art complex of elec-
trons flashing through this technological poem as it screamed
across the sky.

Occasionally the radio crackled to life and a voice from some en route air traffic control center would come on, "Now, Four Golf Lima, contact Atlanta Center on one-two-five-point-niner, and have a good night."

Chip would answer, holding the microphone button on the control column, "Ahh, Atlanta on twennie-five-niner, Four Golf Lima, and so long, sir."

It was a secret, protected place, where they could hide high above the earth, their wing tip strobes igniting the darkness in syncopated rhythms as they hung in apparent stillness in the sound that seemed like silence after so many hours aloft.

They had rented the jet with cash from a discreet contact and set out for South America to talk with Moishe. They had heard the news. The summer was not going to turn out all right. All across the land people had promised that "things" would get "heavy," and they had been correct. Bobby Kennedy had walked into the kitchen and had taken a bullet in the head. He had held out all day long. Brain death occurred at 6:30 P.M. June 5. Whatever was left after that gave up at 1:44 A.M. on June 6, proving once more that what passes for modern medicine has not even begun to fathom what keeps a person alive when he should, by all rights, be dead.

"You know what this means," Chip told Danny as they flew along. Danny said nothing. He flew the plane. "Nixon just became our next president."

Danny looked over at Chip. "Forrest was right."

Danny flew. He flew and flew, but couldn't seem to keep himself awake, as if a powerful drug were pushing him down. He gave Chip the controls and slid into the back to sleep, such as it was, dozing in the narrow little cabin, wondering. Danny didn't have a political bone in his body, but he could not help thinking it was all too much to bear. As they left the southern border of the United States, Danny wondered if behind him, even now, they were just burning it to the ground.

At dawn Danny was back in the right seat, as beneath them the protoplasmic immensity of South America rose out of the sea, as if it might at any moment blow steam and sound, leaving nothing but the rippling green ocean. Danny felt as much that he was driving out of time as place.

When they arrived over the warehouse, they saw that Moishe had had the airstrip paved with black asphalt. He had even had numbers painted on it. At its midpoint, off to one side, was a freewheeling wind *T*, and a tower next to it bristled with antennas.

"How much runway do you think we've got?" Chip asked.

"I wonder if he's set up radio communications," Danny said, twirling the knobs on the COM stack. "Let's try the idiot frequency." He switched to 123.45, which had long been in use on international flights and was called the idiot frequency because any idiot could remember it.

"I'd say we've got an easy mile," Chip said. "Try eight degrees."

"All right, gimme eight."

The radio crackled, but Danny and Chip heard no communications.

"Eight degrees flaps," Chip said.

Danny turned onto base leg.

"Maybe he oughta put up a water tower with a big sign on it that says Moishe's Dope Sales," Chip suggested.

Danny laughed and turned final. "Hundred and five over the fence."

"Check."

Ten minutes later they were sitting in Moishe's air-conditioned office on the squeaky plastic-covered couch.

Danny asked, "Isn't this a little bold, the paved airstrip with numbers on it?"

"They know," Moishe told him as he thumbed through a newspaper. "It might as well be a nice airstrip."

"They don't even care?"

"Not as long as we're paying their salaries, they don't. We want a nice airstrip, we get one." He rattled his newspaper in the air like a man riding a subway. "If we wanted a control tower, we could have that, too."

"That's what the antennas are for?" Chip asked.

"No, that's for the ships, though I think we'll put in a

Unicom frequency, too. We'll let you know." Moishe put the paper flat on his desk. "That man," he said.

"What man?" Chip asked.

"That man of yours, Nixon."

"He's not our man," Danny told him.

"A rube," Moishe continued, ignoring Danny's response.

"I'd have thought you'd like him, with all your Bahamian and Cuban connections," Chip suggested.

Moishe frowned and closed his eyes. "Rank amateurs."

"Some people say he had something to do with the Kennedy assassinations," Chip said.

"Who knows? People will speculate for years, but no one will ever know. Me? I'd say if it wasn't that Arab or whoever he was, then it was businessmen. At least they had something to do with John Kennedy's death. I had no great affection for the Kennedys, but this—" He held out his hand. "You don't go around shooting presidents, senators. That's bad." He waved the subject away, reached into his desk and took out a business card. "Here," he said, "go see Bobby. He'll take care of you."

"We need taking care of?" Danny asked. "Bobby who?"

Moishe shrugged. "Money, Danny. He takes care of money. Here." He pushed the card forward into the empty air and Chip stood up to take it.

"I want something done with *my* money," Chip said.

"Good boy," Moishe said. "You listen to him," he told Danny. "See that your money does not gather dust. In the meantime, what are you doing on my nice new landing strip with that little airplane of yours?"

"That happens to be a fine little technological marvel," Danny said.

"For Sunday driving, yes. For Texas oilmen and the idle rich. But what about workingmen? What about its useful load?"

"We," Chip put in, "are its useful load."

"Suit yourselves," Moishe said. He picked up a pen and wrote on a piece of paper, showing Danny and Chip the top of his head. "If you want to do business with me, this contact will provide you with the introductions you need.

Sam Spaulding. Very good people, Sam. Your credit with me will be four star, so you can make up your own mind how you wish to handle this."

"How do you mean, credit?" Danny asked.

"I mean that if you would like to fly twenty tons in a DC-6, that's fine. You can keep doing that just as you have before. No strings attached. We can even arrange to front you some of the product, which will involve no additional risk for you but will increase your net considerably. For your services, we pay ten dollars a pound from now on."

"Ten dollars?" Chip asked.

"Yes, the business is hot. The rates go up. The planes are still about the same price. Everyone makes money. Now." Moishe leaned forward. "You can also acquire your own aircraft and increase your participation in the program. We supply the product. You supply the airplane and commission someone—Spaulding, for example—to supply the buyer on the other end."

"I'm not sure I understand you," Danny said. "Where do you come in?"

"I supply the product. I am paid for that. You have your own airplane. Spaulding makes the introductions so that you have someone to take the product off your hands. For that you pay Spaulding at a rate that will be in the neighborhood of five dollars a pound. You can move the product any way you like. Buy a boat, I don't care. Just let me know how much you want and I'll have it ready. When you unload on the other end, you make, instead of your five or ten dollars a pound, something like fifty dollars a pound. Because I can then sell to you at about twenty-five and they will buy from you at seventy-five and then sell to their customers for a hundred and seventy-five. Do you follow me?"

"I do," Chip said. "It's beautiful, man." His eyes were bright with excitement. "Two million dollars on one of those planes." He poked Danny in the arm.

"It's really very simple," Moishe said. "You take more risk, you make more money. If you take a boat that holds, say, fifty tons—which is nothing in terms of boats, a little hundred-and-fifty-foot freighter will hold that—you can make, let's see . . ." He began to figure in his head, but Chip cut him off.

"*Five million dollars,*" he gasped.

"Well, not quite, because when your initial quantity gets that large, you'll probably be selling on the other end to people in large enough quantities that you'll have to discount your prices as well, you see. But I'd say you could clear four million anyway on a deal like that. Your total time, block to block, would be two or three months at most. If you're really good, though, you can do something like that in a month. From the time your ship hits U.S. waters, you can unload in a single day. *If*"—he held up a finger—"you're really, really good. We have one ship's captain named Reggie, he's done jobs like this in a matter of weeks in a few cases. It takes a lot of planning, a lot of trust, a lot of honest, competent people and a lot of *chutzpah*, too, though."

Danny and Chip stared at him for a moment, and when they said nothing, Moishe went on. "Of course, our people will make all these connections for you—acquisition of boats or planes, their titles, documentation, registry wherever you want it, crews. Generally speaking, if we deal with boats, we go for Monrovia. Liberian registry. Their laws are more generous, shall we say?"

"Is that why every ship you hear about wrecking itself happens to be a Liberian freighter?" Chip asked.

"Well," Moishe said, smiling slightly, "I do suppose that might have something to do with it, but it doesn't mean you have to be reckless just because you happen to register your ship in Monrovia." He cleared his throat as if Chip had caught him in a tiny fib. "So. You'd probably get a Panamanian crew."

"Why Panama?" Chip asked.

"They have good sailors. The U.S. has good relations there, connection-wise. If God forbid, they should get caught, they'll be taken in, printed, photographed and sent back to Panama. The next week they can work for you again."

"Moishe, Moishe," Danny said. "Can we talk about boats later? We're not going to go out and buy a freighter."

"Why not?" Chip demanded. "Do you realize what kind of leverage you could pull in commodities with four million dollars?"

"Chip," Danny said, annoyed and incredulous, "you can't just walk down LaSalle Street with a wheelbarrow full of hundreds and start buying pork bellies."

"Boys, boys." Moishe held up his hand. "Save it for at home. Do whatever you like. I'm just imparting the wisdom of the ages to you. Take it or leave it. See if I care."

"Moishe, you're breaking my goddamned heart," Danny said.

"What can I say?" Moishe asked, spreading his hands. "You two are reliable. When you're up there with our precious cargo, I don't lose sleep over you. So I treat you well, that's all. Do you want the deal or not? You can do it in airplanes; you don't have to use boats." When they said nothing, Moishe misinterpreted their silence and their sly, grinning exchange as hard bargaining. He threw up his hands. "All right, you're driving me out of business, but all right. I'll front you the airplane." He quickly held up a finger. "But only this once."

"The last deal," Danny told Chip, and they both burst out laughing.

"What's so funny now?" Moishe asked.

"You had to have been there," Danny said.

"So what are the arrangements?" Chip asked.

"Someone will contact you to help with that. When you've finished your first trip, you can go visit Sam yourself. You'll have fun. There's going to be a big party there. It happens every year. That'll be a good place for you to get acquainted. I used to go every year." Moishe sighed. "But I can't anymore. The IRS." He shook his head. "I'll make sure Sam knows you're coming. Don't worry about a thing."

"Where is *there*?" Danny asked.

"Tucson."

Danny and Chip looked at each other. "We can visit Michael," Danny said.

Moishe laughed. "Did Michael give you that cock-and-bull story about his being a professor?"

"What?" Danny asked. "It wasn't true?"

"Oh, it's true, it's true all right." Moishe shook his head in dismay. "Such a professor!"

An old fashioned DC-6 airplane is not a very easy thing to lose, even if you have your heart set on it. Those who were successful at such a venture generally contemplated the principle that the more obvious a thing is, the less likely it is to be seen. At an airport any one airplane would not attract attention, just as one tree in the forest does not attract undue attention among its brother and sister trees but would attract a great deal of attention if, say, it appeared in church one Sunday morning. Therefore, the best way to lose a DC-6 airplane appeared to be, quite simply, to park it at an airport, walk away from it and never come back. Which is what Danny and Chip did after making the arrangements Moishe had mentioned. To Danny's utter astonishment, it worked. Their Castle Bank & Trust accounts showed that they had made $1,942,376.50. According to Chip's figures, they should have had $1,942,978.00 after paying various middlemen. He immediately suggested that they "go back to those chiselers we sold that shit to and demand the rest of our goddamned money." Danny was alarmed, hearing this. He thought Chip had finally gone off the deep end, but Chip smiled thinly and nodded at Danny. "Well, never mind," he added.

They paid Moishe for the airplane, which, as promised, had been furnished up front, no questions asked. That left them roughly $1,750,000. The two of them were practically giddy. They wanted to tell someone, to celebrate somehow. There was no such thing in that business, though. There was no outlet other than the business itself. That was part of the reason Danny did not protest vigorously enough when they sat down a few days later and did some serious arithmetic, saying, what the hell.

The second trip made them more than $2 million.

"Now," Danny told Chip in all seriousness, "for absolutely sure, that was the last deal."

"For sure," Chip agreed. "Fuckin'-A-firmative."

So they sat. Danny did not tell anyone. He and Chip did not take out a full-page ad in *Variety* announcing their success. They did not pass out bonus checks to their employees or throw an office party. They simply sat and drank very expensive wine and cognac. Danny bought a case of 1961 Margaux, which they went through in six evenings. And the little suburban world closed around them. Chip began to bury himself in books again. Danny began following a soap opera on television.

Chip, who had not attended a class in weeks, walked into his final exams and came away with the highest honors possible. He was scheduled to begin graduate school at MIT, where he had applied more out of academic habit than any real desire to attend. That he might actually go there was next to impossible as far as he was concerned.

In the fall Chip and Danny sat one day in Chip's apartment. A big color television set flickered with images of the opening ceremonies of the Olympic Games in Mexico City. Chip was doodling on a pad of paper.

"What would you do if you had an atom bomb?" he asked.

Danny continued to watch the television. He said, "I'd ask for three dollars and a quarter million parachutes. Or is it three parachutes and a quarter of a million dollars? I forget which."

"Really," Chip said. "What would you do?"

Danny turned to face him. "Charles, you are strange, do you know that? You were strange when I met you and you've gotten steadily stranger ever since."

Chip continued doodling. Danny looked down at the pad. It was covered with the hieroglyphics of higher math and physics.

"Don't tell me you've designed an atom bomb."

Chip smiled. "I'm pretty sure it would work. Even if it fizzled, it'd give about a tenth kiloton, which would be enough to knock down any skyscraper."

Danny grabbed the pad of paper, suddenly, saying, "Gimme that."

He studied the schematics and equations. There was a

thing that looked something like a cannon. Next to it Chip had made the label, "Diluted Pu Cylinders, 6.0 in. diameter, 7.5 inch thick U(0.3) reflector. Steel guide sleeve 0.030 in. thick, within reflector cylinder. Diluted U(0.28) M_c = 10.3 Kg Pu." Danny looked at it for a moment, but it did not mean much to him. He knew *Pu* was plutonium and *U* was uranium. He guessed that M_c meant critical mass, which therefore meant Chip had figured he would need 10.3 kilos of plutonium. Most of all, he knew Chip well enough to know that if he said it would work, it would work. "Chip," Danny said, "you wouldn't really think about making something like this. . . ."

"Nah," Chip said, taking back the notebook. "Wouldn't *dream* of it."

Danny believed him. It was just a mental exercise. Danny wondered what the FBI would do if they knew that sitting right here in this little college town, an undergraduate student had just invented an atom bomb, doodling while watching the Olympics on TV. He wondered how Chip would have channeled his bizarre energies if he hadn't become a pilot at an early age. "Chip," Danny said.

"Yeah," Chip said without looking up.

"Would you do me a favor?"

"Sure."

"Would you please stop that doodling?"

Chip laughed and looked at his friend, his oldest and closest friend, this half-breed pilot smuggler. "You know, Paine, I think the two of us have flipped out completely. You're addicted to television and I'm sitting around trying to figure out how to blow up the world. I think we need a vacation."

"I think we need a job," Danny said.

"Let's get the fuck out of here."

A
Failure
of Nerve
at the
Critical
Momeut

7

MICHAEL'S HOUSE, on a rise overlooking the town of Tucson, was made of seasoned blond timbers and appeared to have hundreds of windows of every imaginable size and shape, some of them leaded with colored glass, creating images of flowers and birds and sunbursts. On the lower level, a series of glass rooms overlooked the bluffs. The focus of the house was the large room on the second floor, which Michael called the Sky Room. It had an immense stone fireplace extending to the ceiling, which was made entirely of windows.

"The floor," Michael explained to Danny and Chip, "is actually the deck from the USS *Los Angeles*. The architect salvaged it."

Danny brought out his housewarming present for Michael —two bottles of Château Pichon-Longueville, 1945, and they tasted it and talked. Naturally enough, their conversation was about the business itself. There were so few people with whom Danny and Chip could discuss what they did, it was just natural to take advantage of it. Yet in this conversation Danny sensed an incipient direction, as if Michael had something he wanted to tell him. It was only after they had finished the first bottle and begun the second that Michael revealed what it was.

"How much do you know about the guy who tried to bust you?" he asked.

"Fassnacht? Not enough."

"Well, I'll just tell you a story, okay?" Michael asked. In his voice was an overtone Danny had heard before. It seemed to signal that Michael did want Danny to know something but didn't want to be involved.

"Whatever," Danny said to let him off the hook.

Then Michael told him what had happened to Fassnacht right after Mendoza was killed. He did not mention Mendoza by name. He just told the story in such a way that Danny knew the time frame. Fassnacht had hacked out the new Mexican heroin turf under Mendoza's guidance. Officially Fassnacht worked for the United States government as a federal narcotics enforcer, running aggressive antimarijuana raids deep in the interior of Mexico. One noticed, Michael pointed out, the preponderance of photographs and news releases about marijuana seizures and the curious paucity of reported raids involving significant quantities of heroin. To put a finer point on this discrepancy, if seizures were being made even on a random basis, the quantity of heroin impounded would be a hundred times what it was. Unless, of course, most heroin that came into the U.S. came in with the knowledge and cooperation of those responsible for making such seizures.

Exactly how high up the administrative ladder that knowledge went, no one was willing to say. There had even been some intrepid investigators who, having asked too many questions along those lines, were found swimming in the trunks of their cars at the bottom of the Potomac, a stunt the law enforcers called "stealing more chain than you can carry."

By the end of the decade the heroin trade was in the process of shifting full scale to Mexico in preparation for a time when Southeast Asian supplies would begin to dwindle, along with those of Turkey, Iran and Afghanistan. Soon the government would even be forced to make Fassnacht's defoliation missions public, simply because an operation so massive cannot be kept secret forever.

Nor can such an operation continue without its opponents. Mendoza and Fassnacht found theirs in the person of Santiago Amesquita Garza, who led a small army of antiheroin troops on occasional successful missions and (against policy) ignored the relatively small-time marijuana business. Indeed, he left it to flourish. It was the only thing keeping poppies out of the ground in some parts of Mexico.

In turning against heroin, Amesquita and his men turned against Fassnacht and Mendoza and were therefore marked. When Mendoza was gunned down, Fassnacht assumed Amesquita had ordered it done—whether or not he had was an academic question at best. At the time, Amesquita had quite naturally assumed the killing was an internal affair—typical gang-style rivalry.

"Where do I come in?" Danny asked, knowing Michael could not possibly suspect Danny's involvement.

"Your relationship with your uncle. You were moving some grass, too, so they must have assumed he was looking the other way. Or didn't care."

Indeed, Danny recalled Amesquita's saying, "We're fighting dogs. Why should we worry about killing the fleas first?"

"If nothing else," Michael continued, "just the fact that you were running Mexican leaf irked them. It had to have been grown on soil they wanted for poppies."

"I was just a kid," Danny protested. "I wasn't even running grass then."

Michael shrugged. It wasn't important to make it logical. It was just important that Danny know what the story was. The story was that shortly after Mendoza's death Fassnacht found himself in the rather uncomfortable position of sitting in a shack in the high Arizona desert with five men, one woman and $3 million. There were plenty of firearms as well. Fassnacht was experienced enough to have known better, but there he was. That much money could not exist in one spot without trouble finding it.

Conversation in the shack stopped suddenly in the middle of negotiations when everyone heard the automobiles. They were distant at first, but they were going very fast.

"Rip-off!" someone shouted, but it was too late.

A tear-gas canister came through the window before anyone was able to get out the door. It hit one of the men full in the face, killing him outright. Fassnacht grabbed a piece of luggage he knew contained $350,000, held it in front of his

chest and ran out the back door. Somehow he made it
through all the gunfire that had erupted—incoming and
outgoing. He ran until he dropped and then hid under a
rock outcropping, listening. The gunfire continued for a
long time, then stopped. Then a team of cars began systematically searching the area.

It was nightfall before they quit and Fassnacht crawled
out, dragging the suitcase with him. It had five bullet holes
in it.

He found the bodies back at the shack, which had been
leveled. They had been mutilated by bullets and rendered
by fire.

Fassnacht blamed that scene on Amesquita. His reasoning didn't matter; he had begun to blame everything on
Amesquita by that time. If it rained, it was Amesquita's fault;
if it did not rain, it was Amesquita's fault. And if it was
Amesquita's fault, it was also somehow Danny's fault.

Their second day in Arizona Danny and Chip drove far
into the hills and up the winding dirt road to Sam Spaulding's ranch. They watched from the car as they passed
stables and meadows, tennis courts and barns. They drove
by a random grouping of Mercedes, Jaguars and Jeeps. Danny
could see people spread out underneath the overhanging
branches of trees and hear the loud rock-and-roll music
drifting out from the main house. Five large black men in
white aprons stained with red and brown sauces, with blood
and charcoal and mesquite chips, attended barbecue pits.
They piled plates high with generous portions of brisket and
beans, potato salad, roasted corn and baby back ribs.

Two Indian women were heating stacks of tortillas and
placing them in wicker baskets covered with towels to keep
them warm. Two small Mexicans stood in a hollow square
of tables, mixing drinks with the speed and flourish of a
juggling team. Their little sideshow seemed to be attracting
a lot of attention.

"This is some domicile," Danny observed.

"They do it with mirrors," Chip explained. "Look at that guy, isn't that Jim Morrison?"

"Sure looks like him."

The house was jammed with people, shouting, laughing, puffing joints or leaning over glass-topped tables to inhale the white crystalline mixture of mannitol and cocaine. As Danny and Chip made their way inside, the crowd deepened and soon they were separated. Danny kept moving, taking in the conversations around him and wondering who all these people were.

"Good blotter, man, really good blotter," a man's voice said behind him.

"I don't know about this purple microdot," another answered. "I'm getting trails like a banshee."

Elsewhere a black man had cornered a small woman who looked like the one who was never asked to dance. The man wore a wide purple felt hat and a yellow jump suit. He was saying, "Come *on*, girl, go 'haid and try it, it'll make you all the way *live*, yeah, like a *maw*-fuckah. I'm all the way luv-lee now, yeah."

"What is it?" she asked.

"Hawg, baby, Angel Dust."

Danny passed out of range of their conversation and was stopped by the crowd again. He found himself next to a man with light hair and enormous muscles, wearing nothing but white overalls. His biceps looked to be eighteen inches around. He was talking to another blond man similarly dressed.

"Me and Bobsy came to pick up a Q-uie. We were gonna pers the giblets and flak the mani to the dwids, but it was such the kind, the pink flake, such the fucking kind, you know, that we just persed the entire Q-uie."

About twenty feet away Danny saw a woman with straight blond hair that hung well past her waist. It was such a striking sight that he stopped and stared. Her back was to him. She did not appear to be engaged in any of the strange conversations taking place. In fact, she didn't seem to belong at all. She simply stood in the center of the room, sipping wine and watching the action with mild, abstracted curiosity. When she turned, Danny could see her face and had the odd sensation that he had seen her before.

His initial impulse was to go over and talk to her, to impress her with war stories and with his great adventures, which would naturally sweep her off her feet and into his arms. It was, of course, a mean impulse and quite impossible. He could not discuss his business with strangers. It was also a notion degrading to her.

Still, he thought, it is a party. Nothing wrong with talking to one of the guests. He walked up to her and she looked at him as if she were expecting him to say something.

"I, well, I just—" he stammered. He smiled, glancing at the floor. "I guess I just wanted to say something really brilliant. I think I've lost track of it."

"Oh, shit, it doesn't matter," she said. She sounded as if Danny were the thousandth person to approach her that evening. He may have been for all he knew.

"My name is Danny Paine," he said. "How's that?" For a second he could not believe his good fortune. It appeared that he had said just the right thing, for her face lit up with surprise. Then she began laughing. "Was it something I said?"

"Oh, yes—no!" She stopped herself. "It was something Moishe said. "You, of course, know Moishe."

"Of course."

"I'm Sam Spaulding."

Danny stood in silence for a moment, attempting to make sense of what she had just said.

"He likes to play that trick. He said, 'Don't worry, he'll find you.' I guess he was right. You see, my name's Samantha, but people call me Sam."

"Well, my name's Daniel Paine, but you can call me Gloria."

Samantha took his arm and pulled him along through the crowd. "Come on, we've got to get to know each other. Where's your partner? What's his name?"

"Charles Wolf."

"Yeah, Moishe called him Chip. Where is he?"

"I think I saw him with an exotic and beautiful woman somewhere back there. We got separated."

"The way Moishe described you I expected a sort of middle-aged guy wearing aviator sunglasses at night. A little gray at the temples. Maybe epaulets on the shoulders."

"Yeah," Danny said as they passed out of the house, "I forgot my smuggling uniform. I'm chief pilot for Cannabis Airlines."

Samantha got the attention of one of the Mexican bartenders and ordered for Danny and herself. They found a table and as soon as they were seated, one of the mestizo women bent down to Samantha and asked if they wanted to eat. Samantha nodded and the woman hurried away.

Danny stared at the woman before him, shook his head and laughed. "I can't believe you're Sam. All that time I kept thinking of some thick-necked heavy. How did you get into this line of work?"

"My former husband." She looked down at the table as if just the thought of it were painful.

"Divorced?"

"Widowed."

"I'm sorry."

"Don't be. I was a wide-eyed girl from SoCal and I thought he was the most romantic figure ever cut. I was lucky to get out of it alive. He was one of those sixties freaks. He thought he was James Dean and Marlon Brando and Bob Dylan and God."

"How did he die? If you don't mind talking about it."

"He bought a P-fifty-one Mustang and chopped two feet off each wing. It made for a *very* tight-turning airplane and about doubled the stall speed. It also exaggerated the plane's already wicked stall-spin characteristics. It was one of those planes where if there was so much as a *sputter* on takeoff, you had to dump the nose like there was no tomorrow. Well, one day he jumped up and punched a hole in the deck with that thing. I guess it just got a little ahead of him."

"I'm sorry," Danny said.

"Like I said, don't be." Samantha sipped her mescal as the mestizo woman brought their food and two cups of cold beer. Samantha chased the mescal with beer.

"I take it you're a pilot, too," Danny said.

"I haven't flown since he killed himself. It isn't because of his death—I'm not afraid or anything like that. I just haven't had the urge. We had just sold the Queen Air and were about to get something else. When he rolled the Mustang up into a ball, I was left without anything to fly. So I just left it that way." She took a bite of her *cabrito* and sipped a beer. As an afterthought, she added, "Of course, I've still got the G-two, but I have a pilot for that."

"You have a Grumman Gulfstream jet?" Danny asked. "That's a six-million-dollar aircraft."

Samantha dropped her eyes, as if embarrassed. "I guess it's that all right."

Danny started laughing, watching her eat. "I'm sorry, I don't mean to laugh. It's not funny."

"Well, what *is?*"

"I guess you are. You're a funny woman, Sam."

A man walked by their table with a meat hook over his shoulder, from which dangled what appeared to be a quarter of a steer. As he passed, he said hello to Samantha, who stopped him and introduced Danny. His name was Doc. He was short—perhaps only five and a half feet tall—but looked as if he could lift twice his weight. Samantha explained that he had worked for the ranch when her husband was alive. He lived in town and came out regularly to keep things running and fix what broke down. He had been a smoke jumper in Oregon a number of years earlier when a backfire his buddies set caught him flat-footed and burned him nearly to death.

"He looks all right to me."

"From the neck up," Samantha said. "He's a tough customer."

The mestizo woman returned with more beer and a basket of tortillas, along with a dish of fresh sliced tomato. As they ate, a woman named Star came by, dressed in black. She moved as if she were on a stage and kissed Samantha on the mouth, handing her what looked like an antique silver cigarette case. Samantha set the box beside her plate and they finished eating as Danny watched Star sweep away into the crowd.

"Danny," Samantha asked, as if she were bringing up a touchy subject, "are you here on business?"

"I guess. I don't know. I mean, who knows? I never intended to get into this business in the first place. I started out running away from home. Next thing I knew, I was a dope smuggler." He looked at her. She was smiling. "Yeah, yeah, I know, I know, that's what they all say."

Samantha nodded. "That sure is what they all say."

"Well, I am seriously looking for a way out of this business."

"Aren't we all?"

"You, too, huh?"

"Only about twice a day," Samantha admitted.

"Well, why don't you just quit? Look at this spread you've got. All these friends. The G-two. What do you need with that bullshit?"

"Well, first of all, these people are not my friends. They are the members of the Greater Southwestern Pharmaceuticals Shippers' Association and together they control billions of dollars' worth of drugs. If someone were to drop a bomb here tonight, nobody west of the Mississippi would get high for years to come."

"Why are you giving this party for them?"

"I sort of inherited it. When Gary was alive—that was my husband, Crazy Gary—he gave this party every year. I somehow got stuck with it. It seems to have a life of its own. We're like any big business, you know. We can do everything but stop."

"Still, you could quit."

"I'm a broker," she said. "I operate virtually without risk. The drug enforcement people count on making busts with product in hand. It's good PR. I never get near drugs or money. I simply put people together, the way a talent agency would."

"So what's the problem? Why even think about quitting?"

"Look," she said, leaning forward, "this is the third largest business in the United States. It is the single largest business in the state of Florida. Get the picture? The stakes are so high even the government can't afford for the public to know. I'm talking about countless billions. The authorities are using satellite surveillance to map the progress and growth of agricultural commodities they can't control. Satellites, that's how big this is. The smugglers have it all over them, though, when it comes to technology on the ground. Money and methods, too. We are better funded, better staffed, better organized than they are. And the stakes I'm referring to amount to nothing less than complete and literal control of entire countries. Bolivia, for example. The tin and copper industry there has gotten so deeply in debt to the International Monetary Fund that just about the only cash flow Bolivia has these days is from cocaine. José Abraham Baptista, the largest coke mover there, *owns* Bolivia."

"And Moishe owns Colombia."

"Not quite. He's one of a handful, though. And I do want to quit. But I'm too much involved." Samantha paused, staring into Danny's eyes. "But you, you're so young. Look at you. You could be an old man in five years."

"I've heard rumors."

She dropped her eyes and smiled. "Who am I to be telling you? I've never run a load of dope in my life."

"You know Moishe pretty well, huh?"

"He used to come and stay here all the time, before it got too hot for him in the States."

"You know, his place down there is incredible. He's got a paved airstrip, air-conditioned offices. It's so open."

"Moishe is the government there," Samantha explained. "Just like I told you. If the U.S. wanted to shut him down— or the regular Colombian government, for that matter— they'd have to mount a full-scale military operation. There's no other way."

"He gave me the name of some financial wizard he knows."

"Yeah, Bobby. He's the best. Right in your hometown, too." Samantha stood up. "Listen, Danny, it was nice meeting you, I really have to go play hostess." She started to leave, then turned back. "Say, do you ride horses?"

"I don't know the first goddamned thing about any kind of transportation that doesn't involve a coefficient of lift. But I'd love to learn."

She laughed. "You're a funny man, Danny. You come out tomorrow around noon and I just might be crawling out of my cocoon. We'll go riding and talk."

"Sure," Danny said.

"Bring Chip," she said, and merged into the crowd.

Danny sat drinking his beer. He noticed that she had forgotten the little silver case Star had left. He picked it up and opened it. Inside were white rocks, their surfaces punctuated with shiny points of light. He picked one up and touched it to the tip of his tongue, which immediately went numb. He put it back and closed the box.

Danny and Chip arrived at noon. The sun burned over everything and the place was as clean as if no one had been there for months. The front door was open. Danny called inside.

"Come on in!" Samantha hollered.

Danny and Chip found Samantha in the kitchen with Katina, whom Danny recognized as an exotic-looking woman Chip had met at the party.

"Charles," she said, unfolding from her chair. She walked over to Danny. "Hi," she said, smiling. "I don't think we met last night. Your partner had me pinned in a corner, where he tried in vain to tell me how they measure the speed of a galaxy by red shift."

"How's that?" Danny asked.

"Beats me. I was so stoned I didn't know what he was talking about."

She had gray eyes and was quick to laugh. Danny liked her immediately.

Samantha was working at the stove, cooking something. "Kat's a genuine screenwriter," she said.

"What are you working on?" Danny asked.

"Well, this morning," Katina said, "I wrote a scene where this guy's on an ariplane. See, he's very scared of flying. So he goes and gets on an airliner, all right? He has to go somewhere, but he's terrified and so is his wife, but off he goes. Well, they take off and they're climbing out and bang! An engine explodes. The plane shudders and rolls and pitches and there is smoke filling the cabin. And the guy takes off his wedding band and eats it."

"Eats it!" Chip hollered.

"Yeah. He eats his wedding band."

"What for?" Chip asked.

"Well, he figures that when the plane crashes and he's diced into unidentifiable bits, they'll find his stomach and the wedding band will be in there and they'll identify him by its inscription so that his wife can give him a regular Christian burial and get a death certificate."

"How lovely," Danny said.

"But does the plane really crash?" Chip asked, apparently taking the story quite seriously.

"Oh, hell, no," Katina said. "Everything is fine. They make a precautionary landing and then, of course, the guy has to retrieve his wedding band, and you know what that means."

"Oh, even better," Danny said, smacking his lips. "Yum, yum."

"All right, everybody," Samantha ordered, "sit down. Time's awastin'." She set a steaming cauldron of chili in the center of the table and went back to the stove. She wore jeans and cowboy boots. The sunlight from the windows winked off the rivets on her back pockets and Danny could not take his eyes off her.

"Are those dimes or pennies in your pocket?" Danny asked.

"Mm?" Samantha asked, turning around, puzzled. "What?" When she realized what Danny was saying, she said, "Male chauvinist pig."

"If he misbehaves," Katina suggested, "let's put him on Dutchess."

"Dutchess?" Danny asked.

"She's a horse," Katina teased. "A real manhater, that

horse. Last man who tried to ride Dutchess was unable to have sex for a month."

"That's what he gets for trying to have sex with horses," Chip allowed.

Samantha bent down to get a pan from the oven and a little part of Danny cried out at the sight. "I just can't help myself," he explained. "You're not a male chauvinist just because you appreciate a great natural wonder."

After a breakfast of chili and eggs—of which Chip unashamedly ate three full helpings—they were heading toward the stables when Doc pulled up in his truck with a load of hay in the back. He exchanged small talk with Samantha for a moment and then lifted an eighty-pound bail of hay onto his shoulder as if it had been a sack of groceries. They followed him into the barn, where Samantha showed Danny how to saddle a horse. Katina and Chip worked with two others. The entire time they were preparing for the ride, Doc continued to unload the truck, carrying bales on his shoulder up the stairs to the loft without ever breaking stride or even breathing hard.

They rode out to the west for an hour. Dutchess, which Samantha rode, was a tall horse the color of fine wood, with sides as sleek and glossy as lacquered oak. Danny rode a smaller horse named Ochra. Her coat was thicker and less polished, but she was as docile as an old dog and did exactly what Danny wanted, even though he was not altogether certain what that was. Actually Ochra was simply following Duchess. Samantha had put Danny on Ochra to make him look good.

Danny liked it. Ochra was soft and hot to the touch. He had never been that close to an animal so large. Katina and Chip rode two black horses, both of which seemed to want to stretch out and run.

An hour out, they turned north and continued on, down an incline, which the horses negotiated with a sideways gait. "You know what they've been finding out here?" Samantha asked over her shoulder. "Bunch of treasure hunters out here have started digging up cash in plastic bags."

"From what?" Chip asked.

"Drug money," Samantha called back over her shoulder. "Bills in large denominations wrapped neatly in ten-thousand-dollar packets. Some small-time dealers burying their money." She laughed. "It's the eternal problem of the business. What do you do with the money?"

"We're familiar with the problem," Chip said.

"We'll straighten that out," Samantha assured him.

The sun angled down the afternoon sky as they came up over a rise in the middle of open country and there, in the distance, was a small road, an ancient gas station with a glass-topped gravity pump. They rode down toward it, tied their horses, and inside the ramshackle building found a mongrel store, inbred of candy counters and shotgun shells, tire gauges, spark plugs and tins of Copenhagen and Skol snuff, pemmican and Beechnut, Hostess cupcakes, Moon pies and Diamond safety matches. A sign above the counter said, We Gladly Accept Checks If You Are at Least 80 Years Old and Are Accompanied by Your Mother. In the center of the room was an ancient Coca-Cola cooler, its red paint worn through to bare metal in spots. It was filled with chipped ice and beer and soft drinks.

The old man inside hovered near the door, where he could spit when he took a notion to. When no one struck up a lively conversation, he informed them all that he regarded Richard Nixon as a horse's ass and a crook.

"What about Johnson?" Katina asked.

"I s'pose he meant well," the man admitted grudgingly. "But then you go ahead and mean well in your pond and I'll go fishin' in mine, and let's see who gets dinner first."

Katina and Chip finished their RC colas and walked out into the sun to stand by the horses, talking quietly, their faces close together.

When they left the gas station, the sun fell fast behind them and enormous shadows rode ahead of the horses, four stretched-out centaurs, etched on the beige and rocky ground. Danny remarked to himself how strange a place this was, this world, to have put him in this desert with these people, his childhood friend and these two women, virtual strangers whom he already felt he loved, whom he had never touched, either one.

It was a time of possibility for him. Perhaps it was such a time for everyone. A man walked on the moon. Ireland burned. *Mariner VII* rounded the planet Mars. Possibility. Astronauts, true adventurers come home, were welcomed back to the world, the saddest people on earth. Chip and Katina disappeared to her mountain cabin, where she wrote. During their absence Danny visited Samantha almost every day and in the evenings found himself telling her things he had never told anyone. Late at night he would drive back to town with a feeling he hadn't had in so many years that at first he could not identify it. When he did, images of Maggie would blur his vision and he would know he was not really over her.

Up in the mountains Chip and Katina explored one another. Katina asked why he had turned down the opportunity to go to MIT.

"You ever been stereotyped because you're pretty?" Chip asked.

"Sure. All the time."

"Well, my brain's like that. I'm big enough to play football, but they wouldn't let me. I was the brains of the school. It was as if I had no body."

"You do," Katina said, rubbing his chest as they lay in bed in her cabin. "My father is a physician. I was supposed to follow in his footsteps. I think he wanted a son anyway. I went into medical school, too, but the first time I saw a cadaver it was all over. He said I'd end up barefoot and pregnant."

"You showed him."

"He thinks I write trash."

"No," Chip said, getting up on his elbow to look at her. "You know that's not true."

Katina shrugged. "The movies," she said, as if that explained it all.

Chip put his hand on her head and frowned. "You know it's not true, don't you?"

Katina smiled at him. "How did you get to be so tender?"

"By not having any friends. Except Danny, of course, but he's made of uranium or something. He's weird. I never know what he's feeling or thinking. He's like a robot sometimes. I know he feels it all, but he just doesn't show it."

"How'd he get to be that way?"

"You go into his past and you'll start having nightmares just listening. I'd like to watch the inside of his head one evening while he's asleep—watch from a good distance, mind you."

"That bad, huh?"

Chip nodded. They lay in silence for a few minutes and then Chip asked, "Will you promise not to laugh if I tell you a secret?"

"Promise, unless it's a joke," Katina said.

"It's not a joke—not to me anyway."

"Shoot."

"You're the first woman I've ever made love with."

Katina sat up in bed and stared at Chip for a long time.

Chip and Katina came down the mountain, giddy like children, the hot children of the sixties, all mixed up together, arm in arm; they couldn't keep their hands off each other. Danny was glad. Chip had been so remote all his life. Finally he looked as if he could see the world around him and was enjoying it. He had even begun to gain weight.

Reunited on Samantha's ranch, Danny and Chip had an urge they could not place, like an old instinct once so vital, now grown dim through lack of use. It was Doc who brought back to them what it was.

Doc came out to work at the ranch two or three days a week. He rarely said anything to Danny and Chip, except to nod hello. One day, however, he accepted their invitation to join them on the porch for a beer. He mentioned some work that needed doing around the place, work that required more than one man. Danny suggested that he and Chip could help, and before they knew it, they had been recruited as manual laborers and in that work recognized their craving. They reroofed the house with cedar shakes. They renovated a fallen-down gazebo and planted a garden. Without even thinking of it, Danny and Chip, Katina and Samantha gradually became a family, though Doc somehow kept himself out of it, like a dog who has grown shy from too many beatings.

One evening Danny and Samantha were alone at the ranch and he went out to feed the horses, leaving her in the house. Inside the barn, moonlight came through a skylight, illuminating the unstained wood. The lofty structure was filled with smells, sharp and sweet, and with the sounds of horses coughing and twitching. There was a galvanized garbage can full of oats, and with a tin scoop Danny fed each horse. He climbed the wooden stairs to the loft and broke a bale of hay, tossing a few leaves down through a trap door into each horse's stall. The crepitation of horse lips sounded throughout the barn.

Danny sat on a bale and watched through the trap door as the horses ate with calm, dim awareness, the skin on their rumps jerking occasionally, their tails sweeping the air. He put his chin in his hands and contemplated what the passage of time had done, thinking he could probably stay right there for the rest of his life and be as content as he would be anywhere. It was the first time he hadn't felt driven to run somewhere, and he realized that he had not been up in an airplane since he and Chip arrived in Arizona. It was the longest time he'd spent on the ground since he ran away to Mexico as a boy. He knew something had changed in him, but he could not put his finger on its cause or even its exact nature.

"Danny?" He heard Samantha's voice below. "Are you up there?"

"Yes," Danny called, "do you have an appointment?"

He heard her laughter and then her boots on the wooden stairs. Her face rose through the hole in the ceiling, emerging gradually into the moonlight as if surfacing from underwater. Her long blond hair was piled loosely on top of her head and held with pins behind her head. "Mind if I join you? Or are you contemplating the verities in quiet solitude?"

"I'm contemplating my ass off," Danny said, shifting over on the bale to make room and patting the space beside him.

Samantha sat down next to him. They both watched through the hole in the floor. One of the horses sneezed. "Danny. Can I ask you something?"

He looked at his wrist, where a watch would have been had he worn one, and said, "Well, normally I don't accept inquiries after six, but go ahead."

"You are an exceedingly silly boy, do you know that?"

"There've been rumors."

"Danny, how come you've been spending all this time with me? Doing all these things around the place?"

"Do you have to ask?"

"Yeah, I have to ask."

"Well, I don't know that it's proper to say."

"Say it's because you love me."

"It's because I love you."

"Then why haven't you tried to go to bed with me? You haven't even kissed me."

"Women give you diseases," Danny said, and tried not to smile. "I know. My daddy told me."

"Danny! Stop it."

"Well, I don't know then. I kissed a girl once, a long time ago, and it got me into terrible trouble and I swore I'd never do it again. How's that?"

"I don't think that's going to get it either." Samantha paused. "Damn it, Danny. What's the matter with you? Here I am, a gorgeous treasure of womanhood, practically throwing myself at you and you're sitting there cracking jokes. What is it with you?"

"I'm queer."

She stood up angrily, her hands on her hips, and for a moment Danny thought she was going to spout forty feet of flame at him. When she did not, Danny stood up and put his arms around her. She held onto him, saying, "Danny, Danny, Danny, what's wrong?"

When he spoke, it was into the crook of her neck, beside the blond hair, which smelled as clean and free as wind. "I was just sitting up here thinking that I could stay here forever. That's what I was thinking when you came up. I've never felt like that before. It seems like I've never stayed in one place more than a few days before. And I meant what I said."

"What?"

"I love you."

"I love you, too, Danny," she said. "Don't you want to make love with me? Don't you ever get horny?"

He held her away from him for a moment so that he could look at her face. "Do I get horny? Oh, Lord, could I tell you some things about horny."

"Well?"

"I wanted to jump in bed with you the first time I saw you. But I don't know. I guess I decided I was afraid to mess things up. I was afraid that you'd refuse me. Or if you didn't refuse me, I'd just do like I've done before and jump into bed with you and that would become all there was to it. Then I suppose I figured I'd wait and try to get to know you a little and let things develop naturally. Only then there didn't ever seem to be any right moment to bring it up."

"So you didn't do anything at all."

Danny smiled and shrugged, and they held each other.

"I think we've gotten to know each other," she said. "And I think it's time we brought it up."

When they finally undressed and lay down in the hay, they savored the moment, not even touching at first, naked on their backs, inches apart, breathing deeply of the sweet and bitter smells. "Oh," Samantha said.

"What?"

"I feel like I'm on fire. I feel electric."

Danny felt as someone stepping into a hole in the sea, disappearing down and down, and he could hold his breath and dive for himself and never be able to retrieve what was there, twirling with the tide between them, so lucky to be there then, like those must feel who have witnessed a rare act of nature, and Samantha so smart about it all, touching

him at first on his face, to let him lie there, going down
for the third time, knowing that everything could be reborn
in that instant of contact, going down. Danny tasted for
the first time that night what another woman tasted like and
he loved it; he could not stop, pausing only once to ask,
"Samantha, what makes you come?"

"Everything you do," she said, and back he went, she
tasted like the earth, like the ocean, deep and complex and
aromatic and alive.

They made love in the night, so different, entering Samantha as the oxygen had entered him so long ago in those
pure Dreamfuck days of innocence; it was as if he and
Samantha were passing through each other—that urge to be
close so intense that they lost their solid state and mixed
like two colors of smoke from adjacent fires, mixing on a
gentle breeze.

⚊

THE GRUMMAN GULFSTREAM II SAT just short
of Runway 29 right at Tucson International Airport. From
the cabin Danny watched the airfield warped in the trembling distortion of heat, like water in alcohol. He sat knee
to knee with Samantha. Across the aisle Chip and Katina
held a newspaper spread between them, reading. From the
cockpit Danny could hear the copilot say, "Position and
hold." Then Randy, the pilot, came on the intercom and
told them to strap in. He advanced the throttles and Danny
felt the machine gather energy and a moment later they
angled into flight, rolled right and topped a scattered layer
of clouds, breaking into full sunlight.

"I'm starving," Chip said to no one in particular.

"You're getting fat," Danny said.

Katina dug her fingers into Chip's belly and Chip squirmed
away. Samantha stood up and moved toward the rear of the
cabin. "If we don't feed him," she said, "we'll never hear
the end of it."

Danny unsnapped his seat belt and wandered up to the
cockpit door, which had been latched in the open position.

"How's it going?" Danny asked the two men.

"Well"—Randy turned to face him—"she appears to be flying exactly like an airplane."

"A good thing, too," Danny said. "It's a long way down."

"I hear you've got a lot of hours," the copilot said.

"I stopped counting at four thousand," Danny said. "I don't have that much jet time. Some Lear time."

"See this?" Randy asked, pointing to a switch on the panel. "This here's a cutout for the overspeed and the stick puller."

"The Gofaster switch. I flew a Lear once that had that."

Randy nodded seriously, as if to say, bad scene.

"How would it behave at those speeds?" Danny asked. "I understand the Lear will give a little aileron buzz and then"—he slapped one hand into the other—"the big dive."

"Same-same," Randy said. "You wanna fly it?"

"No," Danny said. "Not with passengers."

"Yeah," the copilot said, "sometimes these things can play tricks on you. Randy, tell 'im about that time your boards came out on you."

"Ground spoilers and flight spoilers came out simultaneously in flight. Down we started. I pulled off hydraulic power so they'd come back down and we started to roll over. Spoilers weren't coming down symmetrically. Well, it was either roll over or hit the ground." Randy shrugged. "I let her roll all the way inverted, then back right side up again." He laughed.

"How'd it come out?" Danny asked.

"Well, I'm here."

"Jesus," Danny said. "It's a good thing you didn't have any passengers."

"Oh, Sam was back there. When I had the plane back under control, she hollered up something like: 'Hey, you've got a lotta practicing to do before you get that act up to show quality.' Can you believe that?"

Robert Whitlock had his offices in the top floor of the Palmolive Building. They had been laid out with Iranian rugs, antique furniture and priceless objects. The telephones, when they rang, emitted a soft chirping sound, rather than the three-alarm emergency scream Western Electric had designed.

Whitlock sat behind the comfortable clutter of papers on his desk across from a stone fireplace, above which hung an Egyptian sarcophagus. It was the only Egyptian sarcophagus in any private collection in the Western world.

Danny was surprised at how young Whitlock was. He had expected a man of at least fifty, but Whitlock was no more than thirty-five. His face was just tan enough to indicate that he knew how to take time off, but not so dark as to be considered "California." He had the look of someone who could make serious political commentary on the television from a post in Washington.

"You know," he said to Danny after the introductions had been made, "I met your father back in 1960."

"Really?" Danny asked with mild curiosity.

"Yes," Whitlock said. He laughed. "He was very upset at the time. He was working for Nixon's presidential campaign and a fellow in the media, Drew Pearson, I believe, printed something Nixon didn't like—something about Howard Hughes. Good man, your father. Very able."

"Yes," Danny said. "He's that."

Whitlock moved some papers as if to clear the air of the social obligations he'd just dispatched and asked, "So, how much would you like to invest? Will it be jointly?"

"No, not jointly," Chip said. "We each have roughly two million dollars. Cash. We wanted to discuss cash-intensive businesses, investments where it is very difficult to trace—or even impossible to trace—the movement of large sums. I've been looking at commodities. I understand the CFTC hasn't been able to figure out the first thing about how the big grain companies handle their trade."

Whitlock nodded earnestly and raised his eyebrows. "You have that one right," he said. He sighed and moved some papers on his desk. "Well, we've done well with programs in the two- to eight-million-dollar range. And commodities trading figures prominently in this. Also oil at the moment and probably into the foreseeable future."

"How strong is support for the shah in Iran?" Chip asked. "What's going on with the Kurdish rebels there?"

"I assure you," Whitlock said, "the shah is in to stay. We're selling him enough arms to make Iran the strongest country in the Mideast. He's getting everything but a nuclear arsenal."

"Good," Chip said.

"Good," Danny said sarcastically, "he's a murderer."

"Who cares?" Chip asked.

Whitlock seemed mildly taken aback at the exchange. Danny looked hotly at Chip but said nothing more. "Anyway," Whitlock continued, "I would strongly suggest you get into the oil market. There are other advantages peculiar to your situation as well. You see, if we want to put money into the Middle East, it's very difficult to trace. We can go direct from the Bahamas to Teheran or Saudi banks without ever crossing paths with the IRS. We can put up a secondary foundation in commodities, which is the other area I referred to. What we're going to see is a continuation of the degradation of wheat prices we've already seen. However, I expect them to shoot up dramatically. Our people in State tell us that ground truth testing in Russia seems to indicate that the scene is set for bad crops ahead. That would mean Russia on the open market, looking to buy grain. We're looking into coffee in Brazil, too. Whatever happens, we'll be there. And we can move money around in there; it's very cash-intensive. As Chip suggested, even the transactions of big grain companies, doing business with dollars that have come across the open market, could not be traced. The government has been trying and can't make heads or tails of it. So with our little investment we should have no problems. If we ever do have problems, of course, there will be all the backdated records to show, but let's hope that does not come to pass." And there he knocked on the deeply lustrous wood lamina of his desk top, showing that like a good businessman, he did not rule out superstition as a tool of the trade. "Are you following me so far?"

"Yes," Chip said. "Go on."

"I think you lost me, but I'm sure Chip will get it," Danny said.

Whitlock laughed. "Well, our next problem, of course, is that once this money is flowing through these channels in this legitimate fashion, we will be making some rather handsome profits, which brings up the nasty subject of taxes. So then we come to the little matter of tax avoidance."

"Tax evasion?" Danny asked.

"No, no." Whitlock held up his finger. "Tax *avoidance*. The word is crucial, you see, for it describes the difference between a crime and a perfectly accepted practice. Tax evasion is a federal crime punishable by stiff fines and prison sentences. Tax avoidance is perfectly legal and accepted. It is a game we play with the Service. They write the laws as tight and unbeatable as they can. Then we get together and find holes in the law. We do whatever is allowed by going through those holes. They cannot prosecute us because their law is faulty, not our practices. Then they close the hole by changing the law and we look for new holes."

"I love it," Chip said. "I just love it. It's art."

Danny looked at him with concern.

"Anyway," Whitlock continued, "we have a beauty right now. Silver futures."

"Silver futures," Chip whispered passionately. "It's absolutely poetic."

"It gets better," Whitlock said with a smile. "It's called a butterfly spread. We buy silver futures—we go long. As the price of silver goes up, we make money hand over fist. Near the end of the year, though, we buy an equal number of short contracts—we sell silver futures, while holding our long position. The net result on paper is that we have made no money. But we do this, say, December twenty-ninth and dump the short contracts January third. As far as the Service is concerned, we have had no taxable profit for the year in question. In reality, though, we have stormed the castle."

"That's legal?" Danny asked.

"It's definitely legal," Whitlock assured him. "The Service hasn't yet caught on because not too many people know about it. Of course, those who do aren't exactly advertising. Naturally the Service will shut it down one day."

Danny and Chip had a series of meetings with Whitlock during their visit to Chicago, and by the time they were ready to return to Tucson actual money had changed hands, documents and files had appeared, a legend created. It was only in the dimmest way that Danny began to see what Whitlock was doing for them. He was performing a sort of alchemy by which they changed mysteriously from serious criminals to what came to be known as white-collar criminals. Danny had a vague, uneasy sense about it, too, though it hadn't yet occurred to him that everything he had done had been designed to avoid becoming like Forrest and that now, because of everything he had done to avoid becoming like Forrest, he was being forced to become just like Forrest. The illusion of control where there is none. The Tar Baby Syndrome.

As Randy greased the G-II onto 29 Right at Tucson International Airport, Danny was certain he had made the last deal and that it had been a deal with Whitlock. There was a sense of relief in that. Even Chip's drive to pursue money in larger and larger quantities was deflected for a time as he and Danny settled into the easy, rural life there, happily under the illusion that they were becoming legitimate businessmen now. They stayed for more than a year without even noticing it.

SAMANTHA AND DANNY SAT on the porch one morning drinking coffee. There was a gusty breeze and a high, pale half-moon was halfway down the western sky, the infinite, egg blue sky. Samantha read *Newsweek* while Danny thumbed a newspaper. She passed the magazine to him and pointed out an item headlined THE WATERGATE FIVE.

Danny read it and laughed. "Man, Forrest's favorite politician screwed the pooch. How about that?"

Samantha did not find it amusing. "Danny, you told me Forrest was starting to work for him again."

"Ohhh," Danny said, dismissing it, "he worked with him during the Eisenhower campaign way back in 'fifty-six. He worked for Nixon's own campaign in 'sixty. He's just some kind of consultant now. A lot of Republican lawyers work for Nixon."

"Well, what the hell is this?" she asked, slapping the magazine. "Communist China? I mean, breaking into the Democratic National Headquarters? It's just—" She stammered, her anger rising. She could not find the words. "It's incredible."

"It's nothing," Danny said. "Anyway, Forrest wouldn't be involved in something like that."

"Well, anybody who works for Nixon is suspect. Nixon is a fascist pig."

Danny sighed. "You sound like some kind of sixties Marxist." When Samantha said nothing, Danny laughed and

said, "Okay, okay, let's go out this afternoon and smash the
state or something. It'll be good for us." He was trying to get
Samantha to loosen up, but she was determined to be nasty
about it. He had not known her to have such a temper. She
could really be intractible when she set her mind to it. "Hey,"
Danny told her, "take it easy. The old fossil can take care
of himself."

"I don't care what the *old fossil* can do," Samantha
snapped. "People like that *ought* to go to jail."

"Listen," Danny said, irritated by her outburst, "you don't
even know my father. An appointment as a consultant to
the White House is not something a guy like my father turns
down. Those are his people, so let him alone. You don't
know what you're talking about."

She folded her arms and sat looking off into the distance.
Danny watched her, thinking. It shouldn't be that surprising.
Why should Samantha approve of Forrest any more than
half the young people in the country would? Danny had said
some of the same things to Forrest's face. Still, that was
different and Samantha should know it. Danny could call
his own father a right-wing son of a bitch. Samantha could
not. And now that he thought about it, the item in the
magazine began to worry him. What were those lunatics
doing breaking into the Democratic headquarters?

That fall Danny boarded a commercial flight to Chicago
for a meeting with Robert Whitlock. Whitlock had moved
his offices from the old Palmolive Building to one of the
upper floors of the John Hancock Center, the largest building
in the world, a dizzying black monolith with great girders
lacing X's up its tapering sides all the way to the sky. Two
RCA antennas sat atop the structure like NASA rockets.
Viewed from some distance, the entire assembly looked like
an atomic earwig in some low-budget Japanese science-fiction
film.

"Talked to your father lately?" Whitlock asked when
Danny walked in. "I certainly hope he's not mixed up in any
of this Watergate mess."

"Why would he be? Anyway, what is so important about it?"

"In itself, nothing. But if the drug links ever came out, it could turn this country upside down."

"What drug links?"

"Let me put it this way," Whitlock said. It was the same tone of voice Michael had used in Tucson when he told of the assassination attempt on Fassnacht. "I asked the president's attorney about drugs once—the drug links in all this. And he said—and these were his own words, mind you —he said, 'Bob, you don't even want to know. You want to grow old, you want to stay healthy. Don't even ask.' That was the president's *attorney*, Dan. So . . ." Whitlock shrugged.

"There must be more to it than that."

"Sure there is. No one in the administration told me specifically. As I said, their attitude is: 'Don't ask.' But if I started telling you just some of the bits and pieces, you'd think I was one of those conspiracy theorists."

"I'd assume there has to be quite a large conspiracy if drugs are the third largest business in the U.S.," Danny said.

Whitlock nodded, his lips pursed. "Ever heard of Cay Sal?"

"No," Danny said. He held up his finger. "Wait, yes I have. Where did I hear about Cay Sal?" He searched his memory. He distinctly remembered someone mentioning Cay Sal to him once. A long time ago. "Eddie," he said.

"What?"

"A guy who is no longer with us. Once Chip and I were going to fly a plane for him. We were supposed to refuel at Cay Sal."

"Sometime, if you're just knocking around down there, try to approach Cay Sal unannounced and see how far you get."

"No, thanks."

"Cay Sal was a staging area for the Bay of Pigs invasion. It's only a few miles from Cuba, on the other side of the island from Cienfuegos. Now it's strictly military. It is also, as you know, a stopping-off place for certain drug flights. How do you suppose that is arranged?"

Danny remembered what Amesquita had said once in Mexico. If Fassnacht is the visible arm of the government, how high up does it go? He shook his head. It was too much to think about. "I'm out of all this," Danny said. "I don't want to know any more."

"Yes," Whitlock said. "Precisely." He straightened some papers on his desk and went on. "I have a little computer company for you. My advice is to buy it. Yesterday. It's called ComVex and it will put you in a position of considerable power."

"Nothing like a little power to break up an afternoon."

By that time his meetings with Whitlock had become routine. Whitlock would outline the status, chalking up their wins and losses. He would summarize what he had in store, any new developments, such as this computer company. It had all ceased to matter to Danny. Where it had seemed to grab hold of Chip like a fever, it had never really mattered to Danny, except in that first rush, when the sheer size of the numbers had taken him by surprise and given him that giddy feeling which, if examined too closely, proved to be more surface and reflection than truly deep channel. When he and Chip had flown airplanes full of pot, they had put something on the line—their lives for one thing, their freedom for another—and it had come back a thousandfold in intangible currencies. But now where the business—the wild astronomy of it—seemed to fuel Chip and make him grow, it simply made Danny feel empty and useless, like the punch line to a joke that's already been told.

He left Whitlock and wandered south along Michigan Avenue, breathing the cool air of a midwestern fall, wondering why he could not seem to generate any traction, why he felt as if he were simply sliding away. He stopped at a newsstand to buy a paper. He gave the man a dime and flipped the paper over to the front page. Right there he saw what he finally had to admit he had been expecting for years, day and night, without ever admitting how much of him the vigil had taken. He didn't even see the headline; all he saw was Maggie's by-line.

"I don't fucking believe it."

"What's that?" the newsstand owner asked. "I say he's gonna get us into World War Three, so you better fucking believe it, sonny."

Danny stepped into the path of a passing car, which swerved and honked. He walked south until he reached the catwalk near the river that led around the side entrance of the newspaper offices, a squat steel and glass building that always put Danny in mind of the man who had pioneered the use of glass bricks in suburban 1950s residential structures.

On the fourth floor Danny pushed open the door and saw row upon row of desks, every last one of them loaded with paper in seemingly random piles beneath searing blue fluorescent tubes. Typewriters and telephones sounded over the low murmur of voices. Danny scanned the room until he spotted Maggie. All he could see was the top of her head, but he could have recognized it anywhere.

He had a sudden moment of panic, remembering the day he had chased a city bus away from this very building in the worst thunderstorm of recent memory. He remembered having made a fool of himself. Everyone in the news room seemed to be riveted with disproportionate intensity to the tasks at hand. Perhaps no one would notice this time.

Danny hesitated, then moved among the desks, aware now that no one cared.

Maggie looked up from her paper. She drew a breath and held it, putting her hand to her mouth. The newspaper fell to the floor as she stood, watching Danny, who had stopped a few feet from her.

"What did Perry White always say in the *Superman* series?" Maggie asked, deadpan.

"Great Caesar's Ghost," Danny replied.

"Well, Great Caesar's Ghost then."

"Can we talk now?"

"Yes," she said.

Outside the building they walked two blocks before saying another word. They reached a restaurant called Ricardo's, went in and took a booth.

Danny looked at her then, really looked at her and took

in the image, as if someone had crow-barred open a lid and let sunlight pour into a mine shaft. In a moment he felt himself open, and out of him rose every single thing he had imagined saying to her if they ever met again. All the nights he had spent imagining her, conjuring her face or the fluid of her voice.

"You have gray in your hair," Maggie told him. "You look healthy and prosperous." She smiled, just the smallest movement of her cheek muscles.

"I am." He was painfully aware that Maggie had spent years without him, eating meals, having parties, talking on the telephone, riding bicycles, having ice cream sandwiches and vacations and lovers and adventures.

He felt a shifting of weight within him, like the telltale signal of an emotional avalanche. He looked at the room that fanned out to one side from the center of the universe where Maggie sat in a burgundy-colored leather-covered booth and lifted his hand to a bartender, who came to their table. Maggie ordered white wine. Danny ordered club soda.

"I want to hear everything you've been doing," Maggie said with what was obviously a contrived attempt to be bright and conversational.

"I've missed you, the entire time, that's what I've been doing."

"Don't," she said, cutting him off. "Please don't."

He looked at Maggie's face, at the set of her chin, and thought: She can feel it, too. Can that be? Could she still care after this much time? Still, she was right; they could not approach that subject, not yet, not here and now; they would simply dissolve in it. They had to maintain the illusion of control.

Maggie continued. "It's one reason I never tried to get in touch with you." She looked down at the table for a moment. "There," she said firmly. "That's that discussion. Now let's talk about something else. Tell me what you've been doing. Really."

"I'm a businessman," he said, and laughed ironically.

"Oh, come on."

"Before Buddha. I swear it." A marvelous thought occurred to him then. Maggie was the only person to whom he could tell the whole story—the only one who wasn't a part of it now. He could trust her.

"Just like Forrest, eh?" Maggie suggested. When she saw the expression on Danny's face, she knew she had said the wrong thing. She could see that the comparison hadn't pleased Danny. "I've still got a big mouth. That hasn't changed."

"No, no, it's not your fault. You're absolutely right, of course." Danny knew. Maggie had come in out of nowhere and five minutes into his life had nailed him precisely. And it began to come back to him: They were a matched set somehow, somewhere deep within—yes, in the movement of planets or their genes. Danny knew he was just visiting anywhere else.

"That explains the difference in the way you look," Maggie said. "Like a new-breed businessman. A little gray beginning to appear but still very young. Expensive casual clothes." She smiled. "I'd expect, then, if you're a businessman, that you're very successful. Probably rich."

Danny nodded. "I am rich. I am very, very rich. And it doesn't mean a goddamned thing to me."

"I wouldn't expect it would, Danny. You were always too smart for that."

"Someday I'll tell you the whole story. It'll take more than a day, but I'll tell you. Right now I want to know what you've been doing. I don't have any idea what you've been up to. Where do you live? When did you come back to the paper? Where were you all that time? Are you in love? Do you still ride a white French bicycle? Do you still hate brussels sprouts? Do you still wear white underpants with little blue flowers on them? Are you still tone-deaf?"

Maggie laughed. "To answer your last question first, I couldn't carry a tune up a scant incline with a parbuckle."

"What's a parbuckle?"

"It's too hard to explain; look it up." She regarded him with affection and suspicion. "You sure have a good memory."

"It's Mexican. We know our friends well. We know our enemies even better."

"And which am I?"

"You'll always be a friend, even if you can't stand me."

"I am your friend. Even if I've been a little scarce lately. I mean, I think of myself as your friend. I kind of screwed things up between us, but at the time I didn't know any better."

"What do you mean?"

"I mean, I left you."

"But the way I treated you—it was my fault," he insisted, shocked that Maggie would say such a thing.

"Your fault? The way you treated me? You treated me wonderfully."

"That's ridiculous. You just did the sane thing and walked out. I screwed up our relationship from beginning to end. I drove you out."

"Bullshit. If I had acted the way I acted, I wouldn't have put up with me."

The two of them stopped and stared at each other in silence. Maggie giggled. Danny giggled, too. Suddenly they could not seem to stop giggling, as the bartender came by to ask them if they wanted another drink, and finally, they were shrieking with laughter, howling and leaning back in their seats as if they were mad or drunk or as if they could not stand to be any other way around each other because it would be too painful if they weren't laughing.

"I never knew you felt that way," Danny said.

"I never knew *you* felt that way."

"There's an echo in here."

"I just assumed you hated me for leaving—you certainly would have been justified."

"Maggie, I loved you then and I love you now. I just—"

"Don't—" Maggie held up her hand. "Don't, Danny. There are some things I have to tell you."

"Okay, do you or do you not ride a white French bicycle?"

"I'm married."

It wasn't as if he hadn't anticipated that. He had considered it more than once over the years. Hearing her say it, though, he realized that his armor could never be strong enough. His head felt light, as if he'd stood up too suddenly. "Are you in love?"

"Brian and I get along fine. Who knows from love? I have a daughter. I don't even like children and I love her more than anything I've ever known. That's all there is, Danny."

"That and the stories."

"And the stories."

"I want to know about your work," Danny said.

Maggie gave him a look that seemed to say: Don't patronize me, buddy.

"I mean it; I'm not making small talk."

"I thought you laughed at reporters."

"I did. I don't care about reporters; I care about you. Anyway, I've changed. I even subscribe to a paper at home."

"Where's home?"

"Tucson."

"Thu-Sanh?" Maggie asked. "Like China?"

"No, Tuck-Son, like Arizona."

"Big dope town."

She can read my mind, Danny thought. But then that was nothing new.

"The Bonanno family has headquarters there, doesn't it?"

"How do you know that?"

"I'm a reporter, remember? I get all the stories. I may not be rich, but I sure get the information." She was teasing him and he knew it.

"All right, all right, I'll tell you my story if you tell me yours. Where were you when you disappeared from town?"

"Vietnam."

For a moment Danny thought she was still teasing him, but when he saw her expression, he asked, "Are you serious?"

"I'm as serious as bone cancer."

"How long?"

"Eighteen months."

"You were?"

Maggie laughed. "You should see the way you look. I

must say, I thought of you. I wanted to see the look on your face when I told you and now I'm seeing it. It was worth the wait."

"I don't doubt that. They classified me 4-F because I couldn't talk on the telephone and then *you* end up in Vietnam because you wanted to see what it's like." Danny shook his head in amazement. "I promise I won't ask you what it was like."

"I know. For some reason I still trust you. I don't know why—I've never known why—but I trusted you from the very beginning and I still do."

"I don't know that I've ever been worthy of that, but I appreciate it. Especially after all I did."

"What did you do? I thought about that a lot afterward. You must have a real guilt thing because I can think of only two things you did that really bothered me. First, you and I had that little fight when you screwed some perfect stranger who, in all likelihood, you never saw again and whose name you probably don't even remember."

"Melissa," Danny said with a mischievous smile.

"Second," Maggie said, ignoring him, "you got busted. But you got busted for something you didn't do, remember? Yes, they did tear our place apart, but they didn't find anything. They didn't even book us. They just made a mistake."

"Well . . ." Danny made as if to counter her, but then he said nothing.

"I know, I know." Maggie waved her hand. "You *were* involved, but the fact still remains that that bust was a flim-flam. You got away with whatever it was you were doing. The only really truly unforgivable thing you did was to lie to me about what you were doing—and in the end you said you'd given that up, so there it is, see?"

"I don't know." He still wasn't ready to go through the entire story for her, not yet, not there.

"Hey, let's don't do any more post-mortems, at least not on our relationship. I'll agree to call it even if you will."

"Our account is settled," he said, and then he stopped himself. No, he thought, don't lie to her anymore. If you can't tell the truth, don't say anything at all. "Let me rephrase that. On that particular point—of whose fault it was—you can consider the account settled."

"A cautious businessman at that."

They began to play that old favorite game Whatever-Happened-to-What's His/Her Name. Maggie commented that it had been a shame about Michael and Virginia breaking up and asked where Michael was. She said they were so well suited to each other, original space people of the sixties.

"There was always something strange about Michael, though," she added.

"You noticed?"

"Noticed what?"

Danny explained to Maggie what Michael had been doing and where he was now.

"Jesus," Maggie said when he'd finished. "I'd like to get my claws into that story."

"Someday you will," Danny told her. "Someday you will."

They ran through a few more names and a few more stories, like old buddies, and then Maggie stuck her foot into her mouth again by asking about Elaine.

"So how's the kid?" she asked innocently.

"What kid?"

"Elaine's ki—" Maggie stopped. It simply had never occurred to her that Danny might not have known for all this time. She put her hand to her mouth in that characteristic gesture of hers and looked at the ceiling when she saw Danny's face. Maggie exhaled long and loud through her hand and brought her eyes down from the ceiling to look at Danny, who appeared to be in complete systemic shock. "Oh, Danny. "Oh, no. I didn't realize—"

"Elaine has a *child?*"

Maggie nodded, her hand still covering her open mouth. She closed her eyes and moaned. "Danny, I had no way of knowing you didn't know."

"*My* child?"

"Yes. Yes." She bit the back of her hand.

"But I never—it couldn't, I mean—" Danny did not seem to be able to make a complete thought.

"Goddammit!" Maggie shouted. "Now it makes perfect sense. I wondered why she'd told me that."

"What?"

"She told me that she was off the pill and that you came inside her anyway."

"Elaine told you *that?*"

Maggie nodded. "You revenge-fucked her, Danny."

He felt his face flush. The words mortified him so because they were true. It was a revenge fuck and that mean impulse had resulted in a child.

"Her revenge was not telling you," Maggie said. "I should have known—she never told me things like that. She knew I'd let fly with it, too; she waited—goddammit!"

"Where do they live?"

"No, Danny, forget it. Leave it be; you've already done enough damage."

"But the child—"

"Forget it, Danny," Maggie insisted. Then she covered her eyes with her hand and said, "Oh, Christ, what a mess."

"But is she working? What happened to her husband? How does she support the kid?"

"She got divorced when Tom signed up for his third tour in Vietnam. He's still there. And *it* has a sex and a name. She named the boy Juan."

"Juan," Danny said. "Oh, God. Juan."

"She works part time. She quit the paper when she was pregnant. She does free-lance typing and editing. She makes ends meet."

"I should at least support her."

"Danny, don't do yourself any favors."

Danny was in a state of emotional exhaustion when he reached Forrest's house. He hadn't called ahead. He simply wanted to stop by and see his father. He still had a key and let himself in, calling, "Forrest, you home?" as he did so. There was silence, then footsteps above. He climbed the stairs to the second floor as Faye was coming out of the bedroom. She wore a short dress and looked as if she had slept in it. Danny could not help looking at her long, beautifully formed legs. He noticed that she wore no stockings or shoes. She looked completely flustered.

"Danny!" she said with mock warmth. "What a surprise."

"Hi, sorry I disturbed you, I thought Forrest would be here."

"He should be back this afternoon," she said. Just then a man appeared at the bedroom door and Faye quickly added, "I was just showing Jeff the house. Jeff, this is Forrest's son, Danny. Danny, Jeff Lembert. Jeff is an attorney from Washington. I was just taking him to the airport and we stopped by here on the way."

Danny didn't have to be told any more and Jeff Lembert, whoever he was, did not have to pretend that Danny was blind and deaf. In his bedroom, Danny thought. In his own fucking bedroom. Danny thought of the first night he met Faye when he brought out the wine and she instantly and instinctively conspired to conceal its value from Forrest, without a word passing between them. Danny said something to Faye, something about telling Forrest that he would be over that evening, and then he left. Faye and her boyfriend were so stunned they didn't even follow him down the stairs.

That evening when Danny arrived at his father's house, Faye answered the door. She said nothing about the afternoon, but she transmitted with her eyes a look so complex and full of meaning that Danny knew immediately he would not say anything to Forrest, not now, perhaps not ever.

Faye rushed to the bar with exaggerated gaiety, saying, "Chivas rocks, am I remembering right?"

"Sure," Danny said. He remembered the first time he'd met her, that somehow he'd ended up drinking scotch. He didn't like scotch then and liked it no better now, yet he said nothing. He didn't like the circumstances either.

She handed him the glass of smooth, smoky liquid and he sipped it. What the hell, he thought. Let it go. It had been a week since his meeting with Maggie and he was still feeling the shock. All week he had thought of something

Moishe had once said to him. "Daniel," he had said, "your biggest problem is you've never done any time."

Forrest came down the stairs, saying, "Look what the cat dragged in." He took Danny by the shoulder and shook his hand. "Life is grand, son"—he winked—"if you don't weaken." He took a closer look at Danny. "Straighten up, what's troubling you?"

"Just tired."

"I want you to know I'm proud of you."

For a hot, uncomfortable moment Danny had the illusion that Forrest knew about his son. Or perhaps about his decision not to say anything about Faye's boyfriend. Or about something even deeper and more personal. "What?" Danny asked.

"Buying ComVex," Forrest said, giving Danny an elbow as if the reference were to a sexual conquest he'd made rather than the purchase of a computer company. "Smart move. You're going to make a killing."

"Thanks," Danny said. He felt confused, as if he were slightly stoned.

"If you do what I think you're going to do, you'll knock IBM on its ear with their mainframe dictum."

"Oh, I don't know about that," Danny said. "I guess a lot of people will want to get away from big computers and get some small hardware that they can run themselves."

"Don't move too fast," his father said. "I've got to divest myself."

"You mean take your clothes off?"

"Well, with all the IBM stock I've got, I guess you could say I don't want to get caught with my pants down."

Danny looked at his father as if he were drunk or possibly even dangerous.

"Come sit down," Faye said to them. She put a glass of scotch in Forrest's hand. "Freshen your drink?" she asked Danny.

"No, I—" He stopped, shook his glass and sat down. His head felt light from drinking scotch on an empty stomach. He realized that he hadn't eaten a full meal since he met

with Maggie. He felt as if he were running with one wheel
in the sand. To avoid appearing odd he began talking again
about his computer company.

"It's wonderful," Faye said.

"It's a killer," Forrest said.

"It's business," Danny said. He finally put his finger on
what it was about Forrest tonight that seemed different. It
was so simple: Forrest was treating Danny like a peer for
the first time. Danny, in Forrest's eyes, had arrived as a
businessman. Maggie had been right.

Danny somehow made it through the dinner but by its end
was drunk. He forced himself to stay a while longer, though.
He wanted to talk with his father before returning to
Tucson.

He excused himself and went to the bathroom, where he
splashed water on his face. He had noticed that he wasn't
the only one getting drunk. Faye seemed to be putting it
away with a purpose, whether it was from relief or some
darker motivation, he couldn't guess. She had hardly met his
eyes all night.

When Danny returned to join Forrest and Faye in the
living room, Faye stretched out on the couch, yawned, put
her feet up and a minute later was sound asleep.

"I want you to know how proud of you I am," Forrest
said.

"How do you know I won't use my money to overthrow
the government?" Danny asked with a grin.

"Because as a businessman you will learn, if you haven't
already, that there is no government. There is only business.
This is America."

They sat in silence for a few minutes. "What did you
think when you were shot down in World War Two?" he
asked his father. "When you were flying that big plane and
looked out and your left wing was gone?"

Forrest smiled a bitter smile. "All I thought of was getting out. You have no idea how important your own rear
end becomes in a situation like that. Well, maybe you do;
you're a pilot, too. And then, when I realized I wasn't going

to get out, I felt very sad. I thought about my mother and how sad it would make her. I thought about my wife."

"Well, that's pretty unselfish."

Forrest raised his eyebrows. "Yeah, I suppose it is." Again they fell into silence. Forrest got up and poured coffee. "Say," he asked as he returned to the room, "how did you get capitalized initially?"

"I smuggled dope."

Forrest laughed. "That's good. Very good." He clapped Danny on the shoulder. "Not a bad policy, I guess. A man's business is a confidential matter."

"Yeah, just between God and the IRS." Danny rattled the ice in his glass. "Speaking of which, what do you know about this Watergate thing?"

Forrest pushed out his lower lip and shook his head as if it were merely an embarrassment, like an uncle who overstays his welcome. "Some overzealous amateurs. Nothing to worry about. What are you getting at?"

"I'm not getting at anything. I'm worried for you. I don't want anything screwed up for you."

"Well, that's kind, Danny. Really, I appreciate your concern, but this little business—this has nothing to do with me."

"If you say so, Forrest."

Forrest stood up. "You look tired."

"Yeah, listen, I've got to be wheels in the wells by eight ayem. I've had a rough week."

"Say," Forrest said as he led Danny toward the door, "you're not involved with Gates Learjet out there in Tucson, are you?"

"No, Forrest, I'm not."

At the front door Forrest told him, "Don't worry about me. Pay attention to your business. I've been around too many blocks, so don't concern yourself."

"Yeah," Danny said, patting him on the shoulder. "Keep it in your boots, Forrest."

9

"NEWS ABHORS A VACUUM," was how Maggie would explain it. Where a story could not be had, one could be invented, and where information was incomplete, speculation would rush in until the story was overflowing. A few facts were known, beyond which the story began to blur at the edges. One version of the story had it that Fassnacht's own men, in an attempted coup, had slipped him a dose of ketamine large enough to kill a donkey, which instead destroyed what was left of his ability to reason.

One fact not widely known was that someone had made off with $37 million worth of pure heroin that Fassnacht's organization was transporting from the Mexican manufacturing sites to the East Coast and Canada. One day it was there, in ten-kilo packages, waiting to be moved. The next it was gone without a trace.

Some speculated that this was what put Fassnacht over the edge finally. Whatever the case, the community of cops and robbers that makes up the drug world is a small society with an efficient communications system. Word traveled, but it was sometimes difficult to decipher the signal-to-noise ratio, so, as always, one was left with the stories, uncertain which comprised a truth of sorts and which were simply the hysterics of an overloaded system.

It was known that Fassnacht blackmailed a surgeon from the University of Mexico Medical Center. The man, a Dr. Melitón Diego, had supplied the methods used on children in the hideous smuggling incidents of the early sixties. No one had ever been charged with those crimes. The files were officially open. Diego hadn't been aware at the time that those methods were going to be used on children, but now it was academic. He was obliged to do anything Fassnacht wanted.

Fassnacht then kidnapped Amesquita. Here again his methods were said to have been equally deranged and effective. He hired a well-dressed, well-spoken prostitute to go to Amesquita with the story that her daughter had gone off with a couple they knew and had not returned. The story matched perfectly the ones Amesquita had been told in the early sixties and he followed the woman to her house, where Fassnacht was waiting with one of his journeymen killers, who, along with Fassnacht and Dr. Diego, drove Amesquita into the high sierra.

There was an abandoned barn with high ceilings and cathedral light where owls perched, hiding from daylight, where wasps and bees nested and rats picked through the balls of bones left by the owls that lived in the rafters.

Amesquita knew he was a dead man. He was bound and gagged but not blindfolded, which he interpreted as a clue that he was not coming back. He had begun looking for an avenue of escape the moment he saw Fassnacht's lampshade white face before him. None had presented itself. If he could just have the use of his hands for a few seconds, he could kill Fassnacht, if not the other man. Fassnacht knew this, of course, so it was not likely that Amesquita would gain the use of his hands again. Amesquita cursed himself for his mistakes—what must have been the oath a tightrope walker utters when, after years on the wire, his foot finally slips, a curse between himself and God. Amesquita cursed himself as far back as the day he stood in the envanescent rain on the highway to the airport and told Ramón to kill Fassnacht, only to change his mind and push the barrel of the rifle down. A failure of nerve at the critical moment— that, Amesquita knew, was what always got you. Which was just another way of saying that nice guys finish last.

The barn was empty except for a few old tools, a plow

point, rusted to dust, a wooden table elevated off the floor some three feet. Fassnacht and his killer shoved Amesquita and Dr. Diego inside, closing the door. Diego said nothing the entire time. He was clearly stupefied with fear, confused and out of place. Once inside, he asked Fassnacht, "What are we doing here?"

"Just be patient," Fassnacht said. His companion said nothing. He held a shotgun casually, his right hand on the grip, his index finger laced through the trigger guard, the short barrel draped lazily over the crook of his left arm. A high, dusty light came through openings in the walls and roof, giving the scene the quality of a Vermeer painting. Amesquita thought it was quite beautiful. A beautiful place to die. He had wondered who Diego was, though he did not know his name was Diego and did not even know he was a surgeon. All he knew was that he, too, appeared to be a captive rather than a captor. He was not one of Fassnacht's men—he did not have that air of sadistic arrogance, certainly not of control. Diego was afraid, which worried Amesquita further.

Amesquita felt a terrific movement inside him as his automatic panic systems tried to empty his bowel. He fought against it. Fassnacht gave his shotgun and sidearm to the other man and then approached Amesquita. "Turn around," he said. Amesquita did as he was told, slowly, watching over his shoulder. A few seconds was all he needed, a few seconds of distraction, a few seconds with his hands free, with Fassnacht close, so that he could tear the man's throat out for him. Fassnacht unlocked the handcuffs and backed away fast, before Amesquita knew he was free. "If he moves," Fassnacht told the other man, "kill him."

"Sure," the man said. It was the only thing he'd said the entire time. He pointed the shotgun at Amesquita and Fassnacht took his own weapons back.

"Now," Fassnacht said to Amesquita, "take the ropes off your legs and undress."

Amesquita bent down and untied his ankles. He removed his suit coat, placed it on the table and turned around to face them. Fassnacht nodded, gesturing with the shotgun.

"Go on. All the way." Amesquita untied his shoes and slipped them off. Then he took off his tie and draped it over the table next to his coat. He unbuttoned his shirt slowly, feeling each white button with his fingers, wondering: Should the last moments of life be richer than any other moments? And does one's life, as they say, flash before one's eyes? Where are my regrets? Will they all appear before me? Have I done any good, being here on earth? All I need is one second. As his bargaining power had diminished, so had his demands. One second—a moment's distraction—and he could get out. He could be gone through the mountains and be safe. He knew that if Fassnacht had simply wanted to kill him outright, it would have been over the moment he had walked into the whore's house in Cuernavaca. So Fassnacht must want either information or revenge—or both.

All he needed was a small distraction. If there had been a kerosene lamp with which to start a fire, Amesquita could have knocked it over while undressing. But all he had was the beautiful sunlight, coming through the spaces and openings high in the old barn. He wondered if somehow sunlight, too, could be used as a weapon. Yes, if you have something to hide.

A little animal scurried across the floor, but neither Fassnacht nor his man looked at it. The surgeon, Diego, nearly jumped out of his boots, though, and the man pointed his shotgun at him suddenly. Amesquita tensed, but that was not his moment, for Fassnacht jerked his shotgun at Amesquita and smiled, indicating that he was not going to let that happen. He, for one, was not going to let his attention wander. The tiny drama had begun and ended inside a single second, yet at its end Amesquita knew he'd had another failure of nerve at a critical moment, for if he had truly believed that Fassnacht would not summarily blow him away—and all evidence pointed to that conclusion—Amesquita would have acted. In that moment he knew his defeat and embraced it the way a single elk embraces his, when, cut from the herd by wolves, he gives in and calmly allows himself to be cut to ribbons.

Amesquita put his shirt next to his coat and tie. He took

down his pants, removed his socks and stood in his shorts, as
brown as the flank of a horse.

"That's good enough," Fassnacht said. "Get up on the
table."

Amesquita backed up to the table and put his callused
hands on either side of him to push himself into a sitting
position on it, his feet dangling above the barn floor.

"Lie down," Fassnacht said. The table was rough wood
and as Amesquita swung his legs up, he could feel a splinter
poke through his back. He let himself down to a supine position and stared at the high-beamed ceiling of the barn. It
was a beautiful place to die. A rumbling, painful knot mean-
dered through his intestines. His heart was going like crazy
and he was terrified, but this did not show. He looked calm.
A swallow crossed his field of vision. He wished for the gift
of flight. To be able to soar like that, just to move his arms,
to flutter toward the ceiling, aloft under his own power and
break into daylight through the opening near the ceiling in
hot pursuit of the swallow. What a lovely thing flight was.
Flight was freedom, it was life, reprieve from the miserable
realities of this earth, and for those who could not fly, there
was slow death down here. Amesquita felt his options had
run out.

"Doctor Diego," Fassnacht said, motioning with his finger
at the frightened man.

Amesquita fixed on the word *doctor*. What is a doctor
doing here? he wondered. He forced himself to lie perfectly
still. His mouth was so dry that he could not swallow. He
blinked several times in rapid succession, a knot of panic
rising within him, and he felt light, as if he might really fly.

"Roll over on your side," the doctor said. "Bring your
knees up to your chest." The man's voice was gentle and
unsteady. Amesquita could tell he did not want to be here,
sensed the doctor was not against him, but he could not
figure what it might mean.

"What are you going to do?" Amesquita asked in Spanish.

"Don't talk," Fassnacht said. "Give him the shot."

"What shot?" Amesquita asked.

"Shut up and hold your knees like he said," Fassnacht ordered.

"Oh," Amesquita said involuntarily, but it came out as a cry of despair.

Amesquita held his knees encircled in his thickly muscled arms, lying on his side, and for a moment he almost felt a sense of relief. Maybe Fassnacht wanted information from him and was going to have this doctor inject him with a drug so that he would talk. Those American agents got all those crazy drugs from their CIA and army. Maybe they were giving him truth serum, and when they found out what they wanted to know, they would let him go or just leave him. Amesquita breathed deeply, hoping against his better judgment that that was the case, for he knew of nothing that he could not tell Fassnacht—nothing he would refuse to tell Fassnacht at this moment. Amesquita did not make his work secret. He simply fought against heroin traffic in any way he could.

Out of what could only have been long habit, the doctor said, "This will hurt a bit," and a searing, jolting pain shot through him such as he had never felt before. The doctor quickly put a hand on Amesquita's face. "Don't move." Amesquita held his knees tighter instead of uncoiling as he wanted to do.

"God," Amesquita breathed. The sweat broke, cold and oily, on his face and chest. "What is that?"

"You won't feel a thing in a moment," the doctor said. "Just hold still for a few more seconds."

"What do you mean?" Amesquita asked, his voice droning on in sad, sensuous panic, like the sounds of sex, thinking: Maybe they're injecting me with poison and I won't feel a thing in a moment because I will be dead. Maybe they are injecting me with flying serum and I will float up to the ceiling and sprout the delicate lace of the owl's trailing edge feathers, which deaden the sound of flight so that he can pursue his prey without alarming it.

Amesquita wanted to jump up and run, but it felt as if the man had run a sword through his back and suddenly, as the pain subsided, it dawned on Amesquita that this was the position they make you hold when they administer a spinal anesthetic and that all at once nothing hurt him. In fact, he could not feel his lower body at all, not his feet or legs, not his groin, his precious groin, not his stomach, no, his intestines had settled, he could not even feel his chest anymore, it was all gone, solid and cold and heavy and no longer his, and he let out his breath in a great gust and the fear gripped him and he felt tears appear on his one cheek as they ran over the bridge of his nose, and involuntarily he said, "Oh, no."

"There," Fassnacht said. "That's better, eh? No pain."

"What are you going to do?" the doctor asked.

"It's not what I'm going to do; it's what you're going to do," Fassnacht said. "Just like I told you."

The doctor began to whimper. Then he began to cry openly, dropping the syringe onto the floor, where it shattered like a tambourine. "I can't," he said.

"Yes, you can," Fassnacht said angrily. "Now, do it."

"I can't," Diego said, slobbering. "I can't."

Fassnacht went to the other man. "Kill him, Richy."

The man lowered his shotgun and withdrew a long-barreled revolver from a holster. He walked up to Diego and put the revolver to his temple. Then he shielded the doctor's head with his other hand to prevent the blood from spurting out onto him when he fired. He drew back the hammer and the doctor became hysterical, crying, "All right! All right! I'll do it, don't shoot me!"

The man lowered the revolver and looked at Fassnacht for direction.

"Well," Fassnacht said as if talking to a recalcitrant child, "then do it, Diego."

Amesquita watched in horror as the doctor rolled his dead body onto its back. Diego unpacked surgical instruments from his bag, crying as he did so. He fitted a scalpel with a new blade. His voice was thin and quiet, a soft scream of anxiety, as he said, "He's not even clean," but he kept working. "I'm sorry," he said to Amesquita, "God forgive me," but Amesquita could not react, and he watched, transfixed, as the surgeon snipped off his boxer shorts and pulled them out from under his cold, heavy body. Then he made an incision with the scalpel, from his neck to his crotch. A bright line of blood beaded along the seam that had been created and Amesquita's breath came fast and shallow and tears blurred his vision. He felt nothing at all. His eyes blinked over and over rapidly as he strained to lift his neck to watch what he did not want to see, but what he could not stop himself from seeing.

His voice was ragged and dry and almost a cough as he said to Fassnacht, "You're mad. You're completely mad. Look what you're doing to me."

Fassnacht said nothing.

The surgeon took out a hammer and a silver chisel. He placed the chisel at a point beneath Amesquita's breastbone so that it was almost parallel to his stomach with the blade pointing up toward Amesquita's head. Then he swung the hammer and cracked the sternum with his first stroke. All the while he continued to cry. Amesquita felt the jarring blow, heard the cracking of his sternum through his skeleton and rolled his head back to look at the ceiling. "Oh," he said, barely able to catch his breath, "oh." The second blow moved the chisel up another two inches, separating the two halves of the sternum and opening his chest cavity. Amesquita fainted.

Diego worked for half an hour, and when Amesquita regained consciousness again, his chest was completely open, as if for open-heart surgery, and Fassnacht was standing over him. Two large stainless steel spreaders held his rib cage from closing under pressure of the muscles. Amesquita's eyes rolled back into his head as he saw the bulge of the two halves of his trunk, the sharp, white ends of his ribs protruding from the red meat, like slabs of *cabrito*. He lifted his head a little, peered into himself and saw his own heart beating and moving near his lungs, which filled and emptied with each breath he took. He fainted again.

The second time he awoke, Diego was just removing a hypodermic needle from a vein in his arm. Amesquita felt

suddenly wide awake with a jerky, manic energy coursing
through him.

"Crank," Fassnacht informed him. "Methedrine."

Amesquita involuntarily glanced inside himself again and
began screaming at the top of his lungs. His mind did not
enter into it; his body—what was left of it to him—simply
poured the air through his vocal cords and filled the echoing
barn with his screams and he could not stop it, he had
never known anyone could scream that loud, it was remarkable and they let him keep it up for a full minute of exhaust-
ing, excruciating dissonance until he simply ran down and
lay there.

Amesquita looked up at the ceiling. He was going to die
here in this barn. He felt absolutely no pain. His body felt
fine, in fact. If he could only ignore the fact that he was
wrenched open like a pig on a slab. He decided he did not
want to look inside his own body again. He would die here.
That was all.

"Who took the heroin?" Fassnacht asked him.

His heroin? Amesquita thought. He wants to know who
took the heroin? I could have just told him that. He didn't
have to do this to me. "You're mad," Amesquita said.

Fassnacht motioned to the surgeon, who reluctantly came
foreward and took up his scalpel again. He began working
inside Amesquita. Amesquita was aware that no antiseptic
preparations had been made and that they were in a filthy
barn on a wooden table with his entire body open to the air.
Even if they put him back together right now, sewed him up
and let him go, he would die from infection. There was
absolutely no chance that he was going to survive this and
he knew it. Even the gift of flight could not save him. That
certain and incontrovertible knowledge gave him a strange
sense of relief somehow. Now all he had to do was wait. As
long as the anesthetic held.

Relief poured through him and he began crying softly as
Diego worked inside him. Amesquita's glistening pink lungs
sobbed rhythmically, and tears began pouring off each side
of his face and down into his ears. How it would be to have
had the gift of flight when it could have done him some

good—to be just now fluttering over the sierra in the cool wind. His sobs broke and echoed in the barn. It was too late. This life was over, no matter what happened now, there was no turning back. "Oh," he said, "oh, oh." Only that single syllable carried so much meaning it was beyond his ability to articulate, a cry for the loss of a loved one—the ultimate loved one.

The surgeon put something on a white piece of Teflon and backed away. Fassnacht picked it up and showed it to Amesquita. It was a kidney. "Take a good look at that," Fassnacht said. "That's you."

Amesquita applied his entire range of powers to concentrate on the task of generating saliva in his dry mouth. He worked his cheeks and the glands came alive. Fassnacht held the Teflon plate close to Amesquita's eyes. Then Amesquita spat in Fassnacht's face and Fassnacht was so shocked that he dropped the Teflon plate and backed away. He flew into a rage, walking around the barn, blinking and wiping at his eyes. Amesquita took a quick glance along the length of his body and saw his organs, slick with fluid and bristling with hemostats to keep him from bleeding to death prematurely. He let his head back down and watched the ceiling. He concentrated on breathing deeply. Fassnacht walked around the barn a few more times and then came back to the table. He was smiling again.

"It's all right if you spit on me," he said. "Because I'm going to make you a proposition. You're feeling no pain now. But that spinal lasts only about five hours. I have all day. Now, if you tell me what I want to know, I'll make it easy on you. You know you're dead anyway—there's nothing we can do to save you. Tell me what I need to know and I'll let you die right now. It'll be quick and painless. The doc here will give you an injection and that'll be it. But if you give me a hard time," Fassnacht said, baring his teeth, "I'm just going to sit here until that spinal wears off. And then you'll tell me." He nodded up and down, up and down.

It was something to think about. Amesquita knew he could lie here and manage to control himself, to keep from losing his mind. He now knew something about himself he

had never known before and he almost found it humorous
that he could have regrets at a moment like this. If only he
had known before that he had that sort of control—that he
could watch himself cut open, actually witness his own
death and not lose his mind—if only he had known that in
life, what powers he would have had. Maybe going mad
right here and now would be a gift, he thought. But he could
receive no more gifts now, he knew. For he was dead. It was
almost marvelous to contemplate.

"Your own people took the heroin," he said softly. "Your
own people have it in a safe house in Toronto, waiting
to take you out so they can move it onto the streets."

"Names," Fassnacht said. "I know you know the names."

"Yes, I do," Amesquita said, his voice almost calm now,
his breathing deep as he caught out of the corner of his eye
his lungs, inflating and deflating as he spoke. "We were
going to bust the house anytime now. We had it all planned.
Rudy Hereña and Lupe García were involved. Also, Victor
Nuñéz and Porfirio Meléndez. But"—Amesquita motioned
with his chin at the man behind Fassnacht, who had started
to move toward the barn door—"Richy Teller was at the
head of it."

The man behind Fassnacht began to run now. Fassnacht
swung around suddenly and fired with his shotgun just as
the other man was turning to raise his weapon. As the man
was thrown back by the blast, his own shotgun went off and
the pellets ripped through the ceiling. Three owls burst from
hiding and began tearing around near the roof of the barn,
scattering chips of wood and clouds of dust before they
found their way out into the sunlight. The surgeon stag-
gered back in fright and stumbled, sitting heavily on the
straw-covered floor. The dust and wood chips settled, some
of them drifting into Amesquita's chest cavity, and he raised
his head to look at his soiled organs, pumping their fluids,
working at their tasks obliviously, and Amesquita knew that
the moment he had been waiting for had finally come—
right now he had the few seconds he had wished for before—
only it had come too late.

Fassnacht walked over to Richy, who lay on the floor on

his back, wounded. "Is it true?" Fassnacht asked. "Where's the house?"

The man nodded weakly. "Forty-four Charles Street," he said. Fassnacht turned his head away and pulled the trigger on his shotgun again. He hung there for a moment, holding his shotgun down at his side, looking at the floor. Then he sighed and walked back to the table. He looked down at Amesquita.

"Who killed Mendoza?" he asked.

"I did," Amesquita said.

"You did," Fassnacht repeated, nodding. "You're lying."

"Why would I lie now?" Amesquita asked, and his lips smiled involuntarily at the question. It seemed so ridiculous. He was wide awake from the Methedrine they had given him, yet he felt weak, as if he were going to drop off to sleep at any moment, but he couldn't, too tired to sleep. He felt a warmth spreading through him. He felt peace.

"I know you were here in Mexico when he was killed," Fassnacht said. "You're lying to protect someone. Give it up. Tell me who killed him."

"No," Amesquita said. "There's nothing more you can do to me now. Go ahead and let the spinal wear off, I don't care." Amesquita smiled. For the first time in many, many years, it was a natural smile, uncrippled and open. "Anyway, I don't think I'm going to last that long." He could feel the warmth spreading, flowing in him, and he saw that it was good. It was all so good. He felt as if he could fly and he just smiled.

"Yes, you are!" Fassnacht shouted.

"No," Amesquita said weakly, and he felt himself actually flying now, like the silent owl, for he realized the secret. The secret was revealed to him in all its fullness. "No," he said again, smiling, "I don't think so." And he died.

&

CHIP HAD BOUGHT LAND in California, rich, irrigated land on which fruit and vegetables were grown. He had renamed the company Wolf Produce and refused to hire union workers. Danny was outraged and incredulous.

"I'd sooner sell the land," Chip told him coldly. "There's not going to be a single union orange grown on my land, and that's that."

"Don't you remember that afternoon after King was shot?" Danny demanded. "Don't you remember how much for the common man you were? Don't you remember any history?"

"I was a stupid kid full of idealism. I'm a businessman now."

"Chip, goddammit, don't you remember anything about the man who raised me? Who was shot for trying to union-ize? Are you trying to tell me you're becoming like those people? Over money?"

"I'm not killing anybody. I'm just doing my own business the way I see fit. This *is* America."

Danny and Chip fell into a period of strained civility. Danny needed to rationalize what Chip was doing, but he could not. He had bought land, too, some of the most god-forsaken land he had ever seen, in Arkansas. By the winter of '73 the bore holes there had begun to show signs of rich bauxite deposits. Danny put Doc in charge of the operation and hired only union labor.

Danny had kept his apartment in Evanston, though he knew it made no sense. He rarely used it. He stayed in hotels when he was in town. The apartment deepened his loneliness and only forced him to face more squarely the fact that he was a tourist everywhere he went. Perhaps he kept it because it was the closest he could come to something he called home. More and more lately it had become ob-vious that the ranch was Samantha's and hers alone. He could share space there, but he would never call it home. Still, he could not bring himself to return to the apartment.

He handled his business without interest, the way one handles an unavoidable chore. Beyond a certain point he had stopped being impressed with large sums of money. In addition, he did not spend it on much of anything. Often he wondered what had happened to Chip, what had changed him, without seeing clearly how he himself had changed.

When the news of Amesquita's death came, an unspoken

reconciliation took hold between Danny and Chip, though Danny had little real appreciation for anyone or anything in those days. The murder of his second uncle, *Tío* Jim, seemed to eat at him slowly, like a degenerate disorder. Gradually he stopped doing anything at all with his time. Chip and Katina had started their own film company and Chip encouraged Danny to work with them, but he didn't. He just sat in the living room of Samantha's ranch house, and sometimes he drank or played old rhythm-and-blues records, waiting for the inner admission he knew he would have to make before deciding what he would do about Amesquita's murder.

Samantha looked the other way for a while, figuring that he needed to sit with his grief, but the period of stillness stretched on and on. One morning, after refusing breakfast again, Danny wandered into the living room with a cup of coffee and put on a Bobby Bland record. He sat on the couch and stared into the air and listened.

"You're driving me crazy," Samantha told him.

"I'm sorry."

"You're a vengeful Mexican, aren't you?" She was not attempting to make a joke.

"I'm guilty and vengeful, and I can't rest."

"There's nothing I can do, is there? That's the way it was with Gary, only he wasn't kind to me like you are."

"I don't appreciate being compared to him."

"You don't appreciate the truth."

Danny did not want to fight with Samantha. Anyway, what was he going to tell her? Yes, dear, I have it in mind to go down there and kill the son of a bitch who killed my uncle, just the way I did the last time, until history reverberates and shakes me loose. No, the game was getting old, he knew that, but he still could not let it rest. What he really wanted to do was to run away from it. For the first time since he had been with Samantha, he felt that familiar urge to run. He wanted to go visit Moishe, to strap a DC-6 to his butt and fly low over the jungle, daring it to take him. But those days were over, he knew. There was no turning back.

Anyway, how could he get Fassnacht, even if he wanted
him? He couldn't just phone up the DEA and ask for an
appointment. The man was still running his cover, seamless as ever, making bigger and bigger pot busts each year.
What attracted Fassnacht was a Cigarette boat flat out at
ninety-five miles an hour in six-foot seas with a cutter in
hot pursuit; a freighter full of weed, bobbing on the waves
—the mother ship, they called it—that was Fassnacht's
natural element.

Danny suddenly sat straight up. Busting marijuana deals,
he thought. Fassnacht went after big marijuana deals. Yes,
that was certainly one way. He *could* have Fassnacht if he
wanted him, could have him like a spider in a bottle.

Shortly after his last dinner with Forrest and Faye, Danny
had phoned Maggie to ask her if she would give him
Elaine's address so that he could send her a letter. She gave
him the address after eliciting from him the promise that
he would do nothing more than write to her. It was all he
had done, and he had had to wait a very long time for her
answer. When Elaine had not responded within the first
month, Danny assumed that she wasn't going to. Her letter
did finally arrive, though, and it made Danny realize all
over again how little he knew her.

He had written her a long letter full of apology, regret
and the hope that he could see the child sometime. He
also explained to her that he had done well in business
and wanted to provide them with money. Elaine wrote
back as follows:

> Dan:
>   Sorry I didn't answer sooner. Juan and I have
> been very busy with work and his Montessori
> School and so on. Sure, you can see him. Let me
> know when you'd like to come by. Glad to hear
> your business is going well. You didn't say what it
> was. And yes, you can give us money, since you
> offered.
>
>   Best, E.

Danny did not know what he had expected, only that it hadn't been what he got.

Samantha knew the whole story. She did not like it, but she thought it was a good idea for Danny to go see the boy. She knew he would not rest until he did. In those few days before he left, she quietly withdrew her affection from him.

Samantha drove Danny to the airport. As he was getting out of the car, she said, "Are you going to see Maggie?"

"I hadn't planned on it," Danny said. He immediately knew that was a lie. He didn't have to plan on that. Going to Chicago without seeing Maggie would be like going to Agra without seeing the Taj Mahal. Chicago *was* Maggie.

Samantha knew he was lying as well, but she said nothing. He boarded the United Airlines 707 and went to sleep the moment he heard the wheels rumble into their wells, just as he had done the first time Forrest had taken him up in an airplane so many years ago. It told him something. It told him that he was running again.

Elaine had rented an apartment near the university—not far, in fact, from where Danny had lived with Maggie. When he knocked on the door, he could hear her screaming the way mothers have to scream at little boys, in that tone that becomes habit after a few years of it. She was saying something like: "Gerbils can't breathe underwater, honey!"

She opened the door, dragging her long brown hair from her eyes, dressed as she always had, in jeans and a sweat shirt. When she saw that it was Danny, she smiled a little and said, "Oh, hi, come on in. The place is a mess."

He entered the apartment, which was no more of a mess than the one she'd had in 1969. The little boy came running out of the back of the apartment full tilt, holding a soaking wet gerbil and dripping water as he ran. When he saw Danny, he stopped halfway into the living room. He wore tiny jeans and a tiny sweat shirt that said THE KID on it. His face was smeared with something purple—jelly perhaps—and the front of his sweat shirt was dark with water.

"He's been trying to ascertain in what manner gerbils are different from fish," Elaine explained.

"I see." Danny could not take his eyes from the child. "We made that, huh?" he asked, pointing to Juan.

"We sure did. Juan," Elaine said, kneeling beside the boy, "this is your daddy." She pointed at Danny, and they both looked at him, a young man dressed in slacks and a suede jacket.

Juan smiled as if he had been taught to smile when introduced to strangers. Then he held up the gerbil and said, "I got uh fish."

"That's a gerbil, honey," Elaine explained. She turned to Danny and said, "See, I made the mistake of buying him a goldfish and a gerbil in the same week and he can't seem to get their habits straight."

"I got a gerbil," Juan said, still holding up the animal, which squirmed and tried in vain to free itself from the innocent sadism of the child's fingers.

"I see," Danny said again. He walked over and knelt down beside Juan, who feigned interest in the gerbil, embarrassed by the closeness of the stranger.

Juan suddenly stuck out his hand and poked Danny in the chest, saying softly, "You my daddy."

"Yes, I'm your daddy." Now that he was close, he could see that the child actually looked like him. It was the most frightening and exciting sensation he'd ever had. He felt a sudden rush and wanted to scoop Juan up in his arms and take him away, but he did nothing. He certainly didn't expect Juan to leap into his arms. He looked back at Elaine and said, "He's really something."

"You my daddy," Juan said again, nodding his head without looking at Danny, just saying it over again to himself to make sure he had it right or perhaps just repeating the syllables because children do that. He looked up at Danny, then, with reserve and curiosity and suspicion.

"How old is he?"

"I three and haff," Juan said.

Danny's head spun around and he smiled. "Wow," he said.

"He tells jokes, too," Elaine said. "He's a lot like you. He's smart, cute and vindictive."

Danny nodded, accepting the assessment without comment. "Can I take him somewhere? Go out to the zoo or whatever you do with children?"

"I don't think so. I don't want him to get too used to liking you."

"I like you," Juan said, and hugged Danny's leg.

"Don't let it get to you. He says that to all the boys."

It had already gotten to Danny, far more than he had anticipated. He wanted to stay with the child, to go places with him, to live with him. To teach him how not to make a mess of his life as his daddy had done. The only way to learn anything, though, was to do it yourself, and Danny saw in that moment that there was nothing he could teach the child. Juan would have to do just like everybody else did, and he remembered with a smile what Beto used to say to him as he went off to play back in Harlingen: "If you break your leg, don't come running to me."

"Do you think it will be possible for him to visit me at some point? We've got horses and a ranch out there in Arizona. I mean, he could just come in the summer, maybe once a year, I don't know." Danny dropped his eyes, remembering Maggie, long, long ago, saying, "Don't ever beg." Now he was begging again. He felt as if he were facing a mildly deranged judge who had complete power over him and he did not like the feeling. He had to keep reminding himself that he had generated this situation and he was getting exactly what he bargained for.

"I don't think so," Elaine said as if she were declining the offer of a cocktail. "No, I don't think that would be such a good idea."

"Don't you think it's important for him to get to know his father?" Danny heard his own voice go up a few notes as his desperation began to show.

Elaine shrugged, unmoved as always. It wasn't so much that she was cold; she just seemed absent. "No," she said, after considering it a moment. "He'd just learn all that

macho stuff. Riding horses. You'd probably teach him to
shoot a gun, too, take him fishing and hunting and play
contact sports with him. I don't want him to grow up to be
a male chauvinist. I think he's better off the way he is, with
me."

Danny looked away at a far wall. He forced himself to
remain silent. It was Elaine's child if she wanted it that
way—he had given it to her and he could not take it back.
Just as one of those Watergate guys had said, once the
toothpaste is out of the tube, it's awfully hard to get it
back in.

Elaine allowed him to spend the morning playing with
Juan, who showed him all his games and toys and his goldfish, which, he explained, did not have fur.

Danny fixed lunch for the child and watched him spread
the food in widening circles on the kitchen table, then on
the floor. Danny cleaned the table, the floor and the boy.
When it was time for Juan's nap, Danny read stories to
him. By that time Juan had begun to get his mind around
the fact that Danny was his father. The notion excited him
so that he couldn't go to sleep. Danny read him four stories.
One was usually enough, but Juan kept sitting up in the
bed and poking Danny in the chest, saying, "You my
daddy?"

Danny would smile and answer, "Yes."

Then Juan would nod his head with certainty and lie
back down. "You my daddy," he would repeat with a different inflection that confirmed it for him.

When Danny started on the fifth book, Elaine came in
and said, "I think that's probably enough, Dan. Why don't
you go ahead and leave now?"

Danny sighed and pressed his lips together into a thin,
pale line. He closed the book and leaned over to kiss Juan
on the forehead. "Good-bye, Juanito," he said.

"You going to work, Daddy?" Juan asked.

"Yes, I'm going to work."

"Bye, Daddy."

"Bye, son."

Out in the living room Danny stood by the door with Elaine. "Say, I've always wondered something."

"What?"

"Why did you name him Juan?"

Elaine shrugged. "Well, I thought about that. I was pretty bitter at first, you know. But after all, he is what he is, I can't change that. So he's part Mexican. I thought he ought to be aware of it."

"You're all right," Danny said. "You're really all right."

Elaine sighed in response.

"I thought I'd start out by sending you five thousand dollars a month and see how that works out. I can always send more if you like."

Elaine's eyes widened and her scalp moved. It was the strongest reaction he had ever seen her display. "Five thousand dollars a month!" She looked toward the bedroom as if Juan might have heard. "Danny," she whisperd, "that's sixty thousand dollars a year."

"It's nothing, believe me."

"My Christ, what sort of work do you do?"

"I'm a dope smuggler."

Elaine laughed. "That's very funny. But whatever you do, are you sure you can afford that much money?"

"I'm sure."

Early the next morning Danny drove along the snowy streets of Evanston, realizing that for the first time he had a purpose for his money. Up to that point the money had had a life of its own, growing and dividing, spreading and ingesting properties or companies. Danny watched it from afar. Now, though, he could do something with some of it.

He drove aimlessly, stopping when the lights were red, moving with the rush hour traffic when the signals changed to green. Maybe Elaine was right, he thought. Maybe it would be better not only for Juan but for him that they be apart. He would not make a good father.

He followed the traffic along the grade that led to south-

bound Lake Shore Drive. He pushed the gas pedal and
the rented sedan hesitated, then moved forward sluggishly.
The traffic flowed around him, then behind him, and he let
his thoughts continue to run their course, right up until he
exited the drive at Michigan Avenue and drove to the
newspaper offices to find Maggie.

She jumped up when she saw him. Then she grinned.
"You're back," she said with surprise.

"Yeah, my back."

Maggie laughed and shook her head, as if to say, same old
goof. "Yeah," she said. "Your back."

"Since my just back," Danny continued, "can you get out
of here on short notice?"

"What did you have in mind?"

"An adventure."

"I'm too old for adventure." Maggie shook her head.

"You talk like a middle-aged suburban housewife."

"I *am* a middle-aged suburban housewife."

"Oh, go on, you're not even thirty yet. Anyway, it'll put
the glow in your cheeks. What do you say?"

"Well, I suppose I could spring for a small adventure."
She looked up at Danny and smiled. "It's good to see you,
you know that?"

"I'm glad you said that. I need someone who's glad to
see me."

"Shall I call the baby-sitter and tell her I'll be home late?"
Maggie asked with a crooked smile of affection and suspicion
that she seemed always to reserve for Danny. Only this time
he had no idea what he had done to deserve it. He simply
wanted to run and he didn't feel like doing it alone.

"Yes, do that."

Maggie made the call and fifteen minutes later they were
on the road.

"Where are we going?" Maggie asked. "None of my business, of course."

"Do you still belong to that flying club at Pal-Waukee?"

"Yeah, you want to take a ride in the Warrior?"

"I'd like that."

"Technically it's against the regulations for you to fly a club plane, but I trust you."

"I never cease to be amazed that you do."

Once they were aloft, the ride was quite bumpy, and half an hour later they were circling a sprawl of buildings by a nice-looking landing strip with the number 5 painted on one end, 23 on the other. Danny picked up the microphone and called Unicom, asking for winds and favored direction of landing. The man's voice said it was 200 at 15 and Runway 23 was in use.

"You know what that is?" Maggie asked.

"Yeah," he said as he rolled out on downwind. "It's a resort."

"It's a hotel."

"Yeah." Danny picked up the microphone and let go of the control wheel. "Here, let's see how your cross-wind landings are doing these days. I'll call our positions."

Maggie took the wheel. "Thirty degrees cross wind at fifteen knots," she said, and raised her eyebrows.

"No sweat, you can handle it."

They rode over hills into some very bumpy air, descending. Maggie turned left and ran through her checklist. When she turned final, she put down ten degrees of flaps and kept the power up to avoid thermal shock to the engine. She also wanted it warm in case they had to go around. At uncontrolled fields such as this one it was not uncommon to come in on final approach and find someone pulling onto the runway right beneath you, fat, dumb and happy.

When Maggie could see that they had the runway made— and that it was clear—she cut the power and pulled back on the yoke to slow up the plane as she straightened the nose with right rudder. She dipped the left wing into the wind and the little Warrior squatted on the concrete, rolling along on its mains until it ran out of lift, and she applied the brakes gently.

"Very, very slick," Danny said.

"Just like you taught me." She taxied the plane to a parking area, where they tied it down. A station wagon from the resort complex arrived and gave them a ride to a bar overlooking some rather unexciting ski hills. Since it was the middle of the week, there were only a few people skiing and the lift lines were deserted.

They had a cup of coffee and watched the skiers. "You must do a lot of skiing out west," Maggie observed.

"Some. It's great fun. Can you ski?"

"What do you think?" she asked sarcastically.

"Want to try it?"

"In a skirt and blouse?" she asked, indicating the clothes she was wearing.

"We'll fix that up in the shop downstairs."

"Well, we've come this far. We're supposed to have an adventure. All we've had so far is light chop."

Danny and Maggie had themselves completely outfitted in the ski shop, in spite of Maggie's protests about the money Danny was spending. They stumbled out to one of the easier hills, where he showed her how to snowplow and turn. She approached the project with great caution and enthusiasm, doing everything exactly as he showed her, just as she had done when he taught her to fly. Soon he was leading her down the medium-size hill.

Maggie screamed with glee as she rode down, turning to keep from picking up too much speed. On the chair lift up, Maggie put her hand over her eyes, saying, "Oh, God, it's so far down. I don't like this part."

"Christ, we came here at forty-five hundred MSL, Maggie."

"It's not the same."

"Yeah, I guess you're right. These things break and spill people down onto the ground all the time, don't they?"

"Danny!"

They skied all afternoon, riding the lift together, skiing down and meeting at the bottom. As the sun began to go behind the hills, Danny put his arm around Maggie and they dragged themselves back to the lodge, laughing and talking. Maggie changed back into her clothes and they returned to the bar to watch the show that was supposed to take place, with professional skiers on the highest hill carrying torches or some such silly thing. Hardly anyone was there to watch, but the waiter assured them, when they asked, that the show would go on nevertheless.

"When do you have to be back?" Danny asked.

"I don't have to be if I don't want to be."

"How come? Won't Brian wonder?"

"He's not there."

"Where is he?"

"In San Francisco." Maggie folded a small cardboard hat that announced some sort of expensive winter drink. As Danny watched, she tore it along the crease, folded it again, tore it again. She continued the process until it was in shreds before her.

"Well," Danny said softly, "if we don't have to fly back tonight, we can have a drink."

"All right," Maggie said without hesitation and without looking up, busying herself rearranging the bits of card she had torn up.

Danny waved at the waiter, who came to take their orders. Maggie said, "I'd better call and make arrangements for Lisa." Without looking at Danny she stood and walked away. When she returned, they had several drinks without talking.

"I never knew you to drink like that," Danny observed.

"I don't, normally." She laughed and wiped her lower lip with her index finger. "I think I'm a little drunk."

"We need something to eat."

"I don't feel like sitting in a fancy restaurant."

"Let's order something from room service," Danny said, signaling the waiter for the check.

Maggie laughed out loud. "Now that is as slick as I've ever heard, Danny, really."

"Whatever do you mean?"

"Somehow you managed to get us past checking into the hotel and all the way to room service without so much as a 'May I?' Now, that's good. Almost too good." She drank the last of her drink and stood as Danny paid. "That's always been the problem with you. You're sometimes too slick for your own good." She followed him out, still talking, almost to herself now. "Just like the night we met."

"A million years ago."

"You know, you never did tell me what the police were chasing you about that night."

"There's that."

"Are you going to tell me now?"

"No."

"Oh!" Maggie shouted as she let herself flop onto the bed. "What an adventure!" She lay on her back, still in her coat, her arms outstretched.

"What shall I order?" Danny asked.

"Vodka. Meat and vodka and potatoes and limes."

"Yum." Danny picked up the phone, saying to himself, "Meat and vodka and . . ."

After he placed the order, they explored the accommodations together. There was a telephone in the bathroom, which set Maggie off. "They're right," she said, "of course, they're right; every time you get into the bathroom the thing rings. People must give off psychic signals that produce in other human beings an irresistible urge to pick up the phone and call."

In the main room there was a console between two queen-size beds, from which the lights, television, drapes, heat, air conditioning and radio could be controlled. Maggie touched the switch that said DRAPES and a little electric motor started whining and drew back the curtains to reveal glass doors, beyond which was a seamless stretch of white, dotted with trees. Moonlight diminished in pastels toward a frozen pond with weeping willows beside it.

"Isn't it beautiful?" Maggie asked.

"You don't have to be so nervous. I'm not going to rape you."

Maggie turned and blushed. "You know when I was last in a hotel room alone with a man?"

"I might hazard a guess."

"June ninth, 1965. And I am very nervous."

"Well," he said, walking over to her and putting his arms around her, "don't be. You don't have to do anything but eat dinner with me, get drunk if you care to and watch some television. Then get some rest for the flight home tomorrow."

"Do you mean that? You won't feel cheated?"

"What makes you think I'm so fired up about going to bed with you?"

She blushed again and hugged him, throwing both arms around his neck.

While they were waiting for dinner, they sat at a table near the glass doors and watched the moonlight move across the snow. They could hear the growl of snowmobiles in the distance. Danny and Maggie talked about Elaine and compared notes about children, what little Danny knew of them. A waiter wheeled their dinner in and served them, opening a bottle of wine with a flourish. When he'd gone, Danny watched Maggie eating and felt a great warmth, just being with her.

When they had finished eating, Maggie said, "I'm so full. I never eat this much; it was delicious."

"Is this a nice adventure?"

"This is a nice adventure." Maggie reached across the table and covered his hand with hers. "You're very nice, Danny. You were always very nice, but I think you're even nicer now. I like you older."

"Nice?" Danny laughed. "I could think of a lot of ways to describe myself, but nice isn't one of them."

"Well, then," Maggie began, fighting through a great catlike yawn. "Oh!" she said. But she didn't finish whatever she had begun to say. "I'm so tired." She looked at her watch. "My God, it's only eight-thirty."

Danny stood up and walked around the table. Maggie looked up at him with sad, uncertain eyes. Danny took her hands and Maggie stood. She allowed him to lead her to the bed. They faced each other for a moment before Danny pulled back the covers. He reached up to unbutton her blouse and she did nothing to stop him, their eyes locked together there, and her green eyes clicked back and forth, back and forth, as if she could not decide which of Danny's

eyes to watch. Danny slipped her blouse off and Maggie
even turned around to let him undo the hasp on the back
of her bra, which fell away, revealing her breasts, small but
larger than Danny's hand, self-supporting in the yellow incandescence of the room.

"People will see," Maggie said softly, meaning through
the glass doors, but Danny did not answer. He opened the
catch on her skirt and unzipped it, taking it down to the
floor, and it was only when she stood completely naked that
he spoke.

"Lie down," he said, looking at her naked before him, as
he had not looked at her in so many years. He felt his heart
break for it.

Maggie hesitated, then got into the bed. Danny picked
up the edge of the cover and drew it over her. Only her
head remained, her hair fanned out on the white pillow-
case. Danny sat next to her on the bed and worked the controls on the console until the lights were dim except in one
corner by a table near the glass doors. He put his hand on
Maggie's forehead and stroked her hair back from her eyes.
"I still love you," he said. "I never stopped loving you. I
fell in love with you when I first saw you and I've been in
love with you ever since then and I'll always be in love with
you."

"Don't say it, Danny."

"It's true."

"I know, I know how true it is, but it's too late."

"Yes. I guess it is."

Maggie fell asleep almost immediately and Danny watched
her sleeping for an hour before he, too, undressed and got
into the other bed. The bottle of vodka stood untouched
on its tray, the bucket of ice melting. From time to time the
structure of ice would fail and he could hear the pieces shifting. Moonlight flooded the room and Danny watched it for
a while. He could hear Maggie sleeping, her breath like the
surf heard a hundred miles away. He looked over and she was
in her sleeping position, which he knew so well. If he had
been in bed with her, the shape of her left arm would have

circumscribed and defined him. For the first time since she had left him, he did not feel pain playing that deadly hypothetical game. He felt content and quiet and it occurred to him that if only he and Maggie could stay right here at this place in the country, everything would be all right. And he knew it was a lie.

He fell asleep easily and awoke just after midnight. He heard water running in the bathroom. He lay perfectly still and opened his eyes. The setting moon ignited the landscape in indistinct pastel shades. Then he felt the covers lift behind him as Maggie entered the bed. The covers closed around them and she took her sleeping position behind him, a perfect mold of his shape, only smaller, her skin on his, and he felt an energy surge from her to him as if he were a coastline lighting up after a long power failure, blinking to life sector by sector.

He turned slowly toward her and she lifted her arm which encompassed him as he rolled, then enclosed him again and he lay there, his face against her breast, and she put her hand on his head and held him. It was just after midnight in the country and the moon was setting as Maggie turned onto her back and drew Danny over her like a blanket. It was so easy, so simple, their skin hot together, holding each other for a long time, just holding, arms and legs entangled like children absently napping in the afternoon, it was brief and twice, then three times. Then four, like children again, like lovers for the first time, every time, they made love all night, and when the glass doors began to swell with gray light across the snowscape, they fell into endless, impenetrable sleep, annealed together in undiscovered alloys of themselves.

In the morning, when they were dressed and having breakfast, Maggie said, "I don't want you to take this as a precedent." Between them on the table were two tiny white roses in a vase.

"Making love with you?"

"Yes. It was wonderful and I'm glad we did it. But I don't want you to think we can do that all the time."

"Why not?" It did not surprise him, nor did it diminish his elation. He simply wanted her to articulate it.

"I couldn't stand to be a suburban housewife with a lover. I just wouldn't be able to handle that."

"I'm not going to argue," Danny told her with a smile. "I feel great. Better than I've felt in years."

Maggie smiled impishly and looked up from her coffee. "It *is* wonderful, isn't it?" She laughed. "It seems sort of like incest."

"As if we were related."

"Now you know why I trust you. You don't give me a hard time about being the way I want to be." She thought for a moment and then added, "I wanted to tell you. I finally figured out why you do what you do. It came to me during a dinner at the Bakery in Chicago."

"You know how to choose a good location for your insights."

"The head of NASA invited a bunch of press people to have dinner with him. It was PR. It was no big deal. Anyway, this man never drank. That night for some reason the NASA administrator started putting away wine like there was no tomorrow. I don't think he realized what he was doing. By the second glass he was crocked. And you know what he told me? He said that every single astronaut who had been to space—to real space—had asked him permission to take a one-way trip. I kind of dropped my jaw and he confirmed that what he meant was that these guys were willing, say, to go to Venus or Jupiter, knowing they wouldn't be able to return. Just to see what was out there."

"Christ."

"It just clarified a lot of things for me."

"I wish I had known that ten years ago."

They sat drinking coffee into the morning and Maggie called to see that Lisa was all right. At noon they flew home.

He spent the rest of the week in Chicago and they saw each other several times before Maggie's husband returned,

though they did not make love again. They spent long after-
noons walking and talking.

"You know I want the stories," Maggie told him.

"They're long and some of them aren't too pleasant."

"I have the time and I've been in unpleasant stories before."

Danny recounted for her the history, then, the thousands
of tons of drugs, Harlingen and Acapulco, Mexico and Colombia, Chip's growing lust for money and power, even
Fassnacht and the horror of Amesquita. But as the week
came to a close he still had not told her about the night they
met.

She called him early one morning at the hotel and said,
"Danny, I think you'd better take a look at the paper."

The headline said AREA ATTORNEY INDICTED ON WATER-
GATE CHARGES and described Forrest's alleged crimes, saying
that he had been released after appearing in federal court.
As Danny sat in his room, reading the story for a second
time, he felt despair surround and cover him like a frost.

"I didn't want to tell you," Forrest said. "Just when everything was going so well for you."

"Yeah," Danny said. "I understand."

They were sitting high up in an office building, overlooking the city of Chicago. Danny saw on his father's desk a
pen and pencil set—gold with a wooden base—with the
presidential seal. He wondered if that's what Forrest got for
supporting Nixon all those years. Danny walked to the
window and looked out over the perfectly clear winter light
that cut the city in sharp, geometric shadows.

"It's just the way I always told you," Forrest said. "Fat,
dumb and happy. You try. You always try to watch your
six. Then, when you think you've got everything covered,
wham!" He smacked the back of his right hand into the
palm of his left. "Out of nowhere."

Danny turned from the window. "How bad is it?"

"Bad. I'd rather not talk here."

"Let's take a ride."

Out along Lake Shore Drive, Forrest put on a pair of sunglasses. He told Danny that he might actually serve time.

"What did you do?"

"What I did was to make a lot more money than I admitted making and then got mixed up with Nixon. I could have gotten away with it if I hadn't given money to the campaign. Or if those burglars hadn't been caught."

"Income tax evasion?" Danny looked at his father and whistled.

"It's sure one thing when you're up in front of that judge yourself. There are people in this society you can hire to do almost anything if you have a little money: doctors, lawyers, maids, carpenters, chauffeurs. You can even hire love and devotion. The one thing you cannot hire is someone to go to jail for you. Only you can serve time, no matter who you are."

"Do you really think they're going to send you to jail?"

"Yes. Me and a load of others. Me especially because not only did they catch me on the same charges as everyone else, all this illegal campaign contribution business and obstruction of justice, whatever the hell that is, but in looking into that, they found out that I'd been putting money away in Swiss accounts and not reporting it. They don't like that at at all, do they?"

"What's going to happen with Nixon?"

"The president is expendable. He has to be; he's hired for only four years at a time. Presidents get themselves shot and what not. So Nixon will probably fall, too. Ahh, I don't know," Forrest said with disgust. "This whole thing is public relations anyway, and when it's over, all these people will go right back to what they've been doing all along. I'm not protesting my innocence. I owe the government some money; there's no doubt about that. But I got caught by a quirk." Forrest shook his head sadly. "Seems like everything happens at once."

"What else could be happening?"

Forrest watched the lake as they rolled along the frozen shore. The surface of the water was choked with blocks of ice up to a distance of 200 yards out, beyond which stood an old pumping station like a mysterious, surreal mansion that had come to rest in the middle of Lake Michigan.

"Goddammit," Forrest said. The word found a hitch in his throat and he stopped there. He swallowed and began again. "Danny, we've never been much for heart-to-heart talks, I know. That's my fault. But I've gotten myself into a real mess, not just legally but personally."

"Faye?"

Forrest nodded, his lips pressed tightly together. "I think I may be losing my second wife."

"Oh, God."

"I should have known. Young girl like that." Again Forrest's voice stopped within his throat. "She's been seeing another man. For quite a while, I gather." He shook his head back and forth. "Danny, I love that woman terribly. Just terribly. That was my mistake. I fell in love with her, son." He took off his sunglasses and wiped them.

"I know," Danny said, knowing that there was nothing he could say to help.

"Danny, all those years I kept myself from falling in love with another woman. I thought I couldn't stand it, not after what happened the first time. And you know what? I fell in love anyway and I think I was right." Forrest seemed about to go on, but he clamped his jaw shut and stared out the right-hand window of the car. Danny could see his shoulders shake and he looked away. He realized that he did love him; he loved Forrest in all his imperfection, loved him from the moment he went to bed with that sixteen-year-old girl in Acapulco who was Danny's mother, whom he had never seen, to this, his weakest and most open moment. Danny loved the man as he loved himself, for that's what he was.

They drove through the bright, snowy streets of Chicago, going nowhere in particular.

As soon as he returned to Tucson, he told Samantha about his visit with Juan and Elaine, how it had made him feel, and his talk with Forrest. She had reacted angrily and jealously and Danny still wasn't certain why. When she finally came to the point, though, he knew that she had suspected all along.

"What do you take me for, some kind of nitwit?" she asked.

Danny was shocked. He had noticed that Samantha's mood was somewhat distant when he arrived, but she could be moody, he knew that. "What do you mean?"

"Maggie," she said. "It's written all over you."

"What about Maggie?" Danny asked. He couldn't meet her eyes.

Danny had never seen Samantha in a rage before and it shocked him when she stood up, kicking over the chair behind her, and shouted, "You think I can't tell that you went to bed with Maggie. Well, I can and I'm not taking it very well."

"It was nothing," Danny said. It was such a naked lie that he immediately wished he hadn't said it.

"Bullshit! You loved her when you met me and you still love her."

"Samantha," Danny said, moving toward her to reason with her, "I love *you*. Maggie's married. She's got a kid."

"Don't touch me," Samantha shouted, and stormed out of the house.

Danny called after her, but she got into her car and drove off.

That evening Danny called Katina to see if Samantha had gone there, but Katina hadn't seen her.

"Did you two have a fight?" Katina asked.

"You might call it that."

"She never told you about her temper."

"I guess I never did anything to make her that mad before."

"What did you do?" There was a silence and Katina added, "She's very jealous, Danny. I hope it wasn't another woman."

"Kat, it wasn't just any other woman. It was more complicated than that."

"Bad, huh?"

"Bad."

"Is there anything I can do?"

"Find her."

"Well, if I know her as well as I think I do, she'll come back."

Danny waited three days, and when she came back, she refused to speak to him. Nothing Samantha had ever done or said had given him any clue to the magnitude of her wrath. When she came out of it, she told him that she was sorry if he didn't like it, but that's the way she was. "I know we're not married and I know it's old-fashioned. Anyway, it has nothing to do with just any woman. But Maggie? Danny, how could you?"

Danny wanted to ask how he could have done anything other than go to bed with Maggie after all those years of waiting, but he said nothing. He did not want to lose Samantha, but he knew then, somehow, that their relationship was over. Perhaps not that day, but it would never be the same.

He wanted to remind her of the talk they had the first night they made love in the loft of the barn. I kissed a girl once, a long time ago. . . . He was amazed to find that, after all this time with Samantha, he had been right in the first place.

⟞

SUCCESS IN BUSINESS, Forrest had told Danny, was largely a matter of bulling your way through. A lot of it had to do with making everyone around you believe you could do the impossible and then, having convinced them, going on to do it. However, Forrest had warned, success also consisted in knowing when you were whipped and cutting your losses. It came, therefore, as no surprise to learn that Forrest's attorneys had devised a strategy for his trial in which Forrest would plead guilty to one count of tax evasion in exchange for other charges being dropped. They hadn't anticipated, however, that Forrest's case would be singled out for stiff penalties. The prosecution made him out to be the worst sort of criminal and the judge went right along with it. While everyone else was being sent to the so-called country club prisons—minimum security places with nice libraries and work programs—Forrest ended up by some quirk of the judicial system in a very bad place indeed. It was as Forrest had told Danny: The law is like a large and not very clever beast. It could misread you at any moment and bite your head off quite inadvertently. You had to move slowly and with great caution around it and, if you could, keep your distance from it large.

Danny visited Forrest as soon as it was possible. He was gone only a day, but it seemed like a month. The prison was almost intentionally Gothic in its appearance—a great, stone edifice, castlelike and of a color so uniformly drab that it seemed to suck light rather than relinquish it. A low stone outer wall surrounded the entire complex, as if to force an escaping convict to slow down momentarily as he fled. In from that wall was a double chain-link fence, eighteen feet high, with barbed wire across the top and peacocks in the space between. Beyond that was the big house—the Steel Château itself, "Max, max, max," the guard who drove him in told Danny. "Nobody gets out, but everybody's welcome." He chuckled. Danny was locked in the back seat, separated from him by a steel screen. The doors on either side had no handles. Danny could feel the panic rising in him, even though he was simply visiting. His mouth was dry and he wished he had not come.

"What're the peacocks for?" he asked.

"Man gets in that space between those two fences, those devils set up a racket like you wouldn't believe," the guard said. He stopped the car. "This is your stop," he added, and laughed as if that were first-class humor material.

He let Danny out and took him through the front door. Instantly Danny knew he was in a bad place, the wrong place, maybe even the last place. He had always laughed at Michael when he used the word *vibes*, but they were so thick here that Danny would have turned and bolted if it hadn't been for the guard's warning not to go anywhere without an escort once inside, "because those fellas on the towers shoot anything moving out here unless it's wearing a uniform."

First they patted Danny down to see if he had any weapons. Then they put him through a metal detector. Then they went over him with a device they said detected explosives. He could feel his pulse quickening, his blood pressure rising, each time they performed another procedure on him, as if the last one would cause him to detonate.

They took him through the first steel door, and when it clanked shut with a sound like two railroad cars meeting, he imagined that he could hear the tumblers melt and weld and become a single plumb of metal.

Twenty feet beyond that, they put him through another steel door even more formidable. Everything beyond was green. That steel door opened to another steel door only five feet away and he was locked into the space between. He could feel himself vibrating with claustrophobic panic. He could not stop his eyes from blinking, and though he tried to swallow, he could not. Then the other door was unlocked and he was let through, gasping as if he'd just surfaced from a long, dangerous dive.

He was in the prison proper now, the main lockup. The green covered every surface, the most depressing color he had ever seen. He thought at any moment he might drop to his knees and begin pleading and begging for them to let him out. It was very difficult to remember that his crimes had not been discovered—only he knew at that point that he could actually leave this place.

He could hear the roar of the prison now, the harsh, mechanical sound of doors and bolts and locks, the rattling of cages and the deep, underlying harmonic of men's voices at a tidal level, as someone approaching the sea will hear it long before he sees it and will smell it even before he hears it. The smell was not death, not locker rooms or even toilets. It was the smell of something that had been tormented past pain and exhaustion and had been left to fester. It had an electric overtone, too, a jittery, berserk quality, as if at any moment it might ignite like a gas in the air.

Danny was led past the main tiers of cells to a room eight by eight feet with a small table and two chairs. Foam-rubber mattress pads, yellow, dried and crumbling, were stacked to the ceiling along one wall. Two bare incandescent bulbs illuminated the windowless room. Forrest sat at the table, ashen. His hair had been clipped short. He hadn't shaved. He wore what appeared to be green pajamas.

"Five minutes," the guard said, and closed the door.

"Oh, my God," Danny said when he saw his father. Forrest stood up and Danny put his arms around him and cried openly, without shame, saying over and over, "Oh, my God, Forrest, my God," and holding his father tighter.

"It's all right, Danny, take it easy, son, I'm hacking it."

"My God, Forrest, they can't leave you here, there's been some kind of mistake."

"They're working on it. I've got people on it night and day, son."

Danny straightened, still holding his father's arm. "I'm going to get my lawyers on this, too."

"It's all right, they'll get me out of here."

Before they could continue to the more personal conversation Danny had imagined they would have, the guard came and said his time was up and virtually dragged him away.

On the flight back to Tucson Danny remembered what Moishe had said about never having done any time. It hadn't meant much to Danny then, but now it was a reeling, yawning reality.

He returned to find that Katina had moved out of Chip's house. He found Chip there, fatter than before and snorting coke.

"It's like I told you before," Chip said. "I need to put it to the wall again. I'm vegetating here. Atrophy, man. I think I drove Katina crazy. She'll come back. We just had a fight."

"I've got a health plan for you. We're going to the country to get straight together."

"Fuck health."

"I've got another plan."

Chip looked up with interest.

A few days later, Samantha also wanted to know what Danny planned to do with himself. "I am not going to tolerate your sitting around here, sulking again," she warned. "I can't take that anymore."

"I'm going to make a deal."

"What sort of deal?"

"I'm going to make the biggest, most expensive deal they've ever seen."

Samantha stared at him for a moment. "You're serious, aren't you?"

Danny nodded.

"And you want me to broker it, right?"

He continued to nod, slowly, steadily. "And I'm taking Doc off the bauxite thing in Arkansas and putting him on this."

"What if I refuse to cooperate?"

"Makes no difference now," Danny said. "I don't really care."

"If you don't have buyers, you'll lose everything."

"I know how much I'll lose. That's not why I'm doing it. I'm going to catch Fassnacht."

The
Last
Deal

10

IF YOU SPUN THE GLOBE to the intersection of fifteen degrees north, seventy-five degrees west, it would be apparent that the shortest navigable water route from La Guajira, Colombia, to the United States would take you across the Caribbean, through the Yucatán Channel and around Cuba to the west coast of Florida. It would be shorter to take the Windward Passage between Cuba and Haiti, but since the Cubans had removed all the lights along the coast, it would be virtually impossible to make that run at night. Furthermore, all northerly routes from South America were so heavily patrolled by the time Danny began to consider all this that it would have been extremely risky to attempt any straightforward passage. An infamous Coast Guard cutter, *Dauntless*, patrolled the Caribbean, and numerous other official and equally deadly vessels from Cuba, Mexico and the U.S. could be encountered at any moment while sailing that area.

Consequently, an alternate route had been devised that involved laboriously sailing against the current down along the Venezuelan coast toward Guyana, then north to the Leeward Islands and from there to the Florida coast (or, recently, farther north—in some cases as far as Martha's Vineyard).

However, Danny considered the entire East Coast too hot. Florida itself was so hot by then that Danny would not have stopped there for fuel. The police—various police of every description and persuasion—and smugglers played such a deadly game there that no one could tell anymore who was on whose team. There were bands of outlaws who acquired counterfeit police credentials (or simply killed police to get the real ones) and made "arrests" to steal the drugs. Once a group of police attempted to arrest another group of police after a stakeout and shot five of them in the confusion. It was chaos, amateur night, with double and triple cross, blackmail, torture and murder running around the clock.

A few miles east were the Exumas, where entire islands were owned outright by drug-smuggling operations and where even casual tourists on sailing expeditions ran the risk of being boarded, turned away, robbed or even killed for being in the wrong place or seeing the wrong thing. Every boat carried guns. Trouble was everywhere from the Alabama-Florida border on south as far as one cared to sail. And the IRS was right behind it. Danny wanted nothing to do with any of that action.

He and Chip bought a small salvage company on the Oregon coast, where a river emptied into the Pacific Ocean amid century-old logging communities west of the foothills of the Cascade mountain range. A few miles inland they leased a great warehouse. Nearer the water they set up offices and rented a dock. They moved quietly and gently into the little town there. It was easy with Chip's slow-moving grace next to Danny and Doc, in jackboots and flannel shirts, muscling up to the bar in town and introducing themselves to anyone who cared to share a beer.

Over time, Chip had developed a beer gut from being too fond of food and booze and in some mysterious way (or so it seemed to Danny) from the natural expansion of his empire, as if his body were the visible manifestation of his wealth. Danny could see him growing older and louder before his eyes. Chip's appearance, however, stood him in good stead in their new surroundings. They worked long hours from the very beginning, in the sun and rain and coastal fog that sometimes seemed eternal.

After the first month the salvage company offices were

piled high with papers, manifests of cargo, receipts, bills of lading and spare equipment, rusting or greasy in a clutter that was so diverse it defied interpretation. By the second month anyone in that area—Coast Guard, cop, IRS, logger, customer or bill collector—could walk into the offices early and watch Chip and Doc and Danny working over second-hand metal desks or hang around awhile longer and watch Doc piloting a leased tugboat out to sea. Doc showed Chip and Danny how to maneuver the boat away from land, what lights to run for various operations and the fundamentals of getting a diesel engine to function should it decide to quit at sea.

The Coast Guard officers would blow their air horn whenever they saw them working at sea. Yes, the three men fit right in with that sleepy, hard-working environment, building themselves reputations as unassuming, ordinary fellows, honest and unafraid of getting their hands dirty. Chip charmed the locals at the bar, joking and laughing and carrying on in ways Danny had never known him to. "Yeah," Chip might say, "I'm not afraid of hard work. I can lie down right next to it and go to sleep."

At times Danny would wish he had never started the machinery turning, but he knew he had to stop Fassnacht, knew, in addition, that once set in motion, the thing was as indomitable as the eye of a hurricane.

Moishe assembled in his warehouse on the Colombian peninsula the finest tops and flowers the country could produce. No second-level weed was to go into this shipment, for Danny had specifically explained that he wanted this to be not only the biggest deal but the most expensive one as well. What he did not tell anyone was that if he happened not to come out of it, he wanted to leave a monumental legacy of marijuana to the United States of America.

Danny and Chip purchased two eighty-foot barges. They made a big drama out of obtaining the bank loan and, once they had acquired the vessels, made sure Doc repeatedly towed them out to sea and up the river into the warehouse in full view of the townsfolk, who waved and smiled and admired their hard-working nature.

While this was going on, the captain named Reggie and his Panamanian crew were piloting a ship called the *Palmas*, registered in Monrovia as a Liberian freighter. Reggie worked his way through the Caribbean, checking on ways to get through the Panama Canal without too many questions being asked. He moved four loads of coffee through there and each time he was searched and the registration numbers were checked on the ship's main beam. The bags of coffee were opened at random and in general a rather large fuss was made. The fifth time he went through with a load of coffee, they simply waved and signed him off. Reggie went through one more time just to make sure. They barely looked at the ship. He stopped to exchange small talk with some officials he had gotten to know.

Reggie sent word to Moishe that he was ready and willing to try to move through the Panama. Moishe sent word to Danny that the product would be ready on schedule. Co-ordinates of longitude and latitude were sent by encoded postcard—just a few numbers disguised in official red stamp pad ink as a postage meter identification number; then: "Wish you were here" and all that. On the given day the *Palmas* would stand by on VHF channel 16 in case visual contact was not made.

One morning Danny, Doc, Chip and some extra help motored out to sea under a heavy overcast sky. On board was a great IGY orange buoy attached to a chain that was in turn attached to five tons of concrete.

Some twenty-five miles offshore they dumped the concrete over the side and watched the chain snake down into the subsea ravine and disappear. The buoy followed and remained floating on the surface.

The buoy was IGY orange because Danny wanted to be sure that no matter what color the seas turned, anyone could see it; IGY orange, which had been developed during and took its name from the International Geophysical Year of 1957–58, was one of the very few colors never found in nature. The buoy was anchored with five tons of concrete because Danny wanted further to be sure it did not go wandering off on its own. Because one day it would have his barges attached to it, and those were expensive barges.

The locals who had hired on to help with the project understood. Those barges weren't going nowhere, nosiree.

There was always a good deal of truck traffic through that little town in Oregon, what with shipping, logging, small-time farming and just general movement and commerce. So the additional trucks that had begun to arrive in the days following the installation of the buoy did not attract undue attention.

The barges had been hooked up to the buoy for some time when word came from Moishe. Danny and Chip got into their tugboat one morning as usual and chugged out to sea, honking in response to the Coast Guard and waving at the officers. They rode out to the buoy and anchored the tug. Then they danced all over the barges, opening the drain cocks, and scurried back on top as the barges began to list to their sides. Chip and Danny scrambled onto the tug, and the barges sank to the bottom of the ocean. They watched the waters boil with the task of swallowing those monstrous, rectangular lozenges. The objects disappeared beneath the surface and then no clue remained but the slate-colored waves for insurance men to read. Danny and Chip fired up their engines and rode out to meet their schedule. They had timed it to coincide with the passage of the navigational satellite. With the receiving device they had, they were able to pinpoint their position to within 200 yards, and when they had done so, they began scanning the waves.

On the horizon were exact replicas of the barges they had just watched vanish beneath the slate-colored waves. Only these were not attached to an IGY orange buoy and five tons of concrete. They were attached to the *Palmas*, a 300-foot freighter, rocking on the high swells. There was no way to tell these barges from the originals unless one poked them with a sharp instrument and discovered that they were steel-reinforced fiberglass copies. Or unless one opened them up and discovered that each contained 200,000 pounds of marijuana. The *Palmas* had been loaded off La Guajira

Peninsula, from which Reggie had piloted it through the
Panama Canal without incident. The barges were brought
out to meet it at sea and were loaded from the *Palmas* there
in open water. The *Palmas* then moved to meet Danny and
Chip, and the barges were detached and hooked onto the
tug. Then Danny and Chip started up and motored back
toward land, flying three white lights in a vertical line to
indicate they were towing. As they entered the mouth of
the river that evening, no one even noticed—it was too
familiar a sight, like the clutter of equipment and receipts
in the salvage company office. The Coast Guard officers
honked and Chip waved from the bridge, just as he had
done so many times before. They moved up the river to their
warehouse, towing the barges behind them.

The barges were moved into the enclosed slip so they
could be unloaded out of sight, inside the warehouse. As
Chip and Danny jumped off the tug and went inside, they
could see the fork-lifts and cherry pickers standing stark and
indomitable and mute, like great insects of steel, the fork-
lifts squat and blunt, pure grunting muscle, waiting to heave;
the cherry pickers gawky, white and icy, spiders awaiting prey.
The warehouse was entirely silent. Danny snapped his fingers
once just to hear it. The pop came back to him twice at
one-second intervals, so large was the metal room they
were in.

"Spooky," Chip said. "Where's Doc?"

"The office," Danny said. They crossed the enormous
concrete floor to a metal staircase. Danny went ahead of
Chip, his boot heels pinging on the steel latticework as they
ascended, up and up, toward the glassed-in booth that formed
an office high off the warehouse floor. Danny pushed through
the white-painted metal door. Doc sat at a desk. The office
was no more than twenty-feet square. Before the desk, an
enormous picture window, angled outward and down, commanded a view of the entire staging area, including the narrow slip into which the two barges had been brought. Danny
glanced at the ceiling. There was a hatch, leading onto the
roof.

"All set," Doc said, standing up. "How's it goin', Chip?"

"Okay."

"When do the drivers arrive?" Danny asked.

"You have exactly twenty-four hours to put your scene together. Then—and these guys are punctual—this place is going to be crawling with people."

"I'll expect you," Danny said.

Doc let himself out of the office without further comment. Danny and Chip listened to his footfalls on the metal stairs, then watched through the window as he crossed the vast warehouse and left by a tiny door admitting a startling trapezoid of light, which diminished to a sliver as the pneumatic brake allowed the door to close, and then the warehouse was once again illuminated only by a faint blue glow.

Danny slapped Chip on the shoulder. "Time for you to go," he said. "Keep it in your boots, buddy."

"I ought to stay. What do you say?"

"Charles, we've been through this a hundred times. I've got to do this alone and that's all. You come back in twenty-four hours and it'll be over. Now, thanks for the ride, go get some sleep, have a beer, play some pool in town, but leave."

"Danny, be careful, man."

Yeah, Danny thought as he watched Chip leave, be careful. Isn't it funny how timing is everything? How far back should I go? he wondered. Timing, Fassnacht's timing the night he tried to bust me? Amesquita? Elaine? Or Forrest in the Year of Our Lord 1947.

Timing.

Danny went through it all in his mind, the way he did before a flight. Yes, Fassnacht would know about this deal. That had been taken care of. Danny had been sure to pluck the correct strand, to set the entire informational web humming like a harp. Getting here, to this one small white metal room, high above the concrete floor, had been the most complicated operation Danny had ever undertaken. All the pieces fit together.

And now: silence. Deadly silence.

Don't forget what Forrest always said: Watch your six. Don't get caught fat, dumb and happy. Danny tried to concentrate on running his checklist. Fassnacht knew. He would have gotten his regular narcotics police for this job—make it look extremely legitimate. A warrant. Gangs of probable cause. Information to beat the band.

How would he come in?

Through the front door with a few select men. Yes, some other narc might come bombing down with tear gas, helicopters and a regular army, but not Fassnacht. He would silp in—no, waltz in—with a handful of good men. Straight cops, no one from his Mexican Mud operations. Men he could order around, who would be in awe of a lieutenant and were good at paper work. Maybe even at shooting now and again as well. Fassnacht liked his busts to have flash and style because they made the papers, and more to the point, they were seen by people who would then say, see? Fassnacht is really after those drug pushers. Keep him down there. He's doing fine.

So Fassnacht would order his men onto the barges to start an inventory. Take stock of their loot. Then he would slip away. Fassnacht would know Danny was in the office.

Next item on the checklist: the mask.

Danny reached into the side drawer of the metal desk at which he sat. He took out the gas mask and tried it on.

Next: the cartridge, drill and screws.

In the other side drawer he found them. It was a cartridge of tear gas in aerosol form. With the drill and screwdriver he mounted it in its bracket above the door. It had a spring-loaded pin that would fire it if anyone opened the door now. When Fassnacht got to the top of the stairs (Danny would hear him coming) and pushed open the door, Danny would have his mask on. Fassnacht would be unable to see or breathe. Danny would force him out onto the roof at gunpoint and . . .

And what?

He had known when he set out to arrange this deal, yet somehow it no longer seemed clear. It had been so simple: He would kill Fassnacht. And then the world would be a better place. Amesquita and Linda Márquez and Beto all would be alive again, and Maggie would come back and say it had all been a bad dream.

I should have killed Fassnacht the day after killing Mendoza then. And killed his second-in-command, then his third and fourth, then all the others like Eddie, who are just cells in the organism—no, not even cells—who are just bacteria living in the gut of the organism. Timing, he thought. His timing was all wrong.

Danny stood up and began pacing the tiny office. He looked at the clock. Incredible, he thought. Four hours had passed and Fassnacht hadn't shown up. That was it then; the killings breed, just as the lies do. You can't tell just one story; you have to tell them all.

Danny went to the window and looked out over the warehouse floor. The two barges bobbed gently in the slip. The finest weed the country had ever known in larger quantities than anyone had contemplated.

Danny knew that Fassnacht would want him alone. That was why Danny had arranged to be high off the floor where the other policemen could not observe their stark and final dance. Fassnacht wanted Danny dead. Fassnacht would rush up to the office. A shot would ring out, maybe two, maybe more. Fassnacht would come down the stairs, his pistol smoking, saying, Sorry, fellas, he pulled a piece on me. A very tough break.

Danny knew it. That was why he was sitting in the office. Because he wanted the very same thing. Only he knew that when the shot rang out, it would be on the roof and Danny would be gone, like smoke on a breeze.

He knew the answer then. He knew what Fassnacht was going to do because, in some dark recess, he was part Fassnacht. Know thine enemy; that's how he had gotten Mendoza when those lawmen could not. No, it was more than that: *be* thine enemy or else just let it go.

All his elaborate precautions had merely been a gesture in the other direction, to deny that he was one and the same mutant force. Sure, he had gotten Doc to keep the drivers and equipment operators away for a day—he didn't want

Fassnacht marching in and shooting a bunch of innocent men who were just trying to make ends meet by running a little leaf. By the time those men arrived to do their work Fassnacht would be dead on the roof, his cops rounded up by the first wave of men Chip was to send in. The regular cops wouldn't be hurt—another concession Danny had made to prove his own humanity, his difference from Fassnacht and Mendoza. Those cops would be captured, kidnapped and released far enough away so that the grass could be moved out before they called for help.

Danny opened the center drawer of the desk. The Colt New Police Python was in there. He took it out and checked its cylinder. It wasn't that he didn't trust Doc and Chip. He just didn't like to leave anything to chance. Anyone could make mistakes. He removed all the cartridges from the revolver and replaced them with ones from his pocket.

Danny waited. He drank coffee, and when that was gone he waited some more. The little door down below, across the concrete floor, remained motionless. Sometime during the night he fell asleep briefly, his head down on the desk and awoke with a violent start. He scanned the warehouse.

Nothing.

He turned off the light in the office and watched the warehouse, which was lit with only a few of the thousands of fluorescent tubes mounted in the ceiling and walls. An eerie, blue, metallic scene in which nothing moved. Danny thought: I did everything right. The checklist is complete. Why hasn't Fassnacht shown up? There is something wrong here. Something, something, something. The checklist is complete.

Could it be . . . ? No, Danny thought, standing up. He could not possibly suspect Chip. No, it was simply impossible. Chip could not—would not . . .

But something. If Danny had done every single thing right, where was Fassnacht?

Fatigue was already blurring his mind twenty-four hours after he had arrived at the warehouse when the phone on the desk rang. Danny jumped. The phone rang again and he regarded it, let it ring a third time and picked it up. As planned, Chip's voice said, "If you're answering this, somebody fucked up."

"A-firm."

"I'm coming up."

Danny replaced the handset as if it were a live grenade that should not be jarred unnecessarily. A few minutes later he saw the door down on the warehouse floor open. Chip entered. An entire day. Danny couldn't believe it. He didn't want any of it now, didn't want Fassnacht to show, didn't want his head on a platter, didn't want the grass, the thousand-fold buzz that would spread like a resinous haze upon the land, didn't want the money, the escapade that would follow.

He heard Chip's footfalls.

I did everything right, goddammit, everything. The checklist said so. So why hadn't Fassnacht shown up? It was just not possible that Chip could have had anything to do with it, but something had gone wrong. Someone. Danny got up, replaced the safety wire in the tear gas canister and removed it from its bracket. Chip came through the door.

"What went wrong?" Chip asked.

"You tell me."

"What do you mean by that?"

There was a moment—no, half a moment—in which the two lifelong friends regarded each other, and if something —some energy or substance—could come out of the eyes and cross dead air space to another pair of eyes, then it did so, back and forth between them, like a hot short, and then it was gone in the same dead air and only the taste of coppery ions was left hanging. If the expression visual contact had any meaning, they both now knew what it was.

"I don't know," Danny said, dropping his eyes. "Fassnacht never showed and now, when those drivers start arriving . . ."

"Christ."

"Those guys *have* to pick up their loads or it's going to be their asses—whoever they're dealing with. It wouldn't do us any good to warn them now. I'm just—" Danny suddenly kicked the desk furiously. "Goddammit! I shouldn't have done this. I didn't want anybody else involved. It was between me and Fassnacht."

"Everybody's involved now."

"Jesus shit."

"We'd better move," Chip said softly.

"No telling what Fassnacht's going to do now." Danny made a fist and stared at it. "I was so sure." And the words echoed in his head: *Fat, dumb and happy.* The worst part was admitting what he had been unwilling to concede all along: that he was not controlling the game.

As they reached the main floor of the warehouse, Doc was coming in, followed by eight security guards. They were young men carrying leather cases for their sniper rifles. Trucks had begun arriving through the big sliding door that fed out onto the main highway at the other end of the warehouse.

"All set?" Doc asked.

"Yeah," Danny said, watching the security guards. They looked like kids off the street, dressed for a hunting trip in jeans and down-filled vests. "I'd like to get this thing over with as quickly as possible," he continued. "I want men on those barges moving bales. I want to see those cherry pickers moving. Get someone to carry fuel if necessary. I don't want to see them shut down. Rotate the men if you have to. This has to go like a relay race, Doc."

"You got it," Doc said. He turned and whistled. A man came running over. More men were coming through the door. The big door went up and a truck entered the warehouse. It closed again with a tremendous clatter. Men had already started crawling and hopping all over the barges. A fork-lift started up with a sound like a grizzly being tormented out of his lair. Another started; then a cherry picker fired to life. Bales began to appear from the holds of the barges—large, plastic-wrapped blocks of pressed marijuana each weighing 100 pounds or more. Danny watched for a few minutes as more trucks entered. Then he turned to Doc.

"Me and Chip are going back up to the office," he said.

'Sure," Doc said, and waved to the operators at their fork-lifts and cherry pickers. The machines roared and the men on the barges brought bales out of the holds, passing them to points where the pickers could get at them. The trucks pulled up in line and, as they were loaded, moved off toward the great sliding door that fed onto the highway. During the first hour five tons moved and Danny came back down onto the floor to talk with Doc. The movement was too slow, he said. They'd have to step it up, at least double.

"Get more men on those barges," Doc shouted to one of the workers. He turned to Danny. "The only limit is how fast they can get that stuff outta the barges. The pickers and Hysters can load as fast as they please."

"Well, get it outta there faster then," Danny shouted, climbing back to the office. He remembered what Michael and Moishe and Amesquita had said about listening to voices, but all he could hear was the white noise of fatigue.

In the second hour eight more tons were moved. In the third, twelve. Danny and Chip sat in the office watching the second hand go around on the clock and drinking coffee.

"Where might the guest of honor be?" Chip asked.

"He really fucked us this time," Danny said. "He shows up now with about forty guys wielding shotguns and we're gonna have a pitched battle on our hands."

Danny went down onto the floor again and talked with Doc. "Have you had good radio contact?"

"For sure, for sure," Doc told him. "Everything's going as smooth as buttermilk. We've talked to every single driver and they have ten-minute reporting, so if we don't hear from one of 'em, that means they've been hit, see. Nobody's so much as seen a fucking smokey yet."

"Yeah," Danny said, lost in thought.

"Look," Doc offered, "I don't ask too many questions on jobs like this, but you seem awfully skittish. I mean you said you had some business to take care of, so I held off the drivers for twenty-four hours like you asked, but if there's something I oughta know, maybe you should tell me now? Do you think somebody might rip off this operation?"

"No, no, nothin' like that, Doc." Danny clapped him on the shoulder. "You keep a handle on it. I'm just tired, that's all."

"Whatever you say, Dan."

Danny returned to the office and sat with Chip. He watched the action on the floor below. Cherry pickers nabbed the bales as they came out of the barges, then dropped them on pallets held by the Hysters, which transferred them to the trucks, which rolled out the door. Danny had to admit it was beautiful to watch, this great synchronized machine, working so smoothly. It must have been what Henry Ford felt. Except that dawn came upon Danny and Chip and their enormous warehouse and no sign of Fassnacht came with it. Chip dozed, his head down on the desk in the office. Danny tasted another cup of coffee and grimaced. His tongue would not tolerate any more of it.

"They favor the predawn hours," he said, thinking out loud.

"Mm?" Chip muttered.

"Last night I figured they wouldn't hit until late, but then nothing happened. And none of our drivers are being hit. It just doesn't make any sense."

"Mm?"

"Oh, fuck it," Danny said, and left Chip sleeping on the desk. He went back down onto the floor and found Doc, who was washing down a white pill with Coke.

"Aren't you tired? Jesus, I'm wasted."

"Here," Doc said, shaking a pill bottle at him. "I never rest on these jobs. Too fuckin' dangerous. Wake up with a gun barrel in your mouth."

"Or not wake up," Danny said, pushing the bottle away. "You hang onto those, you're gonna need 'em." He squinted up at the ceiling. "How're the boys doin' up there?"

"Oh, they're fine, I'm sure."

"How long do you figure it'll take to finish getting this shit out of here?"

Doc looked at his watch, then at the men hopping all over the barges, the roaring, spitting machinery, the banks of trucks waiting. "All fucking day," he said.

"Well, keep after it, I guess."

"Wilco."

It was late afternoon and nothing had happened, except that Danny had smuggled 200 tons of tops and flowers right into the heart of America. He contemplated with some satisfaction the fact that some of it would have already reached Colorado, North Dakota, California, Washington —the trucks abandoned, the grass purchased, the bales broken down. People at this very moment were inhaling the hot, peppery smoke, getting zoned out, listening to The Band or the Stones or Bach. In a few days the country would be flooded with the stuff from sea to shining sea.

All the trucks had gone and the only thing left by way of evidence was the litter in the two barges from the few bales that had broken, spilling stems and sticks and leaves. It is no simple matter to vacuum out an old fashioned 168,000-cubic-foot barge, and they did not even pretend that they might attempt it. They would follow their plan out to its end.

Doc was still speeding, sitting in a corner, watching the empty warehouse floor, when Danny and Chip came down, yawning and looking severe.

"I guess I'll be goin'," Doc said.

"Take your little army with you," Danny told him. He offered Doc his hand. "Thanks for everything."

"My pleasure," Doc said. He whistled at the ceiling and eight heads appeared above the beams. Danny looked up and saw one of the men remove a golden bullet from each ear and peer down.

Doc ambled off toward the door, his heels clicking on the concrete floor. Danny thought: Fassnacht is waiting outside, and when I walk out that door, he's gonna paste me. Danny heard Doc's station wagon start outside and then hum away down the highway. One of the sharpshooters came walking by carrying his leather rifle case. Danny slapped him on the back, then stopped suddenly and said, "Hey."

"Yeah?" The man looked no more than twenty-four years old, with fine brown hair clipped short and a thin, motionless face. He wore a down-filled hunter's jacket and blue jeans.

"What's that under your jacket?" Danny asked.

"Flak vest."

"Mind if I borrow it a minute? You're about my size."

"Sure," he said, shrugging off his jacket. He unclipped the hasps on the olive drab vest and handed it to Danny.

Chip looked on and whistled. "Not taking any chances, eh?"

The sharpshooter smiled—one quick movement at the corners of his mouth.

Danny put on the vest and clipped it shut. "I feel silly with this thing."

"You'd feel a right smart sillier," said the sharpshooter, "tryin' to hold in an armload of slimy guts."

"You got a real poetic way with words," Danny told him, buttoning a windbreaker over the vest.

"Dan, why don't I go out there with you?"

"No." Danny moved back from Chip. "It's not you. I'm the issue here."

He walked to the door and opened it a crack. Blinding sunlight came through in a widening trapezoid on the concrete floor. Just my luck, Danny thought, that the sun should be shining here in the land of overcast this one time when I need to see. It would be too bright out there and would take time for his eyes to adjust. What the hell, he thought. Maybe he'll win. Maybe he'll just get us all finally.

Danny threw the door open all the way, imagining Fassnacht's orders to his troops: "Now don't shoot until he's out in the clear. . . ." But nothing happened. He looked out, but the sun blinded him. He stepped into the doorway, bracing himself for something—he didn't know what. A truck rumbled by, carrying logs. It appeared on the crest of a rise, a black and terrific apparition, groaning under the weight of its load, tremendous, agonized reports issuing from its welded and bolted steel joints as it twisted and slaved onward, seeming not to advance one inch. Then it was past him, fading down the highway in the other direction. The road was still except for the gossamer trembling of sunlight heat and all he could hear was the truck changing gears in the distance, whining out to redline, gathering speed, changing gears again.

He took one step into the full sunlight and flinched as

he did so. He wondered what it felt like to be shot. He wondered if the flak vest was actually strong enough to stop a bullet. He wondered if Fassnacht—being himself the federal government—might have also brought along his own sharpshooters, who could put out a starling's eye at 1,000 meters, in which case it would make little difference if Danny wore a flak vest because he would never even hear the shot as the bullet flew ahead of its own sonic crack and took him in the head. He would be dead before he hit the pavement. Danny wondered if it would be better to be dead before you knew it or better to be like Tío Jim, peeled open in all your reality before your own eyes.

Danny had to admit that if Fassnacht were out there, he certainly had a peculiar way of showing it. Not a sound, not a car, not a whisper came from the distance. Danny walked a few meters away from the warehouse and looked all around. He went out to the middle of the highway and looked up one way, down the other. Nothing.

"Chip!" he called.

"Yeah." He heard the voice echo within the warehouse.

Chip emerged into the sunlight, squinting. He jogged over and stood beside Danny, and together they looked up the road and down the road.

"It's awful quiet," Danny said.

"Yeah, too quiet."

The next day Danny, Chip and Doc were at their offices as usual. It was a perfectly ordinary day, except Danny and Chip were on the order of $10 million richer, even after paying the crew. They gave Doc a fat bonus for his trouble.

They monitored the radio reports at the office or out on the boat to make sure they didn't miss any suitable weather for the final step in their plan. A few days passed, then they towed the barges back out to the buoy and left them there just before the storm hit. Sadly the barges disappeared in heavy seas. This time, however, they reported the loss to the insurance company and the bank that held the titles to the barges. They dropped their lease on the tug and, not long thereafter, went out of business for good. All the locals were as helpful as they could be. They knew how tough things could get for a hard-working white man on the Oregon coast.

✦

IN THE SUMMER OF 1975 Danny drove to Safford, Arizona, to pick up his father, who was being released on parole. A few months after Forrest had begun serving his sentence, he had been transferred to the minimum security prison there. When Danny arrived at the guard shack, there were television cameras and vans and a group of reporters standing around, waiting for something to happen.

Danny thought of the theory he and Maggie shared about reporting. Forrest's release was not that big an event. These people were there to see for themselves, not to disseminate information. They were there the way we all are there when a car overturns and burns on the highway.

Danny asked the guard if Forrest could be slipped past the reporters.

"Ain't no way outta here," he said, "except right here."

The reporters filmed Forrest and Danny getting into the car, filmed Forrest's mystified smile as if he were both as important and as baffled as an astronaut come home to earth. The reporters tried to get Forrest to answer their questions, but he merely continued to smile. The car pulled away, kicking up a little puff of red dust.

"What would you like to do?" Danny asked once they were under way. "You can come to Tucson or I can take you straight home."

"I think I need some breathing space. I'm sure glad you came to pick me up."

"I wouldn't have it any other way," Danny said. He looked his father over, assessing his condition. "You look fit."

"There's not a whole lot to do inside," Forrest explained. "I exercised every day for hours. I think it kept me sane."

"Good. Listen, would you like to come out and stay on the ranch for a while before going back? Would that be better for you?"

"Yes. I think so. That is, I don't want to impose . . ."

"No problem. It's cool."

When they reached the ranch that afternoon, Danny brought a cooler out onto the porch and filled it with ice and beer. He popped open a can and handed it to Forrest.

"Beer," Forrest said as if learning to pronounce the word for the first time. "Son of a bitch. Beer."

"It's a kind of foamy, golden liquid," Danny suggested.

"I vaguely remember." He tasted it. "Oh, that's so good. You know, inside, some of the men would get liquor smuggled in, whiskey, vodka, that sort of thing. You could buy it if you had enough money. I never wanted it. But the whole time I thought: If anyone ever offers to sell me a cold beer, I'll buy it. What is it about beer?"

"It's beer, that's what."

Forrest drank for a moment in silence, then asked. "Where's this lady friend of yours? What's her name? Samantha?"

"Yeah, Samantha. She's out of town."

"I was hoping to meet her."

"Sure." Danny did not want to talk about Samantha. He didn't want to tell Forrest about the big fight he had with her over the possibility that Forrest might come to stay at the ranch for a few days. Of course, it wasn't Danny's ranch, so he offered to take Forrest to a hotel in Tucson, but Samantha had ended up leaving town. Danny didn't want to think about it. Samantha had become more and more difficult to live with as time went by. No matter what he did, she seemed to find something wrong. If he took a shower while she took a shower, she would complain that the water temperature fluctuated and it was all horrible. If he did not take a shower while she took a shower, she would complain that he wasn't ready on time. He sometimes wondered what he would do. Most of the time, though, he knew.

The father and son drank beer, rocking and listening to the wood creak and pop beneath their feet. Forrest said, "You have no idea how good this is, Daniel. It's amazing the things you can get used to. The things you can give up."

"How did they treat you?"

"Oh, after that first place Safford seemed like a vacation. But don't misunderstand me. Being locked up is cruel and unusual. I do not recommend it."

"Oh, say, I almost forgot. I've got a present for you." He went into the house and returned a moment later with a wooden box, which Forrest took.

"Where on earth did you get Cuban cigars?"

"Try Cuba for starters."

Forrest ran his fingers over the box, then opened it and smelled the tobacco. "Mm," he said. He removed one and lit it.

"You should see the look on your face."

"I don't need to. Life is grand," Forrest told his son.

"If you don't weaken," Danny added.

"Yes, if you don't weaken."

They drank beer for hours, talking. Forrest didn't say much about prison. Only that he had seen into the soul of man while inside and it had worried him. Danny brought a bottle of brandy from the house and poured two shots into juice glasses to toast his father. "Here's lookin' at you, old man," he said. "You're a fine old fossil specimen."

Forrest smiled. He sipped his brandy. "That is smooth," he said. He regarded the cigar, which had burned down to a stub. "Those Cubans really know their business, don't they?" he asked.

Danny laughed out loud at the irony of his father's remark.

"What's so funny?" Forrest asked.

"You had to have been there."

"You really think I'm a good fossil specimen?"

"None finer in any museum of human history."

"What are you going to do now?"

"I'll have to think that one out."

"You know, all that time when I was without you, when you were in Texas as a little baby, I was so afraid that you wouldn't be my friend. I wanted to have a son in order to have a friend, and of course, it didn't work out that way either. I took you up in that airplane, remember? You were so excited." Forrest looked at the floor. "I thought you were excited to see me. That was ridiculous. Impossible. You didn't know me from Adam. You were excited about the airplane."

"Yes, I was. I didn't have any idea what you were talking about either. I thought when you asked me to come with you that I was going to get an airplane, not a father."

"You got the airplane, all right."

"I did that," Danny said. "I've got another story for you. If you're ready for it." Danny hesitated as Forrest looked at him in anticipation. "You're a grandfather." Danny could see the information percolating through his father. "You want to know how really alike we are?"

"Samantha?" Forrest asked.

Danny shook his head. "It's not even a woman you've heard of. Not even someone I knew well. Your grandson, Juan, is five and a half years old."

Forrest's expression went blank. He started to say something, but it died on his tongue.

"Just like you, Pops. It happened, just like that, and she had the child and they live not all that far from you, as a matter of fact."

"You're joking with me," Forrest gasped.

"Not the slightest bit. She says she likes having the kid, living all alone. I support them now, but she doesn't want me to have the child. She says he'll become a male chauvinist."

"Well, I'll be a son of a bitch."

"A grandfather, Forrest, in the grand tradition of the Paine family."

"I've created a monster."

"Me, too."

"Juan," Forrest said, as if tasting the flavor. "What's he like? Can I see him?"

"Sure you can."

"Lord," Forrest said. He looked positively tickled by it as he tried to get a grip on the information.

By nightfall both Danny and Forrest were drunk. They stumbled into the darkened kitchen and rummaged around in the refrigerator until they found some chili and a plastic bag of tortillas. Danny heated up the food and they ate at the kitchen table before going to bed. Every few minutes, as Forrest spooned chili and nibbled at the end of a tortilla, he would smile, look at the ceiling and say, "Juan."

The second night Chip came to see Forrest. Danny made barbecue and they sat in the moonlight, drinking and eating and talking of old times and airplanes. On the third day they went horseback riding and Forrest told of how he had enlisted in the last division of cavalry when he was seventeen years old. It was decommissioned when the war began and became a mechanized battalion.

On the fourth day Danny told Forrest he had business appointments and disappeared from the ranch. Out in the high desert he parked his car and waited. He could hear the rotors beating long before he saw the helicopter. He had learned the truth of what Amesquita and Michael and Moishe had said. Information. That's the name of the game, the only power. If you listen, little birds speak to you. If you listen long and hard enough, the trees and rocks begin to speak to you. Listen to your inner voices. Danny had been listening. He did not like what he heard.

Danny got out of the car, walked under the turning rotors of the helicopter that had landed nearby and climbed in. A door had been removed as if for combat. At the controls was a man named Dean, a robot in helmet and goggles. He had been a chopper pilot in Vietnam. His mouth, jaw and a good part of his face were plastic. He could no longer eat solid foods, but he looked good. He had flown defoliation missions down in Mexico before he switched sides.

In the back was an empty metal floor—just a cargo area— on which lay a man bound and gagged. He wore a blue windbreaker. Near him was an M-16 rifle. Danny picked it up and checked to make sure it was loaded. Dean turned around and Danny put his thumb up. Dean moved the collective. The helicopter tipped forward and rose away from the desert floor.

Twenty minutes later they were descending into an isolated canyon at the end of which was a ranch house on an acre of sod, with a few trees scattered here and there. Dean made the approach and Danny watched from the open doorway. As they bore down 100 feet above the house, Doc burst from the front door and began running toward the Jeep parked in the driveway. Danny threw the bolt on the M-16. Dean continued the descent. Doc ran across the open lawn toward the Jeep. Danny squeezed the trigger, scattering bullets in a wide arc ahead of Doc. It was not anger that moved Danny, not even revenge anymore. It was as if one machine were pursuing another.

Doc kept running. Danny fired again at Doc's feet. Doc reached the Jeep at a dead run, caught the open-sided truck as if it were a moving freight train and hopped aboard. Danny did not hurry. He felt no fear. He reached up and took the headset from a hook. "Stay on him, Dean," he said.

The chopper shot forward, like an air-filled object released underwater. It swung into a wild, shuddering hammerhead turn and Danny held onto the door handle quite literally for his life, as the bound and gagged form in the blue windbreaker slid across the floor toward him. Danny put his leg out across the yawning doorway and stopped the man before he slid out.

The Jeep raced along the single lane that led out of the canyon, leaving a thick cloud of dust in its wake. The road was straight and there was nowhere for the Jeep to go but down the slim ribbon of dirt road.

Dean flew the helicopter fifty feet above the road, racing out ahead of the Jeep. The chopper shot upward again, did a wrenching 180-degree turn back, then tipped toward the Jeep again, heading on a dead collision course with it. Danny gripped the handle, bracing himself for the impending impact.

With an astounding roar the chopper seemed to pass through the Jeep and out the other side. Danny had closed his eyes. Dean pulled the chopper into a 2-G turn. As the open doorway swung around, Danny had a good view of the Jeep, which had gone into the rocks on one side. Doc was crawling out. Dean pulled the helicopter up next to the overturned truck as Doc was running and stumbling over the rocks. Danny fired another burst at his feet and Doc fell down, covering his head. Danny jumped out and ran toward him, hollering. Doc started to get up again but stopped and waited for Danny to get there.

"Let's go," Danny said. "Come on. Up!"

He stood over Doc, who had a cut above his right eye but seemed all right otherwise. Doc slowly pushed himself to his feet.

"Come on!" Danny shoved the automatic rifle into his side and Doc stumbled, then began walking toward the helicopter. Danny followed him and they climbed in. Dean moved the collective. The machine shot into the sky.

When Doc saw the man bound and gagged on the floor, Danny saw the fear and disbelief settle in him. "Chip!" Doc gasped.

Chip rolled over to face Doc more directly. Doc could see the panic that gripped him in his helpless position there. The gag seemed superfluous. Chip did not appear capable of speaking.

The wind howled around them as Dean raced westward. The day was clear, with high, thin cirrus and little turbulence, CAVU they called it, ceiling and visibility unrestricted, perfect flying weather as they approached the Organ Pipe Cactus National Monument 12,000 feet above ground level. When they reached the middle of the park, Dean hovered the machine in one spot. Danny removed the gag from Chip's mouth. Danny motioned with the rifle and Chip got unsteadily to his feet. His face was twisted with fear.

"Danny, goddammit, you've lost your fucking mind," Chip said.

"One more time, Chip. Who set us up? Who told Fassnacht what was going down?"

"Danny," Chip hollered, "you're crazy, man. I didn't have anything to do with that. Think about it. It doesn't make any sense!"

Danny pushed the barrel of the M-16 into Chip's ear and worked the action. Chip twisted away from the pain. "Now!" Danny shouted.

"Danny, don't," Chip said, a last desperate plea.

Doc watched in horror as Danny pushed Chip closer and closer to the open, howling door. Chip began to scream, but his hands and feet were bound. He was helpless, losing his balance at the lip of the yawning hole. Dean flew the chopper like a robot, hovering over the Organ Pipe Cactus thousands of feet below. Chip began to sob, teetering on the brink of the abyss. Danny heard Doc holler a last warning. He put his foot in the center of Chip's back. He remembered the very first time he ever met Chip, in Forrest's kitchen with Chip's father. A million years ago. Danny shoved with his foot and Chip jerked into the bright, quivering air. He seemed to hang there for a stunned, terrific moment and then he was gone without even a cry.

Doc went into hysterics the moment Chip was gone, slumping to the floor, his hands up to his face in defense. "Danny, Danny, no, no, you've gone crazy, man, please," Doc stammered, edging backward across the chopper floor.

"Let's go, Doc. Your turn," Danny shouted above the engine noise.

"Okay, okay, now take it easy," Doc said, talking very fast, his face turning to a blotchy pattern of white and purple as if he had been poisoned by his own uncontrollable panic.

"Give it up, Doc, I know you set me up. Now what's the deal? What's going down?"

Doc squirmed away from the howling door. Danny moved suddenly and forcefully, taking him by the collar and dragging him physically to the opening. Doc's head slid over the brink and he had a glimpse of the earth far below. Suddenly his power of speech returned and Danny pulled him back into the chopper.

It was then that Danny learned the full extent of Doc's complicity in the affair. The sharpshooters who had waited high above the warehouse floor had filmed the entire last deal. Fassnacht had that as evidence. He also had the sharpshooters themselves as witnesses, along with Doc. They would testify if it came to that. Fassnacht, however, had another plan. Doc was supposed to tell Fassnacht when Danny was returning to Chicago. Doc had already let Fassnacht know that Danny would likely return in the G-II with his father. Fassnacht's agents would be at the Butler Aviation ramp at O'Hare with warrants, but they would never issue them. They would open fire on Danny and kill him, saying later that Danny was armed or appeared to have been armed or whatever they needed to say. All very neat. Worked out to the last detail.

When Danny was finished with his interrogation, he picked up the headset again and said to Dean, "You can go down for Chip now."

"Roger," Dean said, angling the chopper north and descending. Dean let the chopper down quickly and it settled onto its runners near Chip on the desert floor. Chip was gathering up the parachute silk, which was spread around in a great pile. With the chute in his arms, he ran toward the chopper.

Danny clapped him on the back. "Man," he said, shaking his head, "at the last minute there, I almost couldn't do it, Chip. I kept thinking: What if he gets tangled in the ropes? I was scared shitless."

"Think how I felt," Chip said with a laugh. "It worked all right, though. The ropes just fell away. Took me a little longer than I expected to get the windbreaker off so I could pull the reserve chute, but you know, it was really kind of exciting."

"Charles, you're sick." Danny smiled. "I'm glad to see you, though."

They took Doc back to his own house and Danny said, "Come on, Doc, you've got a shorter drop. Get out."

"What are you going to do?" Doc asked.

"Nothing. I could kill you, of course, but what's the point? You go ahead and testify. Or go ahead and tell Fassnacht you told me about his trap. Then *he'll* kill you."

Doc said nothing. Dean moved the collective and the chopper rose away, taking Danny and Chip back to his car in the desert. Danny was back with his father by nightfall, sipping beer and talking about computers and business as if nothing had happened.

"They'll come at you from inside," Forrest warned him.

"The government will do whatever it takes. Send some beautiful woman down to the Bahamas to have an affair with a bank official, then rifle his Rolodex for names. Things like that. While I was in prison, I had one of the people in Switzerland quietly buying gold with all the money the IRS didn't find."

"I've bought some, too," Danny said. "Bought a nice coin collection, in fact."

"Gold is good now. It'll go up. Watch your six with those government people, Danny. I don't want you to get caught fat, dumb and happy like your old man."

On the fifth day at the ranch Danny and Chip took Forrest to Tucson International Airport. Danny had explained to Forrest what was coming down. Danny knew they were watching every move he made now. Without a doubt there were agents on him day and night and the phones were certainly tapped. Forrest had insisted on going along with it anyway. If Forrest were to get on a commercial jet, they would know that Danny knew something was up. So they boarded the G-II with Chip, introducing Forrest to Randy and his copilot. Danny understood even then. He had for months since he first considered the possibility that something might go wrong. Prison was capital punishment. It was that simple. Running was the greatest agony of all, but at least it wasn't the death sentence.

Danny had quietly put out feelers and knew what the scene was in Colombia now. No one could touch him down there. It would take a full-scale military operation to get into or out of Moishe's. Danny knew what he would have to do. He also knew they would be watching him the entire time he did it. One way or another. If he tried to slip them before meeting them face on, they would simply kill him. The only answer was to do everything in full view. Anyway, Danny and Chip both understood that it would be better to go out and meet them than to wait for them to come, giving Fassnacht the perfect excuse to start a shooting war. At Samantha's ranch. At Chip's house, where Katina might be. Danny and Chip didn't want any of that.

Randy took off for Chicago, cruising at flight level 450,

at which altitude they could almost see the curvature of the earth.

"You know," Forrest mused, "if a little plane like this decompressed at forty-five thousand feet, there would be no way in hell to get down safely."

"They couldn't get their oxygen masks on quickly enough," Chip said, pointing to the cockpit.

"They'd be out cold." Forrest snapped his fingers. "Like that. I'm surprised it's never happened."

"It's just one of those risks," Danny said softly, lost in thought.

When they arrived at O'Hare International Airport and taxied to the Butler Aviation ramp, the crowd was spread out on the ramp. Television cameras and a score of radio and newspaper reporters were gathered behind Fassnacht and his police. There were men in flak vests with automatic rifles and gas grenades clipped to their web belts. Fassnacht stood at the head of the crowd, his sunglasses producing flashes across the distance to the plane, where Danny watched from the little window.

"I guess your phone call to Maggie did the trick," Chip said.

"I'm sure glad she came through. It would have been embarrassing as hell to show up here and find the press wasn't interested in big busts anymore."

"Look, there she is," Chip said.

Danny made a little wave with his fingers through the window. He wasn't sure if she saw him. He stood up and said, "Take your shirt off, Chip, and let's get going."

"What for?"

"Just in case," Danny said as he began stripping off his shirt. He made his voice sound like an announcer's. "The suspect appeared to be armed and a warning shot was fired into the fleshy part of his heart. . . ."

"Very fucking funny."

The steps of the airplane were dropped and the crowd pushed forward, enclosing the semicircle below, as if the president of the United States were going to step into their midst. Danny put his hands over his head, his chest bare, and walked down into the bright sunlight to face Fassnacht. The cameras rolled.

Fassnacht's blond hair had turned nearly white and was as dry and thin as flax. It appeared to be falling out. The skin of his face was stretched tight over his skull and seemed to have dried like that of a mummy. He stood in Danny's jail cell, while Danny sat on the metal cot and listened. Danny thought he could see the impression of Fassnacht's teeth through his lips, so tight and desiccated was the man's skin.

"Prisons are very violent places," Fassnacht said. "Very dangerous places. Ask your father."

"Did you come here to tell me that?"

"I wanted to look at you." Fassnacht turned and stared at Danny. Danny held his gaze. It wasn't a challenge to see who would look away first. They were merely looking at each other the way two people who have come to know each other over many years by correspondence or by telephone must look at each other the first time they meet. Danny knew the battle was over for him. He had known for a while now. "You're very clever," Fassnacht was saying. "But then you know that, don't you?" Fassnacht turned and paced the small cell casually, his hands clasped behind his back. "You're certainly better than either of your uncles."

Danny's entire body tensed. Fassnacht's back was to him. Danny could have jumped him, but something stopped him. Fassnacht could feel the move. "Violent prisoners don't get bail," he said without turning around to look. "Attacking a federal officer." He clicked his tongue in disapproval. "Anyway, you know what I say is true, don't you? You've lost. That little stunt of bringing the press out didn't save you. It just postponed the inevitable. You will be found guilty, of course. We have the whole thing on film. Couple of the drivers were our men, so we have that evidence. Loads of witnesses. You'll be sent to some nice prison like that first place your father was in. Hearty meals. The works. And you'll be found hanging in your cell. Or perhaps you'll get into one of those ever-so-common prison fights. Some lifer with nothing left to lose will put a homemade shank into your liver—who knows?"

"What makes you think I won't run while I'm out on bail?" Danny asked.

"Oh, you may. That'll be even easier. We'll have men on you night and day, of course. The IRS has seized everything you've got—everything that's out in the open, that is. They'll have men on you night and day, too. If you run, I'll kill you, that's how simple it is."

Danny knew Fassnacht was right, too. But he also knew that there had to be a way to outsmart them all. He couldn't help remembering what Samantha had once said: We're better equipped, better trained, better funded than they are. So be it.

"I'm going to leave you now," Fassnacht said. "Enjoy your stay." He smiled. "Guard!" he hollered. And in that moment Danny realized that he had probably just made the same mistake Amesquita had made. He should have killed Fassnacht. Now the chance was gone. Amesquita pushed the rifle down at the wrong moment. Danny did not even get that close. As Fassnacht disappeared down the hallway, Danny told himself: No, no, that's not it. That wouldn't end it either. There was no end to it. Let it go, finally. Let it go.

That evening Danny and Chip were out on bail. They went to Forrest's house for dinner. Maggie called. She wanted to see Danny the next morning, but he said he had business. He would see her the following day. The three men were quiet around the table. Danny could not stop thinking about the time he had visited Forrest in prison. He was well aware that he would be headed for a place just like that if he did not leave the country soon. Just thinking of the possibility, he could feel the panic rise within him. He had known he would have to run, and as each moment passed, he became that much more sure of it.

The next day Danny went to visit Elaine and Juan. He

played with Juan all morning and again had the feeling that he should have Juan with him, to steal him away, though of course, he knew it would be impossible. There were no choices like that left. When he got ready to leave, Juan wanted to go outside with him, but Danny refused. He told Elaine there were police following him and he didn't want them to see the boy or her.

"You going to work, Daddy?"

"Yes, son, I'm going to work."

"Bye, Daddy."

"Keep it in your boots, Juanito," Danny said, and the boy laughed.

"My boots!" he said.

Danny and Chip met at the John Hancock Center at noon and took the elevator to the ninetieth floor, where Robert Whitlock waited in his offices.

"I see the Oregon sun didn't do you boys much good," Whitlock said in an attempt at levity.

"What Oregon sun?" Danny asked. "Let's get down to business."

"The IRS has got things locked up pretty tight," Whitlock said. "They're trying to figure out how to charge you with income tax evasion. I don't think they can. Failing that, they want half of everything you own."

"What's the status up until that?" Chip asked.

"Well." Whitlock pulled a folder from a pile. "The land sale in New Mexico went through. They are going to be able to go ahead with construction anyway, it looks like. The IRS doesn't know about that because it's owned by your Swiss company, which has its offices in Toronto. Remember that one, Northern Equipment?"

"Sure," Danny said.

"This new WSBM thing in Atlanta probably won't happen."

"I don't care. I didn't want a radio station."

"It was an awfully good deal. They were asking five million, but I think we could have gotten it for three."

"Fuck it."

"Whatever you say. The Service came down hard on those

silver butterfly spreads. We've been out of those for a time, which is to our advantage. We bought gold and there is no record of that anywhere as far as I know."

"Good man," Chip said.

"Now just before all this happened I shifted about four million dollars to Canada and the Service isn't onto it apparently; at least the bank accounts are open and active. I want to talk to you about coffee. It's going crazy. It snowed in Costa do Sol."

"They don't grow coffee there," Chip said.

"No, Chip, but it gives you some idea. Coffee is going to be in short supply."

"Can we buy it?" Danny asked.

"I think so. I'm going to try through the Canadian outfit."

"Are you basing everything on the weather down there? What about the charts?" Chip asked.

"Let's take a look," Whitlock said. There ensued a conversation laced with the esoteric jargon of commodities technical forecasting, with terms such as *trend lines, exhaustion gaps, head and shoulders formations*, none of which meant much to Danny. He stood up and walked to the window, which commanded a breath-taking view of the lakeshore and Meigs Field, a single-strip airport on an island to the south. The visibility was excellent and Danny watched a small twin-engine airplane break ground and leap into the air like a toy. He wondered what would have happened if he had grown up in a place where there were no airplanes. He wondered if there was such a place on earth. He wondered why, since he liked to fly so much, he hadn't become a fighter pilot, for example. Stunt pilot. Bush pilot in Alaska. No, no, there was something more than simple flight. Flight. To flow. The old Greek forms meaning wealth, riches—literally, to overflow. And from there to the German: to run away, to flee, the act of escape; to float, swim, to further. Danny saw it as the little airplane below banked out over the lake, yes, to be able to mingle with the window before him and drift away, not in a craft—that would no longer do —but just as a vague collection of molecules, perhaps as a passing aroma on the breeze, carried around the hemisphere, you can catch a whiff of it, but you can never catch it. Flight. Standing at the window in Whitlock's office, Danny realized that he had never achieved flight. Only locomotion.

Behind him the conversation had stopped. Danny turned. "I want to talk about trusts," he told Whitlock.

"Trusts for what?" Whitlock asked.

"I want everything I have that the IRS hasn't attached to be put into trust in my son's name. He's only five and a half years old, so I want it in trust for him when he's older."

"You have a son? I didn't know."

"Yes. Incidentally, my father will be overseeing my business from now on."

Whitlock looked puzzled. "How do you mean?"

"I mean, I'm going to be kind of tied up, with my legal problems. So I've told my father everything." He looked at Whitlock for a moment. "Do you understand what I mean?"

"You're not suggesting that we might do something—"

"No, no, Bobby. I trust you completely. Absolutely." He paused. "I'd just feel a bit more secure with a family member involved. You understand, I'm sure."

"Certainly," Whitlock said.

"Please have the trust papers prepared immediately," Danny said. "Like yesterday if you can."

Whitlock placed the tips of his fingers together and raised his eyebrows as if he suddenly understood what Danny was saying. "You're certain you want to do this?"

"Positive. Where is the coin collection I bought?"

"I've got it. It's safe."

"I want it."

"Fine."

"I've given my father power of attorney. He'll be by tomorrow to meet with you."

"Fine," Whitlock said. He stood up. Danny had said nothing about leaving, but Whitlock knew what it meant. "Listen," he told Danny, "good luck, eh?"

Danny extended his hand to Whitlock. "Yeah, thanks."

The next day Danny took a long walk by the university. Two men followed him in a car, idling along stupidly for block after block, until two other men on foot took up the task of watching him. Danny stopped at a telephone booth and called Maggie at her house, his finger on the switch hook of the phone, ready to hang up if her husband answered. Maggie answered.

"When can I see you?" he asked.

"Tomorrow. I'll be free all day."

"Where?"

"Here," Maggie said. "I'll be alone until late at night."

"I'll be there at nine if that's all right."

"Nine in the morning? It's fine."

"Will you have your car?"

"Yes."

"Bye."

He then called Michael.

"I didn't try to reach you," Michael said. "I knew if you needed anything, you'd call. We have a whole routine, Danny. We can get you out of the country just like you'd never existed."

"Shoot."

"There will be a Cessna Four-o-one at Pal-Waukee tomorrow afternoon. It's clean and anyway, no one will be watching. It's two-nine-five November Echo."

"Check."

"Now, are you on foot, driving, what?"

"I've been walking around. There are two guys following me."

"Two? No problem. Tell me exactly what you're wearing."

"Khaki slacks," Danny said.

"What kind of shoes? Tell me everything."

"Clark's Wallabees," Danny said, feeling silly. He described his shirt and coat.

"Tell you what. Just let them follow you. Do some shopping or something. Then call me back in two hours."

"Thanks."

Danny walked around aimlessly. He went to the library

at the university. When the time had elapsed, he phoned Michael again.

"There's a gas station at Asbury and Greenbay Road. Go into the rest room there. There's a guy waiting."

"Outstanding," Danny said.

"After you've met with him, call me right back."

"Will do."

Fifteen minutes later Danny entered the rest room. The two men following him waited outside at what they no doubt considered a discreet distance. Inside was one of the strangest things Danny had ever seen. It was someone made up to look like him.

"Gimme your clothes," the man said.

Danny looked at him, dumbfounded, trying to determine whether the likeness was fantastically good or bad. The man looked like him—had even dressed in similar clothes—but then again, he really didn't look like him.

"Will this work?" Danny asked as he undressed quickly.

The man undressed as well. "It'll work. We do it all the time."

"You *do?*"

The man ignored the question. "Stay in here for half an hour. That should be enough time."

"Okay."

Danny watched the man leave. Michael, he thought. How exceptionally slick. He sat on the closed toilet lid for half an hour and then went to the nearest phone and called Michael.

"The Webster Hotel," Michael said. "You'll be safe there until tomorrow afternoon if you need that much time. The guy who took your place went straight to your dad's house. He's going to explain everything to your father and then stay there all day tomorrow, so they'll just be watching the house. You should have no problems."

"Michael, I don't know how to thank you."

Michael laughed. "Thank me?" he asked with a note of outrage. "Don't you remember who got you into this? I owe you one and this is it."

"Yes, I suppose it is. Well, in that case, fuck you."

"Sure thing, Dan. Say hello for me."

In the morning Danny arrived at Maggie's house at precisely nine o'clock. She lived in one of the grand old houses of that little college town, a once-elegant mansion about the laundry room of which the blueprints said "Maid's Dining Room," and in whose kitchen there had once been zinc bins for flour. The kitchen had been redone by some former owner in Sears, Roebuck Modern with Formica countertops and bar stools, though, and Maggie and Danny sat there drinking coffee and acting like strangers, nervously making small talk until they got used to each other's presence.

"When I saw you at the airport," Maggie said, "with your shirt off like that, so helpless, with all those policemen around you and the cameras and that horrible man—" She stopped and stared at her coffee cup. "I wanted to run up to you and hold you."

"I never even saw the police," Danny said. "All I saw was you."

"What are you going to do?"

"I'm going to use the Cleveland Defense."

"You can't run," Maggie protested.

"You just watch."

"What about Chip?"

"He's doing the same thing. If my guess is correct, they're having a bit of difficulty finding him right about now. We agreed to go separately for security reasons."

"What about Samantha?"

"That's all over." He looked down at the Formica countertop and picked at it, as if something were there. "It's been ending for a while now."

"I'm sorry."

Danny shrugged. "Even if it wasn't over, I'd have to leave. In a way it's better like this. I think Samantha would rather see me alive in either case."

"Of course she would, Danny, but all we're talking about is a prison sentence. They don't execute people for dope, not yet."

"The hell they don't."

Maggie looked at Danny strangely, with a mixture of

shock and curiosity, as if she wanted him to explain further, but she said nothing. It was one piece of information she felt she could do without. She poured more coffee. The light changed its shape on the floor and the clock hummed loudly on the kitchen wall, an old, round office clock with a convex glass lens covering the face and hands.

"So you're going and not coming back," Maggie said.

"I guess that's about the size of it."

Maggie slipped off her stool and put her arms around him. For a long time they held each other, suspended in the quiet murmurings of the old house. The clock hummed. The refrigerator's compressor thunked as it went on. Maggie was wearing a thin cotton dress. Danny could feel her strong body through it. He moved his head back so their faces were no more than a few inches apart. He kissed her then deeply, as he had in the December snows. Maggie didn't know really how he would react, but she knew what to do. She knew the situation was beyond their control for once— for always, really—and both of them such irreconcilable control freaks, not even minding now, as they took the stairway to the bedroom.

Danny held her again, kissing her, and Maggie felt herself relaxing, as he moved her thin cotton dress up the side of her thigh, *the hot hands*, she remembered, *it had been his hands that did it, isn't that right? Did it all those years ago and on the very day he left, right in my bedroom where the light through the curtains revealed everything we were doing. He undressed in the bars of light, his body still hard and young, and I held him inside me, I wouldn't let him go even after we'd made love twice, then twice again, it was our moment at last, our last moment like that.*

Sitting on the bed together in the afternoon light, they dressed. Danny lay back. Maggie put her hand on his leg and patted it.

"What if you got me pregnant?"

"You're too practical to take chances like that."

"I just did."

Danny looked at her from where he lay. For a moment

he thought he detected the slightest note of pride in her voice. "You're not pregnant," he said.

"No, I guess I'm not." And for another moment he thought she regretted it. Perhaps it was just his imagination. "Where will you go?" she asked.

"Remember Moishe?"

"How could I forget the Moishe stories? And what you said is really true? That it would take a land war to get into his place there?"

"No government in the world would touch him. It would be too embarrassing. Too messy."

"Will you ever come back?"

"Officially, I doubt it. But there's the possibility that one night you may get a call. Or someone may come by with an airline ticket or a letter or message. I just don't know now."

"Isn't there anything I can do?"

Danny thought about that. He thought about Fassnacht out there. What would that man do next? The millions of people going about their lives, completely ignorant of the workings of one of the largest businesses on earth. "You could tell some of the stories you've been collecting all this time," Danny said. "Yes, tell 'em."

"I've got them all now," Maggie said.

"All except one."

"I've got that one, too."

"Which one?" Danny asked, puzzled.

"The night we met. You probably don't even remember, but you told me. Then I went and found out on my own, once I realized what it had to be. We were sitting in a parked car in the forest preserve and I asked you. You said you had gunned a man down. Then you laughed. I laughed, too, of course. I thought you were joking. But after we went to that resort together and had our adventure and you *still* wouldn't tell me, I began to think. It scared me. Then I went into the morgue at the paper and looked up November twenty-fifth, 1964. And there it was on the front page. Heroin kingpin slain in gangland shooting, or some such. You killed him, didn't you?"

"Jesus Christ," Danny said. "You're amazing. Do you know why?"

Maggie shrugged. "I thought a lot about that. I knew it had to be a very good reason. I know you wouldn't have killed him unless it was a very good reason."

"He killed my uncle Beto," Danny said.

"I wondered if that was it."

"That and the little children."

"Yes."

Then Danny told her, filling in all the details she could not possibly have known—the man from Justice at Forrest's barbecue, the shotgun from the sporting goods store. He told her everything and then they lay in silence on the bed, as if waiting for the air in the room to boil or for the hand of God to come down, but nothing happened.

Danny looked at the alarm clock. "I've got to get wheels in the wells."

"I'll drive you."

"I don't want you mixed up in this if anything should happen."

"No, I'm going to drive you. I'm not afraid." She smiled. "I've always been mixed up in this. I'm still mixed up."

Even as they rode out Willow Road to the west, past the unilevel industrial sprawl, through spots of forest preserve with deer and pheasant, he saw, yes, there was no revenge, not for Beto or his brother, *Tío* Jim, or the little children; they could only draw him down into a never-ending cycle of battles that no one can win. All there would ever be was the bloody play, that and the stories. Let it go, finally, let it slide, just walk away from it. Maggie has everything now. The stories are hers.

It was an illuminating moment for Danny. This was where he and Forrest parted, their ways did, indeed, divide, and that was called evolution. Yet it had taken so many years and lives. Fassnacht came after Mendoza to outdo his horrors, and there would be another horror after Fassnacht, for they were eternally the same and left behind them only the history, let it go, let it go, the last deal now.

He could feel himself rising as they approached the little airport, feel his spirit lift and rejoice in the abomination and sadness of it all, of achieving it and the price that had been paid, would be paid, the dear freedom, his whole life paid out to it now, such a commitment, walk away now; there is no revenge, revenge is slavery. Let it go. Let it go.

"We're here," Maggie said.

Danny looked up. He had parked the car in the gravel lot without realizing it, and he had been sitting there, mesmerized by the intricate clarity of it all.

"Danny?"

"Yeah."

"What's wrong?"

"I was just figuring something out. Those stories. They're yours now. Tell them."

"I will."

Out on the field Danny checked over the Cessna 401 while Maggie watched. He made sure there was enough oil in the engines, and as he was closing the cowling on one of them, he saw Maggie weeping. He went over and stood before her and she cried, the wind blowing right through her.

"It's not fair," she said.

"Maggie." He tried to console her, but she did not stop crying. He grabbed her forcefully by the arms and said, "Look."

Maggie looked up into his eyes and asked, "What'll you *do*?"

"I'll start a little disco in South America and we'll have all the big name acts there."

"Danny, how can you joke at a time like this?"

"No time like the past."

"Danny!" she shouted, then collapsed into his arms.

He shook her violently. "Listen," he told her.

Maggie stopped crying suddenly. She hiccuped, then laughed through red eyes.

"Look," Danny repeated, out there in the wind and late sun of the airport ramp. "You've got to be a big boy to play the game. It costs a lot to play and you're not going to win either. You may even get hurt playing. But it's a good game nevertheless."

"I know," Maggie said. Danny believed her, too. He had run his position out to the end. He had played well and played long—Danny was a long-ball hitter, but now the game was over.

"Danny," Maggie said.

"I know." He took her shoulders and turned her around. He put his lips next to her ear and whispered, "If you turn around, you'll turn into a pillar of salt."

She immediately spun around, tried to smile, then burst into tears and hugged him, saying, "I'm not afraid of turning into salt. That's not what I'm afraid of."

Then Danny got into his plane and locked the door. Maggie stood out on the concrete, watching. Danny strapped the plane to himself and started the engines with a terrific roar. He put on his sunglasses and waved from the cockpit. Maggie's cotton dress whipped around her. She looked like Botticelli's *Primavera*.

The plane skittered around on its nosewheel and rolled away toward the run-up pad as she stood in the sun and wind, watching, until the plane exploded into the sunset like a falcon genie freed from a jar. And she thought of one icy, windy day at Garrett Theological Seminary, when he made a paper airplane sail all the way to the lake.

She knew as the plane left the earth that Danny was watching the altimeter for the critical height he'd need to get back to the runway if he lost an engine. The plane reached toward heaven, straining and angling upward. Now, now, Maggie knew it, he rocked his wings good-bye and she turned away toward the flight office.

Behind the counter was a radio, which was always kept tuned to the tower frequency, and Maggie listened for the controller.

"Five November Echo, now contact Departure on one-two-five-point-four, good day."

And Danny right behind him: "Five November Echo, aahh, twennie-five-four, *adios*."

MANY PEOPLE ASSISTED in the completion of this book, including Jonas Dovydenas, Eileen Jacobs, Arthur Kretchmer, Carolyn Lorence, Reg Potterton and Marjorie Williams. Special thanks to Larry "Butch" DuBois for Christmas Day; and to the businessmen, male and female, who provided valuable technical detail—they would prefer to remain unidentified. This book was written at Don Barliant's place in Lake Geneva, Wisconsin and at Asa Baber's desk, using an IBM Model 60 Electronic Typewriter. The editors were Thomas A. Stewart and Ileene Smith. The agent is John Hawkins of Paul R. Reynolds, Inc.—L.G.

Laurence Gonzales, author of the novel *Jambeaux*, is at work on his next book.